NO BUSINESS OF MINE

. . .

MISS SHUMWAY WAVES A WAND

. . .

JAMES HADLEY CHASE

Stark House Press • Eureka California

NO BUSINESS OF MINE / MISS SHUMWAY WAVES A WAND

Published by Stark House Press
1315 H Street
Eureka, CA 95503, USA
griffinskye3@sbcglobal.net
www.starkhousepress.com

NO BUSINESS OF MINE
Original copyright © 1947 and published in hardback as by "Raymond Marshall" by Jarrolds Publishers Ltd, London. Reprinted in hardback as by James Hadley Chase by Robert Hale, London, 1976. No previous paperback edition.

MISS SHUMWAY WAVES A WAND
Original copyright © 1944 and published in hardback by Jarrolds Publishers Ltd, London. Reprinted in paperback by Panther Books, London, 1960; and Corgi Books, London, 1977.

"James Hadley Chase at the Movies" copyright © 2018 by Dr. PC Sarkar and Gregory Shepard.

ISBN-13: 978-1-944520-49-6

Cover design and layout by Mark Shepard, SHEPGRAPHICS.COM

First Stark House Press Edition: December 2018

First Edition

NO BUSINESS OF MINE

American foreign correspondent Steve Harmas returns to post-WWII London to visit his old flame, Netta Scott, but quickly learns that Netta has just committed suicide. Harmas is so sure that Netta couldn't possibly have killed herself that he starts investigating, enlisting the aid of Scotland Yard Inspector Corridan. The first thing they discover is that Netta's body has disappeared from the morgue. Then Harmas is attacked outside her flat. Could her nosey neighbor, Julius Cole, be involved? He certainly seems to know more than he's telling the police. And then there's Madge Kennit, a neighbor who offers to trade information for a bottle of whisky. And what of Netta's sister, Anne, who also seems to have disappeared? Harmas and Corridan soon find themselves at odds as they both investigate a suicide that begins to look at lot more like murder.

MISS SHUMWAY WAVES A WAND

It all starts when Ross Millan, newspaper reporter at large, is assigned to find Myra Shumway, who may or may not have been kidnapped by Mexican bandits. His boss wants it to look like she's been kidnapped anyway, so that Millan can rescue her. It's all supposed to be a big publicity stunt. Millan finds Myra alright, and then runs into Doc Ansell and Bogle, two con artists who are understandably miffed that she has just pickpocketed them. Things get interesting when the four of them pool their resources around a better scheme involving an Indian cure for snake bite. That's when Myra encounters some genuine Naguales magic, and the four of them run into real Mexican bandits. Before long, Myra is levitating, a dog starts talking, a bandit turns into a sausage … and all hell breaks loose.

"Chase somehow manages to be almost insanely readable." —*The Observer*

"His best works sometimes read like a pastiche of a Gold Medal original or noir film...They move fast, and at their best manage to recreate the kind of doomed noirish atmosphere of James M. Cain." —David L. Vineyard, *Mystery*File*

"You may be horrified by his characters, but your sympathy races along with them." —*Eastern Daily Press*

NO BUSINESS OF MINE

...

JAMES HADLEY CHASE

CHAPTER ONE

My name is Steve Harmas and I am a Foreign Correspondent of the New York *Clarion*. During the years 1940-45 I lived in the Savoy Hotel with a number of my colleagues and told the people of America the story of Britain at war. I gave up the cocktail bar and the comfort of the Savoy when the Allied Armies invaded Europe. To get me to go was like peeling a clam off a wall, but my editor kept after me, and finally I went. He told me the experience would give me character. It gave me a pain you-know-where, but it didn't give me character.

After the collapse of Germany, I felt I had had enough of war and hardship, and I changed places with a colleague without him knowing anything about it, and returned to America and two-pound steaks on his ticket.

Several months later I was offered an assignment to write a series of articles on post-war Britain. I didn't particularly want the job: there was a whisky shortage in England at the time, but there was a girl named Netta Scott who used to live in London when last I was there, and I did want to see her again.

I don't want you to get me wrong about Netta Scott. I wasn't in love with her, but I did feel I owed her a great deal for giving me such a swell time while I was a stranger in a strange country, and quite unexpectedly I found myself in the position to do so.

It happened like this: I was reading the sporting sheet on my way to the office, still in two minds about going to England, when I noticed that one of the horses running in the afternoon's race was named Netta. The horse was a ten to one outsider, but I had a hunch and decided to back it. I laid out five hundred dollars, and sat by the radio with butterflies in my stomach, awaiting the result.

The horse won by a nose, and there and then I decided to split the five-thousand-dollar winnings with Netta: I caught the first available plane to England.

I got a big bang out of imagining Netta's reaction when I walked in on her and planked down before her five hundred crisp, new one pound notes. She had always liked money, always grumbled about being hard up, although she would never let me help her once we got to know each other. It would be a great moment in her life, and it would square my debt at the same time.

I first met Netta in 1942 at a luxury night club in Mayfair's Bruton Mews. She worked there as a dance hostess, and don't let anyone kid you dance hostesses don't work. They develop more muscles than Strangler Lewis ever had by warding off tired business men who are not as tired as all that. Her job was to persuade suckers like me to buy lousy champagne at five pounds a bottle, and to pay her ten shillings for the privilege of dancing her around a floor the size of a pocket handkerchief.

The Blue Club, as it was called, was run by a guy named Jack Bradley. I had seen him once or twice, and I thought then he looked a doubtful customer. The only girl working in the club who wasn't scared of him was Netta: but Netta wasn't scared of any man.

The story goes that all the girls had to do a night shift with Bradley before they could qualify for the job of hostess. They told me that Netta and Bradley spent the night reading the illustrated papers when she qualified, but that was only after she had blunted his glands by wrapping a valuable oil painting around his thick neck. I don't know whether the yarn was true: Netta wouldn't talk about it, but knowing her, I'd say it was.

Bradley must have made a packet out of the club. It was patronized almost entirely by American officers and newspaper men who had money to burn. They burned it all right in the Blue Club. The band was first class, the girls beautiful and willing, and the food excellent; but the cost was so high you had to put on an oxygen mask before you looked at the bill.

Netta was one of twelve girls, and I picked her out the moment I saw her. She was a cute trick: a red head with skin like peaches and cream.

Her curves attracted my attention: curves always do. They were a blue print for original sin. I've seen some female hairpin bends in my time, but nothing quite in Netta's class. As my companion, Harry Bix, a hard-bitten bomber pilot, put it, "A mouse fitted with skis would have a grand run down her, and would I like to be that mouse!"

Yes, Netta was a cute trick. She was really lovely in a hard, sophisticated way. You could tell right off that she knew her way around, and if you hoped to get places with her it was gloves off and no holds barred; even at that she'd probably lick you.

It took some time before Netta thawed out with me. At first she considered me just another customer, then she regarded me with suspicion, thinking I was on the make, but finally she accepted the idea that I was a lonely guy in a strange city who wanted to make friends with her.

I used to go to the Blue Club every evening. After a month or so she wouldn't let me buy champagne, and I knew I was making progress. One night she suggested we might go together to Kew Gardens on the following Sunday and see the bluebells. Then I knew I'd got somewhere with her.

It finally worked out that I saw a lot of Netta. I'd call for her at her little flat off the Cromwell Road and drive her to the Blue Club.

Sometimes we'd have supper together at the Vanity Fair; sometimes she'd come along to the Savoy and we'd dine in the grillroom. She was a good companion, ready to laugh or talk sense depending on my mood, and she could drink a lot of liquor without getting tight.

Netta was my safety-valve. She bridged all the dreary boredom which is inevitable at times when one is not always working to capacity. She made my stay in London worth remembering. We finally got around to sleeping together once or twice a month, but as in everything we did, it was impersonal and didn't mean a great deal to either of us. Neither she nor I were in love with each other. She never let our association get personal, although it was intimate enough.

That is she never asked me about my home, whether I was married, what I intended to do when the war was over; never hinted she would like to return to the States with me. I did try to find out something about her background, but she wouldn't talk. Her attitude was that we were living in the present, any moment a bomb or rocket might drop on us, and it was up to us to be as happy as we could while the hour lasted. She lived in a wrapping of cellophane. I could see and touch her, but I couldn't get at her. Oddly enough this attitude suited me. I didn't want to know who her father was, whether she had a husband serving overseas, whether she had any sisters or brothers. All I wanted was a gay companion: that was what I got.

We kept up this association for two years, then when I received orders to sail with the invading armies we said good-bye.

We said good-bye as if we would meet again the next evening, although I knew I wouldn't see her for at least a year, perhaps never see her again: she knew it too.

"So long, Steve," she said when I dropped her outside her flat.

"And don't come in. Let's say good-bye here, and let's make it quick. Maybe I'll see you again before long."

"Sure, you'll see me again," I said.

We kissed. Nothing special: no tears. She went up the steps, shut the door without looking back.

I had planned to write to her, but I never did. We moved so fast into France and things were so hectic that I didn't have the chance to write for the first month, and after that I decided it was best to forget her. I did forget her until I returned to America. Then I began to think of her again. I hadn't seen her for nearly two years, but I found I could remember every detail of her face and body as clearly as if we had parted only a few hours ago. I tried to push her out of my mind, went around with other girls, but Netta stuck: she wouldn't be driven away.

So when I spotted that horse, backed it and won, I knew I was going to see her again, and I was glad.

I arrived in London on a hot August evening after a long, depressing trip down from Prestwick. I went immediately to the Savoy Hotel where I had booked a reservation, had a word with the reception clerk who seemed pleased to see me again, and went up to my room, overlooking the Thames. After a shower and a couple of drinks I went down to the office and asked them to let me have five hundred one pound notes. I could see this request gave them a jar, but they knew me well enough by now to help me if they could. After a few minutes delay they handed over the money with no more of a flourish than if it had been a package of bus tickets.

It was now half-past six, and I knew Netta would be home at that hour. She always prepared for the evening's work around seven o'clock, and her preparations usually took the best part of an hour.

As I was waiting in a small but select queue for a taxi, I asked the hall porter if he knew whether the Blue Club still existed. He said it did, and that it had now acquired an unsavoury reputation as it had installed a couple of doubtful roulette tables since my time.

Apparently it had been raided twice during the past six months, but had escaped being closed down through lack of evidence. It seemed Jack Bradley managed to keep one jump ahead of the police.

I eventually got a taxi, and after a slight haggle, the hall porter persuaded the driver to take me to Cromwell Road.

I arrived outside Netta's flat at ten minutes past seven. I paid off the driver, stood back, and looked up at her windows on the top floor.

The house was one of those dreary buildings that grace the back streets off Cromwell Road. It was tall, dirty, and the lace curtains at the windows were on their last legs. Netta's flat, one of three, still had the familiar bright orange curtains at the windows. I wondered if I was going to walk in on a new lover, decided I'd chance it. I opened the front door, began the walk up the three flights of coconut-matted stairs.

Those stairs brought back a lot of pleasant memories. I remembered the nights we used to sneak up them, holding our shoes in our hands lest Mrs. Crockett, the landlady who lurked in the basement, should hear us. I remembered too, the night I had flown over Berlin with a R.A.F. crew and had arrived at Netta's flat at five o'clock in the morning, too excited to sleep and wanting to tell her of the experience, only to find she hadn't come home that night. I had sat on the top of those stairs waiting for her, and had finally dozed off, to be discovered by Mrs. Crockett, who had threatened to call the police.

I passed the doors of the other two flats. I had never discovered who lived in them. During the whole time I had visited Netta I hadn't once seen the occupiers. I arrived, a little breathless, outside Netta's front door, and paused before I rang the bell.

Everything was exactly the same. There was her card in a tiny brass frame screwed to the panel of the door. There was the long scratch on the paint-work which I had made when slightly drunk with the latchkey. There was the thick wool mat before the door. I found my heart was beating a shade quicker, and my hands were a little damp. It seemed to me all of a sudden that Netta had become important to me: I'd been away too long.

I punched the bell, waited, heard nothing, punched the bell again.

No one answered the door. I continued to wait, wondering if Netta was in her bath. I gave her a few more seconds, punched the bell again.

"There's no one there," a voice said from behind me.

I turned, looked down the short flight of stairs. A man was standing in the doorway of the lower flat, looking up at me. He was a big strapping fellow around thirty, broad and well-built but far from muscular. With a frame like a hammer-thrower, he was yet soft, just this side of fat. He stood looking up at me with a half-smile on his face, and the impression he gave me was that of an enormous sleepy tom-cat, indifferent, self-sufficient, pleased with himself. The waning sunlight coming through the grimy win-dow caught the gold in his mouth, making his teeth come alive.

"Hello, baby," he said. "You one of her boy friends?" He had a faint lisp, and his corn-coloured hair was cut close. He was wearing a yellow and black silk dressing-gown, fastened at his throat; his pyjama legs were elec-tric blue, his sandals scarlet. He was quite a picture.

"Go jump into a lake," I said. "Jump into two if one won't hold you," and I turned back to Netta's door.

The man giggled. It was an unpleasant hissing sound and for no reason at all it set my nerves jumping.

"There's no one there, baby," he repeated, then added in an undertone, "she's dead."

I stopped ringing the bell, turned, looked at him. He raised his eyebrows, and his head waggled from side to side ever so slightly.

"Did you hear?" he asked, and smiled as if he were privately amused at some secret joke of his own.

"Dead?" I repeated, moving away from the door.

"That's right, baby," he said, leaning against the doorpost, giving me an arch look. "She died yesterday. You can still smell the gas if you sniff hard enough." He touched his throat, flinched. "I had a bad day with it yes-terday."

I walked down the stairs, stood in front of him. He was an inch taller than I and a lot broader, but I knew he hadn't any iron in his bones.

"Calm down, Fatso," I said, "and give it to me straight. What gas? What are you raving about?"

"Come inside, baby," he said, smirking. "I'll tell you about it."

Before I could refuse, he had sauntered into a large room which stank of stale scent and was full of old, dusty furniture.

He dropped into a big easy chair. As his great body dented the cushions a fine cloud of dust arose.

"Excuse the hovel," he said, looking around the room with an expression of disgust on his face. "Mrs. Crockett's a slut. She never cleans the place and I can't be expected to do it, can I, baby? Life's too short to waste time cleaning when one has my abilities."

"Never mind the Oscar Wilde act," I said impatiently. "Are you telling me Netta Scott's dead?"

He nodded, smiled up at me. "Sad, isn't it? Such a delightful girl; beautiful, lovely little body; so full of vigour—now, just meal for the worms." He sighed. "Death is a great leveller, isn't it?"

"How did it happen?" I asked, wanting to take him by his fat throat and shake the daylights out of him.

"By her own hand," he said mournfully. "Shocking business. Police rushing up and down stairs ... the ambulance ... doctors ... Mrs. Crockett screaming ... that fat bitch in the lower flat gloating ... a crowd in the street, hoping to see the remains quite, quite ghastly. Then the smell of gas—couldn't get it out of the house all day. Shocking business, baby, really most, most shocking."

"You mean she gassed herself?" I asked, going cold.

"That's right, the poor lamb. The room was sealed with adhesive tape ... roll upon roll of adhesive tape, and the gas oven going full blast. I'll never be able to buy adhesive tape again without thinking of her." The words were a vibrationless hum, intimate and secret-sounding. The perpetual smile bothered me too.

"I see," I said, turning away.

Well, that was that. I felt suddenly deflated, a little sick, infinitely sad.

I thought: If you had only waited twenty-four hours, Netta, we'd have faced whatever it was together, and we'd have licked it.

"Thank you," I said at the door.

"Don't thank me, baby," he said, heaving himself out of the chair and following me on to the landing. "It's nice to know I've rendered a little service, although a sad one. I can see you're suffering from shock, but you'll get over it. Plenty of hard work is the best healer. Doesn't Byron say, 'The busy have no time for tears?' Perhaps you don't admire Byron. Some people don't."

I stared at him, not seeing him, not listening to him. From out of the past, I heard Netta's voice saying: "So the fool killed himself. He hadn't the guts to take what was coming to him. Well, whatever I do, I'd be ready to pay for it. I wouldn't take that way out—ever."

She had said that one night when we had read of a millionaire who had bulled when he should have bearded and had blown out his brains. I remembered how Netta had looked when she had said that, and I felt a little cold breath of wind against my cheek.

There was something wrong here. I knew Netta would never have killed herself.

I pulled my hat farther down on my nose, felt in my pocket for a cigarette, offered the carton.

"Why did she do it?" I asked.

"I'm Julius Cole," the pixy said, drawing out a cigarette from the carton between a grubby forefinger and thumb. "Are you a friend of hers?"

I nodded. "I knew her a couple of years ago," I said, lighting his cigarette and then mine.

He smiled. "She would be interested in an American," he said as if to himself. "And, of course, with her figure and looks an American would be interested in her." He looked up, his eyes sleepy. "It would be interesting to know the exact number of girls in this country who were ravished by American service men during their stay here, wouldn't it? I make a point of collecting such statistics." He lifted his broad, limp shoulders. "Probably a waste of time," he added, wagging his head.

"How did it happen?" I said sharply.

"You mean, why did she do it?" he gently corrected me. Again he lifted his shoulders. The silk of his dressing-gown rustled. "It's a mystery, baby. No note ... five pounds in her bag ... food in the refrigerator ... no love letters ... no one knows." He raised his eyebrows, smiled. "Perhaps she was with child."

I couldn't continue this conversation. Talking about Netta with him was like reading something written on a lavatory wall.

"Well, thanks," I said, and walked down the stairs.

"Don't mention it, baby," he said. "So sad for you: so disappointing." He went back into his room and closed the door.

CHAPTER TWO

Mrs. Crockett was a thin little woman with bright, suspicious eyes and a thin, disapproving mouth.

I could see she didn't recognize me. She seemed to think I was a newspaper man after a story, and she peered at me from around the half-open door, ready to slam it in my face.

"What do you want?" she demanded in a reedy, querulous voice. "I 'ave enough to do without answering a lot of silly questions, so be off with you."

"Don't you remember me, Mrs. Crockett?" I asked. "I'm Steve Harmas, one of Miss Scott's friends."

"One of 'er friends, are you?" she said. "Fancy men, that's wot I call 'em." She peered at me, then nodded her head. Her eyes showed her disapproval. "Yes, I seemed to 'ave seen you before. Well, you've 'eard what's 'appened to 'er, 'aven't you?"

I nodded. "Yes. I wanted to talk to you about her. Did she leave any debts? I'll settle anything she owed."

The disapproving look was replaced by one of greed and calculating shrewdness.

"She owed me a month's rent," she said promptly. "Never expected to get that either. Still, if you're paying 'er debts, may as well 'ave it. You'd better come in."

I followed her along a dark passage that smelt of cats and boiled cabbage, into a dark, dingy room crammed with bamboo furniture.

"So she owed money?" I asked, watching the woman.

"Well, no," she said, after a moment's hesitation. "She always paid up: I'll say that for her, but she only 'ad the flat on the strict understanding it'd be a month's notice or a month's rent."

"I see," I said. "Have you any idea why she did what she did?"

Mrs. Crockett stared at me, looked away. "'ow should I know?" she asked, anger in her voice. "I didn't interfere with 'er. I knew nothing about 'er." Her thin lips set in a hard line. "She was no good. I should never 'ave 'ad 'er 'ere. Bringing disgrace to my 'ouse like this."

"When did it happen?"

"The night before last. Mr. Cole smelt gas and 'e called me. When I couldn't get no answer I guessed what she 'ad done—the little fool!" The hard eyes glittered. "Fair upset me it did. Mr. Cole sent for the police."

"Did you see her?"

Mrs. Crockett started back "Who? Me? Think I want to 'ave 'er 'aunting my dreams? Not likely. Mr. Cole identified 'er for the police. Ever so considerate 'e is. Besides, 'e knew 'er as well, if not better than wot I did ... always popping in and out of 'is room whenever 'e 'ears anything."

"All right," I said, taking out my wallet. "Have you a key to her flat."

"Suppose I 'ave?" she said suspiciously. "What's it to you?"

"I'd like to borrow it," I returned, counting pound notes on to the table. Her eyes followed every movement. "Shall we say twenty-five pounds? Ten pounds for the key?"

"What's the idea?" She was breathing quickly, her eyes overbright.

"Only that I'd like to look around her room. I suppose it's as it was ... nothing's been touched?"

"Oh, no, the police told me to leave it alone. They're trying to trace her relatives. Fat chance of finding anyone who'd own 'er, I say. I can't imagine what'll 'appen to 'er things. Anyway, I want 'em out. I want to let the flat."

"Has she any relatives?"

"No one knows anything about 'er," Mrs. Crockett said with a sniff. "Maybe the police'll find out something, and it won't be any good, you mark my words."

"May I have the key, please?" I said, pushing the little heap of money towards her.

She shook her head doubtfully. "The police wouldn't like it," she said, looked away.

"I'm offering you ten pounds to sooth your conscience," I reminded her. "Take it or leave it."

She opened the drawer of the dresser, took out a key, laid it on the table.

"It's people with too much money what gets honest folk into trouble," she said.

"I'll put that in my autograph book," I said, a little sick of her, picked up the key, pushed the notes farther in her direction.

She snatched up the money, rammed it into her apron pocket.

"Don't keep that key too long," she said, "and don't you take anything from the flat."

I nodded, went out.

I walked up the stairs, paused on the first floor to read the name on the card screwed to the panel of the door: Madge Kennitt. I remembered that Julius Cole had said: "the fat bitch in the lower flat, gloating." I nodded to myself, walked on up to Netta's flat. I fitted the key in the door, turned the handle, pushed gently. The door swung open. I entered Netta's sitting room. As I turned to close the door, I saw Julius Cole watching me from the half-open door of his flat. He raised his eyebrows, waggled his head. I pretended I hadn't seen him, closed Netta's door, shot the bolt.

There was a faint, persistent smell of gas in the flat although the windows were open. I looked around the room, feeling sad and a little spooked.

The room hadn't changed much since last I was in it. Some of the furniture had been shifted around, but there were no new pieces. The pictures were the same: all rather risqué prints taken from American and French magazines.

I had once asked Netta why she had such pictures on her walls.

"The boys like them," she had explained. "They take their minds off me. People who bore me are shocked by them and don't come again, so they have their uses, you see."

On the mantelpiece was her collection of china animals. She had about thirty of them. I had given her several. I went over to see if mine were still there. They were. I picked up a charming reproduction of Disney's Bambi, turned it over. I remembered how pleased Netta had been with it. She said it was the best of her collection. I think it was.

I put the ornament down, wandered around the room my hands in my pockets. I was only beginning to realize that Netta was dead, that I wouldn't see her again.

I didn't think I would feel bad about it, but I did. Her death worried me too. I couldn't believe that she had committed suicide.

She just wasn't the type to quit. Before the war I had been a crime reporter. I'd visited hundreds of rooms in which suicides had met their end. There had been an atmosphere in those rooms which this room lacked. I don't know quite what it was, but somehow I couldn't believe a suicide had happened here.

I went over to the light oak writing-desk, opened it, glanced inside. It was empty except for a bottle of ink and a couple of pencils. I looked at the pigeon-holes, remembered them as they had been when Netta and I had been going around together, crammed with letters, bills, papers. Now there was nothing.

I glanced over at the fireplace expecting to see ashes of burned paper. But the fireplace was empty. I thought this odd, pushed my hat to the back of my head, frowned down at the desk. Yes, odd.

A faint scratching at the front door made me start. I listened. The scratching continued.

"Let me in, baby," Julius Cole whispered through the panels. "I want to see, too."

I grimaced, tip-toed across the room, into the kitchen. The small-gas oven door was ajar. There was an orange-coloured cushion lying in the far corner of the room. I supposed she had used it when she put her head in the oven. I didn't like thinking about it, so I went from the kitchen into her bedroom.

It was a small, bright room. The big double divan took up most of the space. There was a fitted wardrobe near the bed, a small dressing-table by the window. The room was decorated in green and daffodil yellow. There were no pictures, no ornaments.

I closed the door, stood looking down at the bed. It had memories for me, and it was several minutes before I walked to the dressing-table and looked at the amazing assortment of bottles, beauty creams, grease-paints that were scattered on the powder-covered glass top. I pulled open the drawers. They were full of the usual junk a girl collects: handkerchiefs, silk scarves, leather belts, gloves, cheap jewellery. I stirred with my forefinger the necklaces, bangles, rings in the cardboard box. It was all junk, and then I remembered the diamond bracelet and the diamond scarf-pin of which she had been so proud. I had given her the bracelet; some guy—she never told me who—had given her the pin. I looked through the drawers, but I couldn't see them. I wondered where they had got to, if the police had taken them for safe custody.

Then I went to the wardrobe, opened it. A subtle smell of lilac drifted out of the wardrobe when I opened the door: her favourite perfume. I was struck by the emptiness in the wardrobe. There were only two evening dresses, a coat and skirt and a frock. At one time the cupboard was crammed with clothes.

There was a flame-coloured dress which I remembered. It was the dress she wore the night we first decided to sleep together. The kind of dress a sentimental guy like me wouldn't forget. I reached for it, took it off the hanger, and as I pulled it out I realized that something heavy was hung up inside the dress.

My fingers traced around the shape of the thing: it was a gun. I opened the dress, found a Luger pistol hanging by its trigger guard from a small hook sewn inside the dress.

I sat on the bed, holding the dress in one hand and the Luger in the other. I was startled. It was the last thing I should have expected to find in Netta's flat.

There were two obvious things to notice about the gun. It had a deep scratch along its barrel, and on the butt was a scar as if something had been filed off the metal; probably the name of the owner. I sniffed at the gun, had another shock. It had been fired, although not recently. The smell of burned powder was faint, but distinct. I laid the gun on the bed, scratched my head, brooded for a few minutes, then got up, went back to the wardrobe again. I opened the two drawers in which Netta used to keep her silk stockings and undies. Silk stockings had been one of Netta's passions. During the time I had known her I had never seen her wear anything but real silk hose. She had laid in a stock just before the war, and a number of American service men, and myself for that matter, had kept her stock up. I turned over the garments in the drawers, but I couldn't find any silk stockings.

I stubbed out my cigarette, frowned, wondered if Mrs. Crockett had been up here and had taken them, or if the police had been tempted. Silk stockings were almost unobtainable, and the temptation was easy to understand. There should have been at least a dozen pairs. When I last saw her—two years ago—she had thirty-six pairs. I know, because one night, when she had asked me to get her some, I had turned her drawer out and counted them to prove to her she didn't need any more. Yes, she should have at least a dozen pairs, if not more. Where were they?

I decided to search her flat. I had been trained during my years as a crime reporter to take a house to pieces so that it wouldn't show. It would be a long, dull job, but somehow I felt it would pay dividends.

I went through each room carefully and systematically. I left nothing to chance, even unwinding the blinds, feeling along the pelmets, taking up the carpets and sounding the floors.

In the bedroom by the fireplace I found a small recess in the floor, under a loose board. It was obvious that something had been kept there, but it was no longer there. In the bathroom, wrapped around the toilet roll I found eight five-pound notes. In the sitting room between a picture of one of Vargas's lovelies and the back of the frame were eight more five-pound notes. At the bottom of a jar of cold cream I found a diamond ring. It looked a good diamond, and the setting was platinum. I hadn't seen it before. It was an odd hiding place, but then so were the hiding places of the five-pound notes.

I went into the kitchen, and after a painstaking search found at the bottom of the flour bin, buried under the flour, a foolscap envelope. I drew it out, dusted off the flour and read the address on the envelope, written in Netta's big, untidy hand:

Miss Anne Scott,
Beverley

Could this be a sister? I wondered, feeling the bulky envelope between my fingers. It seemed full of papers, and was heavy.

The whole business seemed to me odd. I was uneasy, suspicious. I didn't know what to make of it all.

I satisfied myself that there was nothing of further interest in the kitchen, went back to the sitting room.

I laid out on the table all the things I had found. There was the Luger pistol, the diamond ring, the sixteen five-pound notes, and the letter addressed to Anne Scott.

Why should a girl commit suicide when she possessed eighty pounds and a diamond ring? I asked myself. What other trouble apart from money could have made Netta do away with herself? I couldn't imagine anything bad enough. In fact, I was now as sure as I could be that she hadn't committed suicide. Murder? Well, if it wasn't suicide, it had to be murder. It couldn't have been an accident. Accidents didn't happen quite like that.

I lit another cigarette, brooded. I'd have to discuss this with the police. I remembered Inspector Corridan of the Yard. He and I had been friendly when last I was in London. He had taken me around to the various haunts of petty criminals, and the material I had collected with his help had made a good article for the *Saturday Evening Post*.

Corridan was just the man to consult and I immediately reached for the telephone.

After a delay, Corridan came on the line.

I reminded him who I was, and he remembered me.

"Glad to hear from you again, Harmas," he said. "You're lucky to have caught me. I was just going home."

"Are you in a hurry?" I asked, glancing at my wrist watch.

It was nearly nine o'clock.

"Well, I want to get home. Is it anything urgent?"

"Interesting rather than urgent," I said. "I want your advice, and perhaps help. It's to do with a girl named Netta Scott who committed suicide the night before last."

"Who did you say?" he asked sharply.

"The girl's name is Netta Scott. She used to be an old friend of mine. Frankly, Corridan, I'm not satisfied that she did kill herself."

There was a pause, then he said, "Well, I have nothing special to do tonight. What do you suggest?"

"Suppose you meet me in half an hour at the Savoy?" I said. "If you'd make inquiries about the girl, it might simplify things. Any details may be useful." I gave him Netta's address, and he promised to have the information, and hung up. That was one of the things I liked about Corridan. He was never surprised at anything, never asked a lot of unnecessary questions, and was always willing to be helpful no matter how busy he was or how late the hour.

I put the gun, envelope, ring and money in my various pockets.

Satisfied I hadn't missed anything, I turned off the light, opened the front door, stepped on to the landing.

Julius Cole had brought a chair into his little hall and was sitting there smoking, with the front door open, waiting for me.

"Why didn't you let me in, baby?" he asked, smiling his secret smile. "You had no right to be in there yourself."

"Go bowl a hoop," I said, went on down the stairs.

"Don't run away, baby," he said, sliding off his chair and coming to the head of the stairs. "What's it like in there?" He sniggered. "Did she have pretty things? I suppose you've been through all her clothes. I wish I'd been there."

I kept on, without looking back.

Mrs. Crockett answered my rap on her door.

"You've been up there long enough," she snapped, taking the key I handed to her. "You 'aven't taken anything, 'ave you? Most particular the police were about leaving everything as it was."

I shook my head. "It's all right," I said. "Has anyone been in there since she died ... I mean anyone except the police? Mr. Cole for instance?"

She shook her head. "No one, but you, and I'm sure I didn't ought to 'ave ..."

"There were some silk stockings ... they don't seem to be there," I interrupted. "Do you know anything about them?"

"What should I want with silk stockings?" she snapped. "Course I don't!"

I thanked her, made noncommittal noises, walked up the narrow stairs to the front door.

In the street I paused for a moment to look at the house. A light burned in Julius Cole's flat: the rest of the house was in darkness. I wondered about Madge Kennitt, decided she didn't fit in the picture; anyway, not for the time being, began to walk in the direction of Cromwell Road, fifty yards or so ahead of me.

The street was lit by only three lamps, one at the top, the other at the bottom and the third halfway between the other two. It was dark, and there were deep shadows, otherwise I shouldn't have been so easily surprised.

I heard a patter of feet behind me, felt a sudden premonition of danger, ducked, jumped aside.

Something very hard hit my shoulder, brought me to my knees. I flung up my arm, staggered upright and again jumped back. I caught a glimpse of a shadowy figure of a man holding what seemed to me to be a tyre lever above his head. He slashed wildly at me. I heard the lever whistle past my face, stepped in close, and belted the guy in the ribs with everything I had. He dropped the tyre lever, reeled back, his breath coming out of him like a punctured balloon.

"What the hell do you think you're playing at?" I demanded, crowding him.

I could see him now. He was a little runt, young, slim, underfed. I couldn't see much of his face except that he was pasty. His clothes were shoddy, and his hat like a sponge full of grease.

Before I could collar him, he darted out of my reach and went down the street like a streak of lightning.

I stood looking after him, listening to his light footfalls. My shoulder ached and I was a little scared.

"For crying out loud," I muttered to myself, looked uneasily up and down the street, ran hurriedly towards the lights of Cromwell Road.

CHAPTER THREE

I had been in my room only five minutes when the inquiry desk called to say Inspector Corridan was asking for me.

"Tell him to come up, please," I said, pressed the bell for the floor waiter. Corridan and the floor waiter arrived together.

Corridan was a big, beefy fellow, thirty-five, dark with small blue eyes that had a nasty habit of appearing to look right through you.

Even to his friends he was somewhat dour, seldom smiled, never laughed.

He shook hands warmly enough, looked round the room approvingly.

"They make you comfortable here I must say," he remarked, shot a quick glance at the waiter, went on, "I hope you are going to buy me a drink?"

"Sure, and I thought we might have dinner up here," I said.

"Nothing's too good for the London police."

The floor waiter produced a menu and we chose cold consommé, chicken vol au vent, ice-cream. I ordered two double whiskies and a carafe of Algerian wine.

"You newspaper men know how to live," Corridan sighed, sinking into the only armchair. "Often thought it might've been better for me to have gone in for something less exacting and more profitable than police work."

I grunted. "You should grumble," I said, sitting on the bed. "I bet you are up to your ears in graft, with half the criminals in London paying you hush-money."

His mouth tightened. "Your sense of humour is as warped as your morals," he returned, and I could see he wasn't amused.

"Okay, let's skip our morals," I said, grinning. "I'm damned glad you could come."

"Was this Netta Scott a friend of yours?" he asked, wandering to the window. He went on before I could reply. "I see the Thames enough from the Yard, but from this angle and in this light it's really attractive, don't you think?"

"Never mind about the Thames," I said shortly. "You're not being wined and dined because I want to hear about the sights of London."

He gave me a sharp look. "You sound worried. Anything wrong?"

I nodded. "There could be ..." I began when the floor waiter returned with our drinks.

When he had gone, I went on, "About Netta Scott. She was a friend of mine. I met her in '42, and we kicked around together for a couple of years. It was a shock to learn she'd committed suicide."

He drank some whisky, cocked his head approvingly. "Good whisky this," he said. "But obviously you don't want to talk about whisky. I've read the doctor's report. The girl wasn't risking a mistake. She took a stiff dose of laudanum before she gassed herself. But it's a straightforward case ... obviously suicide. The Kensington Division handled it. They had a call at seven o'clock yesterday morning from a man named Julius Cole who lives in the same house. They found the girl with her head in the gas oven and the kitchen full of gas. The windows had been sealed with adhesive tape, but not the door which fitted well. She had been dead about six hours. At a rough guess she killed herself around one o'clock in the morning. There were no marks of violence on the body, and no evidence that it wasn't anything but suicide. She was taken to the local mortuary, having been officially identified by this Cole chap who claimed to know her well by sight. We are now trying to get in touch with her relatives without any success at the moment."

I finished my whisky, felt better for it.

"No question of foul play?" I asked.

His eyes probed me. "No. Why should there be?"

"Your people are quite happy about that?"

"They're never happy about anything, but they're quite satisfied that there's no question of foul play. Suicide happens every day. It may interest you to know an individual's occupation tends to influence the likelihood of suicide," Corridan went on, closing his eyes and settling farther into his chair. "Occupations involving strain, responsibility or very late hours provide the greatest numbers of suicides. Chemists, doctors, solicitors, publicans, night club workers, butchers and soldiers are to be found high up in the list of occupations, whilst gardeners, fishermen, clergymen, school teachers and civil servants are at the foot of the list."

I groaned. "I guess I stuck my neck out that time," I said. "Okay, okay, don't let's have any more of that. Then I take it because night club workers rank high on the list of likely suicides, Netta killed herself, is that it?"

He nodded. "Something like that. Anyway, it helps us to make up our minds. If she were a school teacher, for instance, we might look at the business more closely. See what I mean?"

"And you think a girl like Netta would choose a gas oven? You don't think she'd jump out of a window or use poison?"

"Women hesitate to make a mess of themselves even in death," Corridan returned, lifting his shoulders. "Especially girls as pretty as Netta. Jumping out of windows can be very messy ... I've seen some. Owing to a little thing called the Dangerous Drugs Act suicides by poison are on the decrease. I believe over six hundred women committed suicide by coal-gas last year. I'll get you the exact figures if you're interested."

"That's good enough for me," I said. "And why do you think she killed herself?"

Corridan finished his whisky, put the glass on the table, shrugged.

"It's interesting to consider the reasons which impel individual conduct," he said, crossing his legs and sinking lower in his chair. "A knowledge of the causes of suicide is also of help in determining the question of accident, suicide or murder. The four main reasons why people commit suicide are, in order of their importance, mental conditions, drink, financial worries and love. There are other causes, of course, but these are the four important ones. As far as we know the girl didn't owe money, she didn't drink to excess, and she appeared mentally normal from what Cole and the landlady tell us. Therefore it's reasonable to suppose she had an unhappy love affair."

"The way you coppers get everything down to a rule of thumb kills me," I said, as the waiter wheeled in a table ladened with good things to eat. "Come on, let's get at it."

"Another of those excellent whiskies mightn't be a bad idea," Corridan said, getting to his feet and pulling up a straight-backed chair to the table.

"Make it two," I said to the waiter, "and then leave us to look after ourselves."

We sat down and began on the cold consommé.

"What makes you think she wasn't murdered?" I asked casually.

He shook his head. "What a chap you are," he said. "I've just told you..." He glanced up sharply, frowned. "But perhaps you know more about this than I do. Perhaps I'd better hear what you have to say before I commit myself too deeply." His lips curled slightly at the corners which was his idea of a smile. "Do you think she was murdered?"

"I'm willing to bet five hundred pounds that she was," I said.

His eyebrows shot up. "And you have five hundred pounds?"

"I have. Like to take me on?"

He shook his head. "I never bet with Yanks; they're far too smart."

He pushed his plate away, dabbed his thin lips with his napkin. "Hmm, now I wonder what makes you so sure?"

"I've been to her flat and had a look around," I said. "I found some interesting items which I'll show you in a moment. First tell me, did any of your men take anything from the flat?"

"No. Is there anything missing?"

"A number of pairs of silk stockings, most of her clothes, and a diamond bracelet and scarf-pin."

"Valuable?"

"The bracelet cost two hundred pounds three years ago. It'll be worth double that now. I don't know about the pin."

"How do you know they're missing? Couldn't she have sold them?"

I hadn't thought of that, and said so. "All the same I don't think she did. She was fond of those pieces and nothing would persuade her to get rid of her stockings. No, I don't believe she did sell the stuff."

Corridan eyed me. "Now you're being obstinate," he said quietly.

"I should say it was most likely. She may have been pressed for money at one time."

The waiter interrupted us with the whiskies. We paused before we started on the vol au vent, finished the whiskies while we talked.

"But she wasn't the type to kill herself," I said. "I remember once she said she'd never take that way out of trouble. If you'd have heard her you'd know she wasn't the type."

"How long ago was that?"

"Two years. Oh, I know you'll say people change, but I'm still sure she wasn't the type."

"What else?" The blue eyes probed, the thin mouth came near to a smile again. "Ignoring the jewellery, the stockings and her type, what else have you got?"

"I haven't started yet," I said, "but it'll keep until we've fed. You don't know anything about the girl?"

"She hasn't a record if that's what you mean," he returned, contentedly chewing his food. "She worked at the Blue Club as a dance hostess and she's been fined once or twice for car offences, otherwise we don't know anything about her."

"And the Blue Club? I hear it's taken a dive since I knew it."

"Most of these clubs that catered for Americans have deteriorated since the Americans have gone home. The Blue Club is on our suspect list, but Bradley is a little too smart for us at the moment. We believe the place is a gambling den, and there's drinking out of hours. I'm sure the food is Black Market, but we've never been able to get any of our men in there, and a raid has always flopped. The Chief thinks one of our men tips Bradley off when a raid is going to be made. Anyway, he's always one jump ahead of us, although he can't last much longer."

By now we had finished the meal, and Corridan went back to the armchair. I ordered brandy and cigars, saw he was settled comfortably.

"Well, now perhaps I can convince you," I said, produced the Luger and handed it to him.

He sat for a long moment staring at it, his face expressionless, then he glanced up, his eyes cold.

"Where did this come from?" he asked.

I told him.

He examined the Luger thoughtfully, shook his head, relaxed again.

"If you knew the number of women who have these damn things you wouldn't think so much of it," he said. "Nearly every American soldier brought one back from Germany, and gave it to his girlfriend. What makes you so het up about it?"

"I'm not het up about it," I said, "but it's odd she should have kept it hidden in a dress like that, isn't it?" I suddenly wondered if I was making a fool of myself.

"Well, you can get into trouble having one of these things—she might have hidden it with that in mind," Corridan returned, stretching out his long legs and sniffing at his brandy. "Nothing more concrete?"

I told him about the sixteen five-pound notes, and handed them and the letter to Anne Scott over to him. I also gave him the diamond ring.

"You certainly searched the place pretty thoroughly," he said, cocking an eye at me. "I don't know if you had any right in there ... had you?"

"Maybe not," I returned, chewing my cigar, "but this business worries me, Corridan. I feel there's something wrong somewhere." I went on to tell him about the man who had attacked me.

He showed some interest at last.

"Did you see him?"

"It was damned dark, and I was startled. All right," I went on when he half smiled. "I was scared pink. So would you've been if it had happened to you. The guy sprang out at me with what looked like a tyre lever, and he had a damned good shot at bashing my brains in. I couldn't see much of him, but he seemed young, slight, and could run like hell. I think I'd know him again if I saw him."

"What do you think he was after?"

"The gun perhaps," I said, "that's why I suggest you have it checked. You see there's a scratch on the barrel and it looks as if at one time a name was engraved on the butt. I believe the gun might tell us something."

"You've been reading too many detective stories," he grunted.

"Still, there's no harm checking the gun." He sniffed at it. "Been fired, I'd say a month or so ago. Smells of lilac, too."

"Her favourite perfume," I told him. "Well, that's my story. I hoped you'd be more impressed, but I should have known better. The trouble with you is you've no imagination."

He stroked his long fleshy nose. "Maybe I haven't, but I've a lot of horse sense, and I still think she committed suicide." He picked up the envelope, tapped it on his finger-nails. "Shall we see what's in here?"

"Can we?"

"The police can do anything," he said with a wink. He took out a pencil, slid it under the flap of the envelope, rolled it gently backwards and forwards. After a little persuasion the flap lifted.

"Easy once you know how," he said, looking at me with his half-hearted smile. "You have to have the right touch, of course."

"I'll keep my mail out of your reach," I said. "Well, what's inside?"

He glanced into the envelope, whistled. With finger and thumb he hooked out what seemed a stack of over-printed paper.

"Bearer bonds," he said.

I leaned forward. "Seems a lot of them," I said, gaping.

His fingers flicked through them. "Five thousand pounds worth," he said. "Now I wonder where these came from?" He glanced inside the envelope. "No note. Hmm, this is a little odd I must say."

I laughed at him. "Now you're starting. The whole thing's odd to me. Well, what are you going to do about it?"

"I think I'll take a trip to Lakeham and see Miss Scott. I'd like to know where these bonds came from. If she can't tell me, I'll have to check them. That may be a longish job; still, I want to know."

"Could I come with you to Lakeham?" I asked. "I'll play Watson to your Holmes. Besides, I'd like to meet the sister. Maybe she doesn't know Netta's dead. I think I should be there when the news is broken."

"By all means come," he said, getting to his feet. "Shall we say tomorrow morning? We can go down by car."

"Swell. But don't think you're through yet," I said. "There's one more thing I want you to do. Where can I see Netta? I want to see her before she's buried."

"A bit morbid, aren't you?" he shot at me. "What good can that do you?"

"I'm funny that way," I said, stubbing out my cigar. "Suppose you come along too? I want you to see her if only to be in a better position to judge when the lid comes off this business, as I'm sure it will. I have a hunch we're on to something that's going to be big, and you'll thank me in the long run for putting you wise."

"I've never met such a chap," Corridan muttered, went over to the telephone, called the Yard.

I stood by while he ordered a police car to pick us up outside the Savoy.

"Come along," he said, "if it hadn't been such a damn good dinner I'd have told you to have gone to blazes, but I suppose I'll have to pay for my entertainment. Who knows, you may invite me again."

"Maybe I will at that," I said, following him along the corridor to the elevator.

It took us under a quarter of an hour to reach the mortuary, and the officer in charge, startled to have a visit from Corridan, came out to greet us.

"Netta Scott," Corridan said abruptly. He was always short with his inferiors in rank. "You have her here. We want to see her."

The constable, a young, red-faced country-looking fellow, shook his head. "Not now, sir," he said. "She was here, but she was taken to the Hammersmith mortuary an hour ago."

Corridan frowned. "Oh? On whose orders?"

"I don't know, sir," the constable replied, looked blank.

"You don't know?" Corridan barked, "But surely you had an official order before you let them take the body?"

The constable changed colour. "Well, no, sir," he said. "I'm new here. I—I didn't know an order was necessary in this case. The driver of the ambulance said there'd been a mistake, and the remains should 'ave gone to Hammersmith. I let him take the body."

Corridan, his face dark with fury, pushed past the constable, went into the office, slammed the door.

The constable stared after him, scratched his head. "Now I wonder what's up," he said, looking at me. "Do you think I did wrong, sir?"

I shrugged. "Search me," I said, feeling uneasy. "But you'll know before long."

After several minutes, Corridan came out of the office, walked past the constable, jerked his head at me. At the door he paused, looked back.

"You'll hear a lot more about this, my man, before very long," he snapped at the constable, walked to the police car.

I got in beside him, and as we drove off, I said, "Well, do we go to Hammersmith?"

"Hammersmith didn't send for the body," Corridan growled.

"Anyone but a fool would have known it was a plant. A couple of hours back an ambulance was reported stolen. Someone—believe it or not—has kidnapped Netta Scott's body. It's fantastic! Why, for God's sake?" and he thumped the hack of the driver's seat with his clenched fist.

CHAPTER FOUR

The next morning, I awoke with a start. The telephone was ringing, and sitting up in bed, I grabbed the receiver, stifling a yawn as I did so. I peered at my bedside clock and saw it was ten minutes past eight, grunted,

"Who is it?"

"Inspector Corridan asking for you," the porter said.

"All right, send him up," I returned, snatched up my dressing-gown and rushed into the bathroom for a hasty shower.

I had slept badly, and was still feeling a little piqued at the abrupt way Corridan had returned me to the Savoy. He had said, "Sorry, Harmas, but this is police business now. Can't take you along with me," and that was that. Of course, he was rattled, and I realized that he had something to get rattled about, but I thought he had a nerve to ditch me after I'd given him so much data to work on; but Corridan was like that. When he started on a job, he worked alone.

I was just coming out of the bathroom when I heard a rap on my door. I opened it; Corridan entered. He looked tired, was unshaven.

"Have you only just got up?" he snapped, tossing his hat on a chair. "I haven't even been to bed."

"You don't expect me to sob over that item of news, do you?" I returned. "After the way you dropped me last night?"

He looked more surly than ever, sat down. "Get me some coffee, there's a good fellow, and don't grouse," he said, "I've had a hell of a night."

I picked up the telephone, called the floor waiter, ordered coffee.

"You have only yourself to blame," I said. "If you'd have kept me with you, I'd have halved your work."

"I'm seeing the Chief in half an hour's time, and I thought I'd look in on my way to tell you the news," Corridan said. "First the gun. It belonged to a fellow named Peter Utterly, a lieutenant in the U.S. Army. He's been repatriated, but we persuaded the authorities on the other side to get a statement from him. Apparently he knew Netta Scott, gave her the Luger as a souvenir. You'll remember I told you that was the probable explanation of the gun."

"You've been quick," I said, a little disappointed that the explanation should be so commonplace.

"Oh, we work fast when necessary," Corridan said, looked dour.

"So much for the gun. We traced the ambulance. It was found on Hampstead Heath, but the body is still missing. We have a description of the driver, but it could fit any young fellow. Where the body's got to defeats me, and why it was stolen defeats me still more."

"There must be an explanation," I said, waving to the waiter who had just entered to put the coffee on the table. "Unless it was a practical joke."

Corridan shrugged. "We'll get to the bottom of it," he said, glanced at his watch. "Let's have that coffee. I have to be off in a moment."

While I was pouring the coffee, he went on, "I've had the bonds checked. They are forgeries. That's always something to worry about. Can you suggest why this girl should be hiding forged bonds in her flat?"

"Not unless someone gave them to her, and she thought they were genuine," I said, handing him the cup of coffee. "Of course, I've been out of touch with Netta for a long time now. She may have got into bad company, but I doubt it."

He sipped the coffee, grunted. "I think that's likely," he said. "The diamond ring you found has a history. It's part of a considerable amount of jewellery stolen a few weeks ago. The owner of the jewellery, Hervey Allenby, identified the ring late last night. Our people have been waiting for the stuff to come into the market. This ring is the first sign of it. How do you think she got hold of it?"

I shook my head, perplexed. "Maybe someone gave it to her," I said.

"Then why should she hide it at the bottom of a jar of cold cream?" Corridan returned, finishing his coffee. "Odd place to keep a ring unless you have a guilty conscience, isn't it?"

I said it was.

"Well, it'll sort itself out," Corridan went on. "I still don't think we have any grounds to suppose the girl was murdered, Harmas. After all that's the thing that was worrying you. You can leave this other business to me."

"So you're going to play copper, are you?" I said. "Well, I think someone knocked her off. If you'll take the trouble to use that hat rack you call a head, I'll explain in two minutes why it wasn't suicide."

He eyed me coldly, moved to the door.

"I'm afraid I can't spare the time, Harmas," he said. "I have a lot to do, and newspaper men's theories scarcely interest me. Sorry, but I suggest you leave this to those competent to handle it."

"There must be times when Mrs. Corridan is very proud of you," I said sarcastically. "This is one of them, I should think."

"I'm single," he said. "Sorry to disappoint you. I must be getting along." He paused at the door. "I'm afraid there can be no question of you coming with me to see this Anne Scott. This is official business now. We can't have Yankee newspaper men barging in on our preserves."

I nodded. "Okay," I said. "If that's the way you feel, think no more about it."

"I won't," he said, with a sour smile, quietly left the room.

For a moment or so I was too mad to think clearly, then I calmed down, had to grin. If Corridan thought he could keep me out of this business he was crazy.

I bundled into my clothes, grabbed the telephone and asked Inquiries how I could hire a car. They said they'd have one ready for me in twenty minutes after I'd explained I could get petrol on my Press card. I smoked two cigarettes, did a little thinking, then went downstairs.

They had found me a Buick. I was too scared to ask them how much it would cost, took the hall porter aside and inquired my way to Lakeham. He said that it was a few miles from Horsham, and suggested I should leave London via Putney Bridge and the Kingston By-pass. The rest of the run, he told me, would be simple as Horsham was well signposted.

In spite of its rather obvious age, the Buick ran well, and I reached the Fulham Road in less than a quarter of an hour and without having to ask the way. At this time of the morning, the traffic was coming into London, and I had practically a clear road ahead of me.

As I passed the Stamford Bridge football ground, one of the landmarks described by the hall porter, I noticed in the driving mirror a battered Standard car which I was fairly certain I'd seen behind me at Knightsbridge. I thought nothing of it until I reached Putney Bridge when I spotted it again. Being still a little jittery from the attack of last night, I began to wonder if I was being tailed.

I tried to catch sight of the driver, but the car was equipped with a blue anti-dazzle windscreen, and I could only make out the silhouette of a man's head.

I drove up Putney High Street, stopped at the traffic lights as they turned red. The Standard parked behind me.

I decided I would have to make certain that this man in the battered Standard was following me. If he was, I'd have to shake him. I wondered if Corridan had set one of his cops on to tailing me, decided it wasn't likely.

I was glad I had the Buick because it was obviously more powerful than the Standard which looked to me to be only a fourteen horsepower job against my thirty-one. As soon as the traffic lights changed to yellow, I shoved down the accelerator pedal, made a racing get-away. I roared up the hill leading from Putney, changed into top, missing second, and belted forward with the speedometer swinging dangerously near eighty miles an hour.

I saw people staring after me, but as no policeman hove into sight, I couldn't care less. I let the Buick have all the petrol it could take until I reached the top of the hill. Then I eased off the throttle, looked rather contentedly into the mirror, had the shock of my life.

The Standard was about twenty feet from my tail.

I was still uncertain that I was being tailed. It might be that the guy had decided to show me I wasn't the only one with a fast car. I now had a healthy respect for the battered Standard, whose shabby body obviously concealed a first-class engine, tuned for speed.

I kept on; so did the Standard. When I reached the beginning of the By-pass, and he was still a hundred yards or so behind me, I decided to be foxy.

I flapped my hand out of the window, pulled up by the side of the road, watched the Standard shoot past me. As it went by I spotted the driver. He looked a youth. He was dark, a greasy slouch hat was pulled down low, but I saw enough of his face to recognize him. He was the runt who'd tried to make a batter out of my brains the previous night.

Now feeling certain he had been tailing me, I watched the Standard go on, and I reached for a cigarette. I guessed he would be pretty mad by now, wondering what he could do. He couldn't very well stop—couldn't he? I had to grin. A couple of hundred yards farther up the road, he pulled up.

That settled it. I was being tailed, and I took out a pencil from my pocket and scribbled the licence number of the car on the back of an envelope.

Now I had to shake him. I didn't hesitate. I owed him something for giving me a scare last night. I started the Buick, drove up to the Standard, braked sharply and was out of the car before the runt knew what was happening.

"Hello, pal," I said, smiling at him. "A little bird tells me you're following me. I don't like it." While I was speaking I took my penknife out, opened the blade. "Sorry to give you a little work, sonny," I went on, "but it'll do you a world of good."

He just sat glowering at me, his lips drawn off his yellow teeth. He looked like an infuriated ferret.

I bent down, stuck my penknife into one of his tyres. The air hissed out; the tyre went flat.

"These tyres aren't what they were, are they, son?" I asked, folding the blade down, putting the knife in my pocket. "I'll leave you to change the wheel. I have an appointment right now."

He called me a word which in normal times would have annoyed me, but I felt he had some justification.

"If you'd like to collect a tyre lever, we'll have another little joust," I said amiably.

He repeated the word, so I left him.

He was still sitting there as I drove past, and he was still sitting there when I reached the bend in the road some six hundred yards farther on. I guessed he was a sore pup all right.

I reached Horsham in half an hour and I was sure now that I wasn't being followed. The traffic was negligible, and for miles I drove with nothing behind me.

From Horsham I took the Worthing road, branched off after a few miles and approached Lakeham. The country was magnificent, and the day hot and sunny. I enjoyed the last few miles, thinking I should have explored that part of England before instead of spending so many days and nights in stuffy, dirty London.

A signpost told me I was within three-quarters of a mile of Lakeham, and

I slowed down, driving along the narrow lane until I reached a few cottages, a pub and a post office. I guessed I'd arrived.

I pulled up outside the pub, went in.

It was a quaint box-like place, almost like a doll's house. The woman who served me a double whisky seemed ready to talk, especially when she heard my accent.

We chatted about the surrounding country and this and that, then I asked her if she knew where a cottage called Beverley hung out.

"Oh, you mean Miss Scott?" she said, and there was an immediate look of disapproval in her eyes. "Her place's about a mile farther on. You take the first on your left and the cottage lies off the road. It has a thatched roof and a yellow gate. You can't miss it."

"That's swell," I said. "I know a friend of hers. Maybe I'll look her up. Do you know her? I was wondering what she was like. Think I'd be welcome?"

"From what I hear, men are always welcomed there," she said, with a sniff. "I've never seen 'er. No one in the village sees 'er. She only comes down for the weekends."

"Maybe she has someone to look after the cottage?" I suggested, wondering if I had made the journey for nothing.

"Mrs. Brambee does for 'er," the woman told me. "She ain't much 'erself."

I paid for my drink, thanked the woman, returned to the Buick.

It took me only a few minutes to find Beverley. I saw it through the trees as I drove up the narrow lane. It stood in a charming garden, a two-storied, thatch-roofed, rough-cast building, as attractive as any you could wish to see.

I parked the Buick outside, pushed open the gate and walked up the path. The sun beat down on me, and the smell of pinks, roses and wallflowers hung in the still air. I wouldn't have minded living there myself.

I went up to the oak nail-studded front door, rapped with the shiny brass knocker, feeling a curious uneasy excitement as I waited. I was uneasy because I didn't know if Netta's sister had heard about Netta, and I wasn't sure how I should break the news. I was excited because I wondered if Anne was like her sister, and how we would get on together.

But after a few moments, I realized, with a sharp feeling of disappointment, that there was no one in, or at least, no one was going to answer my knock. I stood back, glanced up at the windows of the upper floor, then peered into the first window within reach on the ground floor. I could see the room stretching the length of the house, and the big garden through the windows at the back. The place was well furnished and comfortable. I moved around the house, until I reached the back. There was no one about, and I stood for a moment, hat in hand, looking across the well-kept lawn and at the flower-beds, a mass of brilliant colours.

I passed the back door, hesitated, tried the handle, but the door was locked. I moved on until I reached another window, paused as I noticed the curtains had been drawn.

I stared at the curtained window, and for no reason at all I suddenly felt spooked. I took a step forward, tried to see into the room, by peering through a chink in the curtain. I could see it was the kitchen, but my view was so limited I could only make out a dresser from which hung willow pattern cups and plates in rows along the ordered shelves.

Then I smelt coal-gas.

Feet crunched on the gravel. I swung around. Corridan and two uniformed policemen came striding towards me. Corridan's face was dour, his eyes showed irritation and anger.

"You better bust in quick," I said, before he could speak. "I smell gas."

CHAPTER FIVE

I sat fuming in the Buick outside the cottage, and watched the activity going on in and out the front door.

Corridan had been extremely curt and official when he had recovered from his surprise at seeing me.

"What the hell are you doing here?" he had demanded. Then he, too, smelt the gas. "This is no place for you. It's no good glaring at me. This is police business, and newspaper men are not wanted."

I began to argue with him, but he brushed past me, saying to one of the policemen, "Escort Mr. Harmas off the premises, please, and see he keeps out."

I felt inclined to clock the policeman on his beaky nose, but I knew it wouldn't get me anywhere so I returned to the car, sat in it, lit a cigarette and watched.

Corridan and the other policeman succeeded in breaking down the front door. They entered the cottage, while the second policeman remained at the gate to scowl at me. I scowled right back.

After a few moments, I saw Corridan opening the windows, then move out of sight. The sickly smell of gas drifted across the lawn. I waited a quarter of an hour before anything else happened. Then a car drove up and a tall dismal-looking guy carrying a black bag got out, had a word with the policeman at the gate, and together they went inside.

I didn't have to be clairvoyant to guess the guy was the village croaker.

After ten minutes, the dismal guy came out. I was waiting for him near his car, and he gave me a sharp, unfriendly look as he opened his car door.

"Pardon me, doc," I said, "I'm a newspaper man. Can you tell me what's going on in there?"

"You must ask Inspector Corridan," he snapped back, got into his car, drove away.

The policeman at the gate grinned behind his hand.

After a while the other policeman came out of the cottage, whispered something to his colleague, hurried off down the lane.

"I suppose he's gone to buy Corridan a toffee apple," I said to the policeman at the gate. "But don't tell me. Just let it mystify me."

The policeman grinned sympathetically. I could see he was the gossiping type and was bursting to talk to someone.

"'E's off to get Mrs. Brambee wot looks after this 'ere cottage," he said, after a quick look around to make sure he wasn't overheard.

"Someone dead in there?" I asked, jerking my thumb to the cottage.

He nodded. "A young lady," he returned, moving closer to the Buick. "Pretty little thing. Suicide, of course. Put 'er 'ead in the gas oven. Been dead three or four days I should say."

"Never mind what you say," I returned. "What did the doc say."

The policeman grinned a little sheepishly. "That's wot 'e did say as a matter of fact."

I grunted. "Is it Anne Scott?"

"I dunno. The doc couldn't identify 'er. That's why Bert's gone for this 'ere Mrs. Brambee."

"What's comrade Corridan doing in there?" I asked.

"Sniffing around," the policeman returned, shrugging. From the expression on his face I guessed Corridan wasn't his favourite person. "I bet 'e's trying to make out there's more to this than meets the eye. The Yard men always do. It 'elps their promotion."

I thought this was a little unfair, but didn't say so, turned around to watch two figures coming down the lane. One of them was Bert, the policeman, the other was a tall, bulky woman in a pink sack-like dress.

"Here they come," I said, nodding in their direction.

The woman was walking quickly. She had a long stride, and the policeman seemed pressed to keep up with her. As they drew nearer, I could see her face. She was dark, sun-tanned, about forty, with a mass of black greasy hair, rolled up in an untidy bun at the back of her head. Straggling locks of hair fell over her face, and she kept brushing them back with a hand as big as a man's.

She ran up the flagged path. Her eyes were wild, her mouth was working. She looked as if she were suffering from acute grief and shock.

Bert winked at the other policeman as he followed the woman into the cottage.

I lit another cigarette, settled down in the car, waited a little anxiously.

A sudden animal-like cry drifted through the open windows, and was followed by the sound of wild hysterical sobbing.

"It must be Anne Scott," I said, troubled.

"Looks like it," the policeman returned, staring in the direction of the cottage.

After a long while the sobbing died down. We waited almost half an hour before the woman appeared again. She walked slowly, her face hidden by a dirty handkerchief, her shoulders sagging.

The policeman opened the gate for her, helped her through by taking her elbow. It was meant sympathetically, but she immediately shook him off.

"Take your bloody hands off me," she said in a muffled voice, went on down the lane.

"A proper lady," the policeman said, chewing his chin-strap and going red.

"Maybe she's been reading Macbeth," I suggested, but that didn't seem to console him.

It was now almost an hour and a half since I had seen Corridan. I was hungry. It was past one-thirty; but I decided to wait, hopeful I might see something more or get a chance of telling Corridan what I thought of him.

Ten minutes later he came to the door and waved to me. I was out of the car, past the policeman in split seconds.

"All right," he said curtly as I dashed up to him. "I suppose you want to look around. But for God's sake don't tell anyone I've let you in."

I decided that after all I hadn't wasted my money feeding this lug.

"Thanks," I said. "I won't tell a soul."

There was still a strong smell of gas in the cottage, which grew stronger as we entered the kitchen.

"It's Anne Scott all right," Corridan said gloomily, pointing to a huddled figure lying on the floor.

I stood over her, felt inadequate, could think of nothing to say.

She wore a pink dressing-gown and white pyjamas, her feet were bare, her hands clenched tightly into fists. Her head lay hidden in the gas oven. By moving around, carefully stepping over her legs, I could see into the oven. She was a blonde, about twenty-five; even in death she was attractive, although I could see no resemblance to Netta in the serene rather lovely face.

I stepped back, looked at Corridan. "Sure she's Anne Scott?" I asked.

He made an impatient movement. "Of course," he said. "The woman identified her. You're not trying to make out there's a mystery in this, are you?"

"Odd they should both commit suicide, isn't it?" I said, feeling in my bones that something was very wrong.

He jerked his head, walked into the sitting room.

"Read that," he said, handed me a sheet of note-paper. "It was found by her side."

I took the note, read:

Without Netta life means nothing to me. Please forgive me.
                                                              ANNE.

I handed it back. "After fifty years in the police force, I feel justified in saying that's a plant," I said.

He took the paper. "Don't try to be funny," he said coldly.

I grinned. "Who do you suppose it was addressed to?"

He shook his head. "I don't know. Mrs. Brambee tells me a lot of men used to come down here. There was one fellow—Peter—who Anne used to talk a lot about. Maybe it was for him."

"Would that be Peter Utterly?" I asked. "The guy who gave Netta the gun?"

Corridan rubbed his chin. "Doubtful," he said. "Utterly went back to the States a month or so ago."

"Yeah, I'd forgotten that," I said, wandering over to the writing-desk that stood in the window recess. "Well, I suppose you'll look for this guy?" I opened the lid of the desk, glanced inside. There were no papers, no letters. All the pigeon-holes had been carefully cleared. "She tidied up before she threw in her hand," I pointed out. "Any letters or papers anywhere?"

He shook his head.

"No means of checking if the handwriting of the note is really Anne's?"

"My dear fellow ..." he began a little tartly.

"Skip it," I said. "I've a suspicious nature. Find anything interesting?"

"Nothing," he returned, eyed me narrowly. "I've searched the place thoroughly; there's nothing to connect her with forged bonds, diamond rings or anything like that. Sorry to disappoint you."

"I'll get over it," I said, grinning. "Just give me time. Find any silk stockings in the place?"

"I didn't look for silk stockings," he snapped back. "I've more important things to do."

"Let's look," I said. "I have a thing about silk stockings. Where's the bedroom?"

"Now look here, Harmas, this has gone far enough. I've let you in."

"For your rupture's sake, if not for me, calm down," I said, patting him on his arm. "What's the harm in looking? Netta had silk stockings and they vanished. Anne may have had silk stockings and they may still be here. Let's look."

He gave me an exasperated glare, turned to the door. "Wait here," he said, began to mount the stairs.

I kept on his heels. "You may need me. Always a good thing to have a witness."

He led the way into a small but luxuriously furnished bedroom, went immediately to a chest of drawers and began to paw over a mass of silk undies, sweaters and scarves.

"You handle that stuff like a married man," I said, opened the wardrobe, peered in. There were only two frocks and a two-piece costume hanging up. "She didn't have many clothes, poor kid," I went on. "Maybe she couldn't get coupons, or do you think she was a nudist?"

He scowled at me. "There're no stockings here," he said.

"No stockings of any kind at all?"

"No."

"Seems to confirm my nudist theory, doesn't it?" I said. "You might like to turn this stocking angle over in your nimble, sharp-witted mind. I'm going to do that myself, and I'm going to keep at it until I find out why neither of these girls had any stockings."

"What the hell are you driving at?" Corridan burst out. "You have a shilling-shocker mind. Who do you think you are—Perry Mason?"

"Don't tell me you read detective stories," I said, surprised. "Well, what happens now?"

"I'm waiting for the ambulance," Corridan said, following me downstairs. "The body will be taken to the Horsham mortuary, and the inquest will also be held there. I don't expect anything will come out at the inquest. It's pretty straightforward." But he sounded worried.

"Do you really think she learned about Netta's suicide and followed suit?" I asked.

"Why not?" he returned. "You'd be surprised how suicides follow in families. We have a bunch of statistics about it."

"I was forgetting you worked by rule of thumb," I returned. "What was the idea of keeping me out until you sniffed around?"

"Now see here, Harmas, you have no damn business here at all. You are here on sufferance," Corridan retorted. "This is a serious business, and I can't have rubbernecks watching me work."

"Calling me a rubberneck is as big a lie as calling what you do work," I said sadly. "But never mind. I'll behave, and thanks for the break anyway."

He looked sharply at me to see if I was kidding, decided I was, compressed his lips.

"Well, that's all there's to see. You'd better be moving before the ambulance arrives."

"Yeah, I'll be off," I said, wandering to the front door. "You wouldn't be interested in my theory about this second death I suppose?"

"Not in the slightest," he said firmly.

"I thought as much. It's a pity, because I think I could have put you on the right lines. I guess you'll have a guard on the body this time? You don't want it stolen like the other was, do you?"

"Oh, rubbish," he said crossly. "Nothing like that'll happen. But I'm taking precautions if that's what you mean."

"Oddly enough, that's exactly what I do mean," I said, smiled at him, opened the door. "Be seeing you, pal," I went on, left him.

I winked at the policeman at the gate, got into the Buick and drove slowly down the lane. I had a lot to think about, and I didn't quite know where to start. I thought it mightn't be a bad idea to have a word with Mrs. Brambee. That seemed the obvious starting-point.

I knew her cottage couldn't be far, as Bert, the policeman, had only been a few minutes fetching her. I didn't want Corridan to know what I was up to, so I drove to the end of the lane, parked the Buick behind a thicket, and walked back. I was lucky to meet a farmhand who pointed Mrs. Brambee's place out to me. It was small and dilapidated with a wild, overgrown garden.

I walked up the weed-covered path, rapped on the door. I had to knock three times before I heard shuffling feet. A moment later, the door jerked open and Mrs. Brambee confronted me. At close quarters she seemed half gypsy. She was very swarthy and her jet-black eyes were like little wet stones.

"What do you want?" she demanded in a harsh voice that somehow reminded me of the caw of a crow.

"I'm a newspaper man, Mrs. Brambee," I said, raising my hat; hoped she'd appreciate good manners. "I'd like to ask you a few questions about Miss Scott. You saw the body just now. Are you absolutely sure it was Miss Scott?"

Her eyes snapped. "Of course, it was Miss Scott," she said, beginning to close the door. "I don't know what you're talking about. Anyway, I don't intend to answer questions. You get off."

"I could make it worth your while," I said, jingling my loose change suggestively. "I want the inside story of this suicide, and my paper will pay generously for it."

"You and your paper can go to hell," she shouted violently, slammed the door, only I had my foot ready for just such a move.

"Now be nice," I said, smiling at her through the three-inch opening between the doorpost and the door. "Who is this guy Peter you were telling the Inspector about? Where can I find him?"

She jerked open the door, put her hand on my chest and shoved.

I wasn't expecting such a move, and I staggered back, lost my balance, fell full-length. Her shove was like the kick from a horse.

The door slammed and I heard the bolt shoot home.

I got slowly to my feet, dusted myself down, whistled softly. Then I glanced up at the upper windows, stiffened.

I had a fleeting glimpse of a girl looking down at me. Even as I looked up, she jerked back from the window and out of sight. I couldn't even swear that it was a girl: it might have been a man—even an optical illusion. But unless my eyes had deceived me, Netta Scott was upstairs, and had been watching me.

CHAPTER SIX

I was glancing through the newspaper, morning coffee on the table by my bed, when a small item of news caught my eye. I sat up, nearly upsetting the tray.

MYSTERIOUS FIRE AT HORSHAM MORTUARY ran the headline. The few lines below the headline stated that at twelve o'clock the previous night a fire had broken out in the Horsham mortuary, and the efforts of the local fire brigade were unavailing. The building had been completely destroyed, and three policemen, who were on the premises, narrowly escaped with their lives.

I threw the paper down, grabbed the telephone and put a call through to Corridan. I was told that he was out of town.

I jumped out of bed, wandered into the bathroom, took a cold shower. I shaved, came back to the bedroom, began to dress. All the time I was thinking.

Someone behind the scenes was controlling this set-up, like a puppet-master pulling the strings. Whoever it was had to be stopped.

If Corridan wasn't smart enough to stop him, then I was going to have a try. Up to now, I'd tagged along in the rear as an interested spectator. I was now going to take a more active part in this business.

I decided first to give Corridan one more chance. I asked the switchboard girl to connect me with the Horsham police. After the inevitable delay I was put through.

"Is Inspector Corridan with you, please?" I asked.

"Hold on, sir," a voice invited me.

Corridan came on the line. "Yes?" he snapped. "What is it?" He sounded like a lion who'd seen someone swipe his dinner.

"Hello," I said. "This is your conscience calling you from the Savoy Hotel. What have you got on your mind this morning?"

"For God's sake don't bother me now, Harmas," Corridan returned. "I'm busy."

"When aren't you?" I said. "That's a sweet little item in the newspaper this morning. What does Anne Scott look like now? Done to a turn or burnt to a crisp?"

"I know what you're thinking," he said savagely. "It was nothing like that at all. These fools here store their petrol in the mortuary of all places, and a faulty electric wire set it off. We've satisfied ourselves that there's no evidence of arson, although it is a most extraordinary coincidence. The body was practically burnt to a cinder. Fortunately, of course, it has been officially identified, so there'll be no trouble at the inquest. Now you've heard the details, for goodness' sake get off the line and let me get on with my work."

"Don't rush away," I said quickly. "I'm not satisfied about this business, Corridan. Coincidence be damned for a tale. Look, I think ..."

"So long, Harmas," he broke in. "Someone's waiting to speak to me," and he hung up.

I slammed down the receiver, selected four of the worst words in my cursing vocabulary, said them, felt better. That settled it, I thought. I was going to get into this business with both feet and the hell with Corridan.

I went downstairs, buttonholed the hall porter.

"Brother," I said to him, "can you tell me where I can hire a reliable private detective?"

For a moment a look of faint astonishment showed in his eyes, then he became once more the perfect servant.

"Certainly, sir," he said, going to his desk. "I have an address here. J. B. Merryweather, Thames House, Millbank. Mr. Merryweather was, at one time, a Chief Inspector at Scotland Yard."

"Swell," I said, parted with two half-crowns, asked him to call me a taxi.

I found J. B. Merryweather's office on the top floor of a vast concrete and steel building overlooking an uninspired portion of the Thames.

Merryweather was short and fat; his face the colour of a mulberry, and covered with a network of fine blue veins. His small eyes were watery, and the whites tinged with yellow. His long nose gave him a hawk-like appearance, which, I should imagine, was good for trade. I wasn't particularly impressed by him, but from what I had seen of private investigators in my country, the less impressive they were the better results they obtained.

Merryweather eyed me over as I entered his tiny, somewhat dusty office, offered a limp hand, waved me to a straight-backed chair. He folded himself down in his swivelled chair which creaked alarmingly under his weight, sunk his knobbly chin deep into a rather soiled stiff collar. His eyes drooped as he gave what he probably imagined to be a fair imitation of a booze-ridden Sherlock Holmes.

"I should like your name," he said, taking a pad and pencil from his desk drawer, "for my records, and the address, if you please."

I told him who I was, said I was staying at the Savoy Hotel. He nodded, wrote the information on the pad, said the Savoy was a nice place to live in.

I agreed, waited.

"It's your wife, I suppose?" he asked in a deep, weary voice which seemed to start from his feet.

"I'm not married," I said, taking out a carton of cigarettes, lighting one. He leaned forward hopefully, so I pushed the carton across the desk. He eased out a cigarette, struck a match on his desk, lit up.

"Difficult things to get these days," he sighed. "I'm out of them this morning. Nuisance."

I said it was, ran my fingers through my hair, wondered what he'd say when he knew what I'd come about. I had a feeling he might have a stroke.

"Blackmail, perhaps?" he asked, blowing a cloud of smoke down his vein-covered nose.

"Something rather more complicated than that," I said, trying to make myself comfortable in the chair. "Suppose I begin at the beginning?"

He made a slight grimace as if he wasn't anxious to hear a long story, muttered something about being pretty busy this morning.

I looked around the shabby office, decided he could never be busy, but was suffering from an inferiority complex, said I'd been recommended to him by the hall porter of the Savoy Hotel.

He brightened immediately. "Damn good chap that," he said, rubbing his hands. "Many a time we've worked together in the old days."

"Well, maybe I'd better get on with it," I said, a little bored with him. I told him about Netta, how we had met, the kind of things we did, and how I had arrived at her flat to find she had committed suicide.

He sank lower in his chair, a bewildered, rather dismayed expression on his face as I talked.

I told him how the body had been stolen from the mortuary, and he flinched. I went on to tell him about Anne, how I had gone to her cottage and what happened there.

"The police moved her body to the Horsham mortuary last night," I concluded, beginning to enjoy myself. I presented him with my pièce de ré-sistance, the clipping from the morning's newspaper.

He had to find his spectacles before he could read it, and when he had,

I could see he wished he hadn't; also wished I hadn't come to worry him.

"The body was burned to a cinder, so I'm told," I went on. "Now you know the set-up, what do you think?"

"My dear sir," he said, waving his hands vaguely, "this isn't in my line at all. Divorce, blackmail, breach of promise, yes. This kind of novelette drama, no."

I nodded understandingly. "I thought you might feel that way about it," I said. "It's a pity. Never mind, I'll probably find someone else to do the work." As I was speaking I took out my wallet, glanced inside as if looking for something. I gave him plenty of time to see the five hundred one-pound notes I was still carrying. Whatever else was wrong with him, his eyesight, as far as spotting money was concerned, was excellent.

He levered himself up in his chair, adjusted his tie.

"What do you suggest I might do to help you?" he ventured cautiously.

I put the wallet away. To him, it was like a black cloud passing before the face of the sun.

"I wanted someone to investigate at Lakeham," I said. "I want to get everything I can on this woman, Mrs. Brambee, and I want a background picture of Anne Scott."

He brightened visibly. "Well, that's something we might be able to do," he said, and looked hopefully at the carton of cigarettes on his desk. "I wonder if you'd mind ..."

"Go ahead," I said.

He took another cigarette, became quite genial.

"Yes, I think we could help you do that," he went on, drawing down a lungful of smoke. "I have an excellent man, very discreet. I could put him on the job." His eyes closed for a moment, then snapped open. "It isn't our usual line of investigation, you know. It might—hum—cost a little more."

"I'll pay well for results," I returned. "What are your terms?"

"Well, now let me see. Shall we say ten pounds a week and three pounds a day expenses?" He looked hopefully at me, looked away.

"For that I'd expect to hire Sherlock Holmes himself," I said, and meant it.

Mr. Merryweather tittered, put his hand over his mouth, looked embarrassed.

"It's an expensive age we live in," he sighed, shaking his head.

I was glad I hadn't told him about the attempted attack on me, or about the guy following me in the Standard car. He would probably have added danger money to the bill.

"Well, all right," I said, shrugging. "Only I want results." I counted thirty-one pounds on to his desk. "That'll hold you for one week. Get me everything you can on Anne Scott, have someone watch Mrs. Brambee's cottage.

I want to know who goes in and who comes out, what she does and why she does it."

"It's a police job really," he said, whisking the money into a drawer and turning the key. "Who's in charge of the case?"

"Inspector Corridan," I told him.

His face darkened. "Oh, that fellow," he said, scowling. "One of the bright boys. Wouldn't have lasted a day in my time. I know him—a Chief's pet." He seemed to withdraw into himself, brooding and bitter. "Well, I shouldn't be surprised if we find out a lot more than he does. I believe in old-fashioned methods. Police work is ninety per cent patience and ten per cent luck. These new scientific methods make a man lazy."

I grunted, stood up. "Well, I guess I'll be hearing from you. Remember: no results, no more money."

He nodded, smiled awkwardly. "Quite so, Mr. Harmas. I like dealing with business men. One knows where one is so to speak."

The door opened at this moment, and a little guy slid into the room. He was shabby, middle-aged, pathetically sad-looking. His straggling moustache was stained with nicotine, his watery eyes peered at me like a startled rabbit's.

"Ah, you've come at the opportune moment," Mr. Merryweather said, rubbing his hands. He turned to me. "This is Henry Littlejohns, who will personally work on your case." He made it sound as if this odd little man was Philo Vance, Nick Charles and Perry Mason all rolled into one. "This is Mr. Harmas who has just given us a most interesting case."

There was no enthusiastic light in Mr. Littlejohns's faded eyes. I guessed he had visions of hanging around more draughty passages, looking through more sordid keyholes, standing outside more houses in the rain. He muttered something through his moustache, stood staring down at his boots.

"I'd like to talk to Mr. Littlejohns," I said to Merryweather. "Can I take him along with me?"

"Of course," Mr. Merryweather said, beaming, "By all means take him along with you."

"We'll go back to my hotel," I said to Littlejohns. "I'd like you to have details of this case."

He nodded, muttered again under his breath, opened the door for me.

We walked to the elevator, rode down to the ground-level in silence.

I waved to a taxi, ushered Mr. Littlejohns in and as I was about to follow, something—intuition, instinct, something—made me turn quickly and look behind me.

The young runt who had tried to dent my skull and who had followed me in the Standard was standing in a doorway watching me.

For a second our eyes met, then he spat on the pavement, sauntered off in the opposite direction.

CHAPTER SEVEN

Henry Littlejohns looked as out of place in the Savoy as a snowman in the middle of August. He sat on the edge of a chair, his bowler hat resting on his knees, a sad expression on his face.

I told him about Netta, took him through every detail of the story, concluded with the burning of Anne's body.

Throughout the recital, he sat motionless. The sad expression remained on his face, but I could tell by the intent look in his eyes that he wasn't missing a thing.

"A very interesting story," he said when I had finished. "It calls for a most searching investigation."

I said I thought he was right, and what did he think of the set-up now that I had given him the facts?

He sat chewing his moustache for a moment or so, then looked up.

"I think Miss Scott's alive," he said. "The fact that her clothes are missing, the body stolen to prevent identification and that you think you saw her yesterday seems proof enough to me. If she is alive, then we shall have to discover who the dead woman was in Miss Scott's flat. We shall also have to find out whether Miss Scott had anything to do with her death; whether it was murder or suicide, whether there was anyone else implicated. It seems to me that if Miss Scott arranged for the dead woman to be mistaken for her, she must have an urgent reason for going into hiding. That's another thing we must discover. The fact that she didn't take the money nor the diamond ring, although she had time to pack her clothes, would point to a third party being present whom she did not trust and from whom she was anxious to conceal the fact that she had such valuables in the flat. We must find out who that third party was."

"You worked all that out in a few minutes," I said, regarding him thoughtfully. "I worked it out too, only I took a little longer, but Corridan hasn't got around to it yet. Now why? Why should Corridan still insist that Netta committed suicide?"

Littlejohns allowed himself a bleak smile. "I have had some experience of Inspector Corridan," he said. "He is a most misleading man. I suggest from my knowledge of his methods that he has arrived at this conclusion but he is not letting you know that he has done so. It may be, sir, that he considers you're implicated in this case, and is allowing you to think he has hold of the wrong end of the stick in the hope you will be over-confident and commit yourself. The Inspector is a deep thinker, and I wouldn't underestimate his abilities for a moment."

I gaped at him. "Well, I'll be damned," I said. "That idea never occurred to me."

For a moment Littlejohns relaxed sufficiently to look almost human. "The Inspector, in spite of what Mr. Merryweather says, is a brilliant investigator. He has caught more criminals by pretending to know nothing when he has known the full facts than any other of the Yard's personnel. I should be most careful what you say or do as far as he's concerned."

"Okay, I'll remember that," I said. "Now the next step is to dig and keep digging until we find something important to work on. I'm sure you're right about Netta. She's alive and she's arranged with Cole to identify this dead woman as herself. That explains why the body was kidnapped. They are keeping the body away from me. Will you go down to Lakeham right away and keep an eye on Mrs. Brambee's cottage? Look out for Netta. I think she's hiding there. I'll do what I can up here and in a couple of days or so we'll get together and see how far we've got."

Littlejohns said he'd go to Lakeham immediately, left with a much more sprightly step than when he had come.

The rest of the day I worked at my first article on Post-War Britain for the United News Agency. I had already obtained a considerable amount of material for the article so I was able to settle in my room and make my first rough draft. I became so absorbed in my work that the problem of Netta and her sister ceased to nag me. By six-thirty I had completed the draft, and decided to leave it until the next day before polishing and checking my facts.

I rang for the floor waiter, lit a cigarette and sat before the open window looking down on the Embankment. Now that I had put the lid on my typewriter, Netta took over my thoughts. I wondered what Corridan was doing. The more I thought about Littlejohns's theory the more sure I was that Corridan knew that Netta hadn't committed suicide, and that I might be hooked up in the case in some way.

The floor waiter, who was fast beginning to learn my habits, arrived at this moment with a double whisky, water and ice bucket. I added a little water and ice to a lot of whisky, stretched out more comfortably in the armchair. Now what, I asked myself, was I going to do to help solve the puzzle of the missing body? As far as I could see there were three things I could do that might lead to something: first, I could find out all I could about Julius Cole. If the girl who had died in Netta's flat was not Netta, then Julius Cole was in this business up to his neck. It would obviously pay to keep an eye on him. Then there was Madge Kennitt, the occupier of the first-floor flat. She might have seen something. I had to find out if anyone had called the night the girl died. I had a hunch that Netta wasn't involved in this business, but had, in some way, been implicated against her will. If that was so a third person had been in the flat on that night. Madge Kennitt might have seen him or her. Finally, I could visit the Blue Club, and try to find out if Netta had any special friends among the hostesses, and if she did, and if I could locate her, to find out from her anything about Netta that might give me a lead.

By the time I had finished my whisky, I had decided to visit the Blue Club. I took my shower, changed into a dark suit and wandered downstairs for an early supper in the almost deserted grillroom.

I arrived at the Blue Club a few minutes to nine o'clock, too early for the main crowd, but late enough to find the cocktail bar full.

The Blue Club was a three-storey building halfway up Bruton Mews behind Bruton Place. It was a shabby, faded-looking place, and you could pass it without knowing it was there. But inside you stepped from a cobbled dreary Mews, into a miniature palace of rather overpowering luxury.

The cocktail bar was on the same floor as the dance room. I wandered in, glanced around, failed to see a vacant seat so I crossed to the bar, propped myself up.

Sam, the barman, recognized me, gave me a broad welcoming smile.

"Hi, Sam," I said. "How are you?"

"I'm fine, Mr. Harmas," he said, polishing a glass and setting it before me. "Nice to see you again. You all right?"

"Pretty good," I said, "and how's your girlfriend?"

Sam had always confided to me about the ups and down of his love-life, and I knew he expected me to inquire what the latest position was.

"I get discouraged sometimes, Mr. Harmas," he said, shaking his head. "That girl of mine has a split mind. One part of it says yes, the other no. As they both operate at once, I'm kept on my toes wondering whether to retreat or advance. It's getting bad for my nerves. What will you drink, sir?"

"Oh, a Scotch," I said, glanced around the room.

I could see the crowd wasn't the kind that'd interest me. The girls were tough, showily dressed and on the make. The men were smooth, looked as if they'd escaped military service, and had too much doubtfully earned money to spend.

"Things have changed a lot, haven't they, Sam?" I said, as I paid twice as much for my drink as I pay elsewhere.

"They have, sir," he agreed, "and a great pity, too. I miss the old crowd. This bunch's just trash. They give me a pain to waste liquor on them."

"Yeah," I said, lighting a cigarette. "I miss the old faces, too."

We chatted for a few minutes about the past, and I told him what I was doing here, then I said, "Sad about Netta. You read about it, I guess?"

Sam's face clouded. "I read about it. It beats me why she did it. She seemed happy enough, and she was doing fine here. She had Bradley eating out of her hand. Any idea why she did it?"

I shook my head. "I've only just arrived, Sam," I reminded him. "I saw the thing in the newspapers, but I was hoping you could tell me what was behind it. Poor kid. I'll miss her. What are the other bims like here?"

Sam pulled a face. "They'll take the hide off your back if they thought they could make it into a pair of gloves," he said gloomily.

"They have a one-track mind—if you can call what they've got minds. I'd lay off 'em if I were you, except Crystal. You should meet Crystal. She's quite an experience. I'll fix it if you're looking for a little female society."

"She's new here, isn't she?" I asked, not recalling the name.

He grinned. "New and fresh," he said. "Came about a year ago. Can I fix you another drink?"

"Go ahead," I said, pushing my glass towards him, "and buy one for yourself. She wasn't a friend of Netta's, was she?"

"Well, I don't know about being friends, but they sort of got on together. The other dames didn't appeal to Netta. She was always fighting with them, but Crystal ... well, I don't think anyone would fight with Crystal. She's a real dizzy blonde."

"She sounds what I've been looking for. Dizzy blondes are up my alley. Is she a looker?"

Sam kissed his fingers, wagged his head. "She's got a topography like a scenic railway, and every time she comes into the bar the ice cubes go on the boil."

I laughed. "Well, if she's free and would like a big guy with hair on his chest for company, shoo her along."

"She'll like you," Sam said. "She's crazy about big muscular men; she tells me her mother was frightened by a wrestler. I'll get her."

I had finished my drink by the time he returned. He nodded, winked.

"Two minutes," he said, began to mix a flock of martinis.

She arrived a good ten minutes later. I spotted her before she spotted me. There was something about her that amused me. Maybe it was her big cornflower blue eyes or her snub nose. I don't know, but you had only to take one look at her and you were pretty sure she was the girl who originated the phrase "a dumb blonde." She was all Sam had said. Her figure made me blink: it made the male section in the room blink too.

Sam waved, and she came over, looked at me, and her eyelids fluttered.

"Oh!" she said. Then: "Oh, Boy!"

"Crystal, this is Mr. Steve Harmas," Sam said, winking at me. "He cuts the hairs on his chest with a lawnmower."

She put her hand into mine, squeezed it.

"There was a tea leaf in the bottom of my cup that looked just like you," she confided. "I knew I was going to have fun tonight." She looked anxiously at Sam. "Have any of the girls seen him yet?"

"You're the first," he returned, winking at me again.

"What a break!" she exclaimed, turning back to me. "I've been dreaming about a man like you ever since I've had those kind of dreams."

"Hey, wait a minute," I said, kidding her. "Maybe I'd better have a look at the other girls. I'm kind of selective."

"You don't have to look at them. They're only called girls to distinguish them from the male customers. They've been girls so long they think a brassiere is a place to eat. Come on, let's have fun."

"What kind of fun can we have in this joint?" I asked. "It's too crowded for my kind of fun."

Her blue eyes popped open. "Oh, I like lots of people. My father says a girl can't come to any harm so long as she stays with a crowd."

"Your father's crazy," I said, grinning. "Suppose you fell in with a crowd of sailors?"

She thought about this, frowning. "I don't think my father knows anything about sailors," she said seriously. "He stuffs birds and things."

"You mean he's a taxidermist?"

"Oh, no," she said, shaking her blonde curls, "He can't drive."

"Let's skip your father," I said hurriedly. "Let's talk about you. How about a drink?"

"I could go for a large gin with a very little lime if the gin was large enough," she said, brightening. "Do you think I could have that?"

I nodded to Sam, pulled up a stool, patted it. "Park your weight," I said. "How do you like it here?"

She climbed up on the stool, sat down, rested her small hands on the bar. "I love it," she told me. "It's so sinful and nice. You've no idea how dull it is at home. There's only father and me and all the animals that need stuffing. You'd be surprised at the animals people bring to father. He's working on a stag some crank wants to keep in his hall. Can you imagine having a stuffed stag in your hall?"

"You could always hang your hat and umbrella on its antlers," I said, after giving the matter thought.

She drank some of the gin. "You're the kind of person who makes the best of everything," she said. "I'll tell father about that idea. He might make money out of it." She sipped more gin, sighed. "I love this stuff. Now I can't get a two-way stretch, it's the only thing that holds me together." An idea struck her, and she grabbed hold of my arm.

"Did you bring any silk stockings over with you?"

"Sure," I said. "I have half a dozen pairs of nylons at my hotel."

She clenched her fists, shut her eyes.

"Six pairs?" she repeated in a hoarse whisper.

"That's right."

"Oh, dear," she said, shivered. "You weren't thinking of giving them to anyone, were you? They couldn't be lying in your old room unattached so to speak?"

"I brought them for someone," I said quietly.

She nodded to herself. "I might have guessed it," she said, sighed. "Well, never mind. Some girls have all the luck. Some get them, others just dream about them. You certainly made my heart go pit-a-pat for a moment. But I shall get over it."

"I brought them for Netta Scott," I explained. "She was a friend of mine."

Crystal turned quickly, her eyes showed surprise. "Netta? You knew Netta?"

"Sure."

"And you brought the stockings ... but, she's dead. Didn't you know?"

"Yes, I know."

"Then you haven't anyone to give ..." She caught herself up, actually blushed. "Oh, I am awful! Poor Netta! I always get depressed when I think of her. I feel I could cry right now."

"If you want those stockings you can have them," I said. "Netta can't use them, so they're unattached as you put it."

Her eyes brightened. "I don't know what to say. I'd love them—they'd save my life, but knowing they were for Netta ... well, it does make a difference, doesn't it?"

"Does it?"

She thought, frowning. I could see she would always find thought difficult: she just wasn't the thinking type.

"I don't know. I suppose not. I mean ... well, where are they?"

"At my hotel. Shall we go over and get them?"

She slid off her stool. "You mean right now? This very moment?"

"Why not? Can you get away?"

"Oh, yes. All we girls are free lances. We make what we pick up—doesn't it sound sordid?" She giggled. "I suppose I'd have to come all the way up to your room and there wouldn't be any crowds in there?"

I shook my head. "No crowds. Just you and me."

She looked doubtful. "I don't know whether I should. My father said he'd be terribly angry if I ever appeared in the *News of the World*."

"Who's going to tell the *News of the World*?" I asked patiently.

She brightened up again. "I wish I was clever. Do you know, I never thought of that. Well, come on. Let's go."

I finished my drink. "Is there a garage at the back of this joint?"

She nodded. "Yes, a big one. Why?"

I patted her hand. "Some Americans like to look at old churches," I said, smiling. "I'm crazy about garages. You'd be surprised at the number of garages there are to look at. They're full of oil and interest."

"But why garages?" she asked blankly.

"Why old churches?" I returned.

She nodded. "I expect you're right. I had an uncle who liked visiting public houses. I suppose it's the same sort of idea."

"Along those lines," I said, walked with her to the door.

As we reached the head of the stairs, I saw a big woman coming up. She wore a black evening dress and a heavy gold collar surrounded her thick neck. Her black hair was scraped back and her broad, rather sullen face was a mask of make-up. I drew back to allow her to pass. She came on, gave Crystal a cold hard stare, didn't notice me, went on.

I stared after her, a tingling sensation running down my spine.

The woman was Mrs. Brambee.

CHAPTER EIGHT

"Do you know what it means when a girl is said to be ruined?" Crystal asked, sitting on the bed and surveying my room with approval.

I put my hat in the cupboard, sat down in the armchair. "I have a vague idea," I said, smiling at her. "But it's a little technical to go into at this stage of our association. What makes you ask?"

She fluffed up her blonde curls. "My father says that if a girl allows a man to take her into his bedroom, she's as good as ruined."

I nodded gravely. "There are times when your father talks sense," I said, "but it doesn't count with me. You're not the ruining type."

"I thought there was a catch in it," she said, sighing. "Nothing ever happens to me. Confidentially, my greatest ambition is to be chased up a dark alley by a man with glaring eyes. I've hung around dark alleys until I'm sick and tired of them, but no man with or even without glaring eyes ever shows up."

"Remember Bruce and the spider and keep trying," I said. "Something's bound to happen sooner or later."

She nodded, sighed. "Oh, well, I've waited so long now, I can wait some more. May I see those stockings or do I have to wait for those too?"

"You cannot only see them, but you can have them," I said, fetched them from my wardrobe. "Catch." I tossed them into her lap.

While she was drooling over the stockings I rang for the floor waiter, and then lit a cigarette.

My visit to the Blue Club hadn't been a waste of time. Meeting Mrs. Brambee had been a stroke of luck, especially as she hadn't seen me. Crystal had told me that she had seen Mrs. Brambee in the club regularly every Thursday night. She appeared to have business with Jack Bradley, and after, she had dinner and went away. No one knew who she was; she always dined alone, and always left the club immediately after finishing her meal.

This information intrigued me. When I first saw Mrs. Brambee she was so obviously the village charwoman that meeting her dressed up in her finery had come as a complete surprise. I decided to pass this information on to Littlejohns. It might help him to find out what kind of game Mrs. Brambee was playing.

Then the visit to the club's garage had also been fruitful. The first car I had seen in the vast cellar, running under the club, had been the battered Standard Fourteen that had followed me on my run to Lakeham.

Slowly, bits of the jig-saw puzzle were fitting themselves together.

For some reason Jack Bradley was interested in my moves. I was pretty sure that the youth who had followed me was acting on Bradley's instructions. I thought Crystal could enlighten me, and turned from the window to ask her. I found her in the act of changing her stockings.

"Don't look now," she said with a giggle, rolling the nylons up her shapely legs. "I'm in what is known as an intimate situation."

"Hey! Get that limb out of sight," I said, as I heard a gentle tap on the door, and the handle turn.

The floor waiter drifted in as Crystal hurriedly adjusted her dress.

His eyes flickered for a second, then he looked at me, coldly inquiring.

"A double whisky and a large gin and lime," I said, trying to look as if Crystal was my sister.

He inclined his head, drifted out again. His back was stiff with disapproval.

"I guess I'll be the guy who'll be ruined," I sighed, sitting in the armchair again. "Will you hurry and get that leg show over before he returns?"

"Don't you like it?" Crystal asked, hurt. "I thought you'd go all popeyed and coy." She put on her shoes, regarded her legs with unconcealed delight. "They are lovely, aren't they?" she exclaimed. "I can't thank you enough." She rushed over to me, sat on my lap and twined her arms around my neck. "You're a good, kind pet and I adore you," she went on, nibbled the lobe of my ear with her sharp little teeth.

I pushed her off, got up and plumped her in the chair.

"Stay still and behave," I said. "I want to talk to you."

"Talk away. I'll listen," she said, hugging her knees and peering at me over the top of them with her big, dizzy blue eyes.

"Have you ever seen in the club a young guy, slight, dark, sallow complexion, wears a grey greasy looking hat, clean shaven, about twenty, who drives that Standard I pointed out to you?" I asked.

"Oh, you mean Frankie," Crystal said at once. "He's a horrible boy. None of the girls like him."

"That doesn't surprise me," I said, called, "Come in," as the waiter tapped, and received the drinks with as much nonchalance as I could muster. When he had gone, I went on, "What does he do?"

"Frankie?" Crystal raised her shapely shoulders. "He hangs around. I suppose he does all Bradley's dirty work. He drives the car, runs errands—those kind of things. Why are you interested?"

"It'd take too long to tell you," I said, putting her off. "You liked Netta Scott, didn't you?"

"I don't like women," Crystal said promptly. "I'm too busy trying to like men. I'm mad about men. Did you know my mother was frightened by a wrestler just before I was born?"

"I know. Sam told me."

"It's had ever such a funny effect on me ..." Crystal began, but I interrupted.

"Never mind about that," I said hastily. "Let's talk about Netta. Sam tells me you two got on together."

"I suppose we did," Crystal said indifferently. "She was a bit odd, but she didn't try to steal my men, and I didn't want Jack Bradley or her other boys, so we didn't ever come to blows."

"Were you surprised when you heard what had happened to her?"

"I was stricken in a heap. I was sure she'd never have done an awful thing like that. It just shows, doesn't it? My father always says ..."

"And we'll leave your father out of this conversation too," I said. "Will you try to remember that? Wrestlers and your father—out! Tell me something about Netta. Did you ever meet her sister?"

Crystal frowned. "I didn't know she had a sister."

"She never mentioned one?"

"Oh, no, but then she might have and I mightn't have listened. You see, if she had said she had a brother ..."

"Yes, yes, I can understand that, but we're talking about her sister. All right. You didn't know she had a sister. Did she ever speak about going to a village in Sussex called Lakeham."

"No. Lakeham? I don't know the place."

"Don't let that worry you," I said kindly, "There must be a whale of a lot of other places you don't know either. Tell me something else. You'll be able to answer this one. Did she have a regular boyfriend while you knew her?"

"Oh, yes," Crystal said, perking up. "She did have someone, but she never talked about him. In fact, she was quite secretive about him. I saw him twice, although Netta didn't know. I was on the look-out for him. The first time I saw him he was driving a marvellous black-and-yellow Bentley. He picked Netta up outside the club." She sighed. "I wish one of my boys had a Bentley."

"What's this guy like?" I asked, interested.

She shook her head. "I never once saw his face. He was big, tall and hefty. Both times I saw him it was dark and he was in the car."

"Could it be anyone in the club, do you think?"

She shook her head. "Oh, no, I know it wasn't."

I suddenly thought of Julius Cole. He was big and hefty. He had been the one who had identified the dead girl as Netta. He had a flat below Netta's. He might qualify quite easily.

"Ever heard of a man named Julius Cole?" I asked.

She shook her head. "You know, I didn't expect this," she said a little peevishly. "I thought we were going to have some ruinous fun. I'm beginning to think you're more interested in your silly old questions than in ruining me."

"Smart girl," I said, grinning at her. "I am. You're not the ruining type. Besides I'm asking these questions for a purpose. I don't think Netta's dead. If she is dead, then she didn't commit suicide, she was murdered."

Crystal stared at me. "I know I'm a little dumb," she said, after a moment's hesitation, "but I can't be expected to understand what you've just said, can I; or can't I?"

"No, you can't," I agreed. "Would you like to know more about it? Would you like also to play at being a lady detective?"

"My father says detectives are common," Crystal returned, her eyes opening wide. "They listen at keyholes, and my father says that's common. I used to listen at keyholes when I was young; I suppose that's why he said it."

"Isn't it possible to leave your father out of this conversation?" I pleaded. "He seems always to be turning up."

"He always is. I wouldn't be surprised if he doesn't burst in here and hit you over the head with a stuffed mongoose."

I sighed. "I'll chance it. Shall we get back to the original question? Do we or do we not work on this puzzle?"

"I wish I knew what you were talking about," she said plaintively.

I decided that if I could make her understand, it might be useful to have her planted in the club to keep me informed of what was going on there. She might pick up some useful information which might give me the lead I was looking for. I was now certain that the Blue Club was tied up in some way with the puzzle of the missing bodies.

So with infinite patience I told her the whole story. She sat staring at me, her mouth a little open, her eyes wide with astonishment.

"Well, now," I concluded, "you know as much about this business as I do. Bradley is tied in somehow. This guy Frankie is in it, too. Julius Cole might be Netta's boyfriend with the Bentley. Mrs. Brambee isn't what she seems. Don't you see, there are a lot of angles. Some of these angles might be cleared up if you keep your eyes and ears open. All you have to do is to listen and watch. Try to find out why Mrs. Brambee sees Bradley every week. If I knew that I might have the answer to one of my problems. Will you do it?"

She sighed. "Oh, well, I suppose so. You'll argue me into it in the long run if I do say no. All right, I'll do it, but don't expect too much, will you?"

I patted her hand. "Do your best, and I'll not ask more than that."

The telephone rang shrilly. I answered it. The Inquiry Desk said Inspector Corridan was asking for me.

"Tell him I'll be right down," I said, hung up.

"Well!" Crystal exclaimed. "I suppose now you're going to get rid of me. And I thought you were going to show me your etchings."

"You're not the first girl who's been disappointed," I said. "Now slip away like a startled mouse. Scotland Yard is downstairs and I don't want him to see you."

"Goodness!" she exclaimed, jumping up. "I don't want to see him either." She grabbed up her precious nylons, slipped on her wrap, sped to the door. Then she paused, rushed back, flung her arms around my neck, kissed me. "Thanks again for the lovely stockings. I like you. Don't let's be so stuffy the next time we meet."

I said I'd see her in a day or so, steered her to the door, opened it.

Corridan was standing outside, his hand raised to knock. He gave Crystal a surprised, rather shocked look, stood aside.

Crystal slid past him, hurried down the corridor without a backward glance."

"Hullo," I said. "I thought I told the Desk to tell you I was coming down."

He wandered in, closed the door. "Oh, I didn't want to bother you to do that," he said. "I hope I'm not intruding." He gave me the nearest he could come to in the leer line. "Friend of yours?"

"Certainly not," I said. "That's the floor waiter's daughter. She was cleaning the bath."

He nodded, roamed around the room. "I've seen her at the Blue Club on my one and only official visit, I believe, or am I mistaken?"

"At times you are quite observant," I said, tartly.

"Oh, I notice blondes," he returned with a dour smile. "Does that mean you were at the club tonight?"

"Fortunately I don't yet have to account to you for my actions, motives or movements," I returned, eyeing him. "But if you're bursting with curiosity I don't mind admitting I was there. Furthermore, I did bring the blonde back with me. I had some silk stockings, and as I had no one to give them to, I thought she might have them. There was nothing immoral about the transaction, although, at a later date, I hope something along those lines may be arranged. Satisfied?"

He didn't appear to be listening.

"I dropped in as I was passing because I thought you'd be interested to hear the coroner's verdict on Anne Scott," he said, pausing to look out of the uncurtained windowed.

"I can guess what it was," I returned. "Suicide while the balance of her mind was disturbed. Tell me, have you satisfied yourself that Netta had a sister?"

He looked at me, his eyelids drooped. "What a rum chap you are," he said. "Of course I satisfied myself there is such a person as Anne Scott and she was Netta's sister. What kind of a policeman do you think I am? You'll find the record in Somerset House if you feel like checking it."

"Okay," I said, shrugging. "I wanted to see how thorough you've been. How about Netta's verdict?"

He shrugged. "The body will have to be found first. We're looking for it."

"I see the Press haven't got the story."

Corridan scowled. "And they're not having it," he said grimly. "As it is the Chief is raising blue murder. The less publicity at this stage the better. We can rely on you to say nothing I hope?"

I grinned. "Sure," I said, "I'll keep your guilty secret. Nothing more to tell me?"

He shook his head. "Not just yet," he returned, "but I'll keep you in the picture." He moved to the door. "Come down and have a drink?"

"I'm coming down, but I can't stop for a drink. I have something important to do."

"It's nearly eleven o'clock," Corridan said, raising his eyebrows. "Come on, and don't be unsociable."

"Sorry, my work is too urgent," I said, walking with him to the elevator.

"By the way," he said casually, as we waited for the elevator to come from the ground floor. "You and Netta were lovers at one time, weren't you?"

I remembered what Littlejohns had said, grinned to myself.

"Not really," I returned. "Just a boy and a girl romance."

He nodded, stepped into the elevator and we rode down in silence.

"Do change your mind," he said when we reached the lobby.

"Sorry," I said, shaking hands. "But I've got to get along. So long. Have a drink on me."

He nodded. "So long, Harmas," he said, turned back. "Oh, there's just one little thing, you'll keep out of this business, won't you? I think I mentioned it before. It's not easy for my men to follow up leads if they've already been disturbed by enthusiastic newspaper men. That kind of thing's all right in your country, but not here. You might bear that in mind."

We exchanged somewhat dirty looks.

"Whoever heard of a newspaper man being enthusiastic?" I said, and hurried off for a chat with Julius Cole.

CHAPTER NINE

I paid off the taxi outside Mrs. Crockett's residence, looked up at the building. There was a light showing in both the first floor and second floor flats; the top flat was in darkness.

I had intended to try if I could find out something more about Julius Cole, but when I saw the lighted windows of the first floor flat, I changed my mind and decided to call on Madge Kennitt instead. I wondered if the police had questioned her. If they had and learned nothing, then I was wasting my time. I could always go upstairs to see Julius Cole if Madge Kennitt had nothing to tell me, I consoled myself.

I mounted the steps, opened the front door and entered the hall.

On the first landing, Madge Kennitt's door faced me. As I reached for the knocker I heard a faint sound from upstairs, looked up quickly. I was in time to see Julius Cole duck out of sight. I smiled to myself.

That guy missed nothing. I rat-tatted on the door, waited.

There was a long pause, then I heard heavy thudding footsteps and the door jerked open.

A short, fat woman stood squarely in the doorway. She was around forty-five, and had a lot of face and chin. Her straw-coloured hair, brittle by constant bleaching was set in a ruthless permanent.

Her moist eyes were as sympathetic as marbles at the bottom of a pond, and her complexion was raddled with rouge and powder which failed to hide the purple bloom of a whisky soak.

"Good evening," I said. "Miss Kennitt?"

She peered at me, belched gently. A puff of whisky-ladened breath fanned my face. I reminded myself to duck the next time she did that.

"Who is it?" she asked. "Come in. I can't see you out there."

She stepped back into the hard light of the sitting room. I followed her. It was quite a room. The main piece of furniture was a reed chaise-longue by the window. It had a curved back and enough cushions to stuff an elephant. One side of the room was given up to dozens of empty bottles of whisky. Just to look at them gave me a thirst. Then there was a rickety table, a straight-backed chair and a well-worn imitation Turkey carpet on the floor. A bucket stood by the chaise-longue, three-quarters filled with cigarette butts. The smell of stale whisky, nicotine and cheap scent was overpowering.

By the empty fireplace a big black cat lay full-length. It was the biggest cat I've ever seen. Its long hair was silky: it looked in a lot better shape than Madge Kennitt.

I put my hat on the table, tried to breathe through my mouth, put on a friendly expression.

Madge Kennitt was looking at me in that puzzled way people have when they've seen a face before but can't place it. Then suddenly her eyelids narrowed, and a sly smirk settled on her thick lips.

"I know you," she said. "I've seen you in and out there. It must be nearly two years since last you came. You're that Scott girl's friend, aren't you?"

"Yes," I said. "I wanted to talk to you about her."

"Oh, did you?" She padded over to the chaise-longue, settled herself down on it like an elephant about to roll in the dust. "Now I wonder what you want to talk to me about her for." Her fat, doughy-looking hand dipped down on the offside of the chaise-longue and hoisted up a bottle of Scotch. "I have a bad heart," she explained, eyeing the bottle greedily. "This stuff's the only thing that keeps me alive." She carefully unscrewed the metal cap, hoisted up a dirty tumbler and poured three inches of whisky into it. She held up the bottle, inspected it against the light, grimaced. "I can't offer you any," she went on. "I'm running low. Besides I don't believe young men should drink for pleasure." She belched again, but I was well out of range. "It's a disgrace invalids like me have so much worry and trouble getting the stuff. Doctors ought to supply it to deserving cases." She looked at me out of the corners of her eyes. "And don't think I like it. I loathe the muck. I can hardly get it down, but it's the only thing that keeps me alive—I've tried everything else." She lowered two inches of the raw spirit down her thick throat, closed her eyes, sighed. For someone who hated the stuff, she took it remarkably well.

I sat on the straight-backed chair, wondered if I'd ever get used to the smell in the room, took out a cigarette.

"Have a smoke?" I asked, waving the carton at her.

She shook her head. "Only smoke my own brand," she said, hoisting up a vast box of Woodbines from behind the chaise-longue, selected one, lowered the box out of sight.

We lit up.

"Miss Kennitt," I said, staring at my cigarette and wondering how much to tell her. "Netta Scott was a friend of mine. Her death came as a great shock to me. I wonder if you know anything about it. I'm trying to find out why she did it."

The fat woman settled herself more comfortably, thumped her floppy bosom, belched gently.

"You were lovers, weren't you?" she asked, a sly smirk crossing her purple face.

"Does that matter?" I asked.

"It does to me," she said, sipped the whisky: "two young people making love reminds me of my own youth."

I couldn't imagine her ever being young or in love.

"Netta wasn't the loving type," I said, after a moment's hesitation as to how to steer her away from this topic.

"She was a sexy little bitch," Madge Kennitt said, winking at the ceiling. "You can't tell me anything I don't know."

I flicked ash on to the carpet, wished I hadn't ever met the hag.

"All right," I said, shrugging. "What does it matter? She's dead. Names can't hurt her."

"I wasn't good enough for her," the woman muttered, drained her glass, hoisted up the bottle again. "I thought she'd come to a sticky end. I suppose she was pregnant?"

"You know as much about it as I do," I said.

"Perhaps I know more," she returned, looking sly. "You've only just got back, haven't you? You don't know what's been going on here during the past two years. Mr. Cole and I know most things."

"Yeah, he doesn't miss much," I said, hoping to draw her. She shook her bleached head, poured more whisky into the tumbler.

"He's a filthy rat," she said, closing her eyes. "Peeping and prying all day long. I bet he knows you're with me now."

I nodded. "Sure. He saw me come in here."

"It won't do him any good. One of these days I'm going to tell him what I think of him. I'll enjoy that."

"Did the police ask you anything about Netta?" I asked casually.

She smiled. "Oh, yes, they asked questions. I didn't tell them anything. I don't believe in helping the police. I don't like them. They came in here, sniffing and prying; I could see they thought I was a drunken old woman. They don't believe I have a bad heart. One of the detectives, a cold, smug-looking brute, smirked at me. I don't like men smirking at me, so I didn't tell him anything." She poured more whisky down her throat, grunted.

"You're an American, aren't you?"

I said I was.

"I thought so. I like Americans. Mr. Churchill likes Americans. I like Mr. Churchill. What he likes, I seem to like, too. I've noticed it over and over again." She waved her tumbler excitedly, slopped whisky on her chest. "What do you do for a living?"

"Oh, I write," I said. "I'm a newspaper man."

She nodded. "I was sure of it. I'm good at guessing professions. When I first saw you, coming in with that little slut, I said to myself you were a writer. Did she know how to make love? Some of these modern chits—especially the pretty ones rely on their looks. They don't know or care how to please a man. I knew. Men liked me. They were always coming back."

"Do you think Netta committed suicide?" I asked abruptly, rather sick of her.

She lay still, staring up at the ceiling. "They said she did," she returned cautiously. "That's a funny question to ask, isn't it?"

"I don't think she did," I said, lighting another cigarette. "That's why I thought I'd talk to you."

She emptied her glass, put it on the floor beside her. It toppled over, rolled under the chaise-longue. I thought she was beginning to get a little tight.

"I don't know anything about it," she said, smiled to herself.

"Pity," I said. "I thought you might. Maybe I'd better talk to Mr. Cole."

She frowned. "He won't tell you anything. He knows too much. Why did he tell the police Netta came home alone? I heard him. Why did he lie about that?"

I tried not to show too much interest. "Didn't she come home alone?"

"Course she didn't. Cole knows that as well as I do." She groped for her bottle, hoisted it up, examined it. I could see it was a quarter full. "This damn stuff evaporates," she said in disgust. "A full bottle not an hour ago, and now look at it. How the hell can I go on hunting for the stuff if it goes like this?"

"Who else was with her?" I asked.

She didn't seem to hear, but leaned over and tried to find the tumbler.

"I'll get it," I said, bent down, hooked out the tumbler, handed it to her. Her reeking breath fanned my cheek.

I had a glimpse of an indescribable heap of rubbish pushed under the chaise-longue: dirty garments, shoes, cigarette cartons, crockery, old newspapers.

She grabbed the tumbler, clutched it to her.

"Who else was with Netta?" I repeated, kneeling at her side, looking at her intently. "Was it another girl?"

Her face showed surprise.

"How do you know?" she asked, lifting her head so she could see me. "You weren't there, were you?"

"So it was another girl," I said, a sudden tingling running down my spine. She nodded, added, "And a man."

Now I was getting somewhere.

"Who were they?"

A look of cunning came into the glassy eyes.

"Why should I tell you? Ask Cole if you're so interested. He saw them. He sees everything."

I returned to my chair, sat down.

"I'm asking you. Listen, I don't think it was suicide. I think it was murder."

She had unscrewed the cap of the whisky and was pouring the spirit into the tumbler. The bottle and tumbler dropped out of her hands, rolled on to the carpet. She gave a thin scream, her face turned grey.

"Murder?" she gasped. "Murder!"

I made a dive for the bottle, but I was too late. The whisky poured out on to the carpet.

I stood over her. "Yes," I said. "Murder."

"I won't be frightened," she exclaimed, struggling to sit up. "It's bad for my heart. Here, give me that whisky. I want a drink."

"Then you'd better open another bottle," I said, watching her closely. "There's none left in this one."

"I haven't got another bottle," she wailed, sinking back. "Oh, God! What am I going to do now?"

"Aw, forget it," I exclaimed, wanting to shake her. "Who were the man and woman who came back with Netta? What time did they leave? Come on, this is important. They may know something."

She lay still for a moment, a great inert lump of flesh, then she looked at me, her small eyes cunning.

"How important is it to you?" she demanded. "I can tell you who the man is, and the girl, too. I know them. I can tell you what time the man left. I saw him. I'll tell you if you get me a bottle of whisky."

"I'll get you one," I said. "I'll bring you one tomorrow. Now, come on! Who were they?"

"I want one tonight—now." She clenched her fat hands into fists. "You can get one. Americans can get anything."

"Don't talk like a fool," I said, exasperated. "It's past eleven o'clock. Of course I can't get whisky tonight."

"Then I'm not telling you."

"I could call the police," I threatened, furious with her.

She smirked. "You wouldn't do that," she said, winking. "I'm on to you.

You wouldn't want to get that little slut into trouble."

"Now, look," I said, controlling my temper with an effort, "don't be unreasonable. I'll get you the whisky tomorrow morning. I'll get you two bottles, and I'll give you right now five pounds if you'll talk. I can't be fairer than that."

She half raised herself on her elbow. Her face was now dark with frustrated fury.

"Get that damn whisky now or get out!" she screamed at me.

I got to my feet, moved across the room, back again. Then I remembered Sam, the barman at the Blue Club. He'd sell me a bottle of whisky if I made it worth his while.

"Okay," I said, turning to the door. "I'll see what I can do. But no fooling, or I'll drink the damn stuff myself."

She nodded, waved me away.

"Hurry!" she said. "I'll tell you what you want to know if you get it. Go on ... hurry!"

I ran down the steps into the street, looked left and right for a taxi. There wasn't a sign of one. I decided it would be quicker in the long run to wait, so I stood on the edge of the kerb, kept watch.

It looked as if I was now on the right track. Netta had brought a girl back with her and I was willing to stake everything I owned that it was this girl who had died in Netta's flat. Who could the man be?

Netta's boyfriend? Someone else? Could it have been Julius Cole?

And who was the girl?

I suddenly felt I was being watched. I didn't look around immediately, but lit a cigarette, tossed the match into the gutter, then glanced over my shoulder. There seemed no one about, but for all that, I was pretty sure someone was tailing me. I thought of Frankie, wondered if he was going to have another try at beating my brains in.

I stood there for ten minutes or so before a taxi returning to the West End, drew up. I told him to take me to the Blue Club, and as we drove off, I peered through the rear window. I spotted a sudden movement.

Inspector Corridan stepped out of a dark doorway, stood in the middle of the pavement, looking after me. He glanced up and down the street as if hoping to find another taxi to follow me, but he was unlucky.

I grinned to myself. So Corridan had followed me to Madge

Kennitt's place. He wouldn't know I had visited her. He probably thought I had been to see Julius Cole. It looked as if Corridan was keeping an eye on me; did think I might be hooked up in this case.

A quarter of an hour later I arrived at the Blue Club. Ten minutes after that, I was trying to pick up another taxi back to Cromwell Road, the precious bottle of Scotch under my arm. It had cost me five pounds, but I hoped the information I was going to receive would be worth that and more.

When a taxi eventually turned up, my wrist watch showed eleven forty-five. I gave the address, sat back, relaxed.

The run to Cromwell Road seemed interminable, but in actual fact, it only took ten minutes. I paid off the taxi, noted that Madge Kennitt's light still burned, grinned to myself. I guessed the old hag was waiting as impatiently for the whisky as I was for the information.

I pushed open the front door and stepped softly across the hall, mounted the stairs. I didn't want Julius Cole to hear me. Madge Kennitt's door was ajar. I paused, frowned. I remembered closing it when I left. Maybe she had opened it to let the cat out, I thought, pushed the door, glanced into the room.

Madge was lying on the chaise-longue, her mouth open, her eyes glassy. Blood welled from a great gash in her throat, poured down her floppy bosom on to the Turkey carpet.

She was as dead as a soused mackerel.

CHAPTER TEN

For a full minute I stood staring at Madge Kennitt too shocked to move, then I stepped into the room, stood over her.

Her sightless eyes glared up at me, the blood dripped steadily on to the floor. I turned away, weak at the knees.

Because I didn't know what to do, I wandered around the room, looking aimlessly for the weapon that had killed her. I couldn't find it.

I stepped to the chaise-longue, peered over the offside.

Three empty whisky bottles and the carton of Woodbines met my eyes. The dust on the floor-boards that side was thick; written in the dust within reach of Madge's hand which flopped lifelessly on the floor was a word. I moved closer, peered at it. It was badly written, and it seemed to me that Madge might have written it either when she was dying or just before the killer had struck. It took me a few seconds to decipher the scrawl. She had written on the floor in the dust the name: Jacobi. It meant nothing to me, but I stored it away in my mind for future reference.

I suddenly remembered Corridan. If he was still hanging about outside and decided to come in to see what I was doing, I'd be in a hell of a spot. I made a dive for the door, ran down the stairs, opened the front door. I looked up and down the street, but could see no one.

Across the street was a telephone box, and I hurried over, dialled Whitehall 1212, asked for Corridan.

While I waited, I glanced idly along the street. The headlights of a car appeared out of what seemed an alley, down the street on the opposite side to where I was telephoning. A moment later a car came swiftly towards me, went on towards the West End. As it passed under a street light, I recognized it. It was the battered Standard Fourteen and Frankie was at the wheel.

Before I could think anything of this, someone came on the line to say Corridan was out on patrol with a police car. I asked for them to get into immediate touch with him and to tell him to come at once to Mrs. Crockett.

"Tell him it's a murder," I said, hung up.

I didn't fancy waiting for Corridan in Madge's room, so I returned to the house, sat on the doorstep. While I waited, I did a little thinking.

I was at last getting somewhere. I'd have probably solved the whole business if Madge hadn't dropped her bottle of whisky; but I wasn't discouraged. I had found out that a girl had been in the flat with Netta, and I was positive that it was she who had died and not Netta. It seemed pretty obvious that she had been murdered, and I wondered with a feeling of sick apprehension, if Netta had taken a hand in the murder. Could the man who had returned with Netta and the other girl be Jacobi, whoever he might be? Had he been listening to Madge and me talking, and had killed Madge before she could give me the information she had promised? Was that what Madge had tried to convey when she had scrawled the name in the dust? What was Frankie doing on the scene of the murder? How much was I going to tell Corridan? If he suspected me before, he had every reason for suspecting me still more now. I should have to handle him with care.

Corridan arrived in a fast police car in less than ten minutes. He jumped out of the car, ran up the steps before I could get to my feet.

"What's this, Harmas?" he snapped, his cold eyes searching my face. "What's happened?"

"Madge Kennitt's been murdered," I said briefly.

"What are you doing here?" he said.

"I came to see her," I returned, told him briefly what had happened. "You saw me leave, Corridan," I went on. "I spotted you as I was driving away. Why were you tailing me?"

"It's just as well that I was, isn't it?" he returned curtly. "I'm beginning to wonder about you, Harmas. You're not making things easy for yourself, are you?"

"You don't think I had anything to do with her death?"

"You could have killed her, couldn't you?" he returned, shortly. "Every time someone dies connected with this case, you appear on the scene. I don't like it. I've told you before to keep out of this, and I'm telling you again for the last time. This is no business of yours. Now, will you please understand that once and for all?"

"Hadn't you better take a look at Madge?" I said.

He snapped his fingers impatiently, went past me into the house.

Two plainclothes men followed him. I brought up the rear.

"Stay in the hall, please," he said to me, entered Madge's flat.

That settled it, I decided. Corridan could stew in his own juice.

From now on, I was going to work on the case and keep all my findings to myself. Then I'd surprise the lug when I'd solved it.

I sat on the stairs, lit a cigarette, waited.

I heard the three men moving about the room, and after a while one of the plainclothes men came out, went across the street to telephone.

When he returned, he glanced at me and I said, "How much longer do I have to wait here? I want to go to bed."

"The Inspector will want to talk to you," he returned, went into the room again.

I lit another cigarette, continued to wait.

The stairs creaked, and I glanced around. Julius Cole was coming down stealthily, holding the skirt of his yellow-and-black dressing-gown in one hand, the other hand on the banister rail.

Looking at the dressing-gown I thought of the yellow-and-black Bentley, wondered if there was any connection.

"Hello, baby," he whispered, his eyes on Madge Kennitt's door. "What's going on?"

"I'd have thought you'd have been on the scene before now," I said, scowling at him. "You'd better beat it. You're in the way, Fatso."

He came on, plumped himself down beside me, smiled his secret smile. I smelt perfume, drew away from him.

"Has something happened to the old hag?" he asked, rubbing his big, white hands together. "Has she lost something? Is it the police?"

"Someone cut her throat," I said brutally. "Odd you didn't see him arrive, or did you?"

"Cut her throat?" he squeaked, his face going slack. "You mean she's dead?"

I nodded. "Yeah," I said, staring at him. "She knew too much."

He was on his feet now, his mouth working, his eyes full of terror.

"You'll be next," I said, kidding him. "You know too much, too." I wanted to loosen him up, and then I was going to move in and take him to pieces, but I guess I punched him too hard. He bolted up the stairs before I could grab him. I heard him rush into his room, slam the door and shoot the bolt.

I hadn't expected quite such a reaction, but on consideration, I realized that he also had seen the man and girl return with Netta. He, too, stood a likely chance of getting his throat cut; and he knew it.

I got to my feet, undecided whether to follow him or not, when Corridan came out of the room. His face was grim.

"Now, let's hear some more from you," he said, planting himself before me. "How long have you known this woman?"

I frowned at him. "Why, I've only just met her. I told you I thought she might have seen something the night Netta was supposed to have died. I came here, talked with her, and she admitted she did know something. Then she upset her bottle of Scotch, wouldn't talk until I'd got her another. I got another from Sam at the Blue Club, but when I got back I found her dead. Someone had stopped her talking for good."

"It's lucky for you I saw you come out when you did," Corridan said coldly. "Even then, it still doesn't mean you couldn't have killed her."

"For God's sake, Corridan!" I exploded.

"You've brought it on yourself," he returned. "You are definitely on my suspect list."

"That's fine," I said bitterly. "After all the meals I've bought for you, too."

"Tell me exactly what she said," he ordered, watching me with uncomfortable intentness.

I couldn't avoid telling him the truth, although it irritated me to do so. It was his job to find out that Netta had come back with two other people, not to receive it as a gift from me.

He listened in silence, seemed very thoughtful by the time I had finished.

"There goes your suicide theory," I said, eyeing him. "I told you all along Netta didn't kill herself."

"I know," he said, looking up sharply. "If she didn't kill herself, then you might have a reason for stopping Madge Kennitt from talking. Thought of that?"

I just gaped at him.

"On the other hand it still could be suicide," he went on. "These two visitors could have left her after doing whatever they had come to do, and then she committed suicide. It depends on what time they left."

"Well, Julius Cole can tell you. He saw them too."

"I'll have a word with him," Corridan said grimly.

"Will you walk to the corner with me?" I asked, remembering Frankie. "I want to check something."

He opened the front door without a word, and together we walked to the entrance of the alley from which the Standard had come. I struck a match, peered at a small pool of motor oil on the cobbles. It would seem from that that the Standard had been parked there for some time.

"Look at this," I said. "When I was trying to get you on the phone, I spotted a Standard car come out of this mews. There's some oil here that leaked from it. I should say it'd been standing there some time. I happen to know the car belongs to Jack Bradley. Does that mean anything to you?"

"Except you seem to know more about this case than I thought," Corridan returned. "How do you know the car belongs to Bradley?"

"I consulted my Ouija board," I returned.

"You're not in the position to be funny," he snapped sharply. "How did you know?"

"Frankie was driving. I knew he was Bradley's stooge."

Corridan grunted. "You know a hell of a lot, don't you?"

"Do you know anything about Frankie?" I asked.

"We've been hoping to get our hands on him for some time, but he's a slippery customer, as well as a vicious one. He's on our suspect list for several robberies, but Bradley always turns up with a cast-iron alibi for him."

"Think he'd run to murder?"

Corridan shrugged. "He'd run to anything if it paid well enough."

As we retraced our steps to the house, I asked him if he had found any clues in Madge's flat.

"None," he said.

"You mean you haven't found one single clue?" I asked, startled, thinking of the name Jacobi written in the dust.

"No," he repeated.

I had an idea, darted away from him, bolted into Madge's flat.

The two plainclothes dicks were together at the far end of the room, looking for finger-prints. I came in so quickly they weren't aware of me until I had reached the chaise-longue. I peered over the far side. The dust had been swept clean. The scrawled name, Jacobi, had vanished. I immediately thought of Julius Cole. Had he got in here while I was waiting for Corridan?

But I hadn't much time for thought as Corridan came into the room, his face dark with anger. I moved away from the chaise-longue, looked around the room.

"What the hell are you playing at?" he demanded. "You've no business in here. I'm getting tired of your behaviour, Harmas. It's got to stop. Why are you in here?"

I decided I wouldn't tell him about the name in the dust. Anyway, not until I had investigated the clue myself. I tried to look ashamed of myself, didn't succeed very well.

"There was a cat here," I said vaguely. "I wondered if it was still in the room."

"What the blazes has a cat to do with it?" he demanded, glaring at me.

I lifted my shoulders. "Maybe the killer took it away," I said. "That's a clue, isn't it?"

"He didn't take the cat away," Corridan snarled. "It's locked up in the other room. Any more bright ideas?"

"Well, I'm only trying to help," I said. "How about you and me calling on Julius Cole?"

"I'm calling on, him," Corridan said. "You're getting the hell out of here. Now see here, Harmas, I'm warning you for the last time. Keep out of this. You're lucky you're not charged with murder. I'm going to check your story and if it doesn't click, I'm going to arrest you. You're a damn nuisance. Now get out."

"If you listen carefully," I said, as I edged to the door, "you'll hear my knees knocking."

CHAPTER ELEVEN

As I was crossing the Savoy lobby to take the elevator to my room, I ran into Fred Ullman, crime reporter to the *Morning Mail*. We had met when I was in London during the war, and he had been helpful in advising me on angles for my articles on London crime.

He seemed as pleased to see me as I was to see him.

"We've just time for a drink," he said, after we had got through back-slapping and explaining what we were doing in the Savoy at this time of night. "I don't want to be too late as I have a heavy day before me, so don't start one of your drinking contests."

I said I wouldn't, led him into the residents' lounge, ordered whiskies, sat down.

Ullman hadn't changed much since last we met. He was a tall, lanky individual, and his most distinctive feature was the bags under his eyes. He was known as the Fred Allen of Fleet Street.

After we had chatted about the past, checked up on the activities of mutual friends, I asked him casually if the name Jacobi meant anything to him.

I saw surprise on his face, and his eyebrows went up.

"What makes you ask?" he inquired. "A couple of months ago that name was in every English newspaper. Have you just got on to it?"

I said I had. "I heard some guy talking, and he mentioned the name. I wondered if I was missing anything."

"I shouldn't say you're missing much," he said. "The affair is as dead as a dodo now."

"Well, tell me," I said. "Even if it's past news, I should know what's been going on."

"All right," he returned, sinking back in his armchair. "The business began when a rich theatrical magnate, Hervey Allenby, decided to do what a number of rich people were doing: buy diamonds and other precious stones against invasion or inflation or both. He bought heavily: rings, bracelets, necklaces, loose stones; stuff that could be easily carried, and of good value. He amassed a collection worth fifty thousand pounds. As he wanted to be able to put his hands on the stuff quickly, he kept the lot in his country house. The purchase of these gems was kept secret, but after four years—three months ago—the news leaked out somehow or other, and before you could say 'mild-and-bitter,' the collection was pinched."

"Quite a nice haul," I said. The name, Hervey Allenby, made me prick up my ears. "Where was this country house?"

"Lakeham, Sussex, just outside Horsham," Ullman returned. "I went down there to cover the robbery. The village is small, but attractive, and Allenby's house is just a half a mile beyond it. The robbery was a real slick job. The house was crammed with burglar alarms and police dogs, and the safe was a real snorter. The thief must have been an expert. The police remarked that there was only one man who could have pulled the job: a fellow called George Jacobi."

"Jacobi was known to the police then?"

"Oh, yes. He was one of the smartest thieves in the game, and had served several long sentences for jewel robberies. You remember Corridan? He was in charge of the robbery. We ribbed him in the Press. None of the boys like Corridan. He's too damn cocky, and we thought this was our chance to give him a roasting. He suspected Jacobi from the start, but Jacobi had such a cast-iron alibi that Corridan hadn't a hope of nailing him."

"What was his alibi?"

"He said he was in an all-night poker game at the Blue Club on the night of the robbery. The waiters and the cloakroom attendant swore they had seen him arrive. Jack Bradley and a couple of other men swore Jacobi played with them the whole night. Mind you, none of these fellows were what you could call reliable witnesses, but there were so many of them, the police knew they wouldn't be able to make their case stand up in court, so they dropped Jacobi and hunted elsewhere."

"Without success?"

"Not a thing. It was Jacobi all right. Corridan said he wasn't worrying. Sooner or later the thieves would try to dispose of the loot and he had a detailed description of every piece that was missing. As soon as the stuff came on to the market, he was going to pounce."

I grunted. "Yeah, I can hear him saying that. Did he pounce?"

Ullman grinned. "No. The stuff hasn't come on to the market yet. There's still time, of course; unless it's been smuggled out of the country.

One of these days the case may open up again, and then it'll be front page news. I think the trouble was that Corridan's a shade too confident and the thieves a shade too smart."

"What happened to Jacobi?"

"He was murdered. A month after the robbery he was found in a back street, shot through the heart. No one heard a shot, and the police think he was killed in a house and dumped from a car. They haven't a clue to the killer, and I doubt if they ever will find him. The affair wouldn't have caused much excitement only they found, concealed in the heel of Jacobi's shoe, one of Allenby's rings. They tackled Bradley again, but couldn't shift him. There the matter rests, and that's as far as they've got."

"No clues at all?" I asked, lighting a cigarette and offering him the carton.

He took a cigarette, lit up. "There was one important clue, although it didn't get them anywhere. The bullet that killed Jacobi had a peculiar rifling. The police reckoned it would be easy to identify the gun if they could only lay hands on it. The ballistic experts said the bullet had been fired from a German Luger pistol, and for some time they suspected one of the American troops of having a hand in the murder."

I immediately thought of the Luger I had found in Netta's flat. It could have been given to her by an American service man. Could that have been the weapon that had killed Jacobi?

"They never found the gun?" I asked.

"No. I bet they never will, either. My guess is there were two men concerned in the robbery. Probably Jacobi did the actual job, and the other man lurked in the background, directing the operation. Most likely he was responsible for getting rid of the loot. I think the two fell out over the split and the second man killed Jacobi, and is sitting on the loot until it's safe to put on the market. Corridan favours this idea, too." Ullman finished his drink, glanced at his watch. "Well, I'd better be moving on," he said. "It's long past my bed-time." He got to his feet. "Although I haven't much use for Corridan as a man, I must say he's damned efficient, and I shouldn't be surprised if he doesn't get the stuff in the end. He's a surly customer, but he does deliver the goods. The trouble with him is he hates newspaper men. He thinks publicity gives the criminal too much knowledge of what is going on. His idea is to say nothing, to keep the criminal guessing, not even to report the crime, and in the end, the criminal will betray himself because he'll be over-anxious to know what the police are doing. It may be a good idea, but it doesn't suit the Press. I wish he wouldn't trample on my finer feelings. I could like the bloke if he had better manners."

I grinned. "Yeah," I said, "so could I. I'd like to steal a march on him one of these days. He's due for a shake-up, and I may be able to give it to him."

"Well, let me have a front seat when it happens," Ullman said, shook hands and went off to join the queue for taxis.

I returned to my room, undressed, put on a dressing-gown, sat in my armchair.

By the merest fluke I had got hold of what seemed to be the key to the puzzle.

Corridan, of course, had no idea that the Jacobi robbery had anything to do with the death of the girl in Netta's flat, Anne's suicide or the murder of Madge Kennitt. If he had seen the name Jacobi scrawled in the dust in Madge's room, he would have been on to the clue before me. But now I was holding the key to the problem, and he was still floundering about trying to find out what connection Madge's murder had with the other two odd happenings.

Thinking it over, it now seemed certain that Netta, in some way or other, was involved in the Allenby robbery. The fact that a ring from the Allenby collection had been hidden in her jar of cold cream was suspicious, but coupled with the fact that her sister had a cottage close to the scene of the robbery and that Jack Bradley was watching me like a hawk seemed to tie her to the robbery without any doubt.

What of the Luger I had found hidden in her dress? Had Corridan checked it thoroughly? Had he discovered that it was the Luger which had killed Jacobi and was holding out on me? Or hadn't the Luger anything to do with the case? That was something I had to find out, and find out fast.

Where did the five thousand pounds worth of forged bonds come into the picture? Had Frankie been after the Luger and the bonds when he had attacked me? If he had been after the Luger and it was the gun that had killed Jacobi mightn't that mean that Jack Bradley owned the gun and he had killed Jacobi?

I lit a cigarette, wandered about my room. I was sure I was getting close to the solution of this business, but I still needed a little more information.

Should I tell Corridan what I had discovered? That was something that bothered me. With my facts he might clear up the whole business in a few days, whereas I might fool around for weeks and never get anywhere. I knew I should call him at once and tell him about finding Jacobi's name written in the dust. That was the one vital clue that'd open up the case for him. I even crossed the room to the telephone, but I didn't make the call.

After the way he had treated me, I wanted to get even with him.

The sweetest way I could do this was to crack the case, walk into his office and tell him how it was done.

I hesitated, then decided to give myself seven more days, and if I hadn't arrived at the solution by then, I'd turn the facts over to him and give him best.

Having made this decision, I got into bed, turned out the light, and lay awake for at least three minutes wrestling with my conscience.

CHAPTER TWELVE

Soon after eleven o'clock the following morning, I called on J. B. Merryweather. I found him sitting at his desk, totally unemployed, although he did make a feeble effort to look immersed in his thoughts when he saw me come in.

"Hello," I said, drawing up a chair and sitting down. "Any news from Littlejohn?"

"Well, yes," he said, straightening his tie and sitting more upright. "I heard from him this morning. He's a good chap; gets on the job right away."

"That's what he gets paid for, isn't it?" I asked, produced my carton of cigarettes. I rolled one across his desk. He snapped it up, lit it. "What has he to report?"

"There is one thing," Merryweather said, rubbing his long red nose. "Rather curious, rather interesting, I feel. I hope you'll think so too. It seems this woman, Mrs. Brambee, was the sister of George Jacobi, the jewel thief, who was so mysteriously murdered a month or so ago. You may have heard of the affair. Would that interest you?" He looked at me hopefully.

I didn't let him see I was more than interested. "It might," I said cautiously. "Anyway any information at this stage of the case may be useful. Anything else?"

"Littlejohns spent the night watching the cottage. After midnight a car arrived and a man spent two hours with Mrs. Brambee."

Merryweather picked up a sheet of paper, consulted it. "The car was a yellow-and-black Bentley. The man was tall, well-built, powerful, but Littlejohns was unable to see his face. It was a dark night," he added, apologetically.

I nodded. "Did he get the registration number of the car?"

"Certainly, but I've had the number checked and there's no record of it. It would seem it's a false number plate that is being used."

"Well, that's not bad for a beginning," I said, pleased. "It won't be wasting time or money for Littlejohns to stay down there." I went on to tell Merryweather about seeing Mrs. Brambee at the Blue Club. "You'd better pass that information to Littlejohns. It may help him. And tell him to get after the driver of the Bentley. I want him traced. No sign of a girl staying at the cottage?"

"No. Littlejohns proposes to visit the place in a day or so on some pretext or other. He has seen quite a lot of Mrs. Brambee in the village, and he proposes to let her get used to the sight of him before he calls. He knows his job all right, I can assure you of that."

I got up. "Okay," I said, "keep in touch. If anything breaks call me."

Merryweather promised he would, and I went to the elevator, rode down to the ground-level.

Well, that explained who Mrs. Brambee was, and to some extent why she was connected with the Blue Club. The pieces of the jig-saw puzzle continued to fall into place quicker than I had thought possible.

The past twenty-four hours had certainly been revealing ones.

I stood on the edge of the kerb, looked up and down for a taxi. A car swept around the corner, drove up to me fast, stopped with a squeal of brakes. For a moment I was startled: it was the battered Standard Fourteen.

Frankie sat at the wheel. A cigarette drooped from his lips, his greasy hat rested on his thin nose. He looked at me out of the corners of his eyes, a cold, vicious expression in them I didn't much like.

"Bradley wants you," he said in a nasal voice. "Get in the back and make it snappy."

I recovered from my surprise. "You've been seeing too many gangster movies, sonny," I said. "Tell Bradley if he wants to see me, he can call at the Savoy some evening, I'll try to be out."

"Get in the back," Frankie repeated softly, "and don't talk so much. You'll do yourself a piece of good if you come without a fuss."

I considered the proposition with some interest and not a little thought. It might be worthwhile hearing what Bradley had to say. I hadn't anything to do at the moment, and I was curious to meet Bradley again.

"Okay, I'll come," I said, opening the car door. "What's he want to see me about?"

Frankie engaged his clutch, shot the Standard away from the kerb so fast I was flung against the back seat. I sorted myself out, promised to smack his ears down should the opportunity arise, repeated my question.

"You'll find out," Frankie said, drawing on his cigarette.

I decided he imagined himself to be a real tough egg, admired his skill as a driver. He kept thirty miles an hour going all through the heavy traffic, weaving his way in between cars, missing fenders by split inches.

"Now did you like the way I shook you off the other day?" I asked pleasantly. "You weren't so smart then, were you?"

He took his cigarette from his mouth, spat out of the window, said nothing.

"And the next time you try to bounce a tyre lever on my head, I'll wrap it around your skinny neck and tie a knot in it," I went on less pleasantly.

"The next time I come after you, you skunk," he returned, "I'll make a better job of it." He sounded as if he meant it.

That held me until we reached Bruton Mews, then I said, "Well, thanks for the ride, sonny. It's a pity they didn't teach you anything better than to drive a car at your approved school."

He looked me over, sneered. "They taught me plenty," he said, moving towards the club. "Come on. I ain't got all day to fool around with a peep like you."

I reached out, caught him by the scruff of his neck. He twisted, wrenched away, swung at me. There was nothing slow about his movements. His fist caught me flush on the chin. I back stepped fast enough to keep from falling, but I took plenty of the punch. It was meant to be a sockeroo, but late nights, physical wear and tear and underfeeding don't put iron into bones. It worried me no more than a smack with a paper bag.

I sank my fist into the side of his neck just to show him what a real punch felt like. He toppled over sideways, went down on hands and knees, coughed, shook his head.

"Tough guy," I sneered.

He shot at me like a plane from a catapult, reaching for my knees in a diving tackle. I side-stepped and reached for his neck, took it into chancery. He tried to get his hands where he could hurt, but I'd been through that stuff at school. I twisted him around and heaved him a little higher, then I took hold of my right wrist with my left hand and turned my right hip-bone into him.

I had my right forearm against his windpipe and all the strength of both my arms in it. He scratched at the cobbles with his feet, went blue in the face.

I eased off; slapped his mug three or four times, back and forth, put the heel of my hand on his nose and pressed. Then I let him go.

He sat down on the cobbles, blood running from his nose, his face the colour of raw meat, his breath whistling through his mouth. It must have been the toughest two minutes he'd ever experienced.

Tears came into his eyes. He put his sleeve to his face, sniffled: just a soft, yellow kid who thought he was tough.

I reached out, grabbed his collar, heaved him to his feet.

"Come on, Dillinger," I said, "let's see Bradley, and don't give me any more of that gangster spiel; you can't live up to it."

He walked ahead, staggering a little, holding a dirty handkerchief to his nose. He didn't look back, but I could see by the set of his shoulders he was crazy with rage and hate. I decided I'd keep an eye on this lad in the future. He might try sticking a knife in my ribs the next time we met.

He rapped on a door at the end of the passage, opened it, went in.

I followed him, found myself in a big luxuriously furnished room.

There was a built-in upholstered corner seat by the window, a black-and-chromium safe in the wall. There were some filing cabinets, a small bar, and the usual broad, heavy executive desk with the usual high-padded leather chair behind it.

Looking out of the window was a man in a dark lounge suit. He had grey hair and plenty of it. He turned. He was going on for fifty and his face was handsome in a dark heavy way. His eyes were slate grey, unfriendly.

I remembered him now. It was Jack Bradley. I had only seen him twice before and that was two years ago. I decided he had aged a lot since last I saw him.

"Hello, Harmas," he said, then caught sight of Frankie. His face set. "What the hell do you think you're doing?" he snarled at Frankie. "You're bleeding over my goddamned carpet."

"My fault," I said, taking out my cigarettes, selecting one. "Your boy made me nervous. I thought he was a tough egg. We fooled around together just to see how strong we were. It turned out he wasn't strong at all."

Frankie's lips twitched. He said three words; one of them obscene. His voice was not loud, but it was bitter.

Bradley took a step forward, snapped, "Get the hell out of here," to Frankie, who went.

I lit my cigarette, hooked a chair towards me with my foot, sat down.

"You'd better watch that boy," I said. "He's in need of a mother's care."

"Never mind him," Bradley said, frost in his eyes. "It's you I want to talk about."

"That's fine," I said. "I like talking about myself. Where shall we begin? Would you like to hear how I snitched the scripture prize when I was a little lad?"

Bradley leaned forward. "Frankie may not be tough," he said, "but I am. You'd better not forget it."

"That's scared me right through to my jaegers," I said. "May I go in a corner and cry?"

"I've warned you," Bradley said, sitting at his desk. "You're getting too inquisitive, my friend. I sent for you because I thought a little chat off the record might clear the air. I advise you not to pass this on to your friend Corridan. It wouldn't be healthy."

"You needn't worry about Corridan," I said. "He and I aren't pals anymore. What's biting you?"

He took a cigar from a silver box on his desk, pierced it, lit it, threw the match away, puffed it once or twice before he spoke again.

He took his time. He didn't rattle me. I was in no hurry myself.

"I don't like American newspaper men who are inquisitive," he said. "They annoy me."

"Are you suggesting I should relay that item of news to the U.S. Press Association?" I kidded him. "I doubt if they'd lose much sleep, but, of course, they might. You never know."

"You're sticking your nose into something that has nothing to do with you," Bradley went on smoothly. "I suggest you stop it."

"No harm in making suggestions," I returned lightly. "What exactly do you mean by that sinister 'something'?"

"We needn't go into that," Bradley said, a cold, angry gleam in his eyes. "You know what I mean. I'm serious about this. I'd advise you to return to your own country. There's a plane leaving tomorrow. It wouldn't be a bad idea if you were on it."

I shook my head. "I have a lot of work to do in this country," I said. "I'm sorry I can't oblige you. Is that all you wanted to see me about?"

He studied his cigar for a moment, said, "I'm warning you, Harmas. If you don't keep your nose out of this, you're going to be taught a sharp lesson. I know what you newspaper men are like. You get keen on a story and you need a lot of persuasion to give it up. I have all the necessary persuasion but I'm not anxious to use it. I thought if I gave you the hint, you'd be a smart fellow and mind your own business in the future."

I stubbed out my cigarette in the copper ashtray on his desk, stood up.

"Look, Bradley," I said, leaning across the desk, "I've listened to your hot air because I wanted to hear how far you'd go. You and hundreds of other fat, sleek rats who've made money out of this war, sold stinking bad liquor to the Service men, and gorged yourselves with black market food are a gross a nickel in my country. I've knocked around and met real tough eggs, not jerks like you who merely smell strong. I've been threatened before, and the guys who've shaken their fists at me have ended up in a nice cool cell or are now fertilizing the soil. I'm not scared of you, or of your panty-waisted Frankie. I'm coming after you, and I'm keeping after you until I've had the satisfaction of knowing the hangman's taken your weight and height and selected a nice strong rope for you. Show me how tough you are, and I'll show you how tough I am. Keep Frankie out of my hair. He's too young for this kind of shindig. But if he does try anything with me, I'll paper a wall with him, and I'll paper another wall with you."

Bradley let me say my piece to the end. There was a faint flush on his heavy face and his fingers drummed on the desk, otherwise he was calm enough.

"All right, Harmas," he said, shrugging, "if that's the way you feel. Don't forget I've warned you."

I grinned at him. "I won't forget," I said, "but you'll find me a little harder proposition to take on than Madge Kennitt."

His face tightened. "I don't know what you're talking about," he said. "I've never heard of Madge Kennitt. You can get out and stay out. This club's closed to you from now on. And take my tip—mind your own business, otherwise you'll be a sick pup."

"Phooey!" I said, and left him.

CHAPTER THIRTEEN

On my way back from the Ministry of Reconstruction and Planning where I had been obtaining material for my third article, I ran into Corridan.

I spotted him hurrying along the crowded pavement, a dour, forbidding look in his eyes, his mouth set in a grim line.

"Hello, sour puss," I said, falling into step beside him. "You look as cheerful as the National Debt."

He scowled round, continued on his way.

"I never met such a chap," he said, stretching his long legs as if anxious to shake me off. "You're like a vulture. When anything happens or goes wrong, you're sure to appear on the scene."

My legs were as long as his, and I kept pace with him easily enough.

"What's wrong this time?" I asked brightly. "Anyone been bumped off?"

"Nobody's been bumped off," he returned coldly. "If you must know that damned Julius Cole has skipped. He climbed out of his bedroom window and hooked it last night while I was trying to get in."

"I don't blame him," I returned. "Not after what happened to Madge Kennitt. I suppose he thought the same thing might happen to him. Any idea where he's got to?"

"No, but we shall find him. I want him for questioning, and a general alarm has gone out all over the country to bring him in. It won't take long, but it's a shocking waste of public money."

"Don't bother your head about that," I said. "There are plenty of other things to worry about. The great thing is to find him alive."

"I wish you'd stop dramatizing this business," Corridan snapped. "You make it sound a damn sight worse than it is."

"I wonder," I shrugged. "By the way, how are you getting along with the Jacobi case?"

He misstepped, glanced at me sharply. "What do you know about that?" he demanded, slowing his pace.

"Oh, I've been following your remarkable rise to fame and fortune," I returned lightly. "A couple of months ago your face and name were spread over every newspaper in connection with Jacobi. Have you found the missing loot yet?"

He shook his head. "Plenty of time for it to appear," he returned curtly. "What makes you bring up Jacobi?"

"Oh, I've been consulting my Ouija board again. I thought it was a little odd that part of Jacobi's loot should be hidden in Netta's jar of cold cream. I wondered too, why you didn't tell me that the ring was connected with such a sensational case."

Corridan smiled grimly. "I don't tell you everything. You appear capable of finding out most things for yourself."

I nodded. "That's so. You'd be surprised how much I do find out."

"Such as what?"

"I don't tell you everything either. One of these days I'll take you into my confidence and we'll have a good cry together."

He made an impatient gesture, looked around for a taxi.

"Have you wondered if the Jacobi affair has anything to do with Netta Scott and Madge Kennitt's murder?" I asked as the taxi, in answer to Corridan's hail, drew up.

"I'm always wondering about everything connected with all my cases," he returned dryly, climbed into the taxi. "I'll be seeing you, Harmas. You can leave all this safely in my hands. You may not think so, but they are extremely capable."

"Let's keep that as something between you and me," I said.

"Some people wouldn't believe it."

I watched him drive away, grinned, and continued on to the Savoy. So Julius Cole had gone to ground. I wouldn't be surprised, I thought, if I heard he had been found in a ditch with his toes in the air.

I entered the Savoy, asked if there were any messages, collected one from Crystal who suggested we should drink some more gin together that night, gave a telephone number and asked me to call her.

When I reached my room, I put through a call.

She answered immediately.

"Hello, this is your U.S. romance speaking to you from the Savoy Hotel," I said. "I received your note and think your suggestion an excellent one. Where do we meet and when?"

"Come and pick me up at my place," she said, gave me an address in Hertford Street.

"I thought you said you lived with your father—the guy who stuffs birds."

"Oh, I'm nearly as big a kidder as you are," she giggled, hung up.

I arrived at her flat a few minutes after seven. It was over an antique furniture shop, and after climbing red-carpeted stairs I came on a small landing which served as a kitchen.

Crystal popped her corn-coloured head out of a door close by, blew me a kiss.

"Go in there," she said, pointing a bare arm at another door. "I'll join you in two twos."

"Too long to wait," I said promptly. "I'm coming in here."

She hurriedly closed the door, said through the panels that she had on only her vest, and she didn't receive gentlemen dressed like that.

"Who told you I was a gentleman?" I demanded, pounding on the door. "It's those sort of mistakes that gets a girl into trouble."

She had turned the key, but I could hear her giggling.

"Go into the sitting room and behave," she commanded.

"Okay," I said, went into the room, flopped down on the big settee. I thought the room was nice. It was comfortable, bright, full of flowers. The kind of room a man and a maid could get awfully matey in.

By my elbow was a table on which stood a bottle of whisky, a bottle of gin, a bottle of dry Vermouth, a soda syphon and a cocktail shaker.

I mixed two martinis, lit a cigarette, waited patiently.

Crystal came in after a while, wearing a scarlet house-coat, white mules and an expectant expression on her face.

"Here I am," she said, sitting beside me. She patted my hand, smiled.

I thought she looked a cute trick, gave her a martini, raised my own.

"May the bends in your figure never straighten," I said, drank half the martini, found it good. "So that stuff about your father was just a gag?"

"Not really. I have a father and he does stuff things, but I've given up living with him. I just couldn't stand it, and he couldn't stand me. I always tell my boy friends I live with him; it saves a lot of trouble when they want to see me home."

"How come I'm invited to your nest?" I asked, smiling.

She fluttered her eyelids at me. "Well, if you must know, I have designs on you."

"My mother says no nice girls have designs on men."

"But who says I'm nice?" she returned, put down her glass, twined her arms around my neck.

We became intimate for the next five minutes, then I levered off her arm, pushed her away.

"Remember the *News of the World*," I said.

"I've got beyond the *News of the World*. Let's have some real ruinous fun." She put her head on my shoulder, draped my arm around her.

"In a little while," I promised, "but don't let's rush it. I meant to tell you: I saw Bradley this morning. For some reason or other he's taken a dislike to me. He won't let me into the Club anymore."

She sat up, her eyes indignant. "Why?"

I pulled her down, pushed her head back on my shoulder. "He thinks I'm too inquisitive," I said. "I don't care, so why should you?"

"I don't know if I want to go to the club again, if he's going to treat you like that," she said crossly. "Only I don't know what else I could do. You wouldn't think of keeping me, would you? I've always wanted to be a kept woman."

"I don't believe in keeping women. I think they should keep me."

"Oh, you're kidding again," she said, thumped my knee. "But seriously, wouldn't you like to keep me?"

"I'd hate it," I said gravely. "It's as much as I can do to keep myself."

She sighed. "Well, all right. I never seem to have any luck. I don't think I'll go to the club tonight. I have a chicken in the refrigerator. Let's have that and spend the evening together."

"That sounds swell."

She got up. "You sit there and look decorative. I'll fix supper."

That suited me. I was good at looking decorative. I filled my glass, lit a cigarette, relaxed. It was nice to watch her moving about the room. I decided suddenly that it mightn't be a bad idea to keep her at that.

"Tell me, sugar," I said, "have you been keeping your eyes and ears open at the club?"

"Oh, yes. The trouble is I don't know what to listen for. I'll tell you something though." She paused in laying the table, turned to look at me. "I was at the club this afternoon and an odd sort of man came in asking for Bradley. He reminded me a little of the man I saw with Netta—the one I was telling you about with the Bentley."

"Go on," I said, interested.

"I don't know if it was the same man, but he was the same build, and there was something familiar about him that rang a bell. He was big and fat and fair. I thought he looked a bit of a pansy."

"Had he a habit of wagging his head? Did you notice that? And was his hair cut very short?"

She nodded. "Do you know him?"

"It sounds like my old pal Julius Cole," I said. "What happened?"

"Well, Bradley came out of his office, glared at him, said, 'What the hell do you want?' This man said, 'I've got to see you, Jack, it's important.' Bradley looked sort of put out, then he took Cole into his office. I didn't hear what happened, of course."

I stubbed out my cigarette, lit another. "Think carefully. Did anything happen at all after that?"

"I saw Frankie go into Bradley's office, and later he came out and went to the garage. He spoke to Sam and said something about going down to the country right away. I could see he was wild with rage, but I can't remember anything else happening."

"You've remembered enough," I said, crossed over to the telephone, turned up Merryweather in the book. I found his private address, put through a call.

He answered himself.

"This is Harmas here," I said. "Can you get in touch with Littlejohns at once and warn him to look out for a man who's on his way to Lakeham?"

Merryweather said he could. There was surprise in his voice. He asked for a description, and I gave him an accurate picture of Julius Cole. "He'll probably arrive in a Standard Fourteen," I said, gave the licence number. "Tell Littlejohns not to lose sight of him, even if it means taking his eyes off Mrs. Brambee. Cole is important. I guess he'll be staying with Mrs. Brambee anyway. Will you get on to that right away?"

Merryweather promised to call Littlejohns immediately, hung up.

Crystal was listening to all this, her eyes wide with interest.

"You know I get a thrill out of hearing your voice when you get businesslike," she said. "It's like being in a movie with Humphrey Bogart."

"You remember what Bogart did to Bacall?" I asked, advancing and making faces at her.

"I seem to remember it wasn't very polite," she said, backing hurriedly away.

I grabbed her, did what Bogart had done to Bacall, asked her how she liked it.

"I'd forgotten," she sighed, holding me close. "Much more, please."

I had a sudden idea. "Tell me, honey, did you ever meet a guy named Jacobi at the club?"

She shook her head. "You mean the one who was murdered? Oh, no, I didn't know him, but I knew his wife, Selma. She used to be one of the girls at the club before she married him. She was a sweet kid and crazy about George. I haven't seen her since he was killed. I don't know where she's living. I wanted to see her because I knew she'd be terribly cut-up at losing George, although he wasn't a great loss as far as I could see."

"Selma Jacobi," I said thoughtfully, "maybe she fits in this puzzle, too."

Crystal tightened her grip around my neck. "Could we forget all this just for a little while?" she pleaded. "I don't believe you care for me one little bit. All you're interested in is your horrid old puzzles."

"Not all the time," I said.

"Could we have a little fun this very moment?" she asked, pressed her lips on mine.

We had fun.

CHAPTER FOURTEEN

They were waiting for me as I came out of Crystal's flat. I guess I asked for it. I should have been on my guard after Bradley's threat, but the hectic couple of hours I'd spent with Crystal had numbed me, and I stepped into the dark street without the slightest suspicion of what was coming to me.

It happened so quickly that I could only give a strangled shout before something crashed down on my head and I blacked out.

I recovered to find myself lying on the floor of a fast moving car, an evil smelling rug over my head and shoulders, someone's heavy feet on my chest. My head ached, and the rug threatened to stifle me.

I lay still, tried to make out what had happened. I guessed this was Bradley's idea of teaching me to mind my own business. I wasn't happy, wondered where I was being taken, and if I was going to have my throat slit. Cautiously I moved my hands. They were free and so were my legs. Maybe whoever had cracked me on the head had underestimated the thickness of my skull.

The two feet lifted, thumped down on me again.

"Keeps quiet, don't he?" a voice said.

"I 'ope you didn't bash 'im too 'ard, Joe," another voice said.

"Not me," Joe said. "I only patted 'is 'ead with my fist. 'E'll be orl right once I tug 'is ears a bit."

I grimaced. Having my ears tugged was not one of my favourite pastimes.

"We oughter be there by now," the second voice went on. "'Ere, Bert, 'ow much farther is it?"

"Just 'ere," the first voice said. "This'll do, won't it?"

"Yes, this is orl right," Joe said.

The car slowed, bumped over uneven ground, stopped. "Nice quiet spot wid no one to interfere wid us," Bert remarked.

Three of them, I thought. Well, three were better than four. I lay still, waited developments.

Boots trod on me; the car doors opened; feet scraped on gravel.

"Get 'im out, and be careful 'e ain't foxing," Bert said. "'Ere, Joe, you 'andle 'im. Ted and me'll stand by just in case 'e starts any funny business."

"I 'ope 'e does," the man called Joe replied. "I don't like bashing a bloke in cold blood."

I began to like Joe a little.

The other two laughed. "That's a good 'un," Bert sneered. "I ain't so particular, nor's Ted. Are you, Ted?"

"I'm looking forward to bashing the bugger," Ted said cheerfully. "I ain't 'ad any exercise for the past two weeks."

Hands grabbed my ankles. I was dragged bodily out of the car. My shoulders hit on the running-board, but I managed to keep my head clear as I thudded to the ground. I remained still, waited patiently for someone to take off the rug.

"You sure you didn't 'it 'im too 'ard?" Ted asked. "'E's a bit quiet."

"But not for long, matey," Joe said. "Let's 'ave a look at 'im."

The rug was dragged off. I felt the cool night air on my face.

Cautiously I looked between half-closed lids. I could see three massive figures standing over me, stars and a dark sky above me, trees and bushes nearby. It seemed to me I was on some sort of common.

"Strike a match, Ted," Joe growled, bending over me, "and let's 'ave a look at 'im."

I tensed my muscles, waited.

The feeble flickering light from the match lit up Joe's broad, broken features. He looked like an all-in wrestler. He had the kind of puss you dream about after a lobster supper. He knelt beside me, took hold of my chin between fingers that felt like iron. I didn't dare wait any longer. Whipping back my knees and twisting sideways, I jack-knifed into him with my feet, catching him in the middle of his chest. It was like kicking a brick wall.

With a roar of rage and surprise, he shot over backwards.

I squirmed around, got up on my hands and knees.

One of the other massive shapes came at me. He leapt high into the air and descended feet first—the old, spectacular all-in wrestling pounce that looks so easy but isn't. I had a split second to get out of the way. I managed it, swung a wild punch at the man's head as he thudded into the soft soil a half a foot away from me. The guy's skull was made of stone, and I felt a jar run up my arm as my fist connected.

I was on my feet now. The third man had arrived with a crouching rush. He caught me on the shoulder with a half-arm swing that sent me spinning backwards. I steadied up, ducked a haymaker that started from his ankles, socked him in the left eye with everything I had.

I didn't wait to see the effect, but turned on my heel and scrammed across the thick grass.

The common was as flat as a plate, seemed to stretch for miles.

Apart from bushes and an occasional tree there was no cover, nowhere to hide. It looked as if my only chance of escape was to run and keep running. I dug my elbows into my sides, tore across the grass, hoped I was in better condition than the other three.

Wild yells and oaths followed me, then silence. I ran on until I heard the car start up, then looked over my shoulder.

They weren't going to run after me. They preferred the easy way.

They were coming after me by car.

Although the grass was thick, it was quite possible to drive a car over it. I knew in less than a couple of minutes they'd be all over me.

I slowed down, but kept moving. I didn't want to be breathless when they did catch up with me, but I wasn't anxious to come to grips with them any sooner than I could help. My future didn't look too good. Maybe they wouldn't kill me, but they'd do the next best thing.

I thought of Bradley, waiting for these thugs to tell him what they had done to me, and I cursed him.

The car was only a few yards off now. Joe and Ted were hanging on, standing on the running-boards. As soon as they got within reach of me, they jumped off, and closed in on me.

I dodged Joe, ran in the opposite direction. Ted came rushing after me. I slowed, let him come up, then dropped on hands and knees. His knees cannoned into my side and he went head first into the grass. Before Joe got within reach I was off again, but this time Bert had manoeuvred the car so I was sandwiched between the car and Joe.

I wheeled around, waited for Joe who came at me, cursing and waving his arms. I ducked under them, straightened, caught him a clout on the end of his nose which sent him reeling back.

But I couldn't keep this dodging up forever. They would catch me in the end, and by that time I'd be so winded I'd be at their mercy. A big tree a few yards away decided me. I swerved past Bert who came lumbering up, ran across to the tree, set my shoulders against it, waited for them.

I had time to look around the expanse of ground. There was not a house or building to be seen, nor could I see any car lights to indicate a main road. The spot was as bleak and as lonely as a Welsh mountain.

The three men sorted themselves out, came forward, stopped before me.

As I surveyed them I thought the dying gladiator was a happy man beside me. I lifted my fists to show them they weren't going to have it all their own way, waited.

Bert and Ted stood to my right and left. Joe was in the centre.

"Now, chum," Joe said, drawing near, "we're gonna bash you, and then you're getting outa this country, see? If you don't, we'll collect you again and bash you some more, see? And we'll go on bashing you until you do go, see?"

"I get the idea," I said, watching them closely. "But don't blame me if you guys get hurt. I don't usually fight with guys below my weight and strength. It's against my principles."

Joe roared with laughter. "That's a 'ot 'un," he said. "We know 'ow to take care of ourselves, matey. It's you who're going to get 'urt."

I had an uneasy feeling that he wasn't going to be far wrong.

"Go on, paste 'im, Joe," Ted urged. "When you're through wid 'im I'll 'ave a go."

"There won't be much left of 'im by the time I'm through," Joe said, doubling his fists.

"I ain't particular," Ted said. "Just so long as you leave me something to work on."

Joe slouched forward, his bullet head low, his thick lips drawn off his teeth. He looked as attractive as a gorilla, twice as dangerous.

I waited for him in the shadow of the tree, glad the moon was behind me.

He kept coming, his big feet shuffling over the grass, making a slight swishing sound. He wasn't quite sure of me, didn't know if I could hurt him or not. He wasn't taking any chances.

"Don't take all night," Ted called impatiently. "I wanna go 'ome even if you don't."

"Don't rush him," I said, suddenly waving my arms, and made a move towards Joe, who cursed, stepped back, then darted forward, his left fist shooting towards my head. I slipped the punch, hit him in the ribs, swung a right to his jaw. He backed away with a grunt, came at me again. A haymaker whistled past my head, a left grazed my ear.

I uncorked a right that caught him in the throat, lifted him off his feet and stretched him flat on his back.

I blew on my knuckles, stepped back against the tree, looked over at Ted.

"You're next, son," I said. "I treat 'em all the same, no favouritism, no waiting."

Ted and Bert gaped at Joe, then, together, rushed at me.

I thought at least I've hurt one of the punks, hit Bert on the nose, collected a punch on the side of the head from Ted that made my teeth rattle. Bert flung himself on me, snarling, his great fists thudded into my body. He was quite a hitter. I felt as if Tower Bridge had fallen on me. I shoved him off, measured him, socked a couple of lefts into his flat, ugly puss. Ted came up, caught me with a right, and I countered with a left. Then suddenly a light exploded inside my head and I felt myself falling.

I came to a moment or so later. I was lying on the grass, someone was kicking my ribs very hard. I rolled away, tried to get up, but another kick sent me flat again.

I heard Joe bawling savagely, "Lemme get at him."

I had time to see him rushing at me, leap high into the air. I managed to twist sideways, grab his foot. He tried to pull away, but I had a hold. I turned his foot, wrenched it, threw my weight on it. I had the satisfaction of hearing a bone go, and Joe's howl of pain, then a hand seized my hair, and a fist like a lump of iron crashed on my chin.

I felt myself rise in the air, and I landed on the thick grass with a thump that knocked the wind out of me.

I was now half crazy with rage, and struggled to get up, but found I hadn't the strength to support myself. I fell forward on hands and knees. A great crushing weight dropped on me and I went flat.

Although I knew what followed, I couldn't do anything to stop them, couldn't defend myself.

Two of them systematically beat me up. One dragged me to my feet, held me upright, while the other bashed my face and chest with his fists. They made a boxing sack out of me. When one got tired, the other took over. It seemed to go on for a long time. There was nothing I could do but take it. So I took it.

At last, they were through. They left me lying on my back blood running into my eyes, my body pulverized. I felt little pain. That would come later. At the moment, I could see the moon through swollen eyes, hear what was going on as if the sounds were coming to me out of a fog.

I was still half crazy with temper, and after a few minutes, I managed to hoist myself to my feet. I reeled around like a drunk, fell down again. My hand closed over a big round flint stone. That gave me a little incentive.

Crawling upon my hands and knees, holding the flint tightly, feeling its sharp edges digging into my fingers, I peered around until I located the three men a few yards from me.

Ted and Bert were giving first aid attention to Joe's ankle. It was nice to hear his curses as they probed the swollen member with their thick, unfeeling fingers.

I levered myself to my feet, swayed backwards, recovered, set out across the grass towards them. It took me a little time, and it was like walking against a strong wind. Ted heard me when I was a few feet away, turned.

"For crying out aloud!" he exclaimed, "I'll bust my mit on his ugly snug this time, s'welp me if I don't."

I found I couldn't get any farther, so I waited patiently for him to come to me. He sauntered up, flexing his right arm. Bert and Joe turned their heads to watch. Bert was grinning; Joe was snarling at me.

Ted planted himself in front of me, set himself.

"Now, chum," he said, "I'm about to demonstrate 'ow I put Little Ernie to sleep in the first round. If this smack you're going to run into don't take your 'ead off your neck, then may I be."

I collected all my remaining strength, shot the flint into his face as his right hand began to move.

The flint caught him an inch or so below his right eye, ripped his cheek open to the bone.

He gave a startled howl, stepped back, tripped and fell. He began to bleed into the grass.

That was about all I could do. I'd broken Joe's ankle and scarred Ted for life. It was a pity I couldn't do more for Bert, but I just hadn't the guts to stand any longer on my feet. I staggered forward, heard a violent oath from Bert, saw him rush at me.

I took his punch on the point of my jaw, went out like a snuffed candle.

CHAPTER FIFTEEN

Crystal was saying, "You may think it odd I should have married such a wreck, but he didn't always look like that. When we first met, he was almost handsome."

I opened my eyes, found I could scarcely see, stared up at the ceiling. There was a smell of antiseptics and flowers in the room. I felt as if I'd been run over by a steam-roller, but the bed felt fine.

A woman's voice said, "You may sit with him for a little while, Mrs. Harmas. He should recover consciousness any moment now, but please don't excite him."

Crystal said airily, "Oh, we're old married folk now. He doesn't get excited when he sees me, worse luck."

A door shut, and Crystal, looking cute in a blue and white check frock and a white turban, moved into my vision. She drew up a chair, began to put her bag on the bedside-table.

I reached out, pinched her. She gave a sharp squeal, jumped, turned.

"I've recovered consciousness," I announced.

"Oh, darling, you gave me such a fright," she exclaimed, furtively rubbed the spot where I'd pinched her, "and you really shouldn't do a thing like that. It's very uncouth." She took my hand, fondled it, looked down at me with adoring eyes. "I've been so worried about you, precious. You've no idea. I've been simply frantic."

"That makes two of us," I said, squeezing her hand. "I've been simply frantic, too."

"Oh, Steve, I do seem to love you," she said, kneeling beside me, and rubbing her cheek against my hand. "Whatever's happened to your poor face?" She blinked back tears.

I struggled up in bed, grimaced as pain rode through me, looked around the room. It was obviously a private ward in a hospital. I sank back with a grunt of disgust.

"How did I get here?" I demanded, "and how did you find me?"

"Now, you mustn't excite yourself, darling," she said, patting my pillow.

"A very kind, thoughtful man telephoned me. He found you on Wimbledon Common, discovered my telephone number in your wallet, called me and an ambulance, and here you are. But, please, Steve, what happened? Whoever did this to you?"

I ran my fingers tenderly over my face, grimaced.

"I had a fight," I said. "Some thugs picked on me and this is the result."

"But why should they pick on you?" Crystal asked, her eyes opening. "You're such a nice boy. Did you say something to annoy them?"

"I guess I must have done," I said, deciding that it wouldn't add to her peace of mind if she knew Bradley was at the back of this. "What was that you were saying about being Mrs. Harmas?"

She looked embarrassed. "Oh, dear, did you hear me?" she returned. "Well, it was the only way I could get in to see you. You're not angry, are you, precious? We can always get divorced when you're better, can't we?"

I patted her hand, tried to smile, but my muscles were too stiff.

"That's okay with me," I said. "If I was the marrying type, I couldn't think of anyone I'd like to marry better than you—if I was the marrying type."

She nodded, looked bitter. "That kills me—if you're the marrying type! Maybe, you'll have to marry me."

"Don't let's get sordid," I said hurriedly. "Tell me, how long have I been here?"

"Two days."

I moved my legs and arms. After the first twinge of pain, they moved easily enough.

"Well, I'm not staying here any longer. I must get up and out of this."

"You'll do no such thing," Crystal said firmly. "There's no question of you getting up until you're quite well."

"Well, okay. That's something we can argue about when we run out of conversation," I said. "Do the police know what's happened to me?"

She nodded. "I'm afraid they do. You see the hospital reported your arrival. There's been a great, hulking policeman sitting by your bed since you came. I managed to persuade him to wait outside this time. He's out there now."

"Wants a statement, I suppose," I said. "Well, maybe you'd better send him in. We can't keep the Law waiting, can we?"

She looked uneasy. "He worries me. I don't think he believes we're married."

"That shows he's a good cop, but I'll convince him. Tell him to come in, honey, and stick around. You do me good."

"Do I really?" Her face brightened. "I'm so glad. I was beginning to think I was bad for you." She bent over and kissed me tenderly.

I patted her.

"Get the cop, sweetheart, or I'll be dragging you into bed."

"You wouldn't have to drag me," she returned, went to the door.

I heard men's voices, then Corridan entered, followed by Crystal who looked scared.

"I didn't ask him in," she said, hurriedly. "He was outside with the other man."

Corridan came over and stood looking down at me. A fatuous smile lit his dour face. It was the first time I'd ever seen him look really happy.

"Well, well," he said, rubbing his hands. "They certainly made a mess of you, didn't they?"

I scowled at him.

"What do you want?" I asked irritably. "You're the last person I hoped to see."

He drew up a chair, sat down, positively beamed at me.

"I heard the news," he said, "and couldn't resist coming to gloat. You've turned up enough times when I've been in trouble, you vulture, now it's my turn." He was oozing with happiness and geniality. "Who's the young lady?"

Crystal made frantic signs to me behind his back, but I pretended to ignore them.

"She's my cousin twice removed," I said. "Maybe, it's three times removed. I've never stopped to work it out. Crystal, my dear, this handsome looking lug is Inspector Corridan. He works at Scotland Yard, and you know what I mean by the word 'works'."

Corridan lost a little of his sunny smile.

"The last time I saw her," he said tartly, "was in your room at the Savoy. You told me then she was the floor waiter's daughter."

"That could still make her my second or third cousin," I pointed out, smiled at Crystal, who was looking bewildered. "Don't let the Inspector make you nervous. Without his wig and false teeth, he's really quite a kindly old thing."

Corridan lost his smile, fixed me with a cold stare.

"You take your idea of a joke a little too far, Harmas," he said with asperity.

"Don't get annoyed, pal," I said. "I'm not in a fit state to be bullied."

Crystal sat in a corner away from us, folded her hands in her lap, tried to look demure.

Corridan leaned forward. "Let's cut out this fooling," he said.

"Who's been knocking you about?"

I sighed, hung my head. "I was teasing a midget, and he lost his temper," I said, closed my eyes.

Crystal sniggered, coughed, cleared her throat. Corridan looked annoyed.

"Now look, Harmas, that sort of thing won't do. You've caused a lot of trouble, and we want to know what's behind it."

"I've told you," I said, patiently. "At least, that's my story, and I'm sticking to it. I have no complaints to make. I shall pay the hospital fees. I really don't see why a flock of flatfeet should come barging in here to know why and what."

Corridan breathed heavily, shifted in his chair.

"You've been assaulted," he explained. "That is a police matter. It is your duty to file a complaint."

"I'm most certainly not going to provide police with work," I said crossly. "I stuck my neck out, and I got what was coming to me. This is a personal matter, and I don't want you or your pals horning in. So forget it."

Corridan studied me for a moment, shrugged. "All right," he said, "if you're still suffering from I'll-steer-my-own-boat complex, there's nothing more to be said. If you're not going to file a complaint that lets me out." He pushed back his chair, stood up. "I think I warned you to keep out of this business, didn't I? It would seem someone else is also trying to persuade you. If this has anything to do with the Kennitt murder, you must tell me who did it or take the consequences."

"I'll take the consequences," I said flippantly.

Corridan snorted. "Has this or has this not anything to do with the Kennitt murder?"

"I wouldn't know. The thugs who beat me up didn't leave their names and addresses."

"So it's thugs now?"

"That's right. I was kidding about a midget. You know me: I'm tough. Takes more than a midget to beat me up. Those guys were twice as big as Joe Louis. Twelve of them set on me and I fought them for two or three hours. And what a fight I gave them! I laid eight of them out—crying for mercy they were. The other four kept coming and I kept hitting them. The siege of Stalingrad was nothing to it." Finally paused as Corridan, giving me an awful look, stamped out of the room.

Crystal ran over to me.

"Oh, you shouldn't have annoyed him like that," she said, shocked. "He might get you into trouble."

I reached out, pulled her down beside me.

"That wouldn't worry me, honey," I said. "The guy's harmless enough, but dumb."

"I don't like him," Crystal said, putting her head on my shoulder. She hurt me, but it was worth it. "I don't like the way he looks at me."

"And just how does he look at you?"

"That's something a girl could only tell her mother," she replied primly.

A few minutes later a nurse came in. Crystal had heard her coming and was standing by the window, trying to look unruffled and not succeeding very well. The nurse shooed her away, then took my pulse, dabbed something on my bruises and told me to go to sleep.

Oddly enough, I didn't seem to need much encouragement, and I didn't awaken until dusk was falling. I felt better, got out of bed, walked stiffly across to the mirror on the wall, examined my features with mixed feelings.

I certainly looked a great deal worse than I felt. I had two black eyes, the end of my nose was red and swollen, two livid bruises showed on my cheek-bones, my right ear was puffy. My chest and arms were black with bruises. The three thugs had certainly done a good job on me.

I returned to my bed, stretched out, decided I wasn't quite fit enough to start any trouble for the time being. In a day or so I should be ready for Bradley. I was going to surprise that rat.

I heard footsteps, followed by a knock on the door. I called; "Come in," hopefully, half sat up.

The door opened and a sad looking little man wandered in. I gaped at him, scarcely believing my eyes. It was Henry Littlejohns.

"For the love of Mike!" I exclaimed, struggling upright. "What brings you here."

"Good evening, Mr. Harmas," he said, in his sad voice. He looked around for somewhere to park his bowler hat, laid it down on the chest of drawers, came farther into the room. "I'm indeed sorry to find you in this unhappy state, sir," he went on, visibly shocked at my appearance. "I trust you are making a good recovery?"

"Never mind all that stuff," I said, impatiently. "I'm fine. Sit down. Make yourself at home. I thought you were in Lakeham."

"So I was, sir," he said, drawing up a chair and sitting down. He pulled up his trousers so they shouldn't bag at the knees, fidgeted with his feet. "At least, I was until this afternoon."

I saw he wasn't at ease, offered my carton of cigarettes.

"No, thank you, sir," he said, shaking his head. "I don't smoke." He regarded me with his sad eyes, chewed the end of his moustache.

"Something to report?" I asked, wondering what was coming.

"Not exactly, sir," he said, drumming on his knees. "I don't suppose you've heard from Mr. Merryweather yet?"

"I've heard nothing from Merryweather," I said, puzzled. "Anything wrong?"

Littlejohns stroked his greying hair, looked self-conscious. "The fact of the matter is, sir, Mr. Merryweather has withdrawn from your case."

"The hell he has," I said, sitting bolt-upright, and wishing I hadn't. "What's the idea?"

"You see, sir, Mr. Merryweather at no time thought the investigation within our usual terms of reference," Littlejohns explained. "The—er—pecuniary aspect of the case interested him—tempted him, you might say, but he now has been threatened—well, he thinks there'll be no useful purpose served in continuing the investigation."

I pricked up my ears. "Threatened?"

Littlejohns nodded gravely. "Apparently two men visited him yesterday morning. They were rough characters, and they made it clear that if he did not immediately stop working for you, they would settle his hash, I believe was the phrase used."

I lit a cigarette, scowled. It seemed Bradley was working overtime.

"You mean Merryweather allowed these two guys to throw a scare into him?"

"They were exceptionally rough characters," Littlejohns said hurriedly, as if anxious to excuse Merryweather's lack of courage. "They smashed his desk, said they had beaten you up and would beat Merryweather up too. He isn't exactly young, and he has a wife to consider. I can't say I blame him for withdrawing, and I hope, sir, you'll take the same view."

He looked so solemn that I burst out laughing.

"That's okay," I said, lay back on my pillow and grinned at him. "I bet they scared the daylight out of the poor old geezer. I don't blame him in the least. They nearly, but not quite, scared the daylight out of me." I looked at him, suddenly puzzled. "But why did you come here to tell me all this? What's it to do with you?"

Littlejohns pulled at his moustache. "I'm very sorry to be taken off this case, sir," he said. "Very sorry. You see, sir, I liked the excitement. You may not believe it, but I've always wanted to be a detective ever since I was a nipper. I've been disappointed with the work up to now. Mr. Merryweather doesn't get much business. The cases that do come our way are the usual divorce cases. Not, as you will appreciate, very congenial work: very dull, if I may say so. I dislike spying on married couples. But I have to do the work. I'm not getting any younger; jobs are difficult to come by. I thought I'd explain my position, sir. I hope you'll forgive me taking up your time. What I was going to suggest ..." He paused, looked embarrassed. "If you'll excuse the liberty, what I was going to suggest was that I should continue with the case. I'd be very happy to take reduced fees, and Mr. Merryweather has nothing for me at the moment. He pays me only when I'm working for him. So I thought I'd offer my services, not that you'd want to continue the arrangement, but I thought there'd be no harm in mentioning it."

I gaped at him. "But, look, if they're threatening Merryweather, that'll also include you."

"I don't believe in being intimidated by threats," he said quietly. "I assure you I wouldn't be put off by that kind of thing. I'm at your service if you still require me."

I grinned at him, suddenly liking him immensely. "Sure, you go ahead. The same terms suit you?"

He gaped, stuttered. "Oh, but surely, Mr. Harmas, they were rather excessive. I would be prepared ..."

"No, you'll have what Merryweather got, so dry up," I said firmly. "Don't make any mistake: you'll earn the money. There are a number of things to do with this case that I haven't told your boss. I'm going to tell you, and you can then decide if you still want the job."

"Thank you, sir," Littlejohns said, his face lighting up. "There is one thing I must report first. I've seen the young lady with the red hair. She came out of the cottage late last night. The black-and-yellow Bentley called for her. I saw her distinctly. She got into the car which drove away along the London road; I was unfortunately too late to follow it."

"Okay," I said. "Perhaps she's decided to come to London. Well, keep an eye on the cottage for a little while. Now, listen to what I have to say."

I told him the whole story without pulling my punches down to Madge Kennitt's murder and the attack on myself. I told him about Jacobi, Selma, his wife, about Bradley and Julius Cole going to the club.

"That's about the lot," I said. "These guys are a tough bunch. You'll have to watch your step."

He scarcely seemed to hear me.

"I'm glad you've taken me into your confidence, sir," he said, getting to his feet. "I think I'll have something for you in a day or so. I would rather not discuss it now, but something you said just now has given me the clue I've been looking for. I'll get in touch with you very soon."

"Hey!" I called as he picked up his hat and made for the door.

"What about Julius Cole? Has he arrived at Lakeham?"

"He arrived three nights ago, and is staying with Mrs. Brambee," Littlejohns said, opening the door. "I'll have something for you in a day or so."

He didn't wait for me to tell him again to be careful.

CHAPTER SIXTEEN

Two days later, still considerably bruised and battered, but with all my old vigour back and a sharp edge to my temper, I returned to the Savoy.

Crystal was there to welcome me. The room was cluttered up with a mass of flowers and smelt like a florist's. There was a bottle of champagne in a bucket, and it only needed a brass band and the Lord Mayor to complete the homecoming atmosphere.

"Darling!" Crystal exclaimed, throwing her arms around my neck and doing her best to strangle me. "Welcome home!"

"Who's paying for the champagne?" I demanded, removing her arms.

"You are, precious," she said brightly. "Let's open it and drink your health. My poor little tonsils are withering for a drink."

"Not at seven pounds a bottle we won't," I said firmly. "That goes back to where it came from. I suppose I'm paying for all these flowers too?"

"I knew you wouldn't mind," Crystal returned slipping her arm through mine and pressing her face against my shoulder. "I'll take them home if you don't like them, but you'll have to pay for them as I'm a little short right now. They do make the room look lovely, don't they?"

"Sure, but what are they going to do to my bank balance? This is as bad as being married. Now, suppose you sit down and let me look through my mail. I've been out of circulation for the past four days. I shall have some catching up to do."

"Oh, there's plenty of time for that," she said. "Aren't you glad to see me? You haven't even kissed me yet."

I kissed her. "There, now sit down and keep quiet for a moment."

"I do love you, Steve, in spite of your poor battered face," she went on, sitting down. "But I do wish you were a more romantic type."

"It's nice of you to call it a face," I said, glancing into the mirror, grimacing. "Sorry about being the wrong type. You'd better get in touch with Frank Sinatra if that's the way you feel."

She lifted her shoulders in a hopeless shrug. "At least I haven't any competition," she said. "That's the only advantage a girl gets in going around with a fish like you."

"One of these days, when I have the time, I'll prove to you I have blood and not warm water in my veins," I returned, smiling at her. I picked up my mail, sorted through it. I read the letter from Merryweather, full of apologies, but withdrawing from the case with pathetic determination. There was a note from Corridan, congratulating me on my recovery, hoping I would soon be going home, and again advising me, now that I was lucky to be still alive, not to interfere with what was obviously not my business. I tossed the letter into the wastepaper basket. The rest of my mail was from America and needed immediate attention.

I shooed Crystal out, promising to meet her that evening, sat down and worked solidly until lunch time.

After lunch, before settling down to the fourth of my articles on Post-War Britain, I turned Jack Bradley up in the telephone book, found he had a flat in Hay's Mews. I noted the address, closed the book with a vicious bang. Sometime during the night, I proposed to call on Mr. Bradley, and he was going to remember my visit.

In the evening I met Crystal and we had supper together at the Vanity Fair.

She was looking enchanting in an ice-blue evening gown which she said had been a reward for a strictly one-sided wrestling match with one of the club's patrons. I tactfully didn't ask her who had won.

"That horrible policeman friend of yours was in the club this afternoon," she said after we had worked through an excellent veal escalope.

"You mean Corridan?" I asked, interested.

She nodded. "He spent half an hour with Bradley, and on his way out, he passed me and said I was to be sure to tell you I had seen him because you like to know what was going on, and to say that curiosity killed the cat."

I laughed. "The guy's getting to be quite a kidder. Now, I wonder what he wanted with Bradley? Have you ever seen him in the club before?"

She shook her head. "Oh, no. Policemen never come to the club as a rule. Bradley was furious as he showed Corridan the door. Corridan must have said something frightfully rude because Bradley never shows his feelings."

"One of these days I too am going to say something frightfully rude to Mr. Bradley," I said grimly.

She put her hand on mine. "You won't do anything silly, precious, will you?"

"I never do anything silly except make love to you."

She glared at me. "You don't call that making love, do you?"

"I don't know what else you call it. I was under the impression that we were on intimate terms."

"One of these days I'll forget I'm a lady," she said darkly, "then you'll know what being on intimate terms really means. It'll be an experience you won't forget in a hurry."

"Hastily changing the subject," I said, patting her hand, "have you heard anything from Selma Jacobi?"

She sighed. "Here it comes," she said, shaking her head. "More questions.

I don't know why I bother to waste the best hours of my life in your company. I haven't heard anything from Selma. I don't suppose I ever shall. I expect she's started an entirely new life. Sometimes I think it'd be a good idea if I did the same thing."

"Never mind about your life for a moment," I returned. "Let's concentrate on Selma. Has she any friends? I mean, close friends who might know where I could find her?"

"You're not going to chase her, are you?" Crystal demanded, her eyebrows shooting up. "She simply isn't your type. She'd bore you in five minutes. You can't do better than stick to me. After all I'm your first and only love."

"This is strictly business, honey," I said patiently. "I'm trying to solve a murder case. If I could talk to Selma I think I could get somewhere. Do you know any of her friends?"

"I love that line about being strictly business. It's the hammiest of them all. But I suppose you'll go on and on until you wear me down so I'd better tell you. There is one fellow who was awfully keen on her at one time, and before George Jacobi turned up they were always going around together. His name was Peter French."

I rubbed my chin, stared at her. Peter ... could he be the Peter Mrs. Brambee had mentioned?

"Do you know where he hangs out?" I asked.

"He runs a garage in Shepherd Market," Crystal told me, went on to give me the address. "He's often told me if I want any petrol I could get it from him. That's the sort of man he is—he knows I haven't a car."

"You're quite helpful in your dizzy way," I said. "Remind me to reward you when we're alone."

After dinner I put Crystal in a taxi as she had decided reluctantly that she had better show up at the Blue Club, and then I walked around to Shepherd Market, only a few minutes from the Vanity Fair.

French's garage was in one of the back alleys of the Market. It was merely a large concrete wilderness, equipped with a bench and a pit, and didn't look the kind of place that made money.

I wandered up. Two men in soiled dungarees, lounging at the open doors, regarded me without interest. One of them, a short fat guy, bald as an egg, took a cigarette butt from behind his ear, lit it, dragged down smoke. The other, younger, his face and hands smeared with oil, eyed the butt vacantly, rubbed his shoulders against the wall.

"Mr. French around?" I asked the baldheaded guy.

He eyed me over. "Who shall I say?" he asked. "I don't know if 'e's in or out."

I grinned. "Tell him I've been recommended by the Blue Club, and I'd be glad if he could spare me a moment."

The baldheaded guy wandered into the garage, disappeared up some stairs at the back.

"You keep open late," I said to the young fellow.

He grunted. "We ain't as late as this usually, but we're waiting for a job to come in."

After a few minutes, the fat guy came back.

"Upstairs, first door on the right," he said.

I thanked him, skirted a pool of oil, walked across the vast expanse of dirty concrete. Halfway across, I paused. In the far corner of the garage stood a magnificent yellow-and-black Bentley. I hesitated, made a move towards it, glanced up to find the baldheaded guy watching me.

"Some car," I said.

He continued to stare at me, said nothing.

I memorised the number plate, wondered if it was the same car that Littlejohns had seen at Lakeham, and that Crystal had said belonged to Netta's mysterious boyfriend. I thought it was too much of a coincidence not to be, walked up the stairs, repeating the number in my mind. I rapped on the first door on my right, heard a man's voice call, "Come in."

I pushed open the door, walked into a big room so luxuriously furnished that I came to an abrupt stop. A fine Chinese carpet covered the centre of the floor; polished boards that really were polished, set off the surrounds. A big desk stood by the window, comfortable and inviting armchairs were dotted about the room. The drapes and colour scheme were bright and modern. It was an extraordinary contrast to the filthy garage downstairs.

A man stood with his back to the vast brick fireplace, a cigar in his thick fingers, a large brandy inhaler on the mantelpiece within reach.

He was around thirty-five, dark, bulky, big. He looked a foreigner, was probably a Jew. His black hair was parted in the centre, grew back from his narrow forehead in two hard, set waves. His black eyes were like sloes, his complexion like the underbelly of a fish. He looked impressive because he was so well-groomed, so poised, so obviously well-to-do, confident in himself and his money.

He eyed me over without much enthusiasm, nodded. "Good evening," he said. "I didn't get your name. It was something to do with the Blue Club, wasn't it?"

"I'm Steve Harmas of the New York *Clarion*," I said. "Glad to know you, Mr. French."

His eyelids narrowed a trifle, but he shook hands, waved me to a chair.

"Sit down. Have a cigar," he said, "and this brandy isn't exactly poison." He gave a depreciatory smirk, added, "I pay eight pounds a bottle for the damn stuff, so it can't be too bad."

I said I'd sample the brandy, but preferred a cigarette to a cigar.

While he was pouring the brandy into an inhaler, I studied him.

I remembered Crystal's description of the man in the yellow-and-black Bentley. It fitted French well enough. He was more likely to be the owner of a car like that than Julius Cole. I couldn't imagine Netta going around with Cole, but I could see her being fascinated by this guy.

"Nice little place you have here," I said, accepting the inhaler. "Comes as a surprise after the garage."

He smiled, nodded. "I believe in comfort, Mr. Harmas," he returned. "I work long hours, spend most of my life in this room. What's the point in not having nice surroundings?"

I agreed with him, wondered if I should make a direct approach or get around to it more cautiously.

"Your bruises are a little too obvious to ignore," he went on, regarding me with friendly curiosity. "If a fellow has a black eye, I don't pass remarks. Probably his girlfriend has lost her temper with him; but when a fellow has two black eyes and the rest of his face resembles a rainbow, I feel it'd be unsympathetic not to offer condolences."

I laughed, "That's swell of you," I said, "and you're not the only one as you can imagine. A good newspaper man, Mr. French, has to be inquisitive. He can't afford to mind his own business. Three powerfully built gentlemen didn't like my methods. They pooled their muscles and attempted to alter the shape of my face, with some success, as you can see."

He raised his eyebrows, pursed his lips. "I do see," he said. "I must say I should be distinctly annoyed if anyone did that to me."

I nodded. "Oh, I'm annoyed all right, but I didn't come here to talk about my face. I came because I thought you might be able to help me."

He nodded, looked a little wary, waited.

"I believe you know Selma Jacobi," I said, deciding to give it to him straight.

He put the inhaler on the mantelpiece, frowned. "Nothing doing, my friend," he said shortly. "Sorry, but I'm not talking to a newspaper man about Mrs. Jacobi. If that's all you've come about then I'll say good night."

"I'm not talking to you as a newspaper man," I said. "My paper wouldn't be interested in Mrs. Jacobi. I'm talking to you as a friend of Netta Scott's."

He stared at his cigar thoughtfully, moved away from the fireplace to the window.

"You knew Netta Scott?" he said. "So did I."

I didn't say anything, wondered if I should ask him if he owned the Bentley, decided I wouldn't.

"But what has Netta Scott to do with Mrs. Jacobi?" he went on, after a pause.

"I don't know," I said, stretching out my legs. "But I have a hunch there is a connection. I think Netta knew George Jacobi. I want to be sure. Maybe Selma could tell me."

"Why do you want to know that?" he asked, still looking out of the window.

"Maybe it'd explain why she committed suicide," I said. "You know about that?"

"Yes," he said, hunched his massive shoulders as if the subject wasn't to his taste. "Why should you be interested in Netta's suicide?"

"I don't believe in letting sleeping dogs lie," I said. "I've told you I'm inquisitive. Netta wasn't the type to commit suicide. I'm wondering if there's more behind it than I think."

He glanced over his shoulder, started to say something, stopped.

There was a long pause, then he said. "I haven't seen Mrs. Jacobi for two or three months, not since she married."

"Know where she lives?"

"She isn't there anymore," he returned. "The place is shut up."

"Where is it?"

He faced me. "What does it matter where it is? She isn't there, I tell you."

"Maybe she'll come back. Look, let me put it this way. The police are looking for you. At least, they're looking for a big guy whose first name is Peter, and who knew Netta. I'm not interested in helping the police. But they'd welcome the chance of talking to you, and they'd be a lot less polite than I am. I want Selma Jacobi's address. Either you give it to me or you'll give it to the police. I don't care which way it is, only make up your mind."

He chewed his cigar which had gone out, always a sign a guy's got something on his mind.

"What makes you think the police want to talk to me?" he asked, his voice cold.

I told him about Anne Scott, and what Mrs. Brambee had said.

"I've never heard of Anne Scott," he snapped. "I didn't even know Netta had a sister."

"Don't tell me; tell the judge. All I'm interested in is finding out Selma's address."

"I don't want the police nosing around here," he said, after a pause. "I'd take it as a favour if you kept your mouth shut. Selma lived at 3B Hampton Street, off Russell Square. Now suppose you take yourself off. I have things to do before I go home, and I've given you quite enough of my time."

I got to my feet. "Have you a photo of Selma?"

He studied me for a moment, shook his head. "I don't collect photographs of married women," he said. "Good night."

"Well, thanks," I said, "you won't be bothered by the police through any information from me." I turned to the door, paused. "That's a fine car downstairs. Is it yours?"

He eyed me. "Yes. What of it?"

"Nothing. You're lucky to have a car like that."

"Good night," he repeated. "I'm beginning to understand how you got your face damaged. I'm also beginning to feel sorry those fellows didn't make a better job of it."

I grinned, said maybe I'd see him again, left him.

CHAPTER SEVENTEEN

At some time, when Crystal had been prattling, she had mentioned that Jack Bradley seldom arrived at the club before ten o'clock for the evening's work.

I decided, as I walked through Shepherd Market, that if I called on him now, I might stand a good chance of finding him in.

Hay's Mews lies off Berkeley Square; and I arrived there in a few minutes.

Bradley's flat was over a garage. Lights were showing through the cream muslin curtains. I would have preferred to have climbed in through the window, but that was not possible. I did the next best thing: I punched the bell.

I waited a few minutes, then heard a step. The door opened. I didn't expect to see Frankie, but then he didn't expect to see me.

"Hello, tough guy," I said.

He took one look, alarm jumped into his eyes, and he opened his mouth to yell.

I was ready for that, and belted him under the chin. I caught him as he fell, lowered him carefully to the floor.

I stepped over him, closed the door, listened.

Ahead of me were stairs leading to the flat. A pedestal stood at the foot of the stairs on which was a bowl of orchids. I sneered at it.

The stairs were carpeted with thick green material that gave comfortingly under the feet, muffled the sound of steps. The walls were apricot, the banister rail dark green.

A voice called, "Frankie ... who is it?"

A girl's voice, strangely familiar.

I stiffened, felt spooked. I knew the voice. I had heard it so many times before, but even at that it was hard to believe that it was Netta speaking.

I took a quick step forward, caught a glimpse of silk clad legs and the hem of a blue dress at the head of the stairs. Then I heard a startled gasp, the hem of the dress and the silk clad legs vanished.

There was a scurrying of feet.

I sprang up the stairs, didn't realize they were so steep, stumbled.

I cursed, regained my balance, went on up, hands touching each step as I went, arrived at a small lobby with three doors facing me.

One of the doors jerked open: Jack Bradley appeared. He wore a green dressing-gown, stiff white collar and black evening tie. His eyes were frozen stones, his mouth twisted with fury.

As I stepped towards him, I saw the .38 automatic in his hand, paused.

"I'll make you pay for this," he snarled. "How dare you break in here!"

I listened, not looking at him. Somewhere a door closed. "Hello, Bradley," I said. "Who was your girlfriend?"

"I'll shoot if you try any tricks," he said. "Get your hands up. I'm calling the police."

"Oh, no, you're not," I said, "and you're not going to shoot. You haven't a gun permit, and the cops can make things awkward for a thug like you if you let guns off without a permit." I spoke rapidly, hoped my bluff would work, edged towards him.

I saw his expression change, a look of doubt in his eyes. That was enough for me. I slapped the gun out of his hand, kicked it down the stairs. He swung at me, but I shoved him aside, entered the room from which he had come.

The room was empty except for its rich furnishings. A smell of lilac hung in the air. So it had been Netta, I thought, again felt spooked.

There was a door at the far end of the room. I ran over, tried to open it, found it locked. I drew back, kicked at the lock, the door burst open. I looked out into the night from the head of an outside wooden stairway. As I stood there, I heard a car start up, drive away.

I turned, found Bradley sneaking up on me, a poker in his hand. I ducked the wild swing, caught his wrist, wrenched the poker out of his hand, I looked at him. His face was white and his eyes glared.

"I remember you once said you were tougher than Frankie," I said. "Here's your opportunity to show me."

I tossed the poker across the room. It knocked over a lamp standard which in its turn knocked over a small table on which stood bottles and glasses. The crash made a nice noise to my ears.

"You'll be sorry for this," Bradley snarled, backing away.

"So you're not so tough," I grinned at him. "You're the guy who tells other mugs to do your dirty work. Okay, Bradley, you're on the spot now. You'd better exert some of that fat and try to get out of it."

I grabbed hold of him by his dressing gown, shook him, threw him after the poker. He weighed about sixteen stone, but the bulk of it was fat.

I walked over to where he lay, sat on the arm of a chair, smiled at him. He didn't attempt to get up, glared up at me with eyes a snake'd be proud to own.

"Remember me, Bradley?" I said. "The guy who doesn't mind his own business? I thought maybe you mightn't recognize me after what your thugs did to me."

"I don't know what you're talking about," he snarled. "Get out of here before I call the police."

"You warned me you'd teach me a lesson, didn't you?" I went on, taking out a cigarette, lighting it. "Well, the lesson didn't stick. But my lesson will. I'm going to ruin that fat puss of yours, but before I start on you, you're going to answer some questions. Who was that girl you were talking to just now?"

"Nobody you know," he said, sitting up slowly. "If you don't get out, Harmas, I'll fix you. My God, I'll fix you!"

I kicked him in his fat chest, sending him over backwards.

"I told you that rats like you are a nickel a gross, didn't I?" I said, flicking ash it him. "You don't know what it is to be tough. Fix me?" I laughed. "You won't fix anyone by the time I'm through with you."

He lay holding on to his chest, his face purple with fury and pain, but he stayed right where he was.

"Come on, who's the dame? Talk or I'll sock you, and keep on socking you."

"It was Selma Jacobi," he snarled. "Now get out!"

I shook my head. "Oh, no, it wasn't," I said, kicking him gently. "It was Netta, wasn't it?"

His face went flabby. The purple drained away leaving his skin like tallow.

"You're mad!" he gasped, struggling up. "Netta's dead."

"You've given yourself away," I said, taking off my coat and rolling up my sleeves. "Get up, Bradley. You can try to do what your three hired thugs tried to do."

He lay as still as a corpse, looked at me with fear in his eyes.

"Leave me alone," he said. "You can't touch me, Harmas. I'm an old man. I have a weak heart."

I laughed. "You mean you're going to have a weak heart," I said, drew back my foot and booted him in his fat ribs. "Get up, you heel."

I had to kick him to his feet, then I hauled off and hit him in the eye, sent him reeling across the room. He clawed at a bookcase as he staggered back, trying to regain his balance. The bookcase swayed, crashed to the floor, spilling books. I picked up the heaviest, flung it at him. It caught him on the chest, and he went over, upsetting a chair.

Standing off, I pelted him with books until he took cover behind a settee. I went in after him, met his bull-like charge as he rushed at me, swept his feeble right lead out of the way, socked him in the other eye, steadied him as he reeled back, hit him in the mouth. My knuckles scraped along his teeth. I felt them give. He staggered away, spitting blood, his lips ballooning up, his eyes closing.

He made a wild dive for the telephone. I let him get his paw on it, then made a flying tackle, grabbed him around the knees, brought him down.

He caught me a glancing blow as we broke, but it had no more iron in it than could be expected from a fat, middle-aged rat who fed on whisky for breakfast.

I tore the telephone wire out by its roots, hit him with the receiver until it shattered in my hand.

I stood off, looked around the room to see if there was anything standing. There wasn't, so I grabbed an oil painting of a fat dame in her birthday suit off the wall, broke it over Bradley's head as he came up for air.

I grabbed the lamp standard, hit him with that.

He lay flat on his back, gasping and wheezing, his face a lot less pretty than mine.

I waited hopefully for him to get up, but he didn't. As I was trying to make up my mind whether to call it a day or stand on his face, Frankie came in. He looked murderous. In his right hand he had a carving knife, and he handled it as if he meant to use it.

He didn't rush at me, but came slowly, the knife held in front of his skinny body, his lips off his teeth, his eyes glittering.

"Hello, Marmaduke," I said, "didn't your ma tell you it was dangerous to play with knives? You might cut yourself."

He crept towards me, snarling.

I decided it wouldn't be healthy to let him get too close. My hand groped behind me for a book, selected one, shot it at him. It hit him on the shoulder, but it didn't stop him. He kept coming, so I gave ground. I suddenly realized that if I didn't watch my step he'd murder me.

We moved around the room, each stepping over the ruins, careful not to trip, never taking our eyes off each other. I guessed he was manoeuvring me close to Bradley, and that Bradley would try to grab my legs. If that happened, Frankie would have plenty of opportunity to ventilate my hide.

I stopped giving ground, crouched.

This move startled Frankie for a moment: he stopped too. I moved a step forward. He made a feeble poke at me with the knife, undecided whether to go back or rush me. I rushed him while he was making up his mind.

I felt the knife slit my shirt-sleeve, scratch my biceps, but by then I had hold of his wrist. He clawed my face as I bent his arm back. It hurt, and I lost my temper for a moment. I snatched him up by the slack of his pants, threw him at Bradley as Bradley was slowly levering himself to his feet.

While they were sorting themselves out, I tossed the knife downstairs. Both Bradley and Frankie were on their feet when I faced around.

Bradley seemed to have found a little courage now Frankie had joined him.

"Kill the swine," he mumbled to Frankie, pushed him forward.

I laughed. I couldn't help it. Frankie was pint-sized and without his knife he wouldn't have scared a midget. He had plenty of guts though, and rushed at me, fingers like claws. My fight wasn't with Frankie; it was with Bradley. I stood off, waited for him, clipped him as kindly as I could on his jaw. I caught him, lowered him to the floor, put a cushion under his head, shook mine at Bradley.

"You shouldn't let a kid like that fight your battles," I said, advancing on him. "Now, let's see if you can answer a few questions. That was Netta here, wasn't it?"

He grabbed a chair, threw it at me. I got out of the way, caught it by its legs, smashed it across his back. I knelt on him, slapped his fat face four or five times, took hold of his ears and banged his head on the carpet.

"Open up, you rat," I said, continuing to hammer his head on the carpet. I wished the floor was concrete, but I put a lot of steam into it and it seemed to hurt his ears, which was something. "That was Netta, wasn't it?"

"Stop it!" he bellowed. "Yes, it was, damn you!"

"Netta back from the dead, eh?" I said, letting go of his ears, but cuffing him to keep him soft. "What did she want?"

"Money," he snarled.

"Did you give her any?"

"Three hundred pounds."

"What did she want it for?"

"To keep out of the way of the police."

"Why?"

"I don't know."

I took hold of his ears, bashed his head on the carpet again.

"Why?" I repeated.

"I don't know," he howled. "Honest to God I don't know." I sat down hard on his chest, flicked his nose with my forefinger. "Don't tell me you gave her all that dough just because she asked you for it. Why did you give it to her?"

"She sold me some rings," he moaned.

"Where are they?"

"Over there."

I dragged him to his feet, steadied him.

"Come on, don't be coy," I said. "Show me."

He staggered over to the smashed desk, pulled open a drawer.

"There," he said, collapsed on the floor.

I picked out four diamond rings, turned them over in my hand, looked at him.

"Jacobi's loot, eh?" I said.

He flinched. "I don't know what you're talking about. She said they were her rings. I don't know anything about Jacobi."

"Yes, you do, you rat," I said. "You haven't much longer to live outside a cell. You'd better talk fast. Where did she get these from?"

"I didn't ask her," he blubbered. "She offered me the stuff for three hundred. I could see they were worth more so I bought them."

"I'm going to hand these over to Corridan," I said, slipping the rings into my pocket. "You know what that'll mean."

"They're mine," he snarled, shaking his fist at me. "I'll have you up for stealing."

"Be your age," I said. "You know as well as I do that they're part of Jacobi's loot. Where can I get hold of Netta?"

"I don't know," he returned, holding a blood-stained handkerchief to his nose. "She didn't say where she was going. You came in at the wrong moment, blast you!"

I thought maybe that was the truth.

"Get up," I said.

He hesitated, but as I threatened him with my foot, he climbed to his feet, stood before me.

"Okay, Bradley," I said, "we're quits. The next time you think of teaching someone a lesson be more careful who you chose for a subject."

I looked him over, decided my face was now handsome compared with his, hauled off, hit him on the point of his fat chin, watched his flop. Then I unrolled my sleeves, put on my coat, walked to the door and scrammed.

CHAPTER EIGHTEEN

I paid off the taxi at the corner of Hampden Street, walked down the narrow cul-de-sac. Three of the big buildings were blitzed, mere shells of charred brick and wood. The last building was a small printer's shop; the windows were boarded up, and the shop had a forlorn, neglected appearance. A door on the far side of the shop was numbered 311.

I stood back, looked up at the curtained windows. The place was in darkness.

I tried the door, but it, as I expected, was locked. I stepped back again, surveyed the upper windows. There was a stack-pipe running close to one of them. I tested it, decided it was strong enough to take my weight, glanced back down the alley, saw no one.

I started to climb, wished I had on a less expensive suit, managed to hoist myself on to the sloping roof above the printer's shop. From there it was easy to reach the window. I looked into the darkness, listened. The traffic hummed in Russell Square, someone in the distance shouted "Taxi!" No sound came from Selma Jacobi's flat.

I took out my pocket knife, levered back the window-catch, pushed up the window. One more glance behind me, then I stepped down into darkness.

I found myself in a bedroom. Immediately my skin began to tingle.

There was a distinct smell of lilac in the room. I drew the blind, then the curtains. I groped for my cigarette lighter, thumbed the flint. The feeble flame showed me the electric light switch. I crossed the room, turned on the light.

The room was small, but comfortably furnished. There was a divan bed in one corner, turned down, inviting. Across the foot of the bed was a blue silk nightdress; on the floor by the nightdress was a pair of blue mules.

To the right of the window there was a dressing-table, crammed with powder boxes, lip stick, lotions; everything a girl needs to keep herself well-groomed. A chest of drawers stood near the door, a wardrobe on the other side of the window.

I pulled open one of the drawers, glanced inside. There was a jumble of silk underwear and silk stockings. I pulled the stockings out.

Some of them had been worn, some of them were still in their transparent envelopes. I grunted, put them back, turned off the light. I opened the door, listened. The silence and stillness made me feel spooked. I heard nothing, except my own breathing and the steady beat of my pulse.

I stepped into a narrow, short passage, saw the head of the stairs at one end and a door at the other. I crept to the door, put my ear against the panel, listened. There was no sound. I turned the handle, pushed open the door, looked into the inky darkness. Again I listened, uneasy, a little scared. My hand groped along the wall, found the electric light switch, hesitated, then snapped it down.

For a second or so I stood looking around the large well-furnished room, then the hair on the back of my neck bristled; I caught my breath sharply.

Lying on the floor, his small hands flat on the blue-and-fawn carpet, his legs screwed up, his eyes sightless, his mouth below the straggling moustache twisted in horror, was Henry Littlejohns.

I stepped forward, saw the broken skin on the side of his head, and the blood that had run down his neck and had spread like an obscene halo around his head. Near him was a heavy steel poker, its knobbed handle stained red.

I avoided the blood, bent, touched his hand. It was warm, limp. I raised his arm, let it fall. It thudded back on the carpet. He hadn't been dead long.

I was so shocked, so surprised that for several minutes I could only stare down at him, feeling nothing, my mind a blank.

Then I stiffened, my heart gave a lurch and began to pound so violently I could scarcely breathe.

At the far end of the room was a door which was now slowly opening. It inched open, stopped, inched open again.

"Who is it?" I said in a voice I didn't recognize as my own. The door jerked open. I took an involuntary step back. Netta stood there.

We looked at each other over Littlejohns's dead body.

Then she said, "Oh, Steve, Steve, Steve, thank God you've found me at last."

I still stood there like a dummy, and she ran over to me, caught hold of my arm.

"It's Netta, Steve," she sobbed, flung herself in my arms.

I couldn't keep my eyes off Littlejohns, but I held her, said nothing.

"Take me away, Steve," she sobbed. "Please take me away."

I pulled myself together, slipped my arm around her, led her into the bedroom. We sat on the divan bed, and I let her cry. There was nothing I could do to stop her.

After a while I said, "Netta, this won't get us anywhere. Come on, snap out of it. I'll help you if I can."

She pulled away from me, her eyes glassy with terror, ran her fingers through her thick red hair.

"You don't understand," she said, her husky voice off-key, cracked. "I killed him! Do you hear, Steve? I killed him!"

I went cold, tried to say something, but succeeded in making only a croaking noise.

She suddenly jumped to her feet, ran to the door. Before she reached it, I caught hold of her. She struggled to get away, but I held her. We stared at each other: both of us scared now.

"You killed him?" I said. "For God's sake, Netta!"

She collapsed against me. I smelt lilac in her hair.

"They'll get me now, Steve," she said, moaned against my chest. "I've kept out of their way until now, but they'll get me for this."

I felt cold sweat on my face. I wanted to run, get the hell out of here, leave her. This was murder; this wasn't something I could fool around with and pass over to Corridan if I made a mess of it. This was murder. I gripped her arms, tried to think. Maybe the moments of happiness this kid had given me two years ago helped to bridge the horror I felt. Maybe that thought stopped me from running out on her.

"Take it easy," I said, holding her close. "What we need is a drink. Have you any Scotch in the place?"

She shuddered, clung more tightly. "It's in there," she said. I knew where she meant. I pushed her gently away, sat her on the bed.

"Hang on," I said. "I'll be right back."

"No!" she exclaimed, her voice shooting up. "You mustn't leave me. Steve! You mustn't leave me." She caught hold of my wrist, her nails bit into my flesh.

"It's all right," I said, trying to stop my teeth chattering. "I'll be right back. Take it easy, can't you?"

"No! You won't come back. You're going to run out on me. You're going to leave me in this mess. You're not to, Steve! You're not to!"

She began to cry again, then suddenly she put her hands to her face and screamed wildly.

The sound went through my head like white-hot wires. I was stiff with fright. I snatched her hands away, smacked her face hard, knocking her backwards across the bed.

I stood over her. "Shut up, you little fool," I said, trembling, sweating. "Do you want someone to come here with that in there?"

She stopped screaming, looked up at me, her eyes empty; one side of her face red where I had hit her.

"I'm coming back," I went on. "Stay still and don't make a sound."

I crossed the passage, went into the sitting room. He was still there, small, defenceless, pathetic. I looked down at him, feeling bad.

I looked at his worn suit, at his shabby boots, at his thick ribbed socks that hung in wrinkles. I looked at the terror in his eyes, the twisted mouth. I reached down, patted his arm.

Clutched tightly between his finger and thumb was a scrap of paper. I bent closer, gently pulled it from between his fingers. It was a glossy scrap of paper—a piece torn from a photograph. I stared at it, puzzled.

A bluebottle walked across one of his fixed eyes, then buzzed around his blood. I shivered, put the scrap of paper in my vest pocket, went to the cupboard by the fireplace and found a full bottle of Scotch. I carried it and two glasses into the bedroom, shut the door.

Netta was lying face down across the bed. Her skirt had nicked up and I could see an inch or so of bare thigh. Bare thighs mean nothing to a guy in a moment like this. Her thigh meant less than nothing to me.

I poured a big shot of whisky into both glasses, noted my hand was no steadier than an aspen leaf. I drank the liquor; it went down like water, hit my stomach; a moment later, I felt alive again.

I leaned over Netta, pulled her up.

"Come on," I said, "get this down into you."

I had to feed it to her. Her hand made mine look like a rock. She got it down, gagged, then stopped crying. I gave her my handkerchief, gave myself another shot of liquor, put the bottle down.

"Have a cigarette," I said, pushing one between her trembling lips, took one myself, lit both.

I sat on the bed, at her side.

"You have to talk, and talk fast," I said. "I'll help you if I can. I don't know what game you've been playing or why, but if you'll give it me straight, I'll do what I can for you. Now, shoot."

She dragged down smoke, pressed back the mass of red hair that was hiding her face. She looked pretty bad. Dark shadows circled her eyes; her nose seemed pinched. She had lost a lot of weight since last I saw her. Worse still, she had a blank, crazy expression in her eyes that scared me. I didn't like that expression. The rest of her looks were bad, but nothing rest and sunshine couldn't put right. But the blank expression was something else: I had seen it in the faces of the French girls after days of air strafing or after we'd rescued them from some Hun. It was that kind of expression.

"I killed him," she said quietly. The whisky had pulled her together as I meant it to do. "I heard a sound, crept in there. It was dark. I saw something move and hit out." She shuddered, hid her face. "Then I put on the light. I—I thought it was Peter French."

I was listening, sitting forward, cigarette between my lips, listening with both ears.

"It won't do, Netta," I said, putting my hand on her knee. "We'll start from the beginning. Never mind about the little guy. Forget him for the moment. Start right from the beginning."

She clenched her fists, not looking up.

"I can't go through all that. I can't."

"You've got to. Come on, Netta. If I'm to help you, I must know how bad it is. Right from the beginning."

"No!" She sprang to her feet, upsetting the glass she had balanced on the divan. "Let me go! I can't stay here with him in there. You've got to get me away."

I grabbed her wrists, shook her, dragged her down beside me on the bed.

"Shut up!" I said fiercely. "You're not moving out of here until you've talked. Do you know what you're asking me to do? You're asking me to stick my neck in a noose."

She gasped, tried to break away, but I held her close.

"I won't do that for anyone, Netta. Not unless I'm sure whoever it is is worth it and deserves it. That goes for you, so if you want my help, sit still and talk, and talk fast."

She went limp against me, her breath coming in shuddering gasps.

"Listen, Netta," I went on, "that little guy was working for me. Maybe you didn't mean to kill him, but you killed him just the same, and nothing either of us can do can bring him back to life again. I liked him, and I feel bad about it. He had a lot of guts. If it'd been anyone else but you I'd be calling the police right now. But I haven't forgotten what you did for me in the past. I owe you plenty, but I'm not helping you until you talk. Now relax and tell me. Tell me everything from the beginning."

She beat her hands together. "But what do you want to know?" she gasped. "Can't you see, Steve, the longer we stay here the worse it'll be? They'll find us ... find me."

"Who was the girl in your flat ... the one who died?" I asked, deciding questions were more direct, would get me quicker results.

She shuddered. "Anne ... my sister."

"Who was the guy with her?"

She looked up. "How did you know ...?"

I took hold of her chin between finger and thumb, looked into her eves. She didn't flinch.

"Quit stalling," I said. "Answer my questions. Who was the guy with her?"

"Peter French."

"What was he to her?"

"Her lover."

"And to you?"

"Nothing."

"Sure?"

"Yes."

"He killed her, didn't he?"

Her face went paler, her teeth chewed her lower lip, but she said it, "Yes."

I drew back, wiped my face with the back of my hand.

"Why?"

"She found out he killed George Jacobi."

"How?"

She shook her head. "She never had the chance to tell me."

"French and you were seen around together. How did that come about?"

"He was trying to find Anne. He thought if he kept near me I'd lead him to her."

"Where was she?"

"Hiding. She found out he and Jacobi were behind the Allenby robbery, and then later that French had killed Jacobi. She was scared, so she hid."

"And French found her?"

She nodded. "He found her in a night club. She was drunk. Anne was always getting drunk. French knew that, and he was afraid she'd talk. He brought her to me."

"Why?"

She twisted her hands in her lap. "He wanted to talk to her, to find out how much she knew. The night club was close and there wasn't much time."

"When did they arrive?"

"About one. I was asleep. I let them in. I could see Anne was terrified, although she was very drunk. She managed to whisper to me that French was going to kill her, and I wasn't to let her out of my sight." Netta hid her face. "I can hear her voice now."

I poured out another shot of whisky, fed it down her throat.

"Keep going," I said. "Then what happened?"

"I didn't know what to do. I wanted to get dressed, but Anne wouldn't let me leave her alone with French, and he wouldn't let her go into my room. I stalled for time, and brought out drinks. He spiked our drinks. I went out like a light. I hadn't a chance to warn Anne. It worked so quickly. I heard Anne scream, and then I knew nothing more."

"Then he murdered her?" I asked quietly.

She nodded dully, struggled with her tears. "I'm so frightened. He'll do the same to me!"

"Take it easy. What happened then? Come on, Netta, I want the whole story. What happened then?"

"I have a confused recollection of getting into my clothes, being half carried down the stairs. Ju Cole was on the landing. French spoke to him, but I was too doped to hear what was said. French pushed me out of the house. The night air pulled me together, and I started to struggle." She closed her eyes. "He hit me, and the next thing I remember was being in his car. I struggled up, and he hit me again. I came to later in a room. There was a woman watching me: Mrs. Brambee. French came in after a while. He warned me he'd kill me if I didn't stay there and do what I was told."

"Ever hear of Mrs. Brambee before?"

She nodded. "Anne had a cottage at Lakeham. French bought it for her. He used to go down weekends or whenever he had the time. Mrs. Brambee looked after the place."

"Why did they keep you a prisoner?" I asked, giving her another cigarette.

"French wanted the police to think I and not Anne died in my flat."

"But why, for God's sake?"

"He knew they couldn't trace him through me, but he and Anne had been around a lot together, and he was scared they'd connect him with her death. There was something going on at the cottage he didn't want the police to find out, and he thought the police would find the cottage if they began to make inquiries about Anne."

"What was going on at the cottage?"

"I don't know."

"How did you find this out?"

"Mrs. Brambee told me. She was scared of French and liked Anne."

"When I turned up, he realized his scheme wouldn't work, is that it?"

"Yes. But Cole telephoned him, told him you had been up and that you would most likely want to see the—the body. French got into a panic, and with a couple of his men took Anne from the mortuary. They rushed her down to the cottage, fixed it to look as if Anne had committed suicide there instead of at my flat."

"Well, I'll be double damned," I exclaimed. "You mean to tell me the girl who died in your flat and the girl found in the cottage were one and the same?"

"It was Anne."

"But one of them was a redhead and the other a blonde."

Netta shuddered. "French stopped at nothing. My hair's not really red. I had a bottle of henna dye and he dyed Anne's hair while she was drugged. Then when he brought her to the cottage he used a peroxide wash, brought her hair back to its natural colour."

I grimaced. This guy was certainly a cold-blooded rat if ever there was one.

"Well, go on, what happened then?"

"I was in the way. The police were looking for my body. French planned to kill me and plant my body where the police could find it. Ju Cole wouldn't let him. Ju and I had always got on together. As long as Ju was with me, I was safe. He told me French had planted one of Allenby's rings in my flat and the police were looking for me. I got scared. I thought the police were after me, and I knew French was waiting his chance to kill me. I made Ju help me escape. I got away, came to London. There was only one place I could think of to hide in ... here. Selma and I were friends. I used to come here in the old days, before she married Jacobi. I knew Selma had gone to America with Peter, after George had been killed. Peter smuggled her over."

"Peter? Peter who?"

She frowned, passed her hand across her eyes. "I was forgetting you didn't know him. Peter Utterly. He was an American, over here in the Army.

He was nice, and when Selma was in trouble, he offered to take her back to his home and to look after her."

"Was he the guy who gave you the Luger pistol?"

"Luger pistol?" she repeated blankly, then nodded. "I'd forgotten that. I promised to keep it for him, but when he went we both forgot I had it. How do you know about it?"

"Corridan has it," I said. "We both thought it was the gun that had killed Jacobi."

She went white. "But they know now it isn't?"

"Sure, they know," I said, patting her knee. "I'm nearly through. Why did you go to Bradley?"

"I had to. I hadn't any money. Bradley has always been decent to me after our first fight. I had no one to turn to. I was scared to come to you. Ju told me you were always going around with the police. I wanted to come to you, but Ju said it was too dangerous. So I went to Bradley. I told him the whole story. He was decent and gave me two hundred pounds. Then you arrived; I got in a panic and ran."

I stroked my nose. "Go on," I said.

"I came back here," she went on, suddenly gripping my wrist. "I let myself in, came upstairs. I heard someone moving about in the sitting room. I thought it was French. I swear I thought it was French."

She broke off to stare into my face. "Steve! You must believe me."

"Go on," I said.

"I thought he had come to kill me. I was crazy with fear. I didn't know what I was doing. I grabbed the poker, waited in the dark. Something moved, came at me. I—I lost my head ... hit out." She hid her face in her hands. "Steve, you must help me. I'm so frightened. Say you believe me. Say you'll help me. Please...."

I got to my feet, walked the length of the room. "How the hell can I help you?" I asked. "They'll find him here sooner or later. They'll find out he was working for me. They'll find out you've been hiding here. The only thing we can do is to tell this story to Corridan. It's the only way, Netta. He'll understand. He'll help you."

She stood up. "No! French will kill me before the police can do anything. If he doesn't, they won't believe me. I know they won't. No one would believe me except you." She put her arms around my neck, held me close. "Steve, I'm asking you to help me. I know you can do it. You can get me out of the country the way Peter Utterly got Selma out. We can go in a day or so. Before they find him." She looked shudderingly over her shoulder. "Peter took Selma back in one of his friend's aircraft. Can't you do the same for me? Can't you get me out of this after what we've been together?"

"Let me think," I said, sat on the bed, lit another cigarette. I stayed like that for several minutes. Then I said, "Okay, Netta, I'll do it. I'll get you out of the country and then I guess we're quits. I owe you something, but I didn't think the price would be as steep as this. But I'll do it."

She fell on her knees beside me.

"But how will you do it?" she asked, gripping my hand.

"Harry Bik will get us out. Do you remember him? I brought him to the Club the night I first saw you. He's shipping kites back to America every week. He'll do it. He's that kind of a guy. We'll smuggle you on to the airfield, and get you across to the other side somehow. We'll do it, Netta, don't worry. When I say I'll do it, I'll damn well do it."

She began to cry again, her face against my knee.

I played with her hair, stared at the framed picture of a cutie in yellow pants above the bed. The look in her eyes called me a sucker.

Maybe I was.

CHAPTER NINETEEN

While Netta was packing a bag, I washed the glasses, wiped them free of fingerprints, put them and the bottle of Scotch back into the cupboard. With my handkerchief I picked up the blood-encrusted poker, washed it, put it back beside Littlejohns.

I entered the bedroom again to find Netta cramming her things into a big Revelation suitcase.

"There mustn't be one thing left here that could lead them to you," I said.

"I've packed everything," she returned, closing the lid.

"Sure?"

She looked around the room, nodded. "Yes."

"Okay," I said. "Now we have to think where you can go until I've fixed the plane. It may take a couple of days."

"I know where to go," she said. "I've been thinking while you were out of the room. I know now."

I looked at her. "Where?"

"Madge Kennitt's flat."

I gaped at her. "What's that?"

"Made Kennitt's flat. No one would think of looking for me there."

"For God's sake!" I exclaimed. "Didn't you know? She was murdered. You can't go there."

"Yes, I can. The place is empty, and the police have finished with it. Mrs. Crockett wouldn't try to let it until the murder's forgotten. It'll be perfectly safe for the next three or four days. But that's not the only reason why I'm going there. Madge laid in a stock of tinned food at the beginning of the war. I know where she hid it. I'm sure it's still there. I've got to eat, and if I go there I don't have to go out at all until you call for me."

"You sure the food's still there?"

"I think so. At least, I can go and see."

I didn't much like the idea, but agreed the food question was difficult.

"But how will you get in?"

"My key fits her lock. It fits Ju's as well. They have all more or less the same locks on all the flat doors."

"Well, all right," I said. "But you'll have to be damned careful."

I suddenly realized that if Cole's key opened Madge's door, then he might have killed her; might have wiped out the name, Jacobi, that had been written in the dust. I filed that piece of information away for future reference.

"I'll be careful," she said.

"Okay, then that's settled. When I've fixed things, I'll come for you in a car. Be ready any night to move quick."

She came to me, put her hands on my shoulders. Terror still lurked at the back of her eyes, but she was quieter, had a grip on her nerves.

"I can't thank you enough, Steve," she said. "Maybe I have been a fool since last we met, but I'm not bad—not really bad, and I never forgot you."

I patted her shoulder, turned away.

"We're both now in a hell of a mess," I said soberly. "If we aren't smart, and if we play our cards badly, we're going to be in a real tough spot. Make no mistake about it. I wouldn't do this for anyone but you, Netta."

She slipped her hand into mine. "I know, and I shouldn't let you do it, Steve," she said. "I lost my head just now, but I've got over that now. If you want to back out, I shan't blame you, and I'll manage somehow. All my life I've had to manage. I can still go on fighting alone."

"Forget it," I said shortly. "We're in this together. But there's one thing that bothers me ..."

She looked searchingly at me. "What, Steve?"

"Peter French. If we quit, he's going to get away with it."

She gripped my arm. "Then let him get away with it. We can't do anything to him without getting ourselves in a mess. Don't start anything like that, Steve. It'll only come back to us."

I nodded. "I guess you're right, only I hate to think a rat like French ..."

Her grip on my arm tightened, her eyes opened wide. "Listen," she whispered.

"What is ...?" I began, but her hand flew to my mouth.

"Someone's in the flat," she breathed. "Listen!"

That gave me a hell of a jar. I froze, looked towards the door.

She was right. Very faintly from downstairs I heard footsteps.

With my heart leaping like a salmon caught on a line, I stepped to the electric light switch, snapped out the light.

"Wait here," I whispered. "Don't make a sound. Watch your opportunity. Get out if you can, but don't leave that bag here. Do you think you can carry it?"

I could feel her body trembling against mine.

"I'll try," she said. "Oh, God! I'm scared. Who is it, do you think?"

"I'm going to find out," I whispered back. "But don't wait for me."

I crept over to the back window, looked down on a sloping roof, into a yard.

"That's your way out," I said, my lips close to her ear. "Give me a couple of minutes, then get on to the roof, slide down, and into the yard. Go to Madge's place. I'll get in touch with you in a day or so."

Her fingers touched my hand.

"Darling Steve," she said.

"Bolt the door after me, kid," I returned, pressed her hand, peered into the passage. I listened, heard nothing, stepped from the room, shut the door.

I heard Netta slide the bolt. I crossed the passage, entered the sitting room, groped my way across to the lamp. I found it after a moment's fumbling, removed the bulb, put it carefully on the floor. I remembered fingerprints, took out my handkerchief, picked up the bulb, wiped it, laid it down again.

I moved back to the door, stood listening, sweat on my face, my heart pounding.

For some seconds I heard nothing, then a faint creak came to my straining ears, followed by another creak. Someone was coming up the stairs.

I stood against the wall on the far side of the door, waited. I heard a door handle turn and knew the intruder had reached the top of the stairs, was trying Netta's door. I hoped she had the nerve not to scream. I felt like screaming myself.

More silence. You could cut the stillness in the flat with a knife.

Then suddenly I felt rather than saw the door behind which I was standing, opening. My mouth went dry, the hair on the back of my neck moved. Inch by inch the door opened, then stopped. I saw a white shape, a hand, groping down the wall for the electric light switch, find it.

The click the switch made as it was snapped down was like a pistol shot in the silent room. The room stayed dark, and I thanked my stars I had thought of removing the bulb. I flexed my muscles, clenched my fists, waited.

There was a long pause, the door didn't open farther; there was no sound except my own thumping heart. I waited, my nerves stretched, my breathing controlled. To my straining ears came a new sound; someone breathing. I wondered if whoever it was could hear my breathing, and if that was what made him hesitate.

The door began to open again. I crouched against the wall, ready to spring.

A dark shadow appeared around the door: the head and shoulders of a man. I could just make out his blurred outline against the blind. I knew I was invisible in the darkness, waited to see what he'd do.

He peered around the room, took another step forward. Then I heard a new sound, a sharp creak from Netta's window, as she pushed it up.

Instantly the man whipped around, dashed across the passage, tried Netta's door again.

"I hear you," he shouted. "Open up! Come on! Open up."

It was Corridan!

For a moment I was in such a panic I couldn't move. Then I heard Corridan throw his weight against Netta's door, heard the door groan.

I didn't dare hesitate a moment longer. I kicked over a chair which fell against a small table. The racket the two things made as they went over sounded to me like a mine going up.

I heard a startled exclamation from Corridan. A moment later he entered the sitting room. I saw him grope in his hip pocket, and I crept towards him, crouching, prayed he wouldn't hear me.

A second after the bright beam from an electric torch he had taken from his pocket fell on Littlejohns.

I heard Corridan catch his breath. In that hard light Littlejohns was enough to shake the toughest nerve. For a moment Corridan seemed paralysed with surprise and shock. In that moment, I jumped him.

We went down together like a couple of buffalo, smashed the small table to matchwood. I slammed my fist in his face, caught the torch from his hand, flung it with all my strength at the wall. It went out.

Corridan twisted under me, hit me a sledge-hammer blow in the chest. I grabbed him, tried to hold him down, but he was much too strong for me.

For two or three seconds we fought like animals. Both of us were half crazy with fear, and we punched, bit and kneed each other in a frenzy of waving arms and legs. Corridan was tough all right. He knew every dirty trick there was to know in fighting. If I hadn't had a Ranger training as a war correspondent, I wouldn't have lasted two minutes with him.

I got a head lock on him after a moment, tried to throttle him by squeezing his throat with my forearm, but he hit me so heavily about the body, I couldn't hold him. I broke from him, jumped to my feet.

He had me around the legs before I could step clear, and I came down on my back. My breath whistled out of my body, and for one second I was helpless. That was a lot of time to a guy like Corridan. He was kneeling on my arms by the time I had my wind back, and it was like being sat upon by St. Paul's Cathedral.

"Let's look at you, you bastard," he panted.

I heard a rattle of matches. If he saw who I was I was done for. I hadn't a chance being caught with Littlejohns.

I made a terrific effort, brought my legs up, managed to boot him at the back of his head. He fell forward on top of me and I got my arms free. But he came back, grabbed at my head, tried to smash it down on the floor. By keeping my neck stiff I defeated this move, sank a punch into his belly that went in a foot.

He gasped, gagged, fell off me. My hand closed around one of the table legs. I swung blindly at him, felt a jar run up my arm as the table leg connected, heard him flop.

I lay gasping for breath, feeling as if I'd been fed through a mangle. I knew I couldn't waste a moment; I struggled up kicked his legs off mine, reached out and touched him. He didn't move. For one horrible moment I thought I'd killed him, but then I heard him breathing. Any second now he'd come to the surface. I had to get out while the going was good.

I got to my feet, staggered out of the room, peered into Netta's room. The window was open. She had gone. I grabbed hold of the banister rail, nearly fell down the stairs. Reaching the front door, I waited a moment while I pulled myself together, opened it, stepped into the dark cul-de-sac. The night air helped me to come to the surface, but I was still groggy as I half ran, half walked to the main road.

I kept on, found myself in Russell Square, then Kingsway. I reached the Strand, and by that time I was walking steadily. I had to get myself a cast-iron alibi; an alibi so good that Corridan couldn't even suspect it. I wondered if he had recognized me. I hadn't made a sound while we fought, and it had been almost pitch dark. With luck, I'd get away with it.

I passed a telephone booth, hesitated, entered, called Crystal. I didn't expect she'd be back from the Club as yet. It was only eleven-fifteen, but to my relief she answered.

"It's Steve," I said. "No, don't talk. This is serious. How long have you been back from the Club?"

"An hour. I had a headache and thought I'd come home. Why?"

"Anyone see you come home?"

"No. What's the matter, precious?"

"Plenty," I said grimly. "I'm on my way over. I've been with you for the past hour, and I'm spending the night with you. Is that all right?"

"Is it all right?" Her voice shot up a note. "You bet it's all right! You come right over."

"I'm coming," I said, hung up.

As I turned to leave the booth I had an idea. I put in two more pennies, called Fred Ullman of the *Morning Mail.*

When he came on the line, I said, "Pin your ears back, Fred. I've got the biggest story that's hit the headlines for years! It's exclusive and all yours. Will you earn it?"

"I'll earn it, if it's as good as that, but you'll have to convince me. What do you want me to do?" he returned.

I leaned up against the wall of the booth and told him.

CHAPTER TWENTY

I returned to the Savoy the following morning soon after eleven o'clock. As I asked the clerk at the Inquiry Desk for my key, I felt a hand touch my arm. I took the key, glanced around.

Corridan, looking very massive and dour, was standing at my side.

"Well, well," I said, with what I hoped was a friendly smile. "My old pal again, always turning up like Boris Karloff. What brings you here? Lost your way?"

He shook his head. His eyes were frosty, his mouth set in a hard line. "I want to talk to you, Harmas," he said. "Shall we go to your room?"

"Let's go to the bar," I returned. "It's just on opening time. You look as if I need a drink."

"I think we'll go to your room."

"Well, if you insist. Come along then. You don't look your usual sunny self. What's troubling you? Don't tell me you've fallen in love, or is it indigestion?"

"This isn't a joking matter," he returned, walking with me to the elevator.

"That's the usual trouble with you," I said. "You haven't a sense of humour."

We entered the elevator, rode up to the second floor.

"If you did have a sense of humour you'd be a truly great man. Take me for example," I said, as we walked along the corridor to my room. "Where should I be if I couldn't crack a gag now and then? I'll tell you. I'd be in the depths of despair. And why? Because I'd think you were going to arrest me."

He shot me a sharp look. "What makes you say that?" he demanded, pausing outside my door while I unlocked it.

"You have the appearance of a well-meaning flatfoot about to make an arrest," I returned. "Only you're going to be disappointed."

"We'll see about that," he said, entered the room, took off his hat, faced me.

I noted the livid bruise on his temple where I had hit him with the table leg, hoped he hadn't any proof to connect me with the assault.

"Hello, hello," I said, eyeing him. "My turn to gloat now. How did you get that bruise? Trying to beat your head against a brick wall, I suppose."

"We'll cut out this fooling if you please," Corridan said. I had never seen him so serious before. "Where were you last night?"

Here it comes, I thought, and wandered over to where I kept a bottle of whisky.

"That is no business of yours," I returned gently. "Have a drink?" I unscrewed the cap, poured whisky into a glass.

He shook his head. "It is my business, and you'd better realize that this is a very serious matter for you."

I sipped the whisky, eyed him.

"Now I wonder what's got into your head, Corridan?" I asked. "In other words, what the hell's biting you?"

"Ever heard of Henry Littlejohns?"

I nodded. "Sure. He's a private dick. Why?"

"You employed him, didn't you?"

"Well, yes. I still employ him for that matter. What's it to do with you?"

"Quite a lot. He was murdered last night."

I gave what I hoped was a surprised start, put down my whisky, said, "Murdered? Good God! Littlejohns murdered?"

It wasn't particularly convincing, and I could see it didn't convince Corridan.

"I warned you, Harmas, the next time you were connected with a murder it was going to be unpleasant for you. Well, you know what to expect, don't you?"

"Now don't let's forsake our sense of humour," I said. "You can't scare me, Corridan, or can you? I've nothing to do with Littlejohns's death, and you know it."

"I think you have," he said, watching me closely.

I stared at him, and experienced a little difficulty in meeting his penetrating eyes.

"Now wait a minute. You aren't serious about this?" I asked, managed a laugh. It sounded pretty ghastly even to me, so I cut it out. "You're kidding, aren't you?"

"I'm not," Corridan replied. "I'd advise you to be serious about this, too."

"All right, let's be serious. Suppose you explain what you're talking about?"

"When did you last see Netta Scott?" he shot at me.

I wasn't quite prepared for that one, and hesitated. He was quick to spot that, and I saw his face tighten.

"I guess it must have been two years ago," I said slowly.

"You didn't see her last night?"

"Last night?" I repeated. "You crazy or something? She's been dead a week. Or do you mean you've found her body?" He wandered to the armchair, sat down.

"Look, Harmas, this won't do," he said quietly. "We both know that Netta's alive."

I looked down at my hands, saw they weren't too steady, shoved them in my trouser pockets.

"I haven't seen Netta for two years," I said steadily.

He studied me, nodded. "Where were you last night?"

"That's something I can't very well tell you," I said, looking away. "It involves a question of honour."

Corridan controlled his temper with an effort. "Look, Harmas, if you don't tell me where you were last night, I'll have no alternative but to take you to the station. I don't want to be official about this, but if you're going to act the fool and lie to me I damn well will be!"

"You're not seriously suggesting that I killed Littlejohns, are you?" I asked, staring at him.

"If you want me to caution you, and make this official, I will," Corridan said. "At the moment I'm treating you like a friend. If you can convince me that you couldn't possibly have been on the scene of the crime, then—I shall be satisfied. If you can't convince me, I'm going to arrest you."

I sat down, pretended to be shocked.

"Well, if it's like that," I said, "I suppose I'll have to tell you. I was with Crystal Godwin."

His face hardened. "Oh, were you? What time did you meet her and what time did you leave her?"

I considered the question, said, "I picked her up outside the Blue Club at—now, what time was it?—at ten-ten. I remember looking at my watch when she turned up. We'd arranged to meet at ten, and I was impatient because she was late. Then we went on to her flat."

"What time did you leave?" Corridan snapped.

"Now this puts me in a difficult position. Strictly between you and me, I left this morning."

He studied me for an uncomfortable moment. "A very obvious alibi, Harmas. That girl would tell any lie to save your skin."

"I believe she would," I returned, hoisting a stiff smile to my face. "After all, I did give her six pairs of silk stockings. I'd expect her to repay me somehow. All the same, Corridan, it's an alibi. If you think your old pal would tell a lie like that, then I'm sorry. I'm more than that—I'm hurt."

"We'll see about that," Corridan returned grimly. "I might be able to shake that young woman. It's not the first time I've persuaded someone against perjury. Perhaps I'll succeed again."

I hoped that Crystal had more backbone than I thought she had, mentally crossed my fingers.

"Well, if you don't believe me," I said, shrugging, "you'd better talk to Miss Godwin. She'll convince you even if I don't. Look me up after you've seen her and apologize nicely. It'll cost you a bottle of champagne."

"I don't think it will," Corridan said, leaning back in the chair. "You once said Netta Scott's favourite perfume was lilac," he went on, changing the subject abruptly. "Do you remember?"

"Did I?" I said. "I say a lot of things and don't mean half of them. Why bring Netta's perfume into this sordid topic?"

"There was a strong smell of lilac in the flat where Littlejohns was murdered," Corridan returned. "You know, Harmas, you'd be advised to tell the truth. We know for certain that Netta Scott's alive. We're looking for her now, and it won't be long before we catch her. We know she's connected with the Allenby robbery, that she was present when her sister was murdered, and that makes her an accessory. We know too that she was in the flat when Littlejohns was murdered."

I raised my eyebrows, didn't say anything, but I was badly shaken.

I'd thought Corridan had been running around in circles, but it now seemed that he knew as much as I did about this case.

"What do you know about a yellow and black Bentley?" he suddenly shot at me.

He'd got that from Merryweather, I decided, lifted my shoulders.

"Only that Littlejohns reported that it was seen outside the cottage at Lakeham. Why?"

"We're looking for the car," Corridan said. "The owner we think is connected with Anne's murder. Do you know where the car is?"

I hesitated, then decided it'd be too dangerous to tell him about Peter French. I could have only got the information from Netta, and it was the kind of trap he'd've liked to see me walk into.

"No idea," I said.

He grunted. "I think, Harmas, you are behaving like a blind fool," he said. "You're trying to protect Netta Scott because you and she were lovers in the past. I'm sure you were trying to protect her last night when Littlejohns surprised you both. And what is more, you hit him, and killed him. How do you like that?"

I was beginning to sweat. "I love it," I said, with a fixed grin. "What an imagination you've cultivated."

He waited hopefully to see if I was going to say anything more, then, seeing I wasn't, went on, "This is a serious matter for you, Harmas. You could also be tied to the Kennitt murder."

"Could I?" I said, startled.

"Yes, the motive's there all right. You could have killed Madge Kennitt because she knew Netta Scott was alive. You were the last one to see her, and if I can find Julius Cole he might be able to tell me what happened while you and Madge were together. I only want one good witness, Harmas, and your goose is cooked."

I finished my whisky. I felt I needed it. This had turned out far worse than I expected.

"You'd better have your head examined, Corridan," I said, a little feverishly. "You've been working too hard or something."

"Don't worry about my head," Corridan returned coldly. "You'd better start worrying about your neck. Ever since you arrived in this country you've been mixed up in murder. I warned you to mind your own business, now perhaps you wish you had."

"And to think we called each other by our Christian names, and you ate the food I paid for," I said, shaking my head. "Well, my mother always told me not to trust a policeman. Go ahead, Corridan, and try to hang something on me. I don't think you'll succeed, but you can try. The trouble with the British law is that the onus is on you to prove me guilty, not for me to prove myself innocent. Until you have a few reliable witnesses I don't think you should get too inflated with your cock-eyed theories."

He got to his feet, turned to the door. "When I lay my hands on Netta Scott and Julius Cole I shall have all the witnesses I want," he said quietly. "Those two, I think, will talk fast enough for me to get my hands on you. Don't forget I haven't yet failed to solve a murder case."

"The exception always proves the rule," I said hopefully. "Maybe you're heading for your first great failure."

He took from his pocket a small cardboard box. I recognized it immediately. It was the box I'd borrowed from Crystal the previous night, and in which I had sent Corridan the four diamond rings I'd taken from Bradley. The rings had worried me. If they weren't connected with the Jacobi case, I was on a spot. I had decided to send them to Corridan anonymously in the hope he would identify them.

"Seen this before?" he asked abruptly.

I shook my head. "Don't tell me one of your fans has sent you a present?"

He opened the box, shook the four rings into the palm of his hand.

"Or these?"

Again I shook my head. "No, what are they? Part of Jacobi's loot?"

He looked sharply at me. "What makes you think that?"

"I still have my Ouija board," I said, smiling. "You'd be surprised at the surprises it gives me."

"They're not part of Jacobi's loot," he returned, fixing me with a hard look. "They came to me anonymously through the post this morning. Did you send them?"

"Me?" I repeated, blank. "My dear Corridan, as much as I like you, I think I should be able to resist sending you four diamond rings."

"You'd better cut out this fooling," Corridan said, his face growing red. "I have an idea these rings came from you."

"Quite, quite wrong. What gives you that idea?"

"It won't be difficult to trace them to you," he went on, ignoring my question. "The box and wrapping will tell me what I want to know."

"If you ask me," I said, beginning to get worried, "some lag stole those rings, had a change of heart, and sent them to you to return to their rightful owner."

"I thought so until we checked the rings," Corridan returned. "But we have no record of them being stolen. Try another yarn, and make it a better one."

"I must say you're damned unpleasant this morning," I said.

"Suppose you try."

"Why should I send you diamond rings? Tell me that."

"You might have stuck your nose into something that doesn't concern you, found the rings, and taken them, thinking they were part of Jacobi's loot. You had no means of checking them, so you sent them to me, knowing I'd recognize them if they belonged to Allenby. Well, they don't. I'm now going to look for the original owner, and if I find him, I'm going to persuade him to prosecute the thief. Maybe he knows who the thief is, and if he turns out to be you, my friend, I'll do my best to get you a stretch." He turned on his heel and stamped out.

I drank my whisky at a gulp, blotted my brow. And I thought Corridan didn't know his business! If Bradley talked it looked as if I was going to be in a nice jam. The first thing to do was to warn Crystal to be prepared when Corridan produced the box. Since it was her box, he might easily shake her if she wasn't forewarned. I called her number, explained what had happened.

"He's on his way right over," I said. "And he'll spring that box on you. Look out for it."

"Leave him to me, precious," Crystal said. "All my life I've wanted to be grilled by the police. I'll handle him."

"Well, don't be too sure of yourself," I warned her. "That guy's nobody's fool."

"Nor am I," she returned, "only over you. Did you enjoy yourself last night?" she added coyly.

"Enjoy is an understatement," I returned, grinning. "It was an experience that's marked me for life. I'll be back for an encore in a little while."

I hung up, lit a cigarette, brooded. I'd have to watch my step now.

Corridan was after my blood, and if he couldn't hang a murder rap on me, he might easily get me a stretch in jail.

I began to pace up and down. A gentle tap sounded on the door. I crossed the room, opened up, gaped.

Julius Cole stood in the doorway, his eyebrows raised, his head on one side.

"Hello, baby," he said, moving into the room. "I want to talk to you."

CHAPTER TWENTY-ONE

A waiter passed, pushing a table on wheels before him. The table was set for someone's belated breakfast: a simple meal of coffee and rolls. He eyed Julius Cole; I noted his look of snobbish contempt. He went on, disappeared around the bend in the corridor, but Julius Cole didn't disappear. He sauntered into my room, smiling his secret smile, wagging his head, very sure of himself.

"Nice to see you again, baby," he said.

I let him in because I was too surprised to exert the effort to keep him out. Somewhere in my sub-conscious mind an alarm bell was ringing, warning me that trouble was on the way.

"What do you want?" I asked, leaning against the door.

Julius Cole looked around the room, peered out of the window.

"How nice," he said, his hands in his baggy trouser pockets. The grey suit he wore was shiny at the elbows, even on the back of the coat he had managed to collect grease spots. His bottle-green shirt was frayed at the cuffs; his white tie was grubby. "I've often wanted to see the Savoy from the inside. I had no idea they did you as well as this. The view alone must be worth the money." He gave me an arch look. "What do they charge for a room like this?"

"Suppose you tell me what you want," I said. "And then I'll call Corridan. He wants to see you."

He sat on the window seat, raised his eyebrows.

"I know," he said. "But you won't call Corridan."

I wondered if it might be a sound idea to hit him in the left eye, but resisted the temptation. I sat down.

"Go ahead," I said. "Something's crawling about in the thing you call your mind. What is it?"

He took a crumpled packet of cigarettes from his pocket, lit one.
Smoke drifted down his narrow nostrils.

"I want to borrow a little money," he said.

"I won't stop you," I returned briefly, "but you're in the wrong room.
Try the desk. They might trust you. I don't."

He giggled. "I don't suppose you'd think it to look at me, baby," he said
softly, "but one of my side-lines is blackmail. I'm here to blackmail you."
He giggled again.

"What makes you think I'd be a good subject to blackmail?" I asked, suddenly wary.

"No one's a good subject to blackmail," he returned, pouting. "Sometimes I wonder if the game is worth the risk." He fingered his tie with slen-
der, grubby fingers. His finger-nails were black crescents. "It's a big risk,
you know. I have to be very careful how I select my victim. Even then I have
made mistakes."

"Chalk this up as your biggest mistake yet," I said grimly. "I don't believe in blackmail; never did."

He stroked his clipped hair, smiled. "But then no one ever does, baby,"
he pointed out. "It depends entirely on the force of circumstances. In your
case, I don't see how you can help yourself."

"By ramming my foot into your fat carcass," I said, eyeing him with dis-
taste.

He flicked ash on to the carpet, shook his head. "So many people have
wanted to do that. I've always taken care to convince them it wouldn't
pay."

"Tell me," I said.

"I heard what you and Corridan said to each other," he said, giggled. "I
was listening outside the door. I could get you hanged. That's not bad, is
it?"

"I don't think you could," I said, shaken.

"Don't be obstinate, baby," he pleaded. "I wouldn't risk coming to London, coming here, unless I was sure it'd pay dividends. It was my luck that
I heard what Corridan said. He wants me and he suspects I saw what happened in Madge Kennitt's flat. Well, I wouldn't disappoint him. I'd tell
him."

"You saw nothing," I said.

"I know, but he doesn't know. I'll tell him you were in love with Netta.
That Madge told you Netta and Peter French murdered Anne. You did-
n't want Madge to tell the police, so you tried to bribe her. She wouldn't
play, and you lost your head and killed her. I saw you do it."

I drummed with my fingers on the chair arm. "You didn't, Cole," I said.

"And you know it."

He nodded. "Of course I didn't, but that doesn't matter. Corridan expects me to say something like that and I will if you force me to."

"They'll want to know why you didn't tell them before," I said.

"Of course, I shall get into trouble, but then I don't anticipate it'll come to that. I was also watching you when you went to Selma Jacobi's flat. I saw Littlejohns enter after you had arrived, but I didn't see him come out."

"You get around, don't you?" I said.

"I've never even seen Selma's place, but I can tell Corridan that, can't I? He wants to get someone for these murders, and he'll jump at my evidence."

I knew Corridan would.

There was a long pause, then I said, "Corridan wouldn't be so pleased to learn you made a monkey out of him when you identified Anne as Netta. He'd give you a stretch for that."

Cole smirked. "Yes, baby," he said; "I've taken that into account too. But they'd stretch your neck, so I'm not really anticipating trouble. I don't think I shall have to go to Corridan because you'll pay me to keep quiet."

I lit a cigarette, smoked for a moment, thinking.

"You see, there's Netta to be considered too," Cole said in his soft, lisping voice. "She'll get into trouble too. Corridan will bring a murder charge against her. He's a hard man." He removed a hair from his coat and put it on the window seat with exaggerated care. "You must admit I have a strong hand. But you needn't worry. I'm not asking for much. I'm always modest in my demands. What do you say to a single payment of five hundred pounds? That's reasonable, isn't it?"

"But you'll be back in a week or so for more. I know the kind of louse you are."

He shook his head. "Don't call me names, baby. It's not kind. I don't do business that way. Give me five hundred pounds, and you're free to leave the country as soon as you like. Five hundred pounds would keep me going for a long time. I'm not extravagant, baby. I have simple tastes."

"I'd like a little time to think this over," I said. "Suppose you come back this afternoon?"

"What's there to think about?" he asked, wagging his head from side to side.

"It's just that I have to get used to the idea of being blackmailed," I returned, wanting to sink my fist in his fat, flabby face. "I also want to think of a way to get out of this. Right now, I don't see a way."

Cole giggled. "There isn't one, baby," he said. "Corridan would love to get his hooks into you. Besides, what's five hundred pounds to you? It's nothing." His grey-green eyes wandered around the room. "You're used to the good things of life. You wouldn't like to spend weeks in a cell. That's what it'd mean, even if they didn't prove you guilty. Weeks in a cell."

"You're quite a salesman," I said, getting to my feet. "Come back at three-thirty this afternoon. I'll either tell you to go to hell or I'll have the dough for you."

Cole shifted his fat carcass out of my reach. "All right, baby," he said, watching me. "Have the money in pound notes." He looked once more around the room, wagged his head. "It's nice. I might even book a room here. It'd make a change after that beastly flat of mine."

"I shouldn't," I said. "Not in that suit, anyway. They're fussy here."

A faint flush stained his pasty face. "That's not kind, baby," he said.

I watched him go, the frame and build of a truck-driver, sauntering along softly, insolently, like a dancer.

When he had rounded the bend in the corridor, I returned to my room, poured out a stiff shot of whisky, sat down by the window.

Things were breaking a little too fast for me. I was being crowded. If I was going to solve this puzzle outside a cell, I'd have to move fast.

I thought for a few seconds, finished my drink, decided I'd have to see Netta. I jumped up, grabbed my hat, made for the door.

The telephone rang.

I hesitated, picked up the receiver.

"Harmas?"

I recognized Bradley's voice, wondered what he wanted.

"How are your front teeth, Bradley?" I asked. "I'm still undertaking painful extractions. If you have any left, let me know. I'll fix it for you."

I expected him to blow his top, but he didn't. He sounded almost mild.

"All right, Harmas," he said. "Never mind that stuff. We're quits now. I gave you a bad time, you gave me one. Let's forget it." I could scarcely believe my ears.

"So what?" I asked.

"But I want my rings back, Harmas. They're worth two thousand pounds. Maybe you did take them for a joke. I'm not saying you stole them, but I want them back."

That was reasonable enough, I thought, but how was I going to give them back?

"Corridan's got them," I said. "You'd better ask him for them."

"I'm not interested in who's got them," he snapped. "I'm only interested in getting them back. You took them. You return them."

I wondered if Corridan would part, doubted it. I began to sweat.

"But I can't get them back without being arrested," I returned. "Suppose you ring Corridan, tell him I took them for a joke, and ask him to return them to you. He'll try to persuade you to file a charge against me, but you needn't do that. That's the only way to get 'em back."

"If you don't deliver those rings by four o'clock this afternoon, I'll file a charge against you and I'll see it damn well sticks," Bradley snarled, hung up.

I brooded for a moment, rang Whitehall 1212. Someone told me Corridan was out of town, wouldn't be back until late. I thanked him, put the receiver on its cradle, scowled.

"Oh, the hell with it," I said.

I hurried to the elevator, rode down to the ground level, took a taxi to Cromwell Road.

I entered Mrs. Crockett's house, mounted the stairs to the first floor, stood for a moment listening. I heard nothing to alarm me, crossed to Madge Kennitt's door, rapped.

I called, "This is Steve, honey."

The door opened immediately. Netta stared at me, her eyes opening wide. I looked over my shoulder, expecting to see Julius Cole watching me. He wasn't. I stepped into the room, closed the door.

Netta was wearing a suit of almost transparent pyjamas. She looked cute, and if I hadn't so much on my mind she'd have given me a buzz. As it was I said sharply, "Put on some camouflage, kid. For interesting places a tourist map has nothing on you."

"What's the matter?" she asked, grabbing a silk wrap, putting it on. "Why have you come? Is something wrong?"

"Plenty," I said, sitting on the arm of a chair. "Things are moving. They're moving too damn fast for me, and I thought I'd better have a word with you."

She sat down on the chaise-longue. I thought of Madge Kennitt and the way she had looked, lying there with her throat cut.

"Don't sit there," I said sharply. "That's where she was found."

"Pull yourself together, Steve," Netta said, not moving. Her eyes had hardened, were watchful. "You're not losing your nerve, are you?"

"Hell, no," I said. "Okay, sit there if you want to." I stared at her for a moment. "There's nothing wrong with your nerve, is there, Netta?"

She shook her head. "Not so long as you're with me. What's wrong, Steve?"

I told her how Corridan and Cole had visited me and what they had said. I told her about Bradley's phone call, too.

She listened without interrupting.

"Well, that's the set-up," I concluded. "How do you like it?"

"There's only one way out of this," she said, after a moment's thought. "We've both got to get out of the country. Even if they don't pin the murders on to you, you'll be in jail for weeks. Then what shall I do?"

"Yeah, I've thought of that," I said. "But if I run away I'm telling Corridan I'm guilty."

She jumped to her feet, ran over to me.

"Steve! Can't you see? You've got to get out while the going's good. You can write to Corridan when you get to America. You can tell him the whole story; but if you wait now, we'll never get away. French will catch up with me. You've got to save me and yourself."

I put my hand on her hip. Under the thin silk it felt nice. I remembered our more intimate days, patted her flank.

"All right," I said. "We'll get out while the going's good, and I'll give Corridan the works from a safe distance. Now, I suppose I'd better try to fix a plane."

"Let's go tonight," Netta said, gripping my arm. "Do you think we could get off tonight?"

"If we don't, we'll never get off," I returned. "Once they know I'm on the run, they'll watch every airport." I pulled her a little closer to me. "Bradley worries me. I might be able to handle Cole, but Bradley has a real grievance. Where did you get those rings from, Netta?"

"I didn't give him the rings."

"He said you did. He said he bought them off you for three hundred pounds."

She shook her head. "Of course not. I've told you what happened. I went to him, told him the truth, asked him for some money. He gave me two hundred pounds. He told you that yarn about the rings to shield me. I remember he always had a lot of jewellery in his office."

I snapped my fingers. "My God! I've been a sucker. I should have guessed he was lying. What a mug I was to have taken the rings. He can get me three months for that. It's robbery with violence."

"But he won't get you three months because you won't be here," Netta said. "How soon can you fix that plane?"

"Right now," I said, going over to the telephone. I dialled a number, waited. "Is that you, Bix?" I asked, when a man's voice came on the line.

The voice said, "Sure!"

"This is Steve Harmas. I'm coming to see you. This is important. When's your next trip?"

"Why, hello, Steve," he said. "Glad to hear from you again. What's the excitement?"

"I'll tell you when we meet. When's your next trip?"

"Twenty-two-thirty hours tonight," he returned. "Want to come with me?"

"You bet I want to come," I said. "I'll be right over." I hung up, turned.

"Cross your fingers, kid," I said. "Maybe I'll be able to persuade him to take us. Get packed, and be ready for me at nine o'clock."

She grabbed hold of me. "You're wonderful, Steve," she cried, her eyes bright with excitement.

"Sure, I'm wonderful," I said, feeling like a heel, "but save the celebration until we're over the Atlantic."

I let her kiss me, but I didn't kiss her in return. It'd have been too much like the touch of Judas.

CHAPTER TWENTY-TWO

By three-twenty I had completed my arrangements for the evening, and had returned to my room at the Savoy to await Julius Cole.

Since leaving Netta, I had seen Harry Bix, explained what I wanted him to do. Intrigued by the story I had to tell, he had immediately agreed to co-operate. I had then taken a taxi to the offices of the *Morning Mail*, and had spent an hour with Fred Ullman. Acting on the suggestions I had made the night before, Ullman had been working like a beaver, and had collected a mass of information which had to be acted upon promptly.

Corridan was down at Lakeham, and, although I made efforts to get in touch with him, was temporarily out of the picture. I knew he'd return by evening, but by then, I had to complete my case or fail altogether. In a way I was glad he wasn't around. His absence gave me a clear field and I took every advantage of it. When he did get back, he would find I had solved the Allenby case, and he was going to get the shock of his life.

But in the meantime, I had to have the cooperation of the police.

During my previous stay in London, I had been friendly with Detective-Inspector O'Malley of Bow Street Police Station. Corridan had introduced us, and O'Malley had been delighted to show me the workings of the magistrate's court. I decided I'd enlist his aid, and called on him. When I explained the reason of my call, produced my evidence, he had insisted on taking me to meet Corridan's chief at Scotland Yard. It was decided that immediate action should be taken.

Now back in my room at the Savoy, I relaxed, confident that if my plans worked out the way I hoped, by nightfall the Allenby case and the murders of Madge Kennitt and Henry Littlejohns would be solved.

I had scarcely time to run through my plans in my mind to be sure that nothing had been overlooked before a tap sounded on my door which told me Julius Cole had arrived.

I levered myself out of my chair, opened the door.

There he was, eyeing me expectantly, waggling his head. He had smartened himself up. Some of the grease stains had disappeared from his coat; he had changed the grubby white tie to a less grubby yellow one. In his buttonhole was a faded sprig of lilies of the valley.

"Hello, baby," he said. "I'm not too early, am I?"

"Come in," I said, holding open the door.

He sauntered in, looked around the room.

"You know, I like it," he said. "The more I see it, the better it looks." He eyed me hopefully. "Have you the money, baby?"

"Sure. It's right there in that desk."

He wasn't able to control his excitement, although he made an effort to do so. His face brightened, his eyes gleamed, he giggled.

"Five hundred pounds!" he exclaimed, rubbing his big, grubby hands together. "I can scarcely believe it."

"Sit down, Fatso," I said, closing the door. "You haven't got it yet, so don't get steamed up."

His smile slipped, but he jerked it up with an effort, eyed me cautiously.

"But you've made up your mind, baby?" he asked. "You're going to be sensible?"

"How do I know that after you've got the money you won't come back for more?" I asked, lighting a cigarette.

"Please don't talk like that," he said, giving me an arch look. "I assure you I don't do business that way. I like to think I'm an honest blackmailer. It may sound absurd to you, but I have my principles. I make a fair price, and I stick to it."

"I wouldn't trust you farther than I could throw you," I said. "Sit down. I want to talk to you."

He hesitated, then lowered his great flabby body into the armchair.

"I wish you wouldn't be so suspicious, baby," he complained, pouting. "My terms are straightforward. You give me five hundred pounds, I keep quiet; you leave the country. That's simple enough, isn't it? I can't do you any harm if you're not here, can I?"

"I haven't gone yet." I said, "There's nothing to stop you from double-crossing me while I'm waiting to leave, is there?"

"But I wouldn't do that," he protested. "It's not in my nature to do mean things."

"Remind me to cry over that lovely sentiment sometime," I said.

"Suppose Corridan makes things hot for you? How do I know you won't tell him it wasn't Netta but her sister who died?"

"Don't be silly, baby," he said. "If I told Corridan that, I'd get into trouble, wouldn't I?"

"It was her sister who died, wasn't it?"

He blinked. "Of course."

"How do you know? Have you ever seen her sister?"

"Of course," he repeated, picked his nose, stared at me thoughtfully.

"Why did you say it was Netta?"

"I don't think we have to go into that, baby," he said, shifting uneasily. "I had my reasons."

"How much is Peter French paying you to keep quiet?" I shot at him.

For a moment he looked startled, then he recovered himself, giggled.

"There's not much you miss," he said. "I can't tell you that. It'd be a breach of confidence."

"All right," I said, shrugging. "Let's get down to business. You're demanding five hundred pounds from me or you'll give Corridan false evidence that will incriminate me with two murders. That is the position, isn't it?"

"That's the idea," he said, smirking. "I'm afraid I couldn't put that in writing. But between you and me that's the general idea, baby."

I nodded, satisfied.

"You can have your money," I said, "and God help you, Fatso, if you try to double-cross me. I'll come after you, and I'll pound you to a jelly."

"You have my word," he said with a pathetic attempt at dignity. "That should be enough. You're an American, of course, so you can't be expected to appreciate that an Englishman's word is his bond."

"Get off your high horse, you fat louse," I snapped, sick of him.

He waggled his head. "Don't you think we've wasted enough time already? Where's the money?"

I went to the desk, opened it, took out the packet of pound notes I had meant to give Netta. I tossed them into his lap.

"There you are," I said, watched him.

He stared down at the money, his eyes popping out of his head.

He touched them, patted them.

"Take them and get out," I said.

"Do you mind if I count them, baby?" he asked, a catch in his voice. "It's not that I don't trust you, but it's more businesslike. Besides, you might have given me too much." He giggled explosively.

"Go ahead, but be quick about it. I can't stand the sight of you much longer."

There was a long pause while he counted the notes. He was trembling with excitement, and completely absorbed in the sound the notes made as they rustled in his fingers.

Finally he straightened, nodded. There was a gleam of incredulous triumph in his eyes. "Well, baby," he said, "I didn't think you'd be so easy. I thought I was going to have a lot of trouble with you." he stuffed the notes into his hip pocket, smiled his secret smile. He wasn't pleasant to look at.

I laughed at him.

"Get out, you fat louse," he looked down at the faded sprig of lilies in his buttonhole. He took it out, laid it on the table. "Something to remember me by, baby," he said, giggled. That was too much for me.

"And here's something to remember me by, Fatso," I said, hauled off and landed him a sock in his right eye.

He reeled back against the wall, his hand to his eye. For a moment he remained there, stunned, then he cringed away, moaning.

"You beast!" he whimpered. "Oh, you beastly, rotten cad!"

I made a threatening move towards him. He rushed to the door, yanked it open. Waiting for him in the passage outside was an over-sized, plain-clothes dick.

Cole blundered into him, received a violent shove which sent him staggering back. The plainclothes dick smiled at him.

"Hello, dear," he said.

Cole, still holding his eye, stared at him for almost a minute, then his face crumpled and his knees sagged.

The dick advanced on him. Cole retreated.

I kicked the door shut when the dick was in the room.

"So you anticipated you were going to have trouble with me, did you?" I said grimly. "Boy! Is that an understatement."

I crossed over to the bathroom, opened the door. "Okay, O'Malley, you can come out now."

Detective-Inspector O'Malley came out, followed by another plain-clothes dick who had a notebook in his hand.

"Did you get it all down?" I asked.

"Every word," O'Malley said, rubbing his hands. "The sweetest little statement I could wish for. If he doesn't get ten years, may I be hung for a liar."

The three dicks grinned at Cole. O'Malley walked up to him, touched his arm.

"I'm Detective-Inspector O'Malley of Bow Street, and these are police officers," he said, waving his hand to the two plainclothes dicks. "It's my duty to arrest you and charge you with attempted blackmail. And I have also to caution you that anything you say will be written down and may be used in evidence at your trial."

Cole's face turned green.

"You can't do this to me," he squeaked. "That's the man who must be arrested. He's a murderer." He pointed a trembling finger at me. "He killed Madge Kennitt and Henry Littlejohns. I saw him do it! You can't arrest me. I'm an honest citizen."

O'Malley grinned.

"You can tell that to the judge," he said soothingly. "You come along with me."

The two plainclothes dicks closed in on him. One of them whisked my money from Cole's pocket, handed it to O'Malley.

"We'll have to keep this," O'Malley said to me. "But you'll get it back after the trial."

"I hope so," I returned with a grin. "I'd hate to think it might go to your sports fund."

The three dicks laughed.

"Come on," O'Malley said to Cole. "We'll make you nice and snug in a cell."

Cole started back. "He's a murderer, I tell you," he shouted frantically. "Arrest him! He'll leave the country if you don't. Do you hear? He'll leave the country."

"Now don't excite yourself, dear," one of the plainclothes dicks said. "If you come quietly I'll give you a nice cup of cocoa at the station."

Cole took his hand away from his eye which was closed and swollen.

"He assaulted me," he shrilled. "I wish to charge him with assault. Arrest him!"

O'Malley looked pained. "Did you do that?" he asked me, shaking his head sadly.

"Me?" I said, shocked. "I wouldn't dream of doing such a thing. He was so anxious to spend his money, he hit his poor eye against the door handle as he rushed out."

O'Malley guffawed.

"You must have been in a hurry," he said, winking at Cole.

I walked up to Cole, smiled. "So long, louse," I said. "The next time you try blackmail, don't pick on a newspaper man. See you in ten years' time."

They took Cole away. He went speechless, dazed, stupefied. At the door, O'Malley looked over his shoulder.

"See you tonight," he said.

"Sure. Corridan'll be back then," I returned. "I wouldn't miss seeing his face when I spring my little surprise for all the Scotch in London."

"Speaking as a teetotaller, nor would I," O'Malley said piously.

CHAPTER TWENTY-THREE

The clock in Mrs. Crockett's hall was striking the half-hour after seven as I crept up the stairs to Madge Kennitt's flat. No one saw me enter the house. It was a relief to know that Julius Cole wouldn't appear on the landing to waggle his head at me.

I listened outside Madge's door, heard nothing, tapped gently.

"It's Steve," I said.

There was a pause, then the door opened. Netta, in a red and white silk dress, let me in.

I entered the room, closed the door.

"Hello," I said.

"You're early, Steve," she said, putting her hand on my arm. "Is it all right?" Her eyes were deep set in dark sockets. She seemed anxious, nervy.

I nodded. "I think so," I said. "I've talked to Bix. He wants to see you."

"Wants to see me?" she repeated, frowning. "But, why?"

"You don't know Bix. He's a crazy guy," I returned. "He says he won't risk his job to fly some dumb-belle to the States. I told him you were the ace of pin-ups, but he thinks the women I go around with wear over-shoes and red flannel. The only way to convince him is for you to meet him. If you kid him along he'll take us. It's just his way of making things difficult. I've fixed for us to have a drink with him right away."

"But there isn't time," she said, worried. "And it's dangerous; the police may see us. I don't like this, Steve. Why didn't you bring him here?"

"I couldn't," I said. "He had to do things. There's nothing to worry about. We're meeting him at a pub off Knightsbridge. I have a car outside. We'll talk over things with him; then he'll go on back to the airport, we'll come back here, pick up your luggage and fellow on. The plane doesn't leave until ten-thirty. There's plenty of time."

I could see she didn't like the idea, but there was nothing she could do about it.

"All right, Steve," she said. "You know best. I'll put on a hat and I'm ready."

I waited for her, wandered around the room, thought of Madge Kennitt, felt spooked.

Netta came out of the bedroom after a moment or so. Her hat looked like a saucepan lid, but it suited her.

"He'll fall for you all right," I said, regarding her. "You look swell." I slipped my arm through hers. "Come on. On your toes. We don't want Mrs. C. to jump us on our way out."

We sneaked down the stairs and into the Buick I had rented for the evening.

As we drove along the Cromwell Road, Netta said, "What's been happening, Steve? Did you give Ju the money?"

I was expecting that one, and had my lie ready.

"Yeah," I said. "He got it, the rat, and I only hope he won't double-cross us before we get out of the country." I gave her a quick look, saw she had turned pale, was tight-lipped.

"When did you give it to him?" she asked, a catch in her voice.

"Three-thirty this afternoon," I told her. "Five hundred pounds. It's a lot of money, Netta."

She didn't say anything, sat staring straight ahead, a hard look on her face.

As we pulled up outside a small pub in a back street off Knightsbridge, she said, "And Jack Bradley? Have you heard anything from him?"

"No," I said. "There was nothing I could do about him. Corridan was out of town. I couldn't get the rings without asking him first. Bradley's ultimatum expired at four o'clock. For all I know the cops are looking for me right now. If they are, they're too late. I pulled out of the Savoy this afternoon. All my stuff is in the back of the car. I'm ready to go."

We got out of the Buick.

Netta looked up and down the street. "You're sure it's safe, Steve?" she asked, hanging back. "It seems madness to me to come here where we can be seen."

"Take it easy," I said. "It's safe enough. This pub's as dead as a dodo. They'd never think of looking for us here." I hurried her across the pavement into the pub.

Harry Bix in his leather flying-blouse on which was painted a diving albatross, his squadron insignia, was propping up the counter, a Scotch and soda in his hand.

There were only two other men in the bar. They sat in a far corner, and didn't even look up as we entered.

Bix, fleshy, powerful, good-natured, straightened when he saw us.

He took one look at Netta, pursed his lips in a soundless whistle.

"Hel-lo!" he exclaimed, grinning from ear to ear. "You certainly picked yourself a pippin. Pin-up girl! I'll say!"

"Netta, this is Harry Bix," I said, pushing her forward. "Shake hands with Army Air Corps No. 1 pilot. And if he doesn't always act as if he was used to wearing shoes, forgive him. He's just out of the jungle."

Netta slipped her hand into Bix's large paw, gave him a dazzling smile which rocked him back on his heels.

"Lady, what makes you go around with a heel like him?" he asked earnestly. "Didn't you know he has two wives, and eighteen children, and he's done a ten-year stretch for criminal assault?"

Netta laughed, nodded. "That's why I like him," she said. "I'm that sort of a girl."

"For God's sake!" he said, startled. "Do you really like him or is it his dough you're after?"

"A little of each," she said, after pretending to consider his question.

"Well, I guess that calls for a drink. How's about starting a famine in whisky or would you prefer something more fancy?"

"Whisky's all right with me," she said.

Bix waved to the barmaid, ordered two double whiskies. He turned back to Netta.

"Where've you been hiding yourself all this time? I thought I knew all the juicy dames in London."

"And I thought I'd met all the lovely Americans until now," she replied.

Bix blew out his cheeks, punched me in the ribs.

"Brother, you're through. Go outside and oblige me by breaking a leg."

"She's just kidding," I said. "That girl's got an ice-cream cone where her heart's supposed to be. Why, ten minutes ago, she told me all Army Air Corps personnel were jerks, didn't you Netta?"

"But I hadn't met Harry then," Netta protested. "I take it all back."

Bix leaned close. "We're the salt of the earth, sugar," he said.

"They say so in the newspapers, and newspapers don't kid their readers."

"Not much," I said.

When the barmaid had served the whiskies and had gone to the far end of the counter, Bix said, "So you want to make a trip with me, do you?"

Netta regarded him, suddenly serious. She nodded. "Will you trust me to get you there safely?" he asked.

"I'd trust you in an aircraft, but nowhere else," she returned.

Bix roared with laughter. "Say, this baby is quite a kidder, Steve. That's a pretty hot line to hand to a guy like me. Lady, I was kidding just now. Dames don't mean a thing to me. You ask Steve; he'll tell you."

"That's right," I said. "Dames don't mean a thing to him, but put him alone with one dame and see what happens."

"Why, you rat ..." Bix began, indignant.

"And suppose he isn't to be trusted?" Netta asked. "I wouldn't scream for help."

"You wouldn't?" Bix asked, his eyes popping. "Is that on the level?" He looked at me. "Beat it, three's-a-crowd, you're in the way."

"Suppose we cut out this cross-talk and get down to business?" I urged. "Now you've seen her, will you play?"

Bix sipped his whisky, eyed Netta, eyed me.

"Yeah, I guess I can't refuse a honey like her," he said. "But it's a hell of a risk."

"Skip it," I said. "You know it's dead easy. Don't listen to him, Netta, he's trying to be important."

"Seriously, is it risky?" Netta asked, her eyes searching Bix's face.

For a moment Bix wrestled with the temptation to exaggerate, decided against it. "Well, no," he admitted, scowling at me. "Once you sell the pilot the idea and you've already done that, it's easy enough. We'll meet at the gates of the airport, go in together, have a drink at the mess. I'll then offer to show you over my kite and we'll go down to the dispersal point. No one will be around if we get down there before twenty-two-fifteen hours. You two will get into the kite, and I'll show you where to hide. We take off at twenty-two-thirty hours. When we get to the other side, there'll be a car waiting for me. All you have to do is to get in the back. I'll dump my kit and some rugs on top of you and off we go. Once we're clear of the airport, you can come up for air, and I'll drop you off wherever you want to be dropped off."

Netta thought for a moment. "It's really as simple as that?"

"That's right. I've done it before, and I'll do it again. But I warn you, I claim a kiss from my passengers."

"You won't kiss me," I said coldly. "I'd rather swim the Atlantic if those are your terms."

"So would I," Bix said hurriedly. "I wasn't talking to you, lug."

Netta smiled at him. "There won't be any difficulty about that," she said. "I think the terms are most reasonable."

We kidded back and forth for twenty minutes or so, sank a number of whiskies, and then, at eight-ten, Bix said he guessed he'd better be getting along.

"See you two outside the airport at twenty-one-forty-five," he said. "And don't get steamed up. It's in the bag." He took Netta's hand. "See you soon," he went on. "Don't forget if you ever grow tired of that lug, I'm next on the list. Redheads go straight to my heart."

"I'll remember," she said, gave him a long stare which seemed to weaken him, then she smiled. "If I see much more of you," she continued, "I think I'll be changing my mind about my lug, although he is a nice lug if you over-look his table manners."

"He can't help that," Bix said, grinning. "He hasn't been house-broken like me."

He took himself off as if he was walking on air.

The moment the door swung behind him, Netta lost her gaiety, looked anxiously at me.

"Are you sure it's all right?" she asked. "He's such a boy. Are you sure you can trust him to get us across safely?"

"Quit fussing," I said. "That guy's done over a hundred operational trips. He's bombed Germany from hell to breakfast and back again. Maybe he does look like a boy, but don't let that fool you. When he says he'll do some-thing, he does it. He's taken a liking to you, and that means we're as good as there."

She heaved a little sigh, took my arm.

"All right, darling," she said. "I won't fuss, but I'm nervous. What do we do now?"

"We go back to the flat, pick up your things and get over to the airport. Come on, Netta, the journey's begun."

Ten minutes later we were back in Madge Kennitt's flat.

"You're travelling light, I hope?" I asked, as I tossed my hat on the chaise-longue.

She nodded. "Just a grip. I hate leaving all my lovely dresses, but I'll be able to buy what I want on the other side." She came over to me, put her arms around my neck. "You've been wonderful to me, Steve. I can't thank you enough. I don't know what I'd've done without you."

For a moment I felt like a heel, then I remembered the way Littlejohns had looked, curled up on the floor, and that stiffened me.

"Forget it," I said. "You ready now?"

She said what I hoped she would say: what I knew the success or failure of my plan depended on.

"Give me five minutes, Steve," she said. "I want to change. This get-up isn't warm enough for an air trip."

"Go ahead. Get into your woollies," I said. "I'm damned if I don't come in and help you."

She laughed uneasily, went to the bedroom door.

"You keep out, Mr. Harmas," she said with mock severity. "It's a long time since you saw me undress, and I'd be shy."

"You're right," I said, suddenly serious. "It is a long time: too long, Netta."

But she wasn't listening. She went into the bedroom, shut the door. I listened, heard the key turn.

I sat on the chaise-longue, lit a cigarette. The palms of my hands were damp, the muscles in my thighs twitched. I was in a regular fever of excitement.

Five minutes crawled by, then another five. I could hear Netta moving about in the next room. Cigarette ash covered the carpet at my feet.

"Hey!" I called, my nerves getting the better of me. "Time's getting on, Netta."

"I'm coming," she said; a moment later I heard the lock snap back and she came out. She was wearing a light wool sweater, coal-black slacks and a fur coat over her arm. In her right hand she carried a fair-sized suitcase. "Sorry to be so long," she said, smiling, although her face was pale, her eyes anxious. "It's only five minutes after nine. Do I look all right?"

I went over to her. "You look terrific," I said, putting my arm around her waist.

She pushed me away almost roughly, shook her head, tried to keep the smile on her lips. It looked lopsided to me.

"Not now, Steve," she said. "Let's wait until we're safe."

"That's all right, kid," I said.

She'd pushed me off too late. I'd already felt what she had on under the sweater, around her waist.

"Come on, let's go."

I picked up my hat, glanced around the room to make sure we'd left nothing, crossed to the door.

Netta followed. I carried her bag. She carried the fur coat on her arm. I opened the door.

Facing me, his eyes frosty, his mouth grim, stood Corridan.

CHAPTER TWENTY-FOUR

Netta's thin scream cut the air with the sharpness of a pencil grating on a slate.

"Hello, Corridan," I said, soberly, stepping back, "so you're in at the finish after all."

He entered the room, closed the door. His pale eyes looked inquisitively at Netta. She shrank away from him, her hand to her face.

"I don't know what you two are doing in here," he said coldly, "but that can wait. I have a warrant for your arrest, Harmas. I'm sorry. I've warned you enough times. Bradley has charged you with stealing four rings and with assault. You'll have to come along with me."

I laughed mirthlessly. "That's too bad," I said. "Right now, Corridan, there's more important things for you to worry about. Take a look at this young woman here. Don't you want to be introduced?" I smiled at Netta who stared back at me, tense, her eyes glittering in a white face.

Corridan gave me a sharp glance. "Who is she?"

"Can't you guess?" I said. "Look at her red hair. Can't you smell the lilac perfume? Come on, Corridan, what the hell kind of detective are you?"

His face showed his astonishment.

"You mean it's ...?" he began.

I shook my head at Netta. "I'm sorry about this, kid," I said. "But you can't beat the rap now." I turned back to Corridan. "Of course. Meet Netta Anne Scott Bradley."

Netta recoiled. "Oh," she gasped furiously, then: "You—you bastard!"

"Soft-pedal the language, honey," I said. "Corridan blushes easily."

Corridan stared at Netta, then at me.

"You mean this woman's Netta Scott?" he demanded.

"Of course she is," I said. "Or Mrs. Jack Bradley, known as Anne Scott, if you like that better. I told you all along she hadn't committed suicide. Well, here she is as large as life, and I'll show you something else that'll interest you."

I grabbed hold of Netta as she backed away.

Her face was grey-white like putty; her eyes burned with rage and fear. She struck at me, her fingers like claws. I grabbed her wrists, twisted her arms behind her, held her against me.

"Take it easy, kid," I said, keeping clear of her vicious kicks. "Show the Inspector your nice line in underwear." I caught hold of her sweater, peeled it over her head. Then tucking her, screaming and kicking, under my arm, I yanked down the zipper on her trousers, pulled in two directions.

Corridan gave an angry snort, stepped forward. "Stop it!" he exclaimed. "What the hell do you think you're doing?"

"Skinning a rabbit," I said, carrying Netta over to the chaise-longue and forcing her face down on it. I had a job to hold her, but I at last got my knee in her back and pinned her.

Corridan grabbed my arm, but I shook him off.

"Take a look at that belt," I said, pointing to the heavy money belt that was strapped around Netta's waist.

Corridan paused, muttered to himself, stood away.

I undid the buckle, jerked off the belt, stood back.

Netta lay on the chaise-longue, her fists clenched, her breath coming in great sobbing gasps.

With a quick shake I emptied the contents of the belt on the carpet at Corridan's feet.

"There you are, brother," I said dramatically. "Fifty thousand pounds' worth of jewellery! Take a look. Allenby's loot."

Corridan gaped down at the heap of assorted rings, necklaces, bracelets on the carpet. Diamonds, rubies, emeralds gleamed like fireflies in the electric light.

"I'll kill you for this!" Netta screamed, suddenly sitting up. She sprang to her feet, flung herself at me.

I shoved her off so roughly that she sprawled on the floor.

"You're through, Netta," I said, standing over her. "Get that into your thick little skull. If you hadn't killed Littlejohns I might have played with you, but you killed him to save your rotten skin, and that let me out. What the hell do you think I am? A sucker? I wouldn't cover up anyone who did what you did to Littlejohns."

Netta crawled to her feet, then flopped limply on the chaise-longue, buried her face in her hands.

I turned to Corridan who was still staring at the heap of jewellery as if hypnotized.

"Well, I hope you're satisfied," I said. "I promised myself I'd crack the Allenby case because you acted so damn high-hat. I've done it."

Corridan's face was a study. He looked at Netta, at me. "But how did you know she had the stuff on her?" he demanded.

"You'll be surprised how much I do know," I said. "She and Jack Bradley were behind the Allenby robbery. I'll give you all the facts, and then you can manufacture the evidence. Do you want to hear?"

"Of course, I want to hear," he said, knelt down, scooped up the jewellery, dropped it back into the belt. "How did you get on to this?"

He put the belt on the table.

"I got on to it because I never believed Netta committed suicide," I said, lighting a cigarette and perching myself on the table. "I was sure she hadn't killed herself after I had searched the flat. Most of her clothes and all her silk stockings had vanished. I've known Netta for some time, and have a good idea of her character. She wasn't the type to commit suicide, and she had a passion for clothes. It seemed to me, after the body had been kidnapped, that some other girl had died in her flat, and Netta, taking fright, had run off with as many of her clothes as she could carry."

Corridan leaned against the wall, eyed me.

"You told me all that before," he said, "and I worked that out for myself anyway."

"Sure," I said. "But there was plenty still to puzzle me. For one thing, who was the dead girl? Then another thing foxed me. Why should Netta, although she'd taken time to pack her clothes, have left sixteen five-pound notes in the flat and that bunch of bonds worth five thousand pounds? That got me for some time until Madge Kennitt told me a girl and a man had been with Netta that night. The girl was obviously the one who'd died. The man either killed her or was Netta's accomplice. It seemed to me the reason why Netta had left the money in the flat was because she didn't trust her companion, and he didn't give her a chance to get the money from its hiding-place without him seeing her do it. So she had to leave it there, but hoped to collect it later, but I found it first." I glanced over at Netta, but she didn't look up. She sat with her head in her hands, motionless.

"Go on," Corridan said quietly.

"Who was the mysterious man, and why didn't she want him to know about the money?" I went on. "I've talked to Netta, and she has told me he was Peter French, who was Anne's lover. That's another way of saying he was Netta's lover. You see, Netta never had a sister. But we'll come back to Peter French in a moment.

"Nine months ago, Netta married Jack Bradley. For some reason they kept the marriage a secret, and they didn't live together except at weekends which they spent in a cottage at Lakeham, bought by Bradley as a hide-out for them both. Netta called herself Anne Scott when she was at Lakeham. She tells me that French killed her sister because she knew he had killed George Jacobi. Since she never had a sister, that was obviously a lie. Who then was the girl who had died in Netta's flat, and was later found in the cottage? I want you to get this clear, Corridan. The girl who was kidnapped from the mortuary and the girl we found in the cottage were one and the same."

Corridan pursed his lips. "But one was a redhead and the other was a blonde," he said. "How do you account for that?"

"Netta explained it to me," I said. "She tells me that French dyed the girl's hair and bleached it back to its normal colour after he had removed the body to the cottage."

"Well, I'll be damned," Corridan muttered.

I nodded. "It wants a little believing," I said, "but after thinking it over, it seems to me that's what happened. If the girl wasn't Netta's sister, and I've proved beyond doubt that Netta never had a sister, then who was she and why was she murdered, and why was the murderer so anxious to prevent her being identified?"

"Have you found that out?" Corridan asked eagerly.

"I think so," I returned. "Not only have I found it out, but Littlejohns found it out, too. That's why he died."

"Who was it then?"

"Selma Jacobi, the wife of George Jacobi who was murdered by Jack Bradley," I said.

Netta sat up, glared across at me.

"It's a lie!" she screamed. "Jack didn't kill him. It was Peter French."

I shook my head. "Oh, no, it wasn't," I said gently. "Let's go back a bit." I slid off the table, began to pace up and down. "Let's go back to the time when the American soldiers were being repatriated. Before then, Bradley had been content to make a big profit by selling bad hooch and fleecing the boys in any other way he could think up. But when they began to leave, his profits shrank. He had to think up some other way of making money. Apart from running gaming-tables, he also decided to go in for large-scale robbery. George Jacobi was an expert in this line. Bradley hooked up with him, and the Allenby robbery was planned. About this time Netta was married to Bradley and Jacobi married Selma. Allenby's place was near Lakeham, and Bradley killed two birds with one stone by buying the cottage at Lakeham. The robbery was organized from the cottage, and he also had a love nest for Netta and himself. Mrs. Brambee, Jacobi's sister, undertook to run the cottage for them. The robbery was successful, and the next move was to find some way to sell the loot. The stuff was too hot; neither Bradley nor Jacobi had the nerve to put it on the market. They sat on it, hoping that it would cool off. While waiting, they quarrelled over the split, and one night Bradley killed Jacobi in the Club, and dumped him in a Soho street."

"Is this guesswork or have you proof?" Corridan asked.

"It's guesswork," I admitted, "but she'll talk before long. They always do."

Corridan glanced at Netta, grunted. "Go on," he said.

"We'll leave Jacobi's death for a moment and talk about Littlejohns," I said, lighting a cigarette. "It's important because it decided me that Netta wasn't the Netta I used to know, and that I couldn't let her get away with murder. I liked Littlejohns. He had guts, and besides, he was working for me. I had told him all I knew about the case, and he had spotted something I missed. He realized that Selma Jacobi figured somewhere in the case, and that she could very well be the dead girl in Netta's flat as well as the dead girl in the cottage at Lakeham. He hadn't seen Selma, but I had seen the dead girl. He wanted to surprise me, poor little guy. He found out where Selma used to live and went there in the hope of finding a photograph of her. He had planned to present me with the photograph, and when I had identified it as the dead girl, he was going to spring his surprise. He found the photograph. A scrap of it remained in his fingers when I found him. But Netta caught him. She realized that he was on to her, and to save her skin, she killed him. That's something I can't forgive, so I trapped her into thinking I was going to get her out of the country, knowing she'd try to smuggle Allenby's loot out with her."

"That still doesn't explain how you knew she had the loot," Corridan said, frowning. "You say this Peter French killed Selma Jacobi?"

I shook my head. "No, I didn't say that. Netta told me Peter French killed Selma. But that's a lie. Peter French knows nothing about this business at all. He was a stooge, put up to lead me away from the real killer."

Netta got slowly to her feet, her face ghastly. Corridan took a step forward.

"Then who killed Selma Jacobi?" he demanded.

"The same person who killed Madge Kennitt," I said, moving across to the kitchen door. "Let me introduce you." I jerked open the door, stood aside. "Come on out," I said. "You've been in there long enough."

Detective-Inspector O'Malley and three plainclothes dicks moved into the room. They looked at me, at Corridan, at Netta.

"That's the guy who killed Selma Jacobi and Madge Kennitt," I said, jerking my thumb at Corridan.

CHAPTER TWENTY-FIVE

"I expect you to exercise tact and control with Harry Bix," I told Crystal as I piloted her across the Savoy lobby to where Fred Ullman and Bix were examining the latest novels on the bookstall. "He's the kind of wolf who knows all the ankles. Don't encourage him, and if you don't stray away from me you should be safe enough."

Crystal said, "Shouldn't you have brought your poke bonnet and tambourine? Who wants to be safe, anyway?"

By this time Harry Bix had seen us, and nudging Ullman, he fingered his tie, giving us a loud hello.

"Well, well," he said, advancing to meet us. "Bluebeard does it again. How you collect these juicy dames beats me. You must have a fatal attraction or something."

I sighed. "Crystal, this is Harry Bix. Don't trust him. Even the wool he'll try to pull over your eyes is half cotton. Harry, this is Miss Godwin. I'll trouble you to keep your hands in your pockets while you talk to her, and just to keep the record straight, she is my property. The gentleman with the bags under his eyes, lurking in the background, is Fred Ullman. Fred, Miss Godwin."

Ullman said how do you do, looked a little bored, but Bix elbowed him farther into the background, beamed at Crystal.

"This is the most exciting moment in my life," he said, taking her hand. "You're not really his property, are you? A dish as lovely as you wouldn't waste herself on a half-dead numskull like him, surely?"

I unfastened their hands, took Crystal firmly by her elbow.

"Paws off," I said. "This is the one blonde I intend to keep for myself. Away to your own hunting-ground." I convoyed Crystal across the lobby into the grillroom. "Come on, let's eat," I continued. "And, Fred, keep that woman-snatcher out of range."

"Why you fellows make such a fuss about women defeats me," Ullman said sourly. "All my life I've kept away from women, and look at me."

"You look; I've seen you," Crystal said tartly.

When we had all settled down at a corner table and had ordered a meal, Harry Bix said, "We are gathered together here tonight, not to be fed from any charitable reasons, but because Arsène Lupin here," he waved in my direction, "wishes to shoot off his mouth on the subject of his own cleverness, and has naturally to bribe us to listen."

Crystal tugged at my sleeve, asked me in a whisper why Bix called me Arsène Lupin, and wasn't Lupin French for rabbit?

I whispered back that the French for rabbit was *lapin,* and that Arsène Lupin was one of the world's greatest detectives.

She then wanted to know what that had to do with me.

"Shush, woman," I said, annoyed. "You're showing your ignorance."

"As a newspaper man I have to make sacrifices," Ullman said wearily. "I am prepared to eat his food and to suffer the sound of his voice so long as he'll explain in detail the story behind Corridan's arrest. That is something the great British public wish to know, and it's my painful duty to tell them."

"Not in detail," Bix pleaded. "There're so many more interesting things to do than to listen to details," and he leered suggestively at Crystal, who leered back.

I tapped him on the shoulder. "That blonde is my property," I reminded him. "If it wasn't in such an inaccessible spot I'd show you where I've branded her with my personal seal, so paws off and I'll trouble you to keep your dirty looks to yourself."

Crystal said she liked his dirty looks, and could she have a few more please?

"Can't you control these two?" Ullman demanded. "I want the story if they don't. Why you bring a blonde to a meeting like this beats me. Blondes are a menace to society."

"That's not very polite," Crystal said, a little hurt.

Ullman eyed her coldly. "The only woman I've ever been polite to was my mother," he told her.

Crystal said she was surprised to hear he ever had a mother, and did the old lady die of a broken heart?

"Quiet," I said hurriedly as Ullman began to grow hot.

Bix said would it be an idea if Crystal and he went for a walk along the hotel corridor while Ullman and I bored each other to death?

"Will you please pipe down," I growled, thumping the table.

"Well, come on," Ullman said impatiently. "You've run me ragged these last days digging up information. How did you get on to Corridan?"

"Suppose I tell you the setup from the beginning?" I suggested. "Then even Crystal, dumb as she is, will be able to follow. Ouch!"

I massaged my shin, told Crystal to behave herself, hurried on before there were more interruptions.

"As you know, Jack Bradley, to recoup his losses, installed two roulette tables in the Club," I began. "There's no future in that kind of racket unless you have adequate protection. Bradley was smart enough to realize that, and he looked around for a likely bird in the police force who'd give him this protection."

"And he picked on Corridan?" Ullman said.

"Don't interrupt," Crystal reproved him. "My father says that people who interrupt ..."

"Never mind your father now," I broke in hastily. "Just pipe down, honey, and let me do the talking." I looked over at Bix. "And that's my knee you're fondling under the table just in case you thought it was Crystal's."

Bix snatched his hand away, had the grace to blush. He looked at Crystal reproachfully. She giggled.

"Yes, he picked on Corridan," I went on as Ullman began to scowl again. "Corridan was, at that time, a rising star at the Yard, and was handling the club rackets. Bradley offered him a big cut of his profits if he'd tip him when a raid was likely to be made. It was easy money; Corridan fell for it. Then George Jacobi appeared on the scene...."

"How much better this'd be if it was illustrated with lantern slides," Bix said regretfully. "Imagine a slide depicting the arrival of George Jacobi in a snowstorm. How gripping that'd be."

"Especially if the slide was upside-down," Crystal said, giggling over the hors d'oeuvre.

"I'll turn you upside-down and ..." I snarled.

"Never mind these cretins," Ullman said. "Go on, for God's sake."

"Jacobi was an expert jewel thief and was planning to steal Allenby's anti-invasion nest-egg, worth fifty thousand pounds," I said, scowling at Crystal, who made faces at me. "But Jacobi knew he couldn't handle a job as big as that on his own...."

"The weak sister!" Bix said in disgust. "If it'd been half that amount I'd've done it."

"So would I," Crystal chimed in. "I'd've done it for a quarter the amount."

"And he suggested Bradley should come in on it with him," I went on, ignoring the interruption. "Bradley thought it'd be an idea to get the police on his side, and he put the proposition to Corridan, offering him a third of the spoils if he acted as inside man after the robbery, steering suspicion from Jacobi."

"That was smart," Ullman said approvingly. "I suppose you got all this from Netta?"

"Yeah. She talked. Boy! How she talked. Well, Corridan was after as much money as he could get his claws on, so he agreed to play. Netta now comes on the scene. Nine months ago, she and Bradley married. Bradley couldn't get her any other way, but he kept the marriage quiet. This arrangement suited Netta as she could continue to live on her own supported by Bradley, and if Bradley ever got tired of her she would be taken care of in the divorce settlement. Bradley bought the cottage at Lakeham for his robbery headquarters and as a love nest for Netta and himself.

"The gang consisted of Bradley, Mrs. Brambee, Jacobi, Julius Cole and Corridan. The robbery was successful, but Bradley and Jacobi quarrelled over the split. Bradley killed Jacobi. Netta was present at the shooting."

"This is improving," Bix said, brightening. "Don't rush over the gory details."

"Jacobi was killed with a Luger pistol which Bradley had brought back as a souvenir of the First World War. His name was engraved on the pistol butt, and although the name had been erased, Bradley knew the police would be able to read it under ultra-violet rays. If the gun was ever found, he'd swing for the killing. Netta was by now tired of Bradley and had fallen for Corridan. She took the Luger while Bradley was dumping Jacobi's body in a Soho street, and decided to make capital out of it."

"What some women will do for money," Crystal exclaimed, shocked. "Why is it I never have a chance to show how unscrupulous I could be?"

"Netta was scared to approach Bradley direct," I went on, "so she suggested to Corridan that he should blackmail Bradley, and the two of them share the proceeds. Corridan agreed, but he wanted the gun. He was using Netta for his own profit, and he didn't trust her. Netta wouldn't let him have the gun. It was her security in case Corridan tried to gyp her."

"I'd trust you with everything of mine, precious," Crystal said, fondling my hand.

"I'll have that down in black and white when there's a spare moment," I said, patting her. "But keep quiet and let me get on. Eat up your nice chicken, and don't spill any down your pretty dress."

"When you two have stopped drooling over each other," Ullman said in disgust, "you might get on."

"Corridan put the screws on Bradley, who paid up," I continued. "As Corridan didn't dare show his face at the Club in case he was seen, and as Netta wasn't supposed to be in this blackmailing racket, Mrs. Brambee was detailed to collect the money each week.

"Well, that was the set-up until Selma Jacobi discovered that Bradley killed her husband. Cole told her this because he wanted to get even for not receiving a cut from the money Corridan was getting from Bradley. But Cole didn't tell Selma that Corridan was hooked up with Bradley. He was scared of Corridan. Selma went to Corridan, knowing he was in charge of the Jacobi investigation, and told him what Cole had told her. Imagine Corridan's feelings. If he took action, he'd dry up his own source of income, and Bradley would squeal on him. If he didn't, then Selma would go to a higher authority at the Yard, and he'd get caught that way. His only way out was to get rid of Selma. He took her along to Netta's flat, drugged her, and between the two of them they set the stage for suicide."

By this time we had reached the coffee stage of the meal.

"For the love of Mike let's have some whisky with this," Bix implored. "Listening to you gives me a thirst."

I ordered whiskies, and a brandy for Crystal.

"Before Selma was murdered," I went on, after the drinks had arrived, "Bradley had found out that Netta and Corridan were lovers. Bradley told Netta he had given orders to Frankie to lay for her and splash her with vitriol. Whether this was Bradley's idea of getting even, or whether Frankie was really going to do it, I don't know. Netta swears he would have done it, and knowing Frankie I think it's likely. Anyway, Netta was terrified and she decided it'd be safer to drop out of sight. Selma's body offered the opportunity. Corridan agreed to help, and they dyed Selma's hair the same shade as Netta's, bribed Cole to identify her as Netta, passed the news on to Bradley that Netta had killed herself. Do you follow all that up to now?" I asked, looking around.

"Keep going," Bix sighed. "My brain's numbed, but the sound of your voice has a soothing effect on it."

"Now I turn up," I continued. "Bradley was going to the mortuary to identify the body, so was I. Corridan had to work fast. He arranged for one of his men to move the body from the mortuary to the cottage at Lakeham. This was for my benefit as I had found the envelope addressed to Anne Scott, and had jumped to the conclusion that Anne was Netta's sister. I was allowed a glimpse of the body, then it was taken to the Horsham mortuary and destroyed by fire before Bradley could see it. Got all that?"

"Complicated, but smart," Ullman said, nodding his head. "Then what?"

Bix groaned. "You're a whale for punishment," he said, sneaking my whisky and drinking it before I could stop him. "Me—I've had about enough."

"The next bit's interesting," I promised. "It shows how clever I am."

"We'd better stay for that," Bix said to Crystal, "otherwise he'll stick us for the check."

"Bradley had given Netta five thousand pounds' worth of bonds as a wedding present," I went on. "He was anxious to get the money back. Frankie had been into the flat and had hunted for the bonds but had failed to find them. I found them, and suspecting that I had them, Frankie attacked me, but I beat him off.

"You can imagine how pleased Corridan was when I presented him not only with the bonds but also with the Luger," I continued. "He cooked up a yarn about the bonds being forgeries, and that the Luger belonged to a guy called Peter Utterly. Fred checked all this, found there was no such person as Utterly, and more important still that there was no such person as Anne Scott, although Corridan had told me her record was in Somerset

House."

"I have two profound observations to make at this point," Harry Bix broke in. "The first is that Corridan seems to have made a complete monkey out of you, and the second is that Fred seems to have done all the dirty work."

I nodded, grinned. "Correct," I said. "Applause for Mr. Ullman."

Crystal was so carried away that she kissed Ullman, who blinked at her, wiped off the lipstick, said, "Well, that's quite an experience. Perhaps I've been missing things. The only woman who ever kissed me was my mother."

"You ought to be sorry for her," Crystal said. "But I do like the taste of your shaving cream."

"Shut up, you two," Bix said, scowling.

"To continue," I said firmly. "The real give-away as far as Corridan was concerned was the murder of Madge Kennitt. I saw him after I had left Madge's flat to get her a bottle of whisky. I spotted Corridan outside the house, then when I returned I found Madge dead. She had written Jacobi's name in the dust, hoping it would give me a clue, which, of course, it did. Corridan arrived with his dicks, spotted the writing and blotted it out, hoping I hadn't seen it."

"But you had," Bix said. "Let's have some more whisky. The excitement is making me feel faint."

"I'd seen it all right," I went on, ignoring him, "and Fred put me on to the facts of the Jacobi case. Merryweather, the private dick I had hired, told Corridan that a black and yellow Bentley car had been seen at the cottage. I've traced the car to Corridan. He realized that he'd have to get rid of it, and sold it to a guy called Peter French. I happened to call on French and see the car, and Corridan found out that I'd seen it. He got Netta to try to persuade me that French was the killer of Madge Kennitt and I nearly fell for it.

"Well, the pace was getting too hot for Corridan. He decided to get the loot out of the country. I could help there, and Netta was the obvious choice to carry the stuff. Corridan had a showdown with Bradley, told him Netta was alive, and she was to take the loot to America. Bradley didn't like the idea, but Corridan had too much on him to raise objections. The loot was handed over to Netta, and she began to work on me. I played into their hands by taking Bradley's rings, and then getting myself hooked up with Littlejohns's murder. Cole helped by pretending to blackmail me, and I played it to look as if I was being stampeded to leave the country."

"I believe the end's in sight," Crystal said, sighing with relief.

"It is," I said. "I arranged with Harry to kid Netta into thinking he would fly us to the States ..."

"And a very fine job I made of it, too," Bix said, beaming.

"I gave O'Malley the facts and he nabbed Cole, and laid a trap for Corridan. As luck would have it, Corridan heard that Cole had been arrested and guessed something had gone wrong with his plans. He took a chance and came on to Madge's flat just as Netta and I were about to leave for the airport. I think his idea was to knock me off and get Netta to persuade Harry to take her and Corridan to the States."

"As if I would," Bix said scornfully.

"Anyway, O'Malley was listening in and Corridan walked into the trap," I concluded. "If those two don't swing, I'll be surprised."

"You mean you thought all that out without any help?" Crystal said, gazing at me with unconcealed admiration. "I'm proud of you, precious. I should never have thought it of you."

"Come on," I said, signalling the waiter, "let's get out of here. If you two fellows haven't anything better to do, amuse yourselves; Crystal is going to amuse me—alone."

"Give me five minutes, precious," she said, getting to her feet. "I'm going to powder my nose and then I'll be very amusing."

When she had gone Ullman glanced at his watch, got to his feet.

"I've got to write this story," he said. "You two guys keep each other company. Say good-bye to Miss Godwin for me, will you? So long and thanks for the details."

Bix made a move to follow him, but I grabbed his arm.

"Listen, lug," I said, "you stick around where I can see you. I want you to stay right here until Crystal comes back, then I want you to fade quietly away."

"What makes you think she cares for you, you sap?" Bix demanded heatedly. "Why, I'll have her eating out of my hand if I can get her alone for two minutes."

"It may surprise you to know she's not that kind of a girl," I said with dignity. "Moreover, she eats off a plate, and if you start anything I don't like I'll make you think the war's started again."

We sat glowering at each other for half an hour, then we both became uneasy.

"Now I wonder where she's got to," I said, looking towards the grillroom door. "No sign of her. She can't be powdering her nose all this time."

I saw suspicion and alarm in Bix's eyes.

"You don't think that rat ...?" he began.

I jumped to my feet, made a dash into the lobby with Bix on my heels. There was no sign of her out there. I went up to the hall-porter, asked him if he had seen her.

"Miss Godwin left about twenty minutes ago, sir," he said, "with Mr.

Ullman. I believe Mr. Ullman was saying something about showing her his Press cuttings."

"And I was going to show her my tattoo marks," Bix wailed.

I tapped him on the chest. "It was the bags under that rat's eyes and his talk about his mother that did it," I said savagely. "The girl's dissolute."

"I like 'em that way, don't you?" Bix asked, leading me towards the bar. I said I did.

THE END

MISS SHUMWAY WAVES A WAND

JAMES HADLEY CHASE

To Merrill Panitt

PART ONE—MEXICO

ONE

I hadn't been In Manolo's Bar five minutes, when Paul Juden, head of Central News Agency, blew in.

"Well, I'll be damned!" I thought and tried to duck out of sight, but he was too quick for me. He came towards me like a herd of buffalo on the last lap home.

"Why, hul-*lo*, P.J.," I said, like I was glad to see him, "How are you? Sit down and rest your brains. You look as if I needed another drink."

"Never mind the funny stuff, Millan." he said, waving to the waiter. "I've been hunting all over the place for you. Where the hell have you been? I've got something for you."

He didn't have to tell me. When the boss of C.N.A. runs across a bar room floor, looking like he'd swallowed the overalls in Mrs. Murphy's chowder, it doesn't mean he's glad to see me, it means he wants me to work.

"You've got something for me?" I repeated bitterly. "That's what they say to a dog. Then they feed him poison."

The waiter came up and Juden ordered two large whisky sours.

"Now, listen, P.J.," I said, when the waiter had gone away, "I want a little peace. I've stuck around the Mexican desert for six months with a string of vultures waiting to pick my bones. I've had more cactus needles sticking in me than a porcupine has quills. Every time I blow my nose, sand flies out of my ears. Okay, I'm not squawking, but I want a little relaxation and, brother, am I going to have a little relaxation."

Juden wasn't even listening. He had taken out his wallet and was fiddling with a bunch of cables. "Maddox has a job lined up for you, Millan." he said. "I had a cable this morning. It looks like a copy of 'Gone With The Wind.'"

"Maddox?" I sank further into my chair. "You don't have to worry about him. He's just a fallen arch in the march of time. Tell him I'm sick Tell him you can't contact me. Tell him anything, but give me a break, will you?"

Juden sorted out a bunch of flimsies as the waiter brought the drinks.

"Well, here's a clot in your bloodstream." I said and lowered two-thirds of the whisky sour.

"Here we are." Juden said, waving the flimsies at me. "It certainly looks like a swell assignment to me."

I waved them right back at him. "I don't want 'em." I said. "I want a little relaxation. I'm catching a train for New Orleans to-morrow. I've had enough of Mexico to last me a lifetime. Tell Maddox to send some other stooge out here."

"Not a chance." Juden said. "This is a rush job. Now, don't waste time, Millan. You know you've got to do it, so why make things difficult?"

Of course, he was right. Was I getting tired of this newspaper game, or was I? I'd been chasing bandit stories for six broiling months and in this country, bandits were a dime a dozen. Ever since Zapata had started the fashion, every damn Indian who could grow a six-inch moustache had turned bandit. It had taken all my time to coach them how to do the job so that I could give the great American public a story worth reading. Well, I had had enough of it. Besides, one of these amateur Dillingers had tried to shoot me. It got so I began to think some other punk would get the same idea.

But Maddox was my bread and butter. If I turned him down, he'd become a piece of toast. You couldn't argue with Maddox. He had the kind of nature that made snakes cross the street when they saw him coming.

"What's the story?" I said. "Don't ask me to read those cables. I want the news broken gently."

Juden dug into his whisky sour. Now, there's a guy who'd landed a sweet job. All he had to do was to open envelopes and pass the baby to someone else.

"Okay, here it is." he said. "The story is entitled 'A Blonde Among Bandits,' or 'Get Up Them Stairs.'"

I finished my drink. "You don't have to be funny." I said, firmly. "All I want is the unvarnished truth. When I want to laugh, I'll tune into the Bob Hope programme."

"A fella named Hamish Shumway called in to see Maddox a couple of days ago." Juden went on. "He's lost his daughter, last heard of in Mexico City. She's vanished into thin air. Shumway thinks she's been kidnapped by bandits. Maddox wants you to find her."

"Well, go on." I said. "What does he want me to do?"

"He wants you to find her." Juden repeated patiently.

"Well, all right, it's a good gag. Remind me to laugh next time we meet. But, what's the assignment?"

"Don't start that stuff, Millan." Juden said, looking like a hunk of chilled beef. "I'm telling you. He wants you to find this girl."

"You mean he wants me to search the whole of Mexico for one particular girl who's stupid enough to lose herself?" I said slowly, hardly believing my ear.

"Something like that. I don't care how you do it so long as you find her."

"You don't care?"

"No ... I don't care a damn."

"Oh, well." I stared at him thoughtfully. "You wouldn't like to cut my throat and save a lot of time, I suppose?"

"Now, wait a minute. It's not as bad as that. Let me explain." Juden said hurriedly. "The stuff you've been turning in recently is enough to make a dog vomit."

"Can I help it if your dog's got a weak stomach?"

"Never mind about the dog. Maddox wants to cover your expenses, so he's thought up this stunt. It'll be a great newspaper story. Look at it this way. A poor old guy without a dime comes to the New York Reporter and asks their help. His daughter's missing. He wants to know if they'll find her for him. What does the Reporter do?"

"Kick the old guy's teeth out and toss him down the elevator shaft after taking his socks off to make mittens for Maddox." I replied promptly.

"The New York Reporter says, 'All right, brother, we'll find her,'" Juden went on, frowning at me. "They put the story on the front page with a photo of the girl. They print a photo of the old man as well, just to show there's no catch in it: 'Blonde Kidnapped by Mexican Bandits. 25,000 Dollars Reward. Father of Missing Girl Grief Stricken. New York Reporter Begins Nation-wide Search.' Get the idea? Then you find the girl, write the story and bring the girl back to New York. Maddox has the father waiting at a civic reception and you hand the girl over to the father. The Reporter gets the credit. It's a swell idea."

"So poor old Maddox's gone nuts at last." I said, shaking my head sadly. "Well, it doesn't surprise me. I always thought his rivets would shake loose in time. How's Mrs. Maddox reacting? It must be a big shock for her. And his daughter. The nice looking one with the squint and pimples. That reminds me, has one of her best friends had a little chat with her yet?"

Juden finished his drink and lit a cigar. "Well, Millan, that's the job. You can be as funny as you like, but there're no two ways about it. Maddox says if you don't find her within a week you'll be working for someone else or not working at all."

"He said that, did he, the puff adder." I returned, sitting up. "Well, you can tell him what he can do with this job. If he thinks he can threaten me, he's mistaken! Why, I could get any of the plum jobs in this game just by asking. I wouldn't even have to ask. I only have to pass a newspaper office and the publishers come running after me. Maddox! Everyone knows the kind of rat he is. Telling me that I can quit! That's a laugh! Where would he get another guy with my brains—well, how the hell do I find this girl, anyway?"

"It shouldn't be difficult." Juden said, grinning. "I've got a picture of her, she owns a big, dark green Cadillac, she is a magician by profession and swell looking. Her name is Myra Shumway and she was last heard of right here in this town."

"Now look, P. J.," I said earnestly. "There must be hundreds of girls in New York who've got themselves mislaid, why not let's find one of them? I want to get back to Broadway."

"Sorry, Millan." he returned. "You'd better make up your mind about it. The story hit the front page this morning."

I took out my notebook wearily. "Okay." I said. "Let's have it. Name, Myra Shumway. What did you say she did?"

"Magician." Juden returned with a broad grin. "That's unusual, isn't it? She worked the Vaudeville circuit with her father until they quarrelled. Then she went off on her own. Now, she works night clubs so I understand. Her pa says she's pretty good at the job."

"I never believe what parents say about their children." I returned coldly. I made a few more notes and then put my notebook away. "What makes Maddox think bandits have got hold of her?"

Juden shrugged. "That's his story. You've got to play this properly, Millan, if they haven't got hold of her, it's up to you to see that they do. Haven't you any tame bandit who'd do the job for a few bucks?"

"What do you mean?" I asked, stating at him.

"Well, she may be enjoying herself some place and forgotten to send her old man a line. We can't afford to let this flop, you know. If she isn't kidnapped, you've got to get her kidnapped. I don't have to draw you a map, do I?"

This began to worry me. "If I thought you were serious, P. J.," I said, "I'd have someone examine your head."

"There's nothing the matter with my head." Juden said shortly. "But there'll be a lot wrong with your job, if you don't get some action and get it soon."

"Do you honestly mean that if this girl's just having a good time, I've got to fix some greaser to kidnap her?"

"Yep, that's the way it is. It shouldn't be difficult. We'll cover the expenses."

"You'll do more than that." I said. "You'll send me a signed statement. If I get picked up there's a hell of a rap tied to kidnapping."

"You won't get a statement, but someone's got to win the 25,000 dollars reward."

"You mean I stand to pick that up?" I asked, interested for the first time.

Juden closed one eye. "It depends if you claim it." he said. "Maddox doesn't expect you to, of course, but if you jumped him at the civic reception, I guess he couldn't very well back out of it."

And I was thinking Juden was a two-faced grafter and he turns out to be a real pal.

"I'll remember that." I said "Have another drink?"

He shook his head, "I'm off home. It's the children's night out and I've got their nurse to look after."

I laughed. It didn't cost me anything and if the guy thought he was funny, who was I to discourage him?

"Okay." I said, "I'll get after Myra Shumway. What kind of a name's that, anyway? And, where's her picture?"

He took a print from his briefcase and tossed it on the table. "If there was a fire in that dame's bedroom." he said, "We'd take a fireman five hours to put it out and five strong men to put the fireman out."

I picked up the print. By the time I'd got my breath back, he'd gone.

TWO

Before I go any further, I want you to know how Myra Shumway first met Doc Ansell and Sam Bogle, and as I wasn't there at the time, I'll just tell the story as I heard it later.

Doc Ansell and Bogle were in Lorencillo's cafe. Have you ever been there? It's a little place hidden behind immensely thick stone walls. The patio is a fine example of the old Mexican regime, so the guide book tells me. If that means nothing to you, it also means nothing to me, so what the hell?

In the centre of the patio is a carved stone fountain around which stand iron tables and benches. Overhead a canopy of leaves from the ancient cypresses and banana trees blot out the sky. You can imagine that it's a pretty nice spot. There are a number of wooden cages along the verandah which house various coloured parakeets who squawk and whistle at you and if you're new to the country you get a great kick out of the typical Mexican atmosphere.

Well, these two guys, Doc Ansell and Bogle, were sitting at a table drinking tepid beer when Bogle glanced up and spotted an egg-yolk blonde who had suddenly appeared from behind a bunch of Indian peddlers. He had one quick gander before she disappeared in the crowd again.

"Sam!" Doc Ansell said sharply. "Do I have to keep telling you women are poison!"

"Was that a mirage?" Bogle asked scrambling to his feet and gazing anxiously into the dimly lit shadows. "Did I see what I thought I saw?"

Doc Ansell laid down his knife and fork. He was a wizened little man with a shock of untidy white hair. "You've got to watch your glands, Bogle." he cautioned. "There's a time and place for everything."

"You're always shooting your mouth of about a time and place for everything. What time do I get? And when in hell do we stay in one place long enough to do anything?" Bogle returned, sitting down again.

"The trouble with you—" Ansell began, but Bogle raised his hand.

"You don't have to tell me." he said, pushing his plate away in sudden disgust. "I know. It's getting so I'm imagining things. How much longer are we stickin' in this country? I'm sick of it. What's the matter with grabbing a train and getting the hell out of here? Couldn't you do with the smell of Chicago for a change?"

"It's a little too soon yet for you to go home." Ansell reminded him gently.

Bogle frowned. He was a big, powerful man and his dirty drill suit fitted him badly. In the past, he had been a gunman, working for Little Bernie during the prohibition period. After repeal, he went to Chicago and tried to pick up a living as a heistman, but he was not smart enough to organize anything big enough to pay dividends. Then one night, he was involved in a gun battle with the police. Two of the police officers were hurt and Bogle did a lam act. He did not stop running until he reached Mexico. There, he felt comparatively safe. For the past six months he had been working with Doc Ansell, selling patent medicines to the Maya Indians.

Ansell and Bogle made an incongruous couple. They lived in different worlds. Bogle was always yearning for the fleshpots of life. He found Mexico insufferably dull after Chicago. He hated the food, the dust and the heat. The native women appalled him. Both socially and financially the small colony of American and English women were out of his reach. Even the whisky was bad. He hated Mexico nearly as much as he hated the police.

On the other hand, Ansell was happy in any country. So long as he was able to sell his various remedies to the gullible he did not mind where he lived.

Before Bogle became his partner, Ansell often had trouble with his patients. Sometimes, he even found it dangerous to return to the same town. But with Bogle at his side, he had no qualms in facing irate patients or going to the lowest native quarters in the various towns he visited. Bogle was an excellent bodyguard, as Little Bernie had discovered. One look at his massive fists and hard little eyes was enough to cool any hasty temper.

So it was then, that Ansell and Bogle had worked together for six months. They drifted from place to place, spending their morning dispensing coloured water in mysterious looking green bottles and, in the afternoons, selling them by quickfire sales talk to anyone foolish enough to listen.

Ansell represented the brains of the concern and Bogle the brawn. It was Bogle who set up the small tent and the collapsible platform. It was Bogle who set out the green bottles in neat rows and beat a small drum to attract attention. The drum was Bogle's own idea and in some districts it produced considerable dividends.

Ansell would sit inside the tent, smoking a battered pipe, until Bogle's hoarse whisper: "A big bunch of suckers waitin'" brought him to his feet. Then he would sweep majestically from the tent, his eyes blazing with fanatical enthusiasm and, cast spells over the bewildered audience.

Bogle would display his gigantic muscles, built entirely by Doctor Ansell's Virile Tablets (a box of fifty for three dollars). Pictures of a drearily scraggy woman would be passed round the crowd with a comparison picture of the same woman equipped with a figure that made the natives' eyes grow round. Doctor Ansell's Bust Developer (a box of twenty-five pills for two dollars fifty) was responsible for this attractive transformation.

Ansell and Bogle preferred Lorencillo's café to any other eating place. Few Americans came to the café and after the noise and bustle of the City, it was somewhere to pass a peaceful evening.

Bogle swished the last two inches of beer round in his glass. "The cops'll have forgotten me by now." he said. "It's nearly a year ago. That's a long time. Besides, you never saw those two guys. I was doing the State a service."

"Talk sense." Ansell returned. "How do you think we'd live? Can you imagine anyone buying my Virile pills in Chicago?"

Bogle was no longer listening. He was stating with eyes like organ-stops at the egg-yolk blonde who had come out of the café and was standing on the steps looking round the crowded patio.

"Well, I'll be damned!" he said, clutching at the table. "Take a look at that!"

Ansell sighed, "She's certainly nice to look at, but she'd begin by stroking your hair and wind up with your scalp. You're moving out of your class, Bogle."

Bogle paid no attention. "Holy Moses!" he exploded suddenly. "She's on her own, Doc. Get her over here before some greaseball snaps her up."

Ansell regarded the girl doubtfully. She was slight. Her hard little face was full of character. Her eyes and mouth were large and her nose, Ansell decided, was her best feature. Her silky blonde hair fell to her shoulders and gleamed like burnished copper in the hard light of the acetylene flares. She was dressed in a neat white tailored suit over a dark red shirt.

Bogle was whispering with hoarse urgency in Ansell's ear, "Get after her, Doc. Didja ever see such an outline? It's like a blue print for Coney Island's roller coaster!"

Two well-dressed Spaniards, sitting near them, were also showing interest in the girl. They had been muttering to each other the moment they had seen her and now one of them pushed back his chair and stood up.

Bogle whipped round, "Don't get yourself in an uproar, pal." he snarled.

"Repark your fanny! I gotta date with that dame … so lay off!"

The Spaniard stared at him blankly, hesitated, then sat down again.

Ansell, anxious that there should be no trouble, rose to his feet.

"Watch your blood pressure." he said sharply.

"To hell with my blood pressure. Get after that dame before I wreck this joint."

Ansell approached the girl rather self-consciously. Everyone in the patio watched him.

The girl leaned against the verandah rail and watched him come. Her eyes were watchful, but friendly. As he came up to her, she suddenly smiled. The large crimson mouth showed white teeth.

Ansell was startled.

"Hello." she said.

"You'll pardon me." Ansell said in his best manner, "But are you waiting for someone? This is a bad place for a young woman to be on her own."

"That's what the guide-book said." she returned sadly, "but I've been here off and on for a week and nothing's happened to me yet. I think the place's a phoney."

Ansell blinked. "I was going to ask you to join me until your escort arrives."

She laughed. She had a full-throated, rich, infectious laugh with a hint of recklessness that quickened even Ansell's thin blood. He looked at her sharply.

"What makes you think I'm expecting an escort, Poppa?" she asked. "Don't you think I can take care of myself?"

Ansell experienced a rare feeling of embarrassment. "I beg your pardon." he said stiffly. "You're a little more worldly than I had supposed. You'll excuse me."

"Now, don't get burned up." she said quickly. "Let's be friendly. After all, Stanley and Livingstone had to get used to each other. Doesn't your boy friend want to meet me? Or is that a permanent leer he keeps on his face?" She walked down the steps and crossed over to where Bogle was sitting.

With a bewildered shrug of his shoulders, Ansell followed her.

Bogle had been watching this scene in astonishment. When she came up, he just sat there, blinking at her.

"Do you want a needle and thread?" she asked, putting slim brown hands on the table and leaning towards him.

Bogle's eyes were like marbles, "Huh?" he said.

"Never mind." She sat down. "I thought maybe you'd lost a button because you didn't get up to receive me. But, perhaps you belong to the modern school." She crossed her legs, adjusted her skirt over a slim silk-clad knee and regarded him thoughtfully. "I can see what you are now. You're quite deceptive from a distance." She put her head on one side and smiled at him. "Let me see. Definitely Chicago. I bet you carried a gun for one of the big shots. Tell me I'm right."

Bogle blinked. He looked across at Ansell helplessly.

"You asked for it." Ansell said, beginning to enjoy himself. "Don't blame me. It was your idea."

"That's very interesting." the girl went on. "So he has ideas? I shouldn't have thought he was one of the World's thinkers, but appearances are deceptive these days, aren't they?"

"Are they?" Ansell said, a little bewildered himself.

"I think so." She met Bogle's unwavering stare coolly. "Have you a tendency to hernia?" she asked him abruptly.

Bogle screwed up his face. "What's she talking about?" he asked feebly.

"Maybe I'm being too personal." she said. "Let me put it this way. During an arboreal existence in the Miocene epoch of the Tertiary era, man, or I should say, pre-historic man lost his tail. He acquired an upright gait and a tendency to hernia. I just wanted to see how far you'd got. Think nothing of it. It's only idle curiosity."

Bogle's face went a dull red and his eyes flashed viciously. "So you're a smart dame, eh?" he snarled. "We had a flock of 'em in Chicago. But, get 'em in a corner and they yell murder."

"I'm fussy who I take in corners." the girl replied briskly. Then she smiled at him. "Don't get mad. I was just fooling. What's your name?"

Bogle looked at her suspiciously, but her frank smile disarmed him. "Sam Bogle." he said. "And listen, sister …"

"That's a lovely name." she broke in. "Was your mother Mrs. Bogle?"

Bogle blinked. "Yeah." he said. "What of it? Who else do you think she'd be?"

"I just wanted to make sure. Some of the funniest things do happen."

"Well, nothing funny happened to me." Bogle said angrily. "So don't go putting ideas into people's heads."

She laughed, raising her shoulders and glanced over at Ansell, "Never mind." she said. "You mustn't take me seriously. And who are you?" she went on to Ansell.

He introduced himself.

"A real doctor?" she seemed quite impressed. "Well, I'm Myra Shumway. How do you do, Mr. Bogle? How do you do, Doctor Ansell?"

Bogle sat back heavily. "I don't get this." he said. "She must be crazy."

"Don't be a churl, Bogle." she said sharply. "Just because you don't understand my appeal, you don't have to be rude. Who's going to buy me a drink?"

"What would you like?" Ansell asked, slightly dazed.

"I think a Scotch might be nice."

Ansell signaled a waiter. "Now, we've got to know each other." he said, "suppose you tell me what you are doing here?"

The waiter came and took the order for drinks. He seemed to know Myra Shumway. They smiled and nodded to each other.

When he had gone, Myra opened her handbag and took out a silver cigarette case. She lit the cigarette, and leaned back, looking at them thoughtfully. "Would it interest you?" she said. "I wonder. Still, I am accepting your hospitality. I've no secrets. Until yesterday, I was foreign correspondent to the Chicago News. I've been cast aside like a worn-out glove." She turned on Bogle. "Do I look like a worn out glove?"

"Not a glove." Bogle said heavily.

Myra absorbed this. "I think I asked for that." she said to Ansell, "I led with my chin."

Bogle was pleased with himself. "I can be funny too, sister." he said.

She nodded, "You can, but you don't have to try."

"All right, all right." Bogle said hastily, "we won't fight. I know something about newspaper guys. They're poison if you cross 'em. I recollect once I didn't fix one of 'em with a case of Scotch. Did that guy turn sour? He smeared my mug right across the front page. Got me into a helluva jam." Bogle scratched his head mournfully, "Mind you, that's some time ago, but these guys don't change."

"It could be that." she returned. "My boss kept silk-worms. You wouldn't believe the number of girls he interested. I guess they thought the silk-worms were going to give them silk stockings, but it turned out to be a modem version of the Etching gag."

The waiter came with the drinks.

"He lost interest in me when I told him I was allergic to silk-worms. Maybe, that's why I've been tossed out." She picked up her drink, "Here's gold in your bridge work!" she said and drank.

The others drank too.

"Well, you can't be interested in me." she went on. "What do you do for a living?"

Ansell fiddled thoughtfully with his glass. "I'm a healer." he said simply. "I've studied the secrets of herbal medicine for years and I have perfected several remarkable remedies. Bogle is my assistant."

She looked at him admiringly, "Isn't that cute." she said. "And what are these remedies?"

Ansell had an uneasy suspicion that she was laughing at them. He looked at her sharply, but her admiration seemed genuine enough.

"Take my Virile tablets for instance." he said. "If you'd seen Bogle before he had taken a course of these pills you wouldn't have believed that he'd been alive to-day. He was thin, weak and depressed …"

She turned and regarded Bogle with interest. Bogle smirked. "Well, he certainly looks like he takes his daily dozen with a knife and fork now." she said. "He's a credit to you."

Ansell pulled his nose thoughtfully. "Then there's my bust developer." he said and exchanged a quick glance with Bogle. "That in itself is a remarkable invention. It's brought happiness to hundreds of women."

Myra looked at him in astonishment, "Psychologically, I suppose?"

"What's she say, Doc?" Bogle asked, looking blank.

"In a way." Ansell returned, ignoring Bogle. "But a good figure's an asset to a woman in any country. I've some remarkable testimonials."

Bogle leaned forward, "You ought to try a box, sister." he said hoarsely. "Two bucks fifty. It's dynamite!"

Ansell broke in hastily, "Now come, Bogle, that's not complimentary. I'm sure Miss—er—Shumway's a very nice figure."

Bogle sneered, "She got tossed out of her job, didn't she?"

"That would have nothing to do with it." Ansell returned. "Of course, I'm not saying it wouldn't make a big difference, but I'm sure Miss Shumway is quite satisfied with her figure as it is."

Myra looked from Ansell to Bogle in bewilderment. "Up to now." she said, "I thought it was pretty good …"

"Don't be over confident." Bogle said. "You can't stand still these days. Progress, that's what you gotta aim for. Look at the way they're developing the land." He produced a pill box from his pocket and slapped it down in front of her. "You've got to think and plan big, sister. Look at the pyramids. The guy who built them had a big mind. A box of this stuff and you're way out front. You get confidence, see? The other dames get left in the cold. If you've got what it takes, it don't matter if you have dandruff. You're okay. And this is the stuff that'll make you okay. It'll take more than a silkworm to louse up your job. Get figure conscious. Here, take the box. It'll cost you two bucks. I'll give you a fifty cent discount because I like you."

Myra shook her head, "But I don't want them." she said.

"That's what you think now." Bogle persisted. "You're young. Salt it away. It lasts forever. You may never see us again. Wait 'til you're old. Wait 'til some guy gives you the air. Then you'll wish you had this by you. Lay it up for your old age, sister. Put it by for a rainy day."

Myra looked over at Ansell. "Why don't you call off this high pressure salesman?" she said, a spark of anger in her eyes.

Ansell said hurriedly, "You mustn't worry Miss Shumway. I know you've her interest at heart, but if she doesn't want …"

"Aw, nuts." Bogle snapped. "She's got to have the stuff. She'll thank me later. I know what I'm doing. Remember the dame in Vera Cruz? Was she grateful? She spit in my eye at the time, but what a build up she gave us a month later! She beat a home-wrecker to it. Yeah—you know it's right, Doc."

Myra opened her bag, took out two dollars and gave them to Bogle. "I give in." she said, and put the pill box into her bag.

Bogle sat back with a delighted smile. This was his first sales attempt and it had worked. Even Ansell was pleased.

Myra looked from one to the other. "If you can do this to me." she said, "I'm sorry for the simple natives."

"You'll thank me." Bogle said earnestly. He had been taught always to leave a satisfied client. "You'll remember this as the luckiest day of your life."

"Now, suppose we forget my figure." Myra said. "It embarrasses me." There was a hard glint in her eyes and she leaned forward to pick up her glass. Her hand knocked Ansell's beer into his lap.

Before he could move, she was on her feet. She whipped out his handkerchief from his breast pocket and began mopping him. Her face was scarlet with mortification.

"I am sorry." she stammered. "I'm not really clumsy. Has it ruined your suit?"

Ansell took the handkerchief from her and dried himself. "Accidents will happen." he said, feeling sorry for her. "Don't worry about a little thing like this."

She whirled on Bogle. "Did it splash you?" she asked, running her hand down the front of his coat.

"No. It's all right."

She turned to Ansell again. "Will you forgive me?"

"Why, of course." he said, sitting down again. "It was an accident."

She lifted her hands to her nose and made a little grimace. "Mind if I wash?" she said. "I'm all over beer." She smiled brightly at them and swept away to the café.

Bogle watched her go. "What do you make of her, Doc?" he asked. "She came over here as tough as rusty nails, then she fell for my line like, a stupid native dope. Think there's anything to her?"

Ansell was puzzled. "I don't know." he said frankly. "She's too nice looking to be on her own. That's what makes me suspicious. She's too good to be true."

Bogle said: "I don't think I'd make that dame. She's got a tongue like a razor. Suppose we blow before she comes back? I know her type. A dame who turns a guy down with silkworms ain't going to play with me."

Ansell signaled a waiter. "You're improving, Bogle." he said, looking pleased. "There was a time a good looking young woman could tie you in knots. Yes, I think you're right. I see no reason why we should stay here. Anyway, we have work to do." He groped for his wallet. "I'm quite sure that she can look after herself—" he broke off and stared wildly at Bogle.

"What's the matter?" Bogle asked sharply.

"My money!" Ansell spluttered, going through his pockets feverishly, "It's gone!"

"Gone?" Bogle repeated stupidly. "What do you mean gone?"

His eyes suddenly darkened and he began to search in his own pockets. The two dollars that Myra had given him for the box of pills and the five dollar bill he had saved were no longer to be found.

The two men stared at each other.

"The oldest, hoariest trick in the world." Ansell said, trembling with rage. "And we fell for it. She knocked beer over me and shook me down for what I'd got. That wasn't enough for her. She frisked you as well."

"What the hell are we waiting for?" Bogle snarled, kicking back his chair. "We've gotta nail that dame."

The waiter came up with the check. He glanced at Bogle's congested face and a look of alarm came into his eyes. "Is anything wrong, señors?" he asked.

"We've been robbed." Bogle snarled. "Get out of the way."

"But the Señorita has gone." the waiter said. "She has never robbed our clients before they settled their check. That is very bad of her."

Bogle and Ansell stared at each other. "What do you mean?" Ansell demanded. "Do you know this girl?"

"Why, yes." The waiter smiled, "she is very beautiful and she has very clever fingers. She comes here often. It is good for her line of work."

Bogle clenched his fists. "What about us?" he said furiously. "Don't we get any protection?"

The waiter lifted apologetic shoulders, "But the señors asked her to their table. I thought you knew her."

"Let's get out of here, Bogle." Ansell said. "We asked for it."

"But, there is the question of the check." the waiter said, looking distressed.

"Take it off the blonde when she's in next time." Bogle said. "And tell her from me that if I ever meet her again I'll take her apart and find out what makes her tick."

The waiter's face darkened. "That is bad business, señor, she may not come back."

Bogle didn't quite like the look in his eye. "I don't want you to lose by it." he said. "Tell me, buddy, have you a girl friend?"

The waiter's face brightened. "I have a very fine girl." he said, flashing his teeth. "There is no other woman like her in the country."

Bogle took out a pill box and gave it to him. "Make sure of that." he said. "That's worth two bucks fifty. I'll make you a present of it."

The waiter examined the box. Then he sneered. "She has had them before." he said disdainfully. "The last time she took them she came out in a rash."

"So what?" Bogle said, pushing him aside. "It gave her something to do, didn't it?" and he walked across the patio with Ansell out into the street.

THREE

Before I tell you how I came to meet Myra Shumway, I'd better give you her background, then we can go straight ahead without interruption.

Myra Shumway had not been telling the truth when she described herself to Doc Ansell as a newspaper correspondent For the past five years she had been a "dip." If you don't know what that means, just stand on any street corner and flash a fat bank-roll. Before long some dame will take it off you and you'll know nothing about it until hours later. That dame was a dip.

Myra's father was a magician who worked small-time vaudeville without much profit. Myra trailed along with him.

When she reached the age of fifteen, her father decided that she should be his assistant. That was all right with Myra and she really worked at the job. By the end of the year there was no one on the Coast to touch her for speed, style and smoothness of execution. She could palm six cards with the speed of light. She could take a man's vest off his back without him knowing it. That went for his suspenders too. In other words, she was good.

One evening something happened which was to change her immediate future. As she was preparing to leave the theatre her father came with a young fellow who wanted to meet her. He was a travelling salesman who had looked in on the town with the hope of drumming up some new business. In the evening he went to the theatre. He saw Myra, was dazzled by her looks and came round the back intending to dazzle her with his money.

Hamish Shumway was agreeable that this young man should take Myra out to dinner. He knew that she had her head screwed on the right way and that if there was to be any funny business she could take care of herself.

The young man's name was Joe Krumm and he seemed a pleasant

enough young fellow. Myra went with him to a restaurant and had an expensive dinner. During the dinner, Krumm did a fatal thing. He showed her the size of his bankroll. It measured an inch and a half round its waist. Myra had never seen so much money in her life. He bragged about it. He told her that he had stacks of dough in the bank. So Myra thought she'd give him a scare and she lifted his roll. It was the easiest job she had ever done. When the time came for him to pay the check, he found his roll had vanished. He nearly had a hemorrhage.

The manager of the restaurant and a couple of waiters stood around watching. They could see the price of an expensive dinner dissolving into smoke.

Myra got scared. People were staring at them. Krumm was nearly crazy and the manager was muttering about the police. She couldn't work up enough courage to produce the roll and tell everyone that it was a gag.

She sat there, her face the colour of a beet, praying that the ground would open and swallow her.

It never crossed Krumm's mind that he'd been whizzed. No one except the waiter had been near him. Myra's acute embarrassment established her alibi. He was too excited to reason that a magician would be just the person to lift his roll. Besides, a nice looking kid like Myra just wouldn't do such a thing.

Then an elderly man who was dining across the room got to his feet and came over. He had his eye on Myra the moment she had come into the restaurant. Egg-yolk blondes were his weakness and he couldn't let such an opportunity pass him by.

He had a few scathing words to say about young puppies who shook restaurant managers down for the price of a meal. He expressed his sorrow that the young lady should be subjected to such an embarrassing situation. Then he produced a bulky wallet and paid the check.

"My car's outside." he said to Myra. "Let me run you home. This young fella's no fit companion for a little girl like you."

Myra never knew to this day how she got out of the restaurant. It was only when the fresh night air was beating on her face as the big car swept her through the dark streets that she began to get over her scare.

The elderly guy introduced himself as Daniel Webster. He asked her who she was. Although Myra was only sixteen, she had kicked around. You don't work vaudeville for a year without learning that A.B.C. is invariably followed by D. She knew that she was going to have a little trouble with Daniel Webster. He hadn't parted with seven dollars just to make the restaurant happy. So she told him her name was Rose Carraway and that she was staying at the Denville Hotel. Both statements were essentially untrue.

Since the Denville Hotel lay in the opposite direction to the one they were going she thought this would be an indication of Webster's intentions. If he stopped the car and turned around, then she was misjudging him. If he carried straight on, then she would know he was on the make. He carried straight on.

When Hamish Shumway realised he was going to have a very attractive daughter on his hands he decided to equip her with means for self-defence. He knew that in his profession attractive young girls wouldn't remain attractive for long unless they went around with their eyes wide open. At an early age Myra was told the facts of life and taught a trick or two. She was perfectly confident, as she sat by Webster's side, that she could handle anything that might come her way.

Daniel Webster saw no reason why he shouldn't extract payment for the restaurant bill at the earliest convenient moment. Once clear of the town, he ran the car on to the grass shoulder and stopped the engine.

Myra was in no way flustered. In fact, she was most anxious to find out whether the advice her father had drummed into her for the past four years really worked. As Webster eased himself away from the wheel and made a grab at her, she swung her arm and hit him squarely under his nose with the side of her hand. She had been advised by her father never to pull a punch. The chopping blow she handed out to Webster had all her young strength and vigour behind it.

The side of her hand landed accurately. The blow broke Webster's bridge-work, made his eyes water and sent a thousand red-hot needles into his brain. He slumped back in his seat like an inflated balloon.

Myra opened the door of the car, stepped on to the grass shoulder and ran, without panic, into the darkness. It was only after several minutes, when she paused to look back, that she realized she was holding Webster's wallet tightly in her hand. She had no idea that she had taken it. It was obviously unwise to go back and return it, as Webster might not take kindly to such a gesture. So she added the contents of the wallet to Krumm's roll and began her long walk back to the town.

In the secrecy of her bedroom she went through Webster's wallet. She found that the evening's entertainment and car ride had netted her four hundred and seventy dollars.

She didn't sleep at all that night. There was much to think about. She made her plans before the cold dawn light filtered round the window blind.

Fortunately, they were to move on to another town that day so there was little chance either of Krumm or Webster ever seeing her again. She hid her first earnings as a dip in her suspender belt, assisted her parents to pack and caught an early train to Springville which was their next port of call.

For two more years she worked with her father. Then without any warning she packed her bag and left. She had no misgivings and no regrets. Myra

Shumway was ready to carve her initials on opportunity's door.

During those two years she had not ceased to pilfer. She had been cautious but consistent. It had been ridiculously easy. That was the trouble. To acquire money so easily was too great a temptation.

She had made all the necessary plans. Her first move was to buy a second-hand Cadillac. She had fourteen hundred dollars in hand and the Cadillac didn't even dent the roll.

She left a note for her father. It was curt and to the point. She told him that she was tired of living the hard way and he wasn't to worry about her. She didn't think he would, but he'd worry plenty about himself.

She put her bag in the back of the car and headed south. She wanted to get as far away as she could from the dreary little towns they had been touring. She had seen pictures of Florida and she wanted to go there. Now, there was nothing to slop her.

For the next two years, she stood on her own feet. She travelled in the Cadillac. Sometimes she worked in night clubs, but most times she just travelled. Her bank was the wallets of chance acquaintanceships. When she ran out of money, she found a sucker and picked his pocket. She was always careful. Her swift fingers were never detected. She could take a wallet, remove a few hundred dollars and put the wallet back without the owner noticing. More often than not the money was never missed.

She came to Mexico because she wanted a complete change of scenery. She liked variety. Mexico seemed to be the right place for her present mood. She had no roots. Her parents and her past were forgotten. The big Cadillac was her home.

When she left Lorencillo's café she decided to head for Vera Cruz. She slipped out the backway where the Cadillac was parked and drove rapidly towards the centre of the town. When she felt that she had put enough space between herself and the café she drew up in a quiet side street, stopped the car and glanced in the mirror above her head. Satisfied that no one was following her, she opened her bag and felt for a cigarette. When she had lit it, she leaned forward so that the light from the dashboard fell directly on her hands and bag. She took from the bag a small roll of money and counted it carefully. She had a hundred and twelve dollars.

"Not bad." she said, under her breath.

She separated the notes into two even packets. One packet she put back in her bag, the other she folded neatly and slid down the top of her stocking. Then she took a large scale road map from the dashboard locker and spread it on her knees.

And that was how I found her.

I left Manolo's a few minutes after Juden had gone with the idea of talking to the police. If they hadn't a record which way this Myra Shumway had headed, then I was going to have a tough job finding her.

I spotted a big Cadillac standing in the shadow of a building and noticed that it was painted dark green. All right, I admit that I jumped a half a foot. It seemed almost like black magic. I crossed the street and approached the car quietly.

There she was, with her blonde hair hiding her face, staring at a road map. One look at that hair told me all I wanted to know. I didn't have to look any further for Myra Shumway. She was right here in front of me.

I didn't rush up and grab her like an amateur sleuth. I stood back and gave the problem a little thought. Here she was as free as a bird, not a bandit in sight, and ready to take a powder at any moment. She was no good to me unless she was kidnapped. I toyed with the idea of talking things over with her and getting things fixed the easy way. Then I thought if she heard about the reward, I should have to split it with her and 25,000 dollars doesn't look half as nice cut in half. Besides, maybe she was tired of her old man's face and wouldn't go back to New York anyway.

No, there was only one way to play this. She had to be foxed.

I wandered up to the car and putting my arms on the door I leaned in. "Do you favour straw hats for race horses?" I said. "Or do you think they'd eat them?"

She looked up calmly, stared at me with big eyes and then returned to her map. "Go jump down a well." she said. "If there isn't one handy, anyone will help you dig it if you tell 'em what it's for."

That set me back a trifle. I was never much good with a smooth wisecracker. Myra Shumway was that and then some.

I tried again, "I'm just trying to break the ice." I said. "Seeing the car and the map I figured I could hitch a ride."

She looked up again, "This isn't a bus, brother." she said. "I don't take passengers."

"You mean you don't take strangers." I corrected her. "Let me introduce myself. I'm Ross Millan."

"You may be a power-house to your mother." she said carefully, "but to me, you're a blownout fuse. Good night." and she turned back to her map.

I let my blood pressure settle down, then I wandered around to the other side of the car, opened the door and climbed in. "It's a grand feeling to get the weight off one's puppies, ain't it?" I said.

She stiffened. "I hope for your sake that I'm not going to have any trouble from you." she said, putting the map away with quiet determination.

"None at all." I assured her. "All I need is a lift to wherever you're going. I'm tired of Mexico City and I want a change of air. I always hitch hike because I'm mean about money."

"Your repressions fascinate me." she returned. I may be wrong but I fancied she sounded annoyed. "But if you don't get out of this car, I'm going to surprise you."

I made myself comfortable, but I kept an eye on her. I've been mixed up with a few tough babies in my time and I wasn't taking any chances. "Before I came to Mexico." I said, "I was a professional strong man. One of my favourite acts was carrying a dame across the stage in my teeth. That's how tough I am."

"Oh?" She seemed startled. "And you gave that up?"

"It gave me up." I said sadly. "The dame was the trouble. You see she was just a dumb kid with a temper like a dentist's drill. She got on my nerves. You know, I kept having to fight a temptation not to bite her. You can see how easy it'd have been. Well, one night I couldn't stand her any longer." I shrugged. "I only meant to nip her, but I guess I got carried away."

Well, that held her for a moment. I could see she didn't know what to make of me. Finally she decided to try a new line.

"I think you'd better go." she said, at last. "Or else I'll scream."

"I wish you would." I returned, twisting round so that I faced her. "It'd give me a chance to smack you. I've always wanted to smack a beautiful blonde, but I've never found an excuse for it."

She suddenly leaned forward and jabbed the self-starter savagely. "I hope you'll end up in jail." she said and engaged the gear.

"Don't get agitated." I said. "It's bad for the complexion. Where are you going … Vera Cruz?"

"I suppose so." she returned, pushing the car down the dark, dusty road. "That is, if it suits you, of course."

"Anywhere suits me just so long as it's away from this dump." I returned. "Just relax, sister. You don't have to be scared of me. I wouldn't do this only I want to get out of town and it's nice to travel free. When we get to Vera Cruz I'll leave you and you'll just have your dreams to remember me by."

"I'll say you'll leave me." Myra returned. "What do you expect me to do? Marry you?"

"That depends on how old fashioned you are." I said. "Me … I don't make social gestures. Tell me, peach blossom, what did you say your name was again?"

"If you don't remember what I told you, I can't be bothered to tell you again."

"So what do I call you?" I said. "Hi you or Hey, sister?"

"I wouldn't lose weight if you didn't call me anything." she replied indifferently. "Just give your larynx a vacation and I'll pretend you're not here."

I glanced at the clock on the dashboard. It showed 11.15.

"Before I accept those terms." I said coldly, "tell me one thing. You're not going to tackle the whole trip to Vera Cruz to-night, are you?"

"Chalco's a few miles on." she returned, "I'll stop there, hand you over to the police and then find myself a hotel."

"On the other hand, if we take turns driving." I said carefully, "we could reach Orizaba first thing in the morning. I know a swell hotel in Orizaba where you'll have every luxury in the world—if the world goes no further than Mexico."

She thought about this. "Well." she said at last, "I wouldn't like to sleep in this car and let you drive. You might get ideas."

"Well, of course, if you're scared of me." I said, shrugging.

"Who said I was scared of you?" That seemed to annoy her, "I haven't met anything on two legs that could scare *me.*"

"That sounds like famous last words. But, if that's how you feel, Apple pie, give me the wheel and take a nap." I said grinning at her.

She hesitated for a second, then stopped the car. She looked at me hard and then a smile came into her eyes. This dame was certainly something to see. Apart from the fact that she represented 25,000 dollars to me, she looked good. When I say good I mean there wasn't another woman in the country who could get within a mile of her. I like blondes. They may be a little dizzy, but they rest my eyes. That's my only form of recreation.

"Listen, brother." she said. "If there's anything coming from you that's not strictly off the top deck, I'll cut your lights out."

"Would you let me see them before I die?" I asked anxiously. "I've always wanted to make Ripley."

"Don't say I didn't warn you." she returned and got out of the car.

I slid over and took the wheel.

"There's more room in the back for sleeping." she said, getting in and leaving me by myself. "Besides, I've got a tyre lever here and I'll bounce it on your head if you get off the main road. And I won't send you a telegram before I do it."

"To hear you talk." I said, starting the car, "No one would know you had a sentimental streak. But, seriously, Angel skin, you could trust me with your life."

"If I did that." she said, "I'd swap my girdle for a straight jacket."

After a while, I guess she must have gone to sleep. I sent the Cadillac tearing into the night. It was certainly a fine bus and the miles kept clicking up on the dashboard. I expected her to wake up after an hour or so and take over, but she kept on sleeping. I guess the kid was tired. She didn't wake up until I was bumping over the cobbles that led to the outskirts of Orizaba. Then I heard a little gasp and she said, "Why it's daylight. Have

I been sleeping all this time?"

"Well, someone's been snoring in my ear." I returned, as I swung the Cadillac into the main street. "If it wasn't you, we've got a stranger on board."

"I don't snore." she said coldly and I could hear her hunting in her bag for the inevitable powder and puff.

"Think nothing of it." I said. "You don't have to be shy with me." I pulled up outside a small hotel in pink stone. "I liked the sound. It made me homesick."

"Homesick?" she asked as I twisted round to look at her.

"Sure." I said. "At one time I used to live on a farm." Then I got out of the car hurriedly.

"Just wait here and I'll fix things. Do you want a room or just a bath and coffee?"

"No room." she said firmly.

It only crossed my mind after I had dug out the hotel manager and had introduced myself, that I was crazy to leave her out there in the car. But I need not have worked myself into a lather, because she was still there when I came out.

"I've got it all fixed." I said, opening the car door. "Bath first and breakfast on the verandah. Eggs, fruit and coffee. That suit?"

She got out of the car with a small grip in her hand. "It certainly does." she said, and for the first time she gave me a friendly smile.

I felt I might be getting somewhere with this dame. "Join me for breakfast down here in about half an hour." I said. "Then we'll both let our hair down and confide in each other."

She shook her head. "I enjoy my own company." she returned. "I've given you a lift as we agreed, now I think I'll say goodbye."

"Don't be ridiculous." I said, taking her firmly by the arm and leading her towards the hotel. "Who's going to pay for my breakfast, if you run out on me?"

FOUR

As Mexican towns go, Orizaba could be worse. From Mexico City it is a long drop to Orizaba. In sixty odd miles you go down six thousand odd feet. That makes a lot of difference in atmosphere. The air thickens and the heat takes on a fiercer strength.

Sitting on the verandah overlooking the square where some small Indian soldiers in their grubby uniforms watched us with blank expressionless eyes, I felt pretty good. The bath had been just right and I was glad to get outside for some food.

On the far side of the square was the flower market. Although it was still early, Indian women were already at work, binding, sprinkling and sorting all kinds of flowers. The heavy scent came across the square and hung round us. "I'm glad we came here." I said. "I feel this is the beginning of a beautiful friendship."

Myra was sitting with her feet on a chair. Her eyes were closed against the hot sun. She had changed into a simple, well-cut linen frock which fitted her figure like it was painted on her. "We part at Vera Cruz." she said without any finality in her voice.

"Do we want to go there?" I asked. "Let's stay here. You can tell me a story every night and when I want a change you can dance for me."

"That sounds awfully nice of you." she said, stretching lazily. "But, I can see no future in it for myself."

"Don't you ever get away from your hard veneer?"

She opened her eyes and reached for the coffee. "No. It's much more than skin deep and it never cracks." She refilled her cup and then stared across at the mountains that seemed to press in on the town.

"That's an awful shame." I said, fumbling for a cigarette. I found I'd used my last *Chesterfield* and glanced hopefully at her. "You must miss a lot of fun that way, sister."

She gave me a cigarette from her case. "Oh no." she said, "I've no time for play. I've got ambitions."

"You certainly have." I said. "But you don't want to overdo it. What did you say your name was again?"

She laughed, "Myra Shumway." she returned.

I didn't need the confirmation. I knew I hadn't made a mistake, but all the same I was glad to know. Besides, we were getting on a more friendly footing and that was important.

"That's a beautiful name." I said.

A small party of Mexican labourers passed, carrying guitars. They crossed the little ruined square and sat down with their backs against the wall of an opposite building. Two of them began to play very softly.

"That's nice." Myra said. "Do you think they'll sing?"

"They will if you ask them to." I returned. "If you give them some money, God knows what they'll do."

While I was speaking, a truck came rumbling into the square, blotting out the thin music of the guitars. As it swept past the hotel, two men slid off the tailboard. A small wizened man and a big fat man.

Myra suddenly pushed back her chair, made to rise, then settled herself again.

"Something bite you?" I asked, watching the two men approach. "We're going to have company. Americans by the look of them."

"You ought to go into vaudeville." Myra returned. Her voice was so acid that I glanced at her, surprised.

"Know 'em?" I asked, wondering why her face had hardened. This kid could look tough when she was in the mood.

"My best friends." she returned bitterly. "You'll love them."

The two men came up to the verandah, mounted the steps and stood over us in silent hostility.

Myra said, "Hello. I've been wondering what happened to you?"

"I bet you have." the fat man said between his teeth.

"This is Mr. Ross Millan." she went on, waving her hand in my direction. "Doc Ansell and Mr. Samuel Bogle. Mr. Bogle's the gentleman with the dirty face."

"Sit down and have an egg." I said, wondering why these two guys looked like a public disaster.

"I don't want an egg." Bogle said, stretching his thick fingers ominously.

"Maybe Mr. Bogle would like a drink?" Myra said, smiling.

"We're going to have more than a drink." Bogle returned viciously. "We're collecting for charity—our own charity."

"He's got a very forceful personality, hasn't he?" I said to Myra.

"Grape nuts for breakfast." Myra said, shrugging. "You know what it does to some people."

"Oh sure." I said. "Perhaps he'd like some now."

Bogle seemed to draw moss of the air around into his lungs. He took a menacing step forward.

Myra said quickly, "Do sit down and have a drink. It gives me a pain in the neck looking up at you."

"Yeah?" Bogle said. "You'll be getting more than a pain—and it won't be in the neck either—if you don't hand over my dough."

Myra looked over at Ansell, "Has he been left out in the sun, do you think?"

Ansell's small mouth tightened. "That line won't get you anywhere." he said firmly, "we want our money!"

I didn't know what this was all about, but I did feel that two to one seemed pretty long odds. "Listen fellas." I said, easing back my chair. "If you can't be civil, I must ask you to make a noise like an airplane and fly away."

Bogle's fists slowly knotted. "Did you hear what that punk said?" He turned slowly on me and pushed his great red face forward. "Open that big trap of yours again and I'll tear your arm off and beat you to death with it."

I smiled at him, not making any move. "Couldn't you beat me to death with something else? The manager of the hotel would probably supply you with something. I don't think I'd like to lose my arm."

Ansell intervened just as Bogle got set to hand me one. "Not so fast, Sam." he said. "Maybe, this gentleman doesn't realize the facts."

Bogle looked suspiciously at me and then at Ansell, "You mean he's a sucker, too?" he asked.

"Why not? You and I were. He seems quite a respectable person." Ansell returned.

I thanked him. "Of course, I don't know what this's about." I said. "But, if I can lend you anything or help you, just say the word." I looked at Myra who had been watching with alert eyes. "Do you know these two gentlemen?"

"We met at a café." she said slowly. "But, it was just a hello and good-bye acquaintance. We had a drink and we parted...."

"Yeah, we parted okay." Bogle said, breathing heavily. "Our dough went with you."

In spite of this guy's bulk, I wasn't standing for that. I stood up, "Are you calling her a thief?" I demanded angrily.

Bogle crowded me. It gave me the impression that a mountain was going to fall on me. "Yeah." he said, showing his tobacco stained teeth. "Do you want to make anything of it?"

I decided that I'd be more use to Myra if I remained in one piece. The Bogle fella looked like he might be a little too much for me. Besides, I never like hitting anyone twice my size. I don't see any sense in it.

"No, that's all right, Bud." I said, stretching my leg and stamping. "I got a cramp."

"Cramp?" he repeated, blinking at me.

"Yeah, nasty thing, cramp." I looked over at Myra. "Do you ever get cramp?"

"Only when I wear pink." she said. "It's a funny thing, but pink cramps my style."

Bogle's blood pressure seemed to be troubling him. He tore his hat off his head and dashed it on to the ground. Then he began punching the air with his fists.

"Gently, Bogle." Ansell broke in. "There's no need to lose your temper."

"I want my dough!" Bogle howled, kicking his hat across the verandah. "I don't want a lot of talk. I just want my money and then I'm going to tear this dame into small pieces and feed her to the vultures."

Ansell drew up a chair. "We mustn't jump to conclusions." he said. "We have no proof that Miss Shumway took our money."

"I'll get proof." Bogle said savagely. "I'll get it if I have to turn her inside out.”

Myra's blue eyes widened for an instant. Then I knew. She had lifted the money. That slaughtered me. It not only complicated matters, but it gave these two guys an opportunity to be really awkward if they felt that way.

“Don't get your truss in a knot.” Myra said sharply. I'll say this for the girl, she'd got plenty of nerve. “What are you talking about?”

Bogle seemed to be praying. But the words that came through his clenched teeth didn't quite line up with divine thought.

“We think you stole our money.” Ansell said, looking at her steadily. “We both had small sums on us, but when you left, the money had gone. I don't like to accuse you, but you'll have to satisfy us that you didn't take it.”

She whirled round on Bogle, “I bet this was your idea.” she said. “I wish I had you at home. I'd use your head in my rock garden.”

Bogle's muscles began to expand. “Iszatso!” he said. “Let me tell you something. You've shot your mouth off long enough. Now, it's my turn. Gimme that dough or I'll turn you upside down and shake it out of you. And if this punk thinks he can stop me, then let's see him do it. They'll have to hose him off the wall by the time I'm through with him!”

Maybe there are a few jaded people on the look-out for a new sensation, but I'm not like that. Being hosed off a wail didn't sound like a pleasant way to spend the morning.

“Myra.” I said firmly, “Give these gentlemen their money and explain, as you explained to me, that it was just a gag. They'll appreciate it as much as I did—I hope.”

Myra hesitated, then shrugged. She took a roll of notes from the top of her stocking and tossed it on the table. “There's your money.” she said angrily. “I hope the rot-gut you buy with it poisons you.”

Ansell picked up the money and counted it. He gave seven dollars to Bogle and put the rest in his pocket.

Bogle drew a deep breath, “And now.” he said, hitching up his trousers, “I'm going to smack her one. Sister, am I going to bounce you off a wall!”

Ansell frowned. “Don't be so primitive, Bogle.” he said. “You should never strike a woman.”

“Not in public, anyway.” I added.

“I'll take her some place quiet.” Bogle pleaded.

“Certainly not.” Ansell said. Now that he had got his money, he seemed to take a much more agreeable view of life. He turned to Myra, “Now, young lady.” he said briskly, “I want to talk to you. I admire cleverness. That was a neat trick you pulled on us. A very neat trick. I deplore your ethics, of course.” he added hastily, “but there can be no mistaking talent. You have great talent.”

Myra seemed inclined to be sore. “Go boil your head, you old owl.” she said and turned her back on him.

Ansell looked upset, "Pity." he muttered; then catching my eye, he went on, "And you, sir? Who may you be?"

"The name is Ross Millan." I said. "I'm a representative of the New York Reporter."

"New York Reporter?" Ansell's eyes opened. "That's one of America's greatest newspapers. I'm pleased to know you, Mr. Millan." He offered his hand, "I'm only sorry that we should meet under such distressing circumstances."

"That's okay with me." I said, shaking his hand. "You don't have to worry about that. Miss Shumway has an advanced sense of humour. I know you boys can take a joke."

"There's too much talk." Bogle growled. "You ain't letting this dame get away with this, are you?"

Myra twisted round, "Why can't you beat it? There're enough rubbish dumps in this town without you adding to them. Take this big pickle-puss away and haunt houses with him."

Bogle swelled with fury, "Did you hear what she said?" he demanded turning on Ansell. "I ain't going to stand for it! I'll—"

"Wait a minute." Ansell said, as Bogle made to get to his feet. "Sit down, Sam. We won't get anywhere like this. Now look, Miss Shumway, if I wanted to, I could hand you over to the police. But that won't get us anywhere. You and I could be useful to each other."

"How?"

"You've got very clever fingers." Ansell told her, settling himself comfortably in the basket-chair. "Perhaps you can do other tricks besides—er— exploring people's pockets."

Myra frowned, "What if I can?" she said cautiously.

"Now look, my dear." Ansell went on, "we can, if we forget our differences, be profitable to each other. On the other hand, if you don't wish to be helpful, then I must hand you over to the police and work out my problems with Bogle."

"That should be a problem in itself." Myra said, looking it Bogle scornfully. "How you've got anywhere with that lump of cheese surprises me."

Bogle closed his eyes. The strain of controlling himself was getting too much for him. "The things I'll do to you when I get you alone." he said in a strangled voice.

"Never mind that, Bogle." Ansell said sharply. "We must stick to the point." He turned back to Myra, "Please don't irritate him. Are you going to be helpful or not?"

"Why, of course." A mischievous gleam had come into her eyes. "You want to know if I can do tricks? Well, I think I could give you a little demonstration." She looked at me, then at Bogle. "Ah! Now if Samuel will help me, I think I'll—yes, the very thing!" She reached across the table and plucked a length of pink ribbon from one of Bogle's ears. She pulled steadily and several yards of ribbon lay on the table before Bogle recovered from his astonishment and jerked away. The ribbon fell in a little pile to the ground and Bogle stared at it in horror.

"Why, Mr. Bogle." I said, "you didn't tell me you were that sort of a girl."

"Did that come from me?" Bogle whispered.

"And to think I said you were empty headed." Myra said sadly. "Why didn't you tell me you used your head as a cupboard? I won't take out the sawdust because your poor head might collapse, but I'm sure you'll be glad to get rid of this." and she removed a billiard ball from his other ear.

Bogle shivered and sprang to his feet. He dug his fingers into his ears feverishly.

"It's all right, Bogle." Ansell said kindly. "She was only demonstrating a trick. She's a magician." He turned to Myra, "I must say that was extremely expert."

Myra shrugged. "If I had my apparatus here, I'd show you something really good. That's just kid's stuff."

Bogle sat down again.

"Why don't you two go off somewhere and get to know each other?" I said to Myra. "This fella Bogle's got a nice face and maybe he just wants conversation. I'll talk to Doc while you two enjoy yourselves."

"Enjoy myself? With him?" Myra said, jerking her thumb at Bogle. "I'd rather walk around with a typhoid epidemic."

I thought she had something there, but I kept my opinion to myself.

"What you need." Bogle said, leaning across the table, "is a smack in the slats."

If the slats were where I thought they were, I felt he had something, too.

"Quiet!" Ansell snapped. "We're wasting too much time." He looked at Myra severely. "Young lady, you're deliberately aggravating him. I warn you, I'm not standing much more of this."

Myra laughed. "I'll be good, poppa, honest I will." she said, and patted his hand. "Now, tell me all about it."

Ansell looked at her suspiciously. "You seem to forget that you can't afford to be funny." he said.

"Aw, skip it, Doc." I broke in. "Why don't you say what you want to say and stop nagging the girl?"

Ansell looked a little surprised, "I'm trying to, but there're so many interruptions."

I turned on Bogle, "Don't interrupt the Doctor any more, Bud." I said. "He's getting tired of it."

"Yes." Myra joined in. "Give that big mouth of yours a rest. We're sick of the sound of your voice."

Bogle was so surprised that he just sat in a heap, his eyes starting out of his head.

"Okay, Doc." I said quickly, before Bogle could recover. "The floor's all yours."

"Do either of you believe in witchcraft?" Ansell asked.

Myra held up her hand. "I do." she said. "How else do you explain our Samuel away?"

Bogle took off his tie and tried to tear it in half. He was blue in the face with passion. He jerked and pulled at the tie, but it was too strong for him.

Myra said, "Let me." and snatched the tie out of his hands. She cut it in half with a fruit knife and handed it back to him. "There you are, Sammy." she said.

Bogle sat in a kind of stupor, staring at the tie. Then he dashed it to the ground.

"Miss Shumway!" Ansell exclaimed angrily. "Will you stop picking on Bogle?"

"Well, I was only trying to be helpful." Myra said, her eyes wide in innocence. "He couldn't manage to do it himself."

"All right, all right." I said hastily. "Why witchcraft? Who believes in witchcraft these days?"

Ansell looked at Bogle, satisfied himself that he was not going to have a fit and tried to collect his thoughts: "I don't suppose you know much of the background of this country. I've lived here for over twenty years and I've seen some very odd things."

"So have I." Myra said, looking at Bogle.

"If you can't stop this woman talking ..." Ansell said to me furiously.

"Be good." I said to Myra.

She lifted her shoulders.

"Go on." I said. "Don't worry about her."

"If I'm to explain this at all." Ansell said, rather hopelessly, "I wish you'd all listen. At one time there was a powerful secret society in this country who called themselves the Naguales. The members of this society were the witch doctors who bossed the Maya Indians. They are almost extinct now, but there's a few of them who still practice in a little village not two hundred miles from here."

"I've heard about 'em." I said. "Aren't they supposed to produce rain at a moment's notice and change themselves into animals? You don't believe that junk, do you?"

Ansell shook his head, "No, I don't. I believe they have certain supernatural powers such as mass hypnotism, and in some rare cases they practice levitation, but that really doesn't concern us. What I'm interested in is their herbal medicines. Have you ever heard of teopatli?"

I shook my head. "What is it? A drink?"

"It's a sure cure for snake bite."

While we were talking, Bogle sat with his head in his hands, in a kind of stupefied daze. He wasn't causing any trouble, so we ignored him.

"How do you mean … a sure cure?" I prompted.

"Listen, young man, I've seen men die of snake bite. It's a pretty nasty business. I've seen men of this little village pick up a coral snake and let it strike at them, and then put this ointment on. They feel no effects at all."

"Probably they've drawn the poison before demonstrating." I said sceptically.

Ansell shook his head. "I've given them a pretty thorough test. Rattle snakes, scorpions and coral snakes. Teopatli fixes any of these bites like lightning."

"All right, where do we go from there?"

"I want to get the recipe from this Indian fella and I think Miss Shumway can get it for me."

Myra stared at him. "Someone's been out in the sun without a nice, big, shady hat." she said. "Wouldn't you like to put your feet up, poppa?"

"If you were a few years younger." Ansell said, between his teeth, "I'd like to smack some manners into you!"

I knew just how he felt.

Myra giggled. "You're not the only one who's thought along those lines." she said, shaking her head. "One of them did try it. They had to put four stitches in his face and give him a pension."

"Take it easy." I broke in. "What makes you think this baby could get the stuff and what would you do with it if you got it?"

Ansell calmed down. "People all over the world are getting bitten by snakes." he explained. "Teopatli really works. Properly marketed it's worth a fortune. It would be an essential part of any traveller's equipment. I could charge what I liked for it."

I considered this. If the stuff was really a cure for any snake bite, then, of course, he had something. There was not only a fortune in it, but also a terrific news story.

"You've actually seen the stuff work?" I asked.

"Of course, I have."

"What's the difficulty? I mean why can't you get hold of it."

Ansell snorted. "Quintl won't part. He's this Indian fells I'm telling you about. For fifteen years I've been after him, but the old devil just grins at me."

"Where do I come in on this?" Myra asked cautiously.

"I saw Quintl a couple of weeks ago." Ansell said. "He tried to fox me as usual, but I put a lot of pressure on him and finally got him in a corner. He told me that soon he was going to die. But before he died, a Sun Virgin would come to him and take from him all his secrets. She would have great powers of magic, her hair would be like beaten gold and her skin like the frozen heights of Ixtacchiuatl. It was just his way of putting me off, but now I've seen Miss Shumway, I guess we could frighten him into talking."

Myra sat up. "You don't want me to impersonate a Sun Virgin, do you?" she demanded.

"Why not?" Ansell asked, his eyes shining. "With your tricks, your looks and a little bluff, you could do it on your head."

I leaned forward suddenly. "Where's this village you're talking about, Doc?" I asked.

"It's ten miles from Pepoztlan."

That gave me an idea, but I wanted time to think about it. "Listen, Doc." I said. "Let Miss Shumway and me talk it over, will you? I think you've got an idea that'd make a great news story. It'd be fine publicity for you if you get the stuff, but I want to sort out the angles."

Ansell got to his feet. "I'll give you half an hour." he said. "I take it that you won't run out on me?"

"We'll be here when you come back." I told him.

"Hey!" Myra said. "Whose side are you on?"

I grinned at her. "Pipe down for a minute, will you?"

Bogle got to his feet after Ansell had shaken him. "Talk!" he said bitterly. "That's all we do. We came out here so I could kick this dame's teeth in and what happens? We sit around and talk! Now, we go away so *they* can talk! Don't we ever do anything else, but talk in this gawdamn place?"

"Cheer up." I said. "You're getting so many wrinkles, before long you'll have to screw your hat on."

He glared at me, then turning on his heel, he slouched after Ansell. They crossed the square and disappeared into a beer parlour that stood at the corner.

I settled further, into my chair. "Well." I said, "you can never tell, can you. How do you like being a Sun Virgin?"

Myra's reply was unprintable.

FIVE

Well, I talked her into it. It took a long time and it was as easy as cracking rock with a sponge.

Some men like strong-minded women. They say they know just where they are with them. Me … I give them away with a box of crackerjacks. The trouble with a girl who knows her own mind is she's one jump ahead of you all the time. If you want to fox her into anything, you've got to do a double jump, and like as not you end up by buying yourself a truss.

Anyway, I sold her in the end. That's all that matters. I got her to see that for a couple of days' work, she'd save herself a stretch in jail and maybe make herself a load of jack.

Why bother with details? It's action that counts. I had a lot to think about and a lot to do, but that's not your worry. All you want to know is how it worked out, not how I did it.

Briefly then, the four of us agreed to put up at the hotel. It was as good a place as any, and until we had worked out the details of our campaign, it was no use us floating around the countryside like peas on a knife. We got ourselves rooms and we settled down. As soon as I was alone, I put a call through to Maddox. When I told him that I'd found the girl, I thought he was going to have a stroke. It seemed he hadn't got his story fixed and he wasn't nearly ready for me to bring her in. Then again, he was dead set on her being kidnapped by bandits because he'd worked out a swell story how she had been carried off from her hotel by thirty desperadoes.

I told him what I had in mind and that slackened the pressure on his arteries. I kept talking and I could hear his blood pressure going down. After a while, he said I was smart and finally he ended up by wanting to kiss me.

The set-up was this. I'd take the girl to Pepoztlan and get the snake-bite angle fixed. That alone would make a swell story. On her way back from Pepoztlan, Myra would be snatched by a bunch of greasers. I knew a little greaser who lived in the hills and who would be glad to do the job for a couple of hundred bucks. I'd take a few photos and then pull a rescue stunt. The rest was plain sailing. The whole business was to be completed within a week.

Maddox thought it was a swell idea. The snake-bite business excited him and he talked about buying himself in. I didn't discourage him, but I made up my mind that if any money was to be made out of thin I was going to be the guy to cash in. I got him to let me spend anything within reason— my reason and not his—and then I hung up. That was that part fixed up.

Then I put a call through to Paul Juden and wised him up on the deal. I told him where to send my bag, demanded some money, and asked him how he was making out with the nurse. He said he'd do everything I wanted and the nurse business was just a gag. He knew I knew his wife.

When I'd done all that, I thought I'd go along and have a talk with Myra. I wanted to know more about this girl. I wanted to take the corners off our friendship and find out just how strong her mind was. So I went along to her room, and put my head round the door. She wasn't there.

I found her messing around the Cadillac under the shade of a banana tree. She looked over her shoulder when she heard me coming and then lowered the hood of the car.

"Come on." I said. "See those mountains? Well, let's go out and look at 'em. I want to stand in the open with the wind against my face and feel that I'm somebody."

She gave me an old-fashioned look, but something must have caught at her imagination because she got into the car without a word. I sat by her side and we jolted gently over the cobbles, through the square on to the main road that led out of Orizaba.

We didn't say anything until we reached the mountain road and when we began to climb, with a sheer drop down into the valley whizzing past our off-wheels, she said suddenly, "We could go on and on like this and we wouldn't have to worry about anything. And when we're tired of each other we could say good-bye and both of us would have still less to worry about."

"And the world wouldn't have any snake-bite ointment and you and I wouldn't feel very happy about it." I said.

"You don't really believe that stuff, do you?"

"I guess I do." I said. "Besides, didn't you promise the old man that you'd play along with him?"

She laughed gaily. "You a newspaper man and you talk about promise." she said. "That's a laugh!"

I looked at her. "What do you want to do, double-cross the old geezer?"

"I'm nor even thinking about him." she returned, slowing the car as we ran past a line of ancient, weatherbeaten houses and refreshment booths, with their awnings over the street. "No one dictates my life. I'm just saying we could go on from here and not go back."

The Cadillac began to mount again, leaving the small town behind. I had no idea what the name of the town was and cared less. We were heading for the wooded country and signs of human life began to thin out. The few Indians, jogging along the roadside, straddling the rumps of their *burros*, became fewer as we went on. Then suddenly she slowed down, swerved off the road and pulled up under the shadow of the forest fringe.

"Let's get out." she said.

I followed her as she moved away from the car, and sank down beside her on the parched, brown grass. She looked up at the brilliant sky, screwing up her eyes against the brightness of the sun, then she heaved a little, contented sigh.

I found her disturbing. I don't know what it was, but her metallic hair, gleaming in the sun, the white column of her throat, the curve of her figure under the blood-red shirt, her small finely boned hands and the courage of her mouth and chin got me. I found myself groping back into the past to remember any one woman I had known who looked as good as this kid. Pale ghosts paraded in my mind, but none of them clicked.

"Look, sister …" I said.

"Just a minute." she interrupted, facing me. "Would you mind not calling me sister? I'm no sister of yours. I've got a name. Myra Shumway. We met. Remember?"

"You'd've been a better girl if you'd been my sister." I said grimly.

"All you tough guys think of is violence. That's your only reply to a woman, isn't it?"

"What do you expect, when they feed us hot tongue and cold shoulder?" I asked grinning. "Besides, a little violence works."

"Get me out of this." she said, suddenly turning so that she was close to me. "You can do it. I don't want to go on with it."

I thought, "If you knew half what I've got lined up for you sweetheart, you'd be climbing trees." But, I just shrugged. "Don't let's go over that again." I said. "You'll thank me in a week or so. You're not scared of this Quinn guy, are you?"

"I'm not scared of anything on two legs …" she began.

"I remember, you told me."

"But, it's crazy." she went on. "It's all right to talk about it, but actually doing it … why, it's crazy! I can't speak the language. They'll know I'm a phoney."

"You leave it to Doc. He's got it all worked out." I said. "Why should you worry?"

She fumbled in her bag and took out a deck of cards. "There's something about you." she said, flipping the cards through her fingers so that they looked like an arc of a rainbow. "I wonder what it is?"

"When I was very young." I returned, lolling back on my elbow, "my mother used to rub me in bear fat. It built up my personality."

She leaned forward and took four aces out of my breast pocket. "Would you say I'm a serious young woman?"

I watched the cards flutter through her slim fingers. "Yeah." I said, feeling my throat thicken suddenly. "More than that. I'd say you were a remarkable young woman."

She looked at me with quick interest, "Really?"

"Hmm, I guess so. We're going to know each other an awful lot better before we wave good-bye. Do you know that?"

She reached over to take the King of Spades from my cuff. I could smell the scent in her hair. It reminded me of a summer spent in England in an old country garden full of lilac trees. "Are we?" she said.

I caught her hand and pulled her close to me. She didn't resist, but let me pull her across the small space that divided us. "I think so." I said, sliding my arm under her shoulders. "An awful lot better."

We lay like that, close to each other, and I could see the overhead clouds reflected in her eyes.

"Will you like that?" she asked, her lips close to mine.

"Maybe—I don't know." Then I kissed her, pressing my mouth hard on hers.

She lay still. I wished she would close her eyes and relax, but she didn't. I could feel the hard muscles in her back resisting me. Her lips felt hard, tight and child-like against mine.

She made no effort to push me away. Kissing her like that was as good as kissing the back of my hand. I dropped onto my elbow again, releasing her. "All right." I said. "Forget it."

She shifted away from me. Her fingers touched her lips carefully, "You meant that to be something, didn't you?" she asked, curling her legs under her and adjusting her skirt.

"Sure." I said. "But what of it? Sometimes it's all right, but not this time. The trick is not to rush this kind of thing."

"No." she said, looking at me seriously. "The trick is not to do it at all."

Then I thought what's wrong with me? What am I trying to do? I'd got a job on my hands. I'd got 25,000 dollars just around the corner with my name on it, and here I am gumming up my chance trying to neck a kid that meant as much to me as last year's income tax return. I guess it was her hair. I was always a sucker for blondes.

"Changed your mind about knowing me awfully well?" she said, watching me intently.

"I guess not." I said. "I'll keep trying. Did I tell you about the red-head I met in New Orleans?"

"You don't have to." she said, scrambling to her feet, "I can imagine it,"

"Not this red-head." I returned, looking up at her. "She had a figure like an hour glass. Boy! Did she make every minute count!"

She began moving slowly towards the Cadillac. "So you're not going to help me?" she said. "Not after I've been nice to you?"

"What's wrong?" I got to my feet and we both walked towards the Cadillac. "You were feeling fine about it this morning."

"I've thought about it." she said, getting into the car. "I don't like the idea any more."

"Give it a chance." I urged, feeling the heat coming at me from off the dusty road. "Be big minded about it."

"What are you getting out of it?" she said, starting the engine "You're selling it too hard to be disinterested."

"A story." I said. "And, Pie-crust, if you were a newspaper man you'd know just what that meant. It's going to be a beautiful story, with lots of publicity, and they'll even print my picture."

"You never give a thought to those folk who have their meat wrapped in your newspaper, do you?" Myra returned, driving slowly back the way we came.

I winced. "I wish you wouldn't." I said. "Wisecracks spoil your romantic appeal."

She slightly increased the speed of the car as we began to descend the steep winding road. Just ahead of us was the little mountain town we had already passed on our way up.

"Let's stop and buy some beer." I said. "My tonsils are dusty."

We entered the town, drove along the cobbled main road, ignored the group of Indians, lounging behind heaps of vari-coloured flowers which they stretched towards us, and pulled up outside a little beershop. There was a long wrought-iron table and bench outside the shop, shaded by a gaily covered awning. A smell of beer and stale bodies came through the doorway.

"We won't go in." I said, sitting at the table. "That smell reminds me of a newspaper office."

She came and sat by my side and pulled off her wide straw hat, which she laid carefully on the table.

A thin, elderly Mexican came out of the shop and bowed to us. There was an odd, worried look in his eyes that made me wonder if he was in trouble.

I ordered beer and he went away without saying anything. "Now, there's a guy who looks like he's got more than his hat on his mind." I said, opening my coat and picking the front of my shirt carefully off my chest.

"These greasers are all alike." Myra returned, indifferently. "They worry over which way a flea will jump. At one time I was sorry for them, but now, I don't worry—" She broke off and looked past me, her eyes widening.

I glanced over my shoulder.

Standing in the doorway of the shop was the fattest man I'd ever seen. He was not only fat, but he was big with it. I guess he must have been seven inches over six foot. He was wearing the usual straw sombrero, a *sarape* hung over his great shoulders, but I could see his neat black suit and his soft Mexican riding boots ornamented with silver inlay.

He leaned against the doorway, a cigarette banging from his thick lips and his black eyes on Myra.

I particularly noticed his eyes. They were flat like the eyes of a snake. I didn't like the look of this party. He didn't belong to the town. I was sure of that. There was too much class about him. I didn't like the leer he as telegraphing to Myra.

"Isn't he cute?" Myra said to me. "I bet he was twins before his mother cooked him in a too hot bath."

"Listen, Apple blossom." I said, keeping my voice low, "keep your funny stuff for me, will you? That hombre won't like it."

The fat man picked his cigarette out of his mouth and flicked it across at me. It landed on the table between us.

If any other greaser had done that, I'd have pinned his ears back, but I've got a superstition about hitting a guy twice my size. I've been over that with you before. But when that guy gets so that he's three times my size, I'll take an awful lot from him before I go into action.

Myra didn't mind pushing me into a fight. That's like a woman. They think uneven odds is a sign of chivalry.

"Why don't you poke that fat boy in his pantry?" she asked.

Maybe the guy couldn't speak anything but his own language, but how was I to know? The most unlikely people get educated these days.

"What do you want me to do?" I whispered. "Commit suicide?"

"You're not going to let a pail of lard insult me?" Myra said, her eyes suddenly flashing. "Didn't you see what he did?" She pointed to the cigarette end that smouldered near her hand.

"That little thing?" I said, hastily. "Why, that was an accident. He didn't mean anything. You pipe down. It's dames like you who cause revolutions."

Just then the thin Mexican came out of the shop. He edged round the fat party as if he were passing close to a black widow. Then he set two beers in front of us and faded back to the shop fast.

The fat party was smoking again and he took his cigarette out and flipped it once more. I had my hand over my glass as the smoking cigarette curled through the air, but it dropped into Myra's glass.

I took her glass before she could say anything and gave her mine. "There you are, sweetheart, and for the love of Mike don't make anything of it."

Myra's face scared me. She'd gone a little white and her eyes looked like those of a cat in the dark.

The fat party suddenly laughed. It was a high tinny sound that went with his sideboards and pencilled moustache. "The señor has milk in his veins." he said, slapping his thick thigh and looking as if he was having the time of his life.

I considered getting up and giving him one, but something warned me off. I've knocked around this country for some time and I've seen plenty of tough greasers, but this party was something special. If I was going to do anything, I'd have to do it with a gun. That was the kind of guy he was and I didn't have a gun with me.

That didn't put Myra off. She gave him a look that would have stopped a runaway horse and said, "Go jump into a lake, you fat sissy; if one won't hold you, jump into two."

You could have heard a feather settle on the ground.

The fat party stopped laughing. "You've got a very big mouth, little rabbit." he said. "You should be careful how you use it."

Boy! Could that guy look mean?

"Get out of the sun, fat boy." Myra said. "Before your dome melts. Take the air—drift—scram—dust off."

The fat party put one hand under his *sarape.* I guess he was going after his arsenal, so I said quickly, "We don't want any trouble, pal, we're just going."

But, he wasn't looking at me. He wasn't even moving any more. He just stood like a great block of granite with his eyes sticking out of his head like long-stemmed toadstools.

I looked at Myra. She had her hands on the table and between her cupped fingers was the head of a little green snake. It darted its spade-shaped head in a striking movement and its forked tongue flickered in and out in a way that gave me the heebies. Then she opened her hands and the snake wasn't there any more and she smiled at the fat party as if they'd known each other for a long time.

I wish you could have seen his face. One minute he was all brag, meanness and confidence and then, in a moment, he was a deflated bag of wind. He covered his eyes with his hand and then shook his head. He seemed to hitch himself together with an effort.

"Didn't you hear me the first time?" she said to him. "Beat it. You're using too much air."

Then the thin elderly Mexican came out quickly and said something to the fat party. He looked sick as he pointed down the road.

The fat party followed his trembling finger and then glared over at us. "We meet again." he said. "Especially will I meet the señorita. She has too big a mouth. I put a hornet in it and sew her lips together." and he went quickly into the shop, leaving the thin elderly Mexican watching a cloud of dust that was coming up the road at a pretty fast lick towards us.

I eased my collar. "Did you get that line about the hornet?" I said. "And you had to crack wise with a guy like that."

She picked up her hat. "Skip It." she said. "He was as yellow as a canary."

"I know. And I loved the way he sang." I returned. "Come on, we'll beat it too. I have a feeling that there's a cloud of trouble heading our way."

We hardly got to the car before a bunch of Federal soldiers came galloping up.

A little guy with a complexion like stale cream cheese pulled his horse over to us and slid to the ground. He was an officer by the look of his dirty uniform and he seemed excited.

I said, "Hello." and automatically felt for my papers. But, he wasn't interested in me. He asked if we had seen a big fat guy anywhere around.

Myra opened her mouth, but I stumbled against her. My elbow hit her in the wind and that held her.

"No one around here." I said. "Maybe some one else has seen him. Have you asked?"

The officer spat in the dust. "They said he was here. Not five minutes ago." he said, fiddling with his revolver butt.

"Well, a lot can happen in five minutes." I said. "Maybe he was in a hurry. Who was he anyway?"

But the officer had lost interest in me and went over to the thin, elderly Mexican. I shoved Myra into the car and got in myself. I wanted to put a lot of space between me and likely trouble.

Myra had got her breath back. "Why didn't you tell him?" she demanded. "You're not scared of him, are you?"

"It's not a matter of being scared." I said starting the engine and throwing in the clutch. "I've been around in this country long enough never to interfere with anyone. It's paid me pretty well up to now, and I'm seeing that it continues to do so."

I sent the car snarling towards Orizaba.

Myra began to laugh. "Did you see that fat boy's face when I did the snake trick?"

"I did." I said grimly. "And I heard what he said about the hornet."

"So what? You don't think that means anything, do you?"

"I know it does." I replied. "A guy like that would do just that little thing and think nothing of it. The next time we meet, I'm going to shoot him first and apologize after."

The idea seemed to shock her and we went back to the hotel without saying another word.

Bogle was sitting on the verandah drinking beer and he waved to us as we came up the steps. "Where've you been?" he asked, putting his mug on the table and getting up. "Doc's worried sick. He thought you'd walked out on him."

Myra said, "Hello, Samuel. You ought to keep in the shade. The light's a little too hard on you."

Bogle watched her disappear into the hotel. He scowled at me. "One of these days she'll shoot her mouth off once too often." he said darkly. "Don't that prove you can't be too careful in picking a blonde? I knew a dame once with hair just like hers. Got the nicest mouth I've ever listened to. You oughta hear the drippy names she used to call me. You'd've been surprised."

It surprised me that Bogle had a sentimental streak in his make-up, but I didn't tell him so.

"Your love life bores me." I said, grinning at him. "Never mind about the drippy names. They won't get you any place. Where's Doc?"

Bogle sniffed. "Oh, he's feeding his face. I didn't feel hungry, but maybe I'd better do something about it now."

"Come and feed with me." I said. "No sense in eating alone."

Bogle brooded darkly. "I'd rather eat alone than with that blonde wise guy." he said at last. "I'll wait. When I sit down to a meal I like to enjoy myself."

"If that's how you feel." I returned and moved towards the lounge.

Just then a kid came quietly up the verandah steps. He was a little Indian boy, very dirty, wearing a dirty white shirt and a pair of ragged trousers. He carried a small wooden box in one of his grubby hands and he looked at Bogle with a calculating eye.

Bogle smirked at him. "Hullo, son." he said. "Coming to have a talk with old Uncle Sam?"

The kid stared at him thoughtfully with his head on one side and shuffled his bare feet on the verandah floor.

Bogle looked over at me. "I like kids." he said simply, exploring his teeth with his finger nail. "This little punk's all right, ain't he?"

The kid shuffled a few paces nearer. "Shine, Johnny?" he said, hopefully.

"You don't have to be scared of me." Bogle said, leering at him. "Come and tell Uncle Sam all about it."

The kid didn't seem full of confidence, but he put his box down and said again, "Shine, Johnny?"

Bogle stared at him. "Wadjer mean … shine?"

"He wants to shine your shoes, you dope." I said, grinning. "He's got beyond Uncle Samuel's bedside chats for kiddies."

Bogle looked disappointed. "Gee! I thought the kid was lonely."

"Shine, Johnny?" the kid repeated monotonously.

"He's got a one-track mind, ain't he?" Bogle said, then seeing the kid was a bit restless, he waved his hand grandly. "Sure, help yourself, son." and he stretched forward one of his great feet.

The kid flopped on the floor and began turning up Bogle's trouser ends.

"Well, I'm hungry." I said. "I'll tell 'em to leave you something."

"What'll I give the little punk?" Bogle asked, watching the kid polishing away at his shoe.

"What you like." I returned. "These kids ain't particular."

Another kid in a dirty red shirt came sidling up the steps. He took one look at Bogle and ran over and shoved White Shirt out of the way.

Bogle blinked. "What do you think you're doing?" he demanded, as Red Shirt began to lay out his shining materials.

"You've got competition." I said, feeling that I might enjoy this. I leaned against the wall and prepared to watch. From past experience I knew what leeches these kids were, once you encouraged them.

Bogle looked quite gratified. "I told you kids liked me." he said, smirking. "They'll even fight over me."

He'd got something because White Shirt recovering from his surprise grabbed Red Shirt by the throat and put on a squeeze.

Bogle was quite shocked. He dragged them apart and held them, one in each great fist.

"Hey!" he said. "This ain't the way to behave. Now, listen, you two ..."

Red Shirt kicked out at White Shirt and succeeded in landing a bone shattering smack on Bogle's leg. Bogle let the kids go like they were red hot and clasped his leg with a grunt of anguish.

The two kids began to mix it all over the verandah.

"Holy Moses!" Bogle gasped. "Can't you stop 'em?"

"Don't bring me into it." I said, watching the kids with interest. "I'll just be the historian."

Bogle got to his feet and managed to separate the kids. "Shut up, you two!" he said fiercely. "No fighting! Now, listen, you can do a shoe apiece. How's that?"

Neither of them understood what he was saying, but they quieted down and looked at him with bright, intent eyes.

Bogle seemed pleased with his tactics. "See that?" he said, sitting down again. "I can handle kids. All you've got to do is reason with 'em."

He was hardly in his seat when the two kids streaked at him and grabbed his right leg. They began thumping each other and dragging his leg backwards and forwards. Bogle hung on to the table, his eyes popping in alarm.

They struggled first one way and then another, worrying at his leg like a couple of bull terriers.

"Reason with 'em, Sam." I said, weak with laughter.

He beat them off finally with his hat and they stood back, breathing heavily. If he'd've been a nice juicy pork chop with a little frill at the end of it, they couldn't have eyed him with more interest.

As they edged towards him again, he raised his hat threateningly. "Keep off, you punks." he growled, then catching my eye. "What the hell do you find funny in this? Tell 'em to behave themselves."

I came over and explained to the kids that they could each clean one of Bogle's shoes and there was no need to fight about it.

They considered this for a moment, then they wanted to know if the payment would also be divided.

I referred this to Bogle.

"Aw, the hell with it." he said, losing patience. "Tell 'em to dust. I thought they were nice kids. Money's all these brats think of. I don't want to be bothered with 'em."

"Hey! Where's all this stuff about liking kids?" I said severely. "You'll disappoint 'em, you know."

Bogle fanned himself with his hat. "Iszatso?" he said violently. "What about me? They nearly broke my gawdamn leg."

"Have it your own way." I said and explained to the kids that Bogle had changed his mind. When it had sunk in, they started howling at the tops of their voices.

They even put my teeth on edge.

"Now, do you see what you've done?" I said.

"Get 'em out of here." Bogle said, confused. "They'll raise the whole neighbourhood."

Myra and Doc Ansell came running out.

"What's going on?" Ansell asked, looking over the top of his sun glasses in surprise.

"Notin'." Bogle said between his teeth. "Just a couple of kids bawling. That ain't anything, is it?"

Myra looked at him with withering scorn. "So you even bully children, you big cheese." she said indignantly. "You ought to be ashamed of yourself!"

Bogle closed his eyes. "You again?" he said, tapping ominously on the table. "Every time I open my mouth, I get a broadcast from you. Listen, these kids want to shine my shoes. Well, I don't want my shoes shined see? Does that call for anything from you?"

The kids stopped howling and looked at Myra hopefully. They sensed that she was on their side.

"And why don't you want them shined?" Myra demanded. "Just look at them! They're like exhumed coffins."

Bogle loosened his collar. "I don't care what they look like. I don't want them shined." he said, furiously. "If I want them shined, I'll shine 'em my-self."

"How ridiculous!" Myra said. "I think you're just being mean. You don't want to pay these kids to shine your shoes. You want them to do it for nothing."

Bogle picked up his pewter mug and flattened it between his hands. "I've changed my mind about having my shoes shined." he said with a hiss.

"Changed your mind?" Myra repeated. "Who did you find crazy enough to swap with you?"

Bogle flexed his fingers. He seemed to have developed acute asthma.

"There's no need to lose our tempers." Ansell joined in, soothingly. "If Bogle doesn't want his shoes shined, then there's nothing more to be said. We came out because we thought someone was being hurt. Come along, Myra, well go back to our meal."

"You might do those kids a lot of harm if you frustrate them." Myra said warmly. "Haven't you ever heard of repression?"

Bogle blinked at her.

"I wouldn't have it on my conscience." Myra went on. "All for the sake of a peso. Don't tell me you can't afford it or have you a hole in your sock?"

"Yeah, yeah." Bogle said, becoming dazed. "Why don't I let 'em shine them? What do I care? Let 'em do anything."

"There now." Myra said. "After all this fuss." She smiled at the two kids and pointed to Bogle's shoes.

They were on him like terriers on a rat. I've never seen anything like it. Bogle, the two kids and the chair went over with a bang that made Bogle's teeth rattle. The two kids fought Bogle, fought each other and went back and fought Bogle again. They pulled off one of his shoes and threw it into the Square. Then they twisted his toes.

Bogle just lay on his back making a humming noise like he had swallowed a bee.

The kids fastened onto his other shoe. They smeared blacking on them-selves, on the floor and on Bogle. White Shirt got so excited that he jumped up and down on Bogle's chest.

Myra and I just clung together and wept.

Ansell took off his glasses. "I do hope they'll be careful." he said mildly. "They'll hurt him in a moment."

As soon as White Shirt had got his breath back, he seized Bogle's other leg. When he found the shoe was missing, he threw it down and rushed at Red Shirt.

Red Shirt didn't like the look in his eye, and tucking Bogle's foot under his arm, he tore off in a circle, spinning Bogle round like a top. Then quite suddenly they both seemed to lose interest in their work and they quit.

Maybe, they thought they were giving too much value for money. They stopped rushing round in circles, looked at each other, nodded, regarded Bogle without interest and then put their shining materials away. They stood over Bogle, smiling at him, with two grubby hands held out for payment.

"You'd better pay 'em." I said weakly. "Or they might start all over again."

Hastily he dug out a few coins which he threw at the kids. While they were chasing the money, he got painfully to his feet and inspected a long tear in his trousers.

"Don't worry about that, Samuel." Myra said. "It was time you got yourself a new suit anyway."

Bogle gave her a blank look. Then he limped painfully across the verandah, into the Square and collected his other shoe. He put it on and regarded his feet with a sour eye. Before, his shoes certainly had looked dusty. Now they looked ready for the ash can.

"I hope you're all satisfied." he said, in a low, strangled voice.

"Just look at those kids." Myra said, wiping her eyes. "They're as happy as larks."

"Yeah." Bogle said, creeping back slowly on to the verandah. "As happy as larks."

Myra heaved a contented sigh. "Well, I enjoyed that." she said. "I wouldn't have missed it for anything. You ought to be pleased you made those kids happy, Samuel. You're quite a nice piece of cheese after all."

She waved to the two kids who were standing watching with bright eyes and then she turned to go back into the lounge.

Bogle took out a silver peso and held it up so the kids could see it, then with a tired but triumphant gleam in his eyes he pointed to Myra's shoes.

They were off the mark like a streak of lightning. Myra hadn't even time to run for it. She gave a wail of terror and then her legs flew up and she came down on the floor with a jar that sounded like music in Bogle's ears.

She disappeared under the two kids.

Bogle sat down and relaxed. There was a sharp, ripping sound of tearing linen. It seemed to do Bogle a power of good. For the first time, since I met him, he looked happy.

"Make a good job of it." he said airily, and then catching my eye, he added, "Didn't I tell you they were all right little punks?"

SIX

The next two days kept me pretty busy. We had decided to go to Pepoztlan on the following Thursday which was just three days ahead of us. There was a lot to arrange. We had to get Myra a dress that would make her look like a Sun Virgin. That had to come from Mexico City and after some trouble Juden got it for us. I reckon his nurse friend had a hand in getting it, because I'm sure Juden would never have found such a humdinger by himself. Even Myra was pleased.

The dress was a cross between a nightgown and an Aimee McPherson surplice. It was simple, but it fitted her and she looked swell in it. There's nothing like white silk to set off blonde hair and Myra looked like she had never said a bad word or done a bad deed when she got it on.

"That kid looks like a saint." Doc said to me when she had gone to take it off. The old guy was nearly crying. "She looks like a saint."

"If you mean a Saint Bernard, I'm with you." Bogle grunted. "That camouflage don't pull wool over my eyes."

I didn't worry what Bogle thought. He didn't count. Ansell was right. Myra looked the part and if she didn't startle this Indian fella then I'd give up.

Apart from fixing her up, rehearsing her in the part and choosing a few good showy tricks out of her repertoire, I had to fix the kidnapping angle.

This wasn't so easy. I wasn't going to let either Ansell or Bogle in on this. I had to find an excuse so that I could get into touch with this Mexican I knew and wise him up what was wanted.

Once I got hold of him, it was easy. He jumped at the idea. I'd known him for some time. His name was Bastino and he was just a small-time bandit who got nowhere. I'd done him a good turn once and I knew I could trust him. All he had to do was to kidnap Myra from the inn where I had arranged for us to stay at Pepoztlan after she had returned from her trip to Quintl. I fixed everything and promised to let him know just when to pull it off. I gave him a hundred bucks as a down payment and promised him another three hundred if he pulled it off.

The set-up looked sweet to me. But, on the morning that we were to move to Pepoztlan, something happened that altered the whole plan.

We were just getting into the car when a guy from the Post Office came running over with his eyes popping out of his head.

"Now, what's the trouble?" I said, going halfway to meet him.

He gave me a telegram and stood back, watching my face with excited interest. I shoved a half a buck into his hand and returned to the car, opening the telegram as I walked.

It was from Juden. When I read what he had to say, I cursed softly under my breath.

The other three watched me.

"This tears it." I said, leaning into the car. "Revolution's broken out in the hills and I've got to cover it."

"What do you mean ... revolution?" Ansell said, sharply.

"Another uprising." I said in disgust. "Can't these guys keep the peace for five minutes? A bunch of bandits swooped on some Federal troops and cut their heads off. Federal troops are on their way from the capital to deal with them. I've got to get over there and give a report on the battle. It may last a week."

"You can't do that." Ansell protested. "I've fixed everything with Quintl. If we don't loose Myra on him now, we'll never do it."

I thought for a moment. He was right. But, on the other hand, I'd got to look after the *Recorder.* The great American public would want to hear more about these Federal soldiers who had had their heads cut off. You don't read about a little thing like that every day.

"Well, I'm sorry." I said. "But you'll have to do this without me. It's simple enough and I think I ought to be through in a few days. I'll meet you at Pepoztlan. Get Myra to see this Quintl and then wait at the inn for me. Okay?"

Myra said, "So you're going to walk out on me after all?"

"Now, don't make it difficult." I pleaded. "You'll do fine. I know you will." I put my hand on hers, "And wait for me, kid, I want to see you again."

"If you ain't in a hurry, I'll get out and heave up." Bogle said, grimacing in disgust. "This sloppy talk gives me a pain."

That seemed to settle it. Myra, her face hardening, started the Cadillac. "Okay." she said. "Run after your stupid little revolution. Do you think I care?" and she drove away fast, leaving a cloud of dust behind her.

That was that.

As I might have expected, the Federal troops made a mess of it. When they got to the place where their comrades had been decapitated there was no sign of the bandits and no sign of any bodies. I wasted a couple of days riding around with them, and then they got sick of it and gave up. All I got out of it was a photograph of the place and a dreary report of the unsuccessful hunt. I sent those off, said good-bye to the Captain of the troop who seemed glad to see me go and rode over to Pepoztlan as fast as I could go.

Pepoztlan was a tiny village on the mountain side. The main road had been hewn out of the mountain itself and the few houses of pink stone over-looked the exposed plateau beyond which lay the Indian settlement.

I found Ansell and Bogle resting in the shade at the inn. It wasn't much of a place, but the wine was good and they did manage to carve up an oc-casional chicken. I'd been there before, so I knew more or less what I was in for.

I arrived on Saturday afternoon. Since Myra was to see Quintl on the pre-vious Thursday, I thought the whole thing had been settled. My next im-mediate job was to get in touch with Bastino and fix the kidnapping.

It came as a surprise when I rode into the patio to find only Ansell and Bogle there.

I slid off my horse, tossed the reins to an Indian and went over to them.

"Where's Myra?" I asked and I admit I felt anxious.

Both Ansell and Bogle looked a little sheepish. It was Ansell who did the talking. "She's still there." he said. "Sit down and have a drink."

"Yeah, this is real tiger's breath." Bogle said, filling a horn mug and shov-ing it into my hand.

"What do you mean … she's still there?"

"She's made a hit with Quintl." Ansell said uneasily. "They wanted her to stay."

I looked from one to the other, "I don't get it. How long do you think she's going to stay there?"

Bogle took off his hat and scratched his head, "Brother." he said, "them Indians scared the pants off me. I didn't want to argue with them."

"Quiet, Bogle." Ansell said sharply. "Let me explain."

"You'd better." I said, feeling mad. "What the hell's been happening?"

"The truth is, she overdid it!" Ansell said. "I warned her, but she kept pulling tricks and I guess the Indians fell for her. They think she's a rein-carnated goddess."

"So what?"

"They won't let her go." Ansell said miserably. "We tried to get her away, but they got nasty about it."

"Knives." Bogle said, with a little shiver. "Great big knives as long as my arm. I tell you, Bud, they scared me."

"So you left her, eh?" I said, feeling blood pounding in my ears. "That was a swell thing to do. What sort of men are you—you yellow-gutted monkeys!"

Ansell mopped his face with his handkerchief. "I was waiting for you to come and then I thought we'd turn out the Federal troops." he explained.

"They'll take a month to get going." I said angrily. "I thought you knew this Indian. Why didn't you tell me you couldn't trust him?"

"It's not that." Ansell said quickly. "I'd trust him with my life. It was her fault. You ought to have seen the tricks she did. They were remarkable. I've never seen ..."

I got to my feet. "We're getting guns and we're going right over there and we'll bring her back. Do you get it?"

Bogle's eyes popped. "Just the three of us?" he said faintly.

"Just the three of us." I returned. "Get horses, while I get the guns."

"You heard what I said about the knives?" Bogle said. "Great big stickers, as long as my arm."

"I heard." I returned. "We got this girl into the mess. We'll get her out of it."

I left them and dug out the innkeeper. "What have you got in the way of guns, pal?" I asked, after we had shaken hands and patted each other.

"Guns?" His little eyes widened, then seeing my look, he grinned. "More trouble, señor?" he said. "Always trouble with the white señor."

"Slow up on the chatter and give me some action." I said shoving him towards the house.

I got action and I got three express rifles and three .38 automatics.

By the time I got back the other two had found horses. I gave than a gun and automatic each and then climbed on to my horse.

"You wouldn't like to put it off until to-morrow?" Ansell said hopefully. "It's going to be hot on the plateau right now."

"It'll be hot all right." I said and rode out of the patio.

The way to the Indian settlement lay across the exposed plateau which was broken only by patches of forest. There was hardly any shade.

After an hour of heat and flies we came to the Indian village. The sordid settlement shocked me. There were six mud huts, thatched with banana leaves. They stood forlornly in the bright sunlight and the whole place seemed deserted.

I jerked my horse to a standstill and sat staring at the huts. Doc and Bogle came up and halted their animals by my side.

"Is this it?" I said. "Are you sure this is the place?"

"Yeah." Bogle said, wrinkling his nose. "Not like Palm Beach, is it?" He rested his arms on the saddle and leaned forward. "Not the kind of glamour parlour Goldilocks is used to."

"Button up!" I said, feeling furious with Ansell for even bringing Myra to such a dump, let alone leaving her here. If I'd gone with them, we wouldn't have gone through with it.

Ansell slid off his horse and walked slowly down the beaten path between the huts. Neither Bogle nor I moved. We sat, with our rifles forward, watching him.

"No one about." Ansell said, coming back. "Maybe they're hunting or something."

In spite of the heat, I suddenly felt my flesh creep, as if a cold hand had touched me.

"You'd better find her." I said quietly.

"Quintl's got a place further in the forest." Ansell said, urging his horse forward.

We followed him.

At the edge of the forest, amid scrub and stones, stood a solid little building made of grey rock.

"This is it." Ansell said, dismounting.

Bogle looked round. "This ain't a country to live in." he said uneasily. "There's something about this dump I don't like. Do you feel it, Bud?"

"Don't be a damned baby." I said sharply, although I, too, disliked the dank atmosphere of the settlement. I guess it was the complete stillness and the silence that gave me the jumps. Even the trees were motionless.

I dismounted and walked up to the rotten wooden door of the building and thumped on it with my clenched list. The heavy silence was broken only by the sound of my fist.

I stopped and listened. Sweat ran down my face with the exertion of beating on the door.

Ansell and Bogle stood a few yards behind me, watching.

"There's no one there." I said, stepping back. "They've taken her away."

"I can smell something like a dead horse." Bogle said suddenly, and he began drawing great breaths of air through his nose.

Ansell said: "For God's sake, keep quiet." He joined me at the door. "There must be someone there." he went on, pressing against the door. "There's no lock. It's bolted on the inside."

I drew back and aimed a kick at the door. It shivered but held firm. I don't know why it was, but I suddenly felt scared. I felt that something was going to happen over which I had no control, but in spite of this I was going to get into that hut.

I turned to Bogle, "Get off that damned horse and help me, you useless punk."

Glad to have something to do, Bogle hurriedly dismounted and came over. He examined the door and then drawing back, he crashed his shoulder against it. The door creaked loudly and Bogle's second charge shattered the bolt and the door crashed open.

A violent, nauseating smell seeped out of the hut. We staggered back before it.

"What is it?" I said, holding my hand over my mouth and nose.

"Someone's been dead in there for quite a time." Ansell said, his face going pale.

Bogle turned green, "I gotta weak stomach." he wailed, sitting down abruptly on the grass. "I can't stand this. I'm going to heave."

I glared round at Ansell. "She's not dead, is she?" I said.

"Don't get excited." Ansell said, struggling with his own nausea. "You wait here. I'll go in." He drew a deep breath and peered timidly into the darkness. His eyes, dazzled by the bright sunlight, could see nothing.

I shoved him aside. "Get out of my way." I said, and walked into the awful, stinking oven of darkness.

I stood just inside the room, breathing through my mouth, feeling the sweat running from me. At first, I couldn't see anything, then as my eyes became accustomed to the gloom I made out a figure sitting on the floor, propped up against the wall. It was Quintl.

The old Indian was wrapped in a dirty blanket. His head was sunk low on his chest and his hands lay stiffly on the mud floor. I fumbled for a match and with a shaky hand, I scratched a light from the rock wall. Moving forward, I peered down at the Indian, holding the little flame high above my head.

The whole of Quintl's face moved in putrefaction. Even the hair on his head seethed with putrefying life.

I started back, dropped the match and half blundered to the door. I had never seen such a disgusting, sickening sight and it seemed to draw my nerves into tight, writhing wires.

I stood gulping in the doorway, too sick even to speak.

Ansell shook my arm. "What is it?" he said, his voice was high pitched. "What are you looking like that for?"

"It's the Indian." I said, trying to control my heaving fluttering stomach. "He's dead. Don't look at him. It's the filthiest thing I've seen." I looked back into the darkness, my heart pounding against my side. "Where's Myra? There's no one in there—just the old Indian."

"There's another room." Ansell said, "Look, over to the right."

I fumbled for another match, struck it and went into the room again. I didn't look at the Indian. I could just see a dark opening at the far end of the room and I walked slowly towards it. Ansell followed me.

I paused at the doorway and peered in. The light from the match pierced the thick darkness for a few feet. I moved forward slowly and I stopped just by the door. The flame of the match flickered and went out.

I had a sudden feeling that this wasn't real. It was like a nightmare of ghostly unknown things that pressed round me in the darkness. If I had been alone, I should have run away. I should have turned and stumbled into the bright sunlight and I would never have gone back into that ghastly, frightening darkness. But Ansell was behind me. I could feel his hand on my arm and somehow I felt I could stand there with him so close to me.

"Do you hear anything?" he whispered.

I listened. The silence was so complete that all I could hear was the pounding of my heart and the little hurried gasps from Ansell.

I fumbled for a match and the bright flame lit the room for a moment, then it died down and the shadows closed in on me again.

In that moment of light I had seen a long starved shadow glide away from the light of the match. It was soundless, like a frightened spirit, and when the flame flickered and went out I was scared.

"There's someone in here." I said. "Doc, where are you?"

"Take it easy." Ansell said, again touching my arm. "I'm right behind you. Who was it?"

"I don't know." I found my hands were shaking so violently that I couldn't strike another match. I pressed the box into Ansell's fingers. "Get a light. There's someone or something in here."

"An animal?" Ansell whispered, his voice quavered.

"I don't know." I said between my teeth and drew the .38.

The match flared up. For a brief second, we again had a clear view of the room. Myra lay on a stretcher bed. Her eyes were closed and she was quite still. Something black and shapeless moved above her head, but as I stepped forward, it dissolved into dancing shadows made by the light of the match.

"Hold it higher." I said.

I could see now. There was no one else in the room except ourselves and Myra.

I shall never forget that brief glimpse I had of her. In the white, sparkling dress, her hair draped over her shoulders, and her cold, hard little face up-tilted towards the roof of the rock building, she looked like a beautiful Greek goddess.

But, right now, I hadn't eyes for that. Fear had seized me and dug into my brain with chilly, steel fingers.

"There was someone in here." I said, gripping Ansell's arm. "I know there was. Where did he go? Doc, hold that match up. He must be somewhere here."

Ansell paid no attention. He bent over Myra. "She's all right." he said in a dazed voice. "She's asleep! Asleep in this stink." He shook her gently, but she did not open her eyes. "Wake up!" he said, shaking her more roughly. "Wake up!"

I blundered over and pushed him away. Feverishly, I pulled Myra into a sitting position. Putting my arm under her knees, I swung her off the bed.

As I did so, something happened that I can never forget. Even now, I sit up in bed sometimes in a cold sweat when I dream about it. It had all the qualities of a bad nightmare.

As I pulled Myra off the bed, I felt something trying to get her away from me. It was as if Myra had become suddenly heavy and I couldn't quite hold her any more. It was as if two long arms were holding my legs so that it was difficult to walk.

But, I struggled on somehow and yelling to Bogle to get the horses, I came reeling out into the sunshine holding Myra tightly against me.

Bogle had scrambled to his feet. His eyes, like poached eggs, showed his panic "What's the matter?" he croaked.

Ansell shot out of the hut, white to the lips. He came running over to me and when he could get his breath he stammered: "Let me look at her."

"You leave her alone." I said. "You've done enough already. Here, Bogle, hold her while I mount." I climbed up on to my horse and Bogle hoisted Myra on to the saddle.

"What's the matter with her?" Bogle said. There was a note of anxiety in his voice.

"I don't know." I said, wheeling away from him. "Let's get out of here. If I have any more of this stink, I'll go crazy."

Kicking my horse into a canter, I rode out across the broad plateau. Ansell and Bogle followed closely behind me.

Once clear of the Indian village, I pulled up in the last of the shade before crossing the plateau. I slid to the ground, supporting Myra and made her as comfortable as I could under a tree.

"Take a look at her, Doc." I said uneasily, holding her warm hand in mine.

Ansell came and knelt beside me, while Bogle gathered the bridles of our horses and stood uneasily, shifting from one foot to the other.

"What's the matter with her?" I asked. "Do something, will you?"

Ansell took her pulse, raised her eyelid and sat back on his heels. "She's in some kind of trance." he said slowly. "We'll have to get her to bed as quickly as we can. There's nothing I can do here." He looked at her again and scratched his chin. "She's quite normal. Pulse good, breathing regular." He shook his head. "We'll have to go on. The risk of sunstroke's too great out here."

"What's been happening?" I said. "Why is she like this? What's the explanation?"

Ansell stood up. "I don't know. It's no use talking now. We've got to get her back to the inn."

I picked her up again. "Do you think she'll stand the journey?"

"Don't worry, man. I tell you there's nothing the matter with her. She's in a hypnotic trance. She'll wake up in a few hours."

I looked at him searchingly, saw the worried look in his eyes and I felt a chill of despair. "I hope you're right." I said and gave her to him to hold while I mounted.

The journey across the plateau was hard going. The heat cut into us and I found Myra's weight exhausting, but we made it at last.

Myra was still unconscious when we reached the inn.

Bogle said uneasily: "I don't like seeing her like that even though she's a sour puss. It don't seem natural."

While he was helping me dismount, Ansell went on in and called the innkeeper. He came out in a few minutes. "They're getting a room ready for her." he said. "Bring her up. I'll show you where it is."

The innkeeper's wife was waiting in a small, quiet room which was cool and shady and flowers stood on a table by the window.

I put Myra gently on the bed. "Look after her." I said to the woman. "Get her to bed."

Leaving Ansell to help the woman, I went downstairs and joined Bogle on the verandah. I ordered two large beers and then sat down a little wearily on the iron bench by Bogle's side.

"Think she'll be all right?" Bogle asked.

I was surprised at the concern in his voice.

"I guess so." I said, not feeling much like talking. "I don't know."

There was a pause, then Bogle said: "What do you think was in that hut?"

I mopped my face and neck with my handkerchief. "I haven't thought about it." I returned shortly, because I didn't want to think about it.

He fidgeted for a moment. "You don't believe that witchcraft stuff Doc was talking about, do you?"

"Hell, no!"

He seemed relieved. "Do you think she's got the snake-bite dope?"

I'd forgotten all about that. I sat up with a jerk. I remembered that I'd have Bastino on my hands to-morrow. He would be coming down from the hills to discuss the final move for the kidnapping. Thinking of Myra up there in that little room and seeing in my mind her white, strained face made the kidnapping impossible. I couldn't submit her to another shock. Then, on the other hand, there was the 25,000 dollars I'd have to pass up and maybe get fired for queering Maddox's stunt.

It seemed to me that I was in a sweet jam, all of a sudden.

Before I could begin to think about it, Ansell came down.

"How is she?" I asked, hurriedly getting to my feet.

"There's nothing to worry about." Ansell said, sitting down. He snapped his fingers at the little Mexican girl who acted as waiter and pointed to my half-finished beer. "She'll be okay in a couple of hours. She's beginning to recover now." He shook his head, "I can't make this out. How did Quintl die? Was he wounded or anything?"

I grimaced. "I don't even want to think about him." I said. "How long do you think he's been dead?"

"I don't know. In that heat, without ventilation, he need not have been dead very long."

"Do you realize that this might affect her mind?" I said suddenly. "We've done a hell of a thing to that girl. There was something filthy in that hut. I swear there was someone in there when I looked into the room where she was lying."

"It's easy to imagine a thing like that in the light of a match." Ansell said, quietly. "There was no one there except Myra. I looked. There was no place for anyone to hide."

"I'm not explaining it, I'm telling you." I said angrily. "I don't like any of it. Do you know what? I feel we're butting into something we don't understand."

The Mexican girl brought Ansell his beer and he took a long pull at it. "You're on edge." he said. "We're not butting into anything. That's no way to talk."

I looked at him, but he wouldn't meet my eyes. "You're lying, Doc." I said evenly. "You're as scared as I am. Only you haven't got the guts to admit it. Something happened in that hut that killed the old Indian. Some power of evil's loose. I felt it behind me all across the plateau. Just like someone was trying to get her away from me. Just like someone's hands were pulling her out of the saddle."

Bogle dropped his glass. "Wadjer mean?" he gasped, his eyes bolting out of his head.

"I wish I knew." I said, kicking back my chair. "I'm going up to see her."

I found Myra lying in bed. A small electric fan whirred busily just above her head and the blind was drawn against the hot afternoon sun.

I drew up a chair. As I sat down, she opened her eyes and blinked lazily. I said: "Hello."

A puzzled frown knitted her brow and she raised her head, looking at me. "Hello." she said. "What are you doing in here?"

"Oh, I just looked in." I said, smiling at her. "You feeling all right?"

She pushed down the sheet and raised herself on her elbows. She was wearing a pair of Ansell's pyjamas. They were a lot too big for her.

"Am I supposed to be ill?" she asked, then the caught sight of the pyjamas. "What in the world ...?"

The puzzled expression changed to alarm. "How did I get into these? What's been happening?"

"Don't get excited." I said. "You're back in the inn again. We came and took you away from Quintl. You remember him?"

"Why, of course. Why did you take me away? Why didn't I wake up?"

She ran her slim fingers through her hair. "What's been happening? Don't sit there looking like a tired sardine. Tell me."

"We found you asleep and we couldn't wake you. So we just carried you off."

"You couldn't wake me?"

"Suppose you tell me what happened to you. Then I'll know where we are."

She frowned, "Why, nothing happened to me." she said. "At least, I don't think so." She pressed her eyelids with her fingers and frowned. "You know I really can't remember. Isn't that stupid? The old Indian rather frightened me. He liked my tricks. Oh, I gave him the show of my life. I was never better. I wish you could have seen his face. I was a tremendous success. Then he took me to a little rock building. I thought Doc and Samuel were following, but I didn't see them again. He left me in this place and I was lonely. I really hated it, especially when it got dark. I lay on a kind of bed and went to sleep. I don't remember anything else."

I found a little trickle of sweat running down into my collar and I patted my neck with my handkerchief. "What happened the next day?" I asked.

"To-day, you mean? I'm telling you. I went to sleep and here I am."

"I see. You don't remember anything?"

She shook her head. "Nothing happened." she repeated with a frown. "I just went to sleep."

"You've been asleep for two days." I said, watching her.

"Two days? Why, you're crazy!"

Then seeing the way I looked at her she went on, "You wouldn't kid me, would you?"

"No. I wouldn't kid you." I said.

She suddenly laughed. "Well, maybe I was tired. I feel kind of weak now. Will you leave me for a little while? I want to think and then I'd like something to eat."

I got up. "Sure." I said. "You take it easy."

Ansell and Bogle looked at me anxiously when I got downstairs. "It's no good." I said. "She doesn't remember anything."

"You don't mean to say she just slept all the time?" Ansell demanded. "But what about the snake-bite remedy? What happened to that?"

"Aw, quit asking questions." I said, suddenly sore, and I went into the kitchen to order her a meal.

When it was ready, Bogle met me in the passage as I came from the kitchen with a tray in my hands.

"Can I take that up to her?" he said, scowling at me fiercely.

"You?" I nearly dropped the tray.

"Why shouldn't I?" Bogle demanded fiercely. "You and Doc's been up, ain't you? Why can't I have a look?"

I grinned at him. "She's not a bad kid, is she?" I said.

"Bad?" Bogle snatched the tray out of my hands. "That ain't the word for it." But he tiptoed up the stairs as if they were made of paper.

As I turned into the lounge, there was a sudden wild yell from upstairs and a crash of broken china.

Doc and I looked at each other in alarm and then we dashed for the stairs.

Bogle came blundering down the passage, his face white and his eyes bolting out of his head. He tried to pass us, but I grabbed him and spun him round.

"What the hell's the matter with you?" I demanded, shaking him.

"Don't go in there." he quavered, sweat running down his fat face. "She's floating round the room. Floating up to the ceiling." and shoving me aside, he continued his mad flight.

"He's gone crazy." I said, staring after him. "What's he mean, floating round the room?"

Ansell didn't say anything, but I could see by his eyes, he was scared.

SEVEN

"Floating in the air." Myra said scornfully. "What kind of an imagination is that?" She was lying full length in a basket chair with her feet up. She still looked pale, but there was a sparkle in her eyes that I was glad to see.

The evening sun had sunk below the mountains and in the fading light, the verandah was quiet and restful. A cool wind rustled the scorched leaves of the overhead cypresses and the square was deserted. Ansell and I lolled in our chairs near Myra, while Bogle sat at the table, fondling a bottle half-filled with whisky.

"Drink's going to be Samuel's downfall." Myra went on. "He can't have his D.T.'s like an ordinary decent citizen. He has to be different. So he sees floating women instead of pink snakes."

I looked across at Bogle. He worried me. Sitting in a heap, drinking whisky steadily, he looked like a man embarking on a long and serious illness. He kept shaking his head and muttering to himself and every now and then a muscle would flutter in his cheek and his eyes would twitch.

"Now, wait a minute." I said. "He must have seen something to get him in that condition. A man doesn't go to pieces like that for fun."

"Phooey!" Myra snapped. "He's trying to be temperamental. You came in two minutes after he'd rushed out. You didn't see me floating in the air, did you?"

"I wouldn't be sitting here, if I had." I said with a grin. "I'd be running somewhere in the desert."

"Well, there you are." Myra said. "He's suffering from delusions."

"Suppose you go over your story again, Sam?" Ansell said kindly.

Bogle gave a little shiver and poured himself out another drink "I'll go screwy if I even think about it." he said in husky voice.

"You don't have to worry about that." Myra told him. "You're as far gone as you ever will be. After all, there is a limit even to lunacy."

Bogle screwed up his fists and faced us. "I don't care what you punks say." he snarled. "I believe my own peepers. I went into that room and there she was lying on the bed. I didn't even have time to ask her how she was when she suddenly rose off the bed with the blanket over her and floated up to the ceiling, stiff, like she was held up by wires."

We all exchanged glances.

"She just floated off the bed, eh?" I said. "You've never seen anyone else just float off a bed before, have you?"

Bogle shook his head. "No." he said simply, "I ain't and what's more, I don't ever want to see it again."

Ansell said in a low voice to me: "Sun stroke."

I nodded. "Now, look pal." I said. "We've had a pretty hard day. Suppose you go to bed? You'll be fine to-morrow."

Bogle groaned. "Do you think I'll ever be able to sleep again?" he said, pouring himself out another whisky.

Myra swung her feet to the ground and stood up. She was wearing a dark blue shirt and a pair of grey flannel trousers. The outfit certainly suited her neat little figure. She walked over to Bogle and took the whisky away from him.

"Go on." she said. "Get off to bed or I'll do more than float over you."

Bogle shrank away from her. "Don't come near me." he said in horror.

"Leave him alone." Ansell said. "It looks to me as if he were suffering from delayed shock."

Myra hesitated, then keeping the whisky bottle she moved back to her chair.

I snapped the bottle out of her hand as she passed. "I'll have what's left." I said and took a long pull from the bottle.

Myra sat down again. "Well, we're right where we started, aren't we?" she said. "We've spent the best part of an hour listening to Samuel's drivel about floating women."

"Yeah." I said. "This isn't getting us anywhere."

"What I want to know." Ansell said, sitting up, "is what happened in that hut? Did you or did you not get anything out of Quintl?"

"Of course, I didn't." Myra said. "I've told you over and over again. He put me in a hut and I went to sleep. I don't remember a thing."

"Well, that's that." I said dismally. "You can kiss your snake-bite remedy good-bye. Now Quintl's dead no one will have it."

"It looks like it." Ansell said. "And yet … why was he in the hut with her? She was alone when she went to sleep, yet we find Quintl with her when we break in. There's something behind all this." He scratched his chin, staring at Myra with questioning eyes. "You don't feel any different, do you?" he asked cautiously.

"You mean do I want to start floating or something like that?" Myra asked tartly. "Are you going nuts, too?"

"Maybe there's something in what Bogle said." Ansell went on. "Maybe he wasn't mistaken."

"A pair of them." Myra said to me. "Good Lord! Put them in strait jackets."

I stared at Ansell in alarm. "What are you getting at?"

Before he could reply a party of horsemen rode into the Square, scattering dust and breaking the stillness of the evening.

"What's this?" Myra asked, looking over her shoulder at the dark group of horsemen. "A rodeo?"

I sat up in alarm. One of the horsemen was immensely tall and fat. That was enough for me. "Quick, Doc." I said. "Get inside and phone for the Federal troops. These guys are bandits."

Ansell stiffened in alarm. "What do you mean?" he asked, sitting like a paralysed rabbit.

"Okay, okay, stay where you are. They've seen us."

Myra looked at me blankly. "What are you talking about?"

"Hornets, my pet." I said grimly, and she caught her breath in a little gasp.

From the group of sixteen men, three detached themselves and walked towards the verandah steps. The others remained with the horses, watching. One of the three men was immensely fat and tall. He walked just ahead of the other two. He came up the verandah steps that creaked under his weight.

It was the fat party we had met on the mountain road and he had a mean look on his dark greasy face as he stood under the lamp, looking at us. Particularly he looked at Myra. Then he took out a pale silk handkerchief and blew his nose. While he was doing this, his eyes remained on Myra's face.

Myra eyed him up and down. She was in no way disturbed to meet him again.

"Haven't we seen that fat boy before?" Myra said to me.

The fat party moved a little nearer. His companions remained in the shadows.

Bogle, suddenly feeling the hostile atmosphere, decided that he ought to assert himself. "Lookin' for anyone, pal?"

The fat party felt in his pocket. "Somewhere I had a very interesting notice." he said. "Now, where did I put it?" He fumbled again, frowning slightly.

"Try your paunch." Myra said, lighting a cigarette and flipping the match into the darkness.

I tapped her arm. "Would you mind keeping quiet?" I said pleadingly. "It's not much to ask in these days of acute crisis."

The fat man pulled out a crumpled newspaper and began smoothing it between his great hands. He peered at it and then at Myra. Then his face lit up and he actually smiled. It didn't reassure me. You know how it would be if you met a snake and it smiled at you, it wouldn't reassure you.

"Yes." he said, "here it is. Very interesting. Very interesting indeed."

"He seems happy enough talking to himself." Myra said, yawning. "Don't you think we can go to bed?"

"I have a sneaking idea that before very long we'll get involved in his monologue." I said helplessly. "I think we ought to be as cautious as possible."

Bogle blinked at the fat party, muttered to himself and then eased his great muscles. "I don't get it." he said. "Who's this guy, anyway?"

"I am Pablo." the fat party returned with a furtive look at Myra. "You are strangers to this country, you would not know me."

Ansell started as if he'd been stung.

"Pablo." Myra repeated. "Sounds like something to rub on your chest."

The fat party smiled again. "The little man has heard of me. Is it not so, señor?"

I'd heard of him, too, and when Ansell said "Yes." very feebly, I sympathized with him.

"Then tell your friends who I am." Pablo went on. "Tell them that Pancho Villa and Zapata finished where I began. Tell them about my fortress in the mountains and of the men that have been bricked up in its walls. Tell them of the excellent fellows that work under me, and of the trains we have dynamited. Come, señor, where is your tongue?"

Ansell looked round at us and nodded his head. "That's the boy." he said nervously.

"If Samuel will play the harmonica, we'll give him a civic reception." Myra said lightly. "After which he'll be presented with a little flag and a string beg to keep his silly looking hat in and then, with luck, we'll all go to bed."

I felt she wasn't being exactly helpful.

Pablo played with his handkerchief. "It is Myra Shumway … that is the name, yes?"

"Fame at last." Myra said, a little surprised. "How are you, Doctor Livingstone?"

"And you, señor, Ross Millan?"

Bogle sat up. "I'm Sam Bogle." he said. "Please to meet you."

"Shut your mouth, you dog." Pablo said, his eyes boring holes into Bogle, "or I will cut your tongue out."

Bogle gaped at him. "Well, I'll be …!" he gasped.

I kicked his chin under the table and told him to take it easy.

Pablo wandered over to the table, drew up a chair and sat down near Myra. He moved very lightly for his bulk.

Myra drew away from him.

"There is much to talk about." he said, reaching for the jar of wine that stood on the table. He poured the sour red wine into Myra's glass, then held the glass up to the light of the lamp. "Your pretty mouth leaves marks." he said smiling at Myra. "Your kisses could be dangerous." and he shook with a spasm of laughter.

"Mind you don't bust your corset." Myra said, alarmed.

Pablo crushed the glass in his hand. The wine and glass splinters spattered the table. Bogle half started from his chair, but I again touched him under the table. I could have smacked Myra. Either she was being the dumbest of all blondes or else she had more guts than I and the rest of us put together. Whichever way it was, she was making things bad for us all.

The men in the Square made a move forward. Several of them dropped their hands to their gun butts.

Pablo wiped his hand on his handkerchief and looked with interest at the cut on his palm.

"That was careless of me." he said, looking at Myra.

"Don't apologize." Myra returned. "I had a cousin who was also a mental defective. He had to have cast-iron feeding utensils. I dare say I could arrange the same thing for you at a cut rate."

"When my women are insolent." Pablo said dreamily, "I peg them out in the hot sun on an ant-hill."

Myra twisted round, facing him. "But, I'm not your woman, fat boy." she said. "You can take your little bandits out of here and feed them through a sausage machine."

I said quickly: "Don't mind her. That's just her sense of humour."

Pablo wrapped his handkerchief round his hand. "Very interesting sense of humour. If my woman talks like that I cut her tongue out. She loses her sense of humour very quick then."

I felt it was time to take a more active part in the conversation. "Tell me, señor, is there something particular that you wish to discuss with us?" I asked, offering him a cigarette from my case.

"Yes." he said, waving away the cigarette. "Something very important." He picked up the newspaper which he had dropped on the floor. I recognized the *Recorder*. "You will see why I am interested in the señorita." and he spread the newspaper on the table.

I knew what was coming, but even then I hardly dared to look at the splash headlines that were smeared across the front page. Somehow, this thug had got hold of the issue containing Maddox's story of the kidnapped blonde. There was a big shot of Myra and in the biggest type of all was the announcement about the 25,000-dollars reward.

"Brother," I thought. "Have you got to be smart to talk yourself out of this?"

Before I could stop her, Myra had snatched up the paper, while Bogle and Ansell crowded round her.

"That's quite a good likeness of you they've got there." I said carelessly. "I always thought the *Recorder* was unreliable, but this is the end. Kidnapped by bandits indeed. That is a laugh."

Myra looked at me over the top of the paper. There was a disagreeable look in her eye.

"Isn't it?" she said, between her teeth. "I'm suffocating with mirth."

There was a long silence while the three of them went through the article, then Myra folded the paper with slow deliberation and put it on the table.

"Twenty-five thousand dollars." she said gently. "And I was going to call you by your first name!"

"But there is more." Pablo said, picking at his great white teeth with his thumb nail. "There is a man called Bastino who lives in the mountains. He is a good friend of mine. He tells me that he is to kidnap this young woman. Later it has been arranged for Señor Millan to rescue her, but Señor Millan says nothing to Bastino about the reward. He pays Bastino a mere three hundred dollars and Bastino feels sore about it. He comes to me and shows me the paper, so I think I had better do something about it." He waved his fat hand. "So here I am."

Myra looked at me. "What a lovely little serpent you've turned out to be." she said with terrifying restraint. "You must let me know when your parents marry, I'll send them a wreath."

Even Ansell was looking at me with hurt eyes.

I eased my collar which threatened to strangle me. "It's all a mistake." I said hurriedly. "If you'll just let me explain...."

"There is nothing to explain." Pablo said. "I do the talking now."

Myra turned on him furiously. "You keep your snout out of this. I've got something to say to this two-faced, double- crossing rattle-snake."

"Now, don't let us quarrel." I said hastily. "You wouldn't have come to any harm and I was keeping the reward as a surprise for you. Just think of all that money and how nice it'll be to spend."

"I'm thinking." Myra said, tapping on the table. "I'm thinking what I'm going to do to you."

Ansell broke in: "And what about us?" be demanded. "We weren't going to be in this either."

I drew myself up. "This is becoming sordid." I said. "Here am I, trying to give the great American public an epic story and all you can do is to yap about money."

"So you were not even interested in the reward?" Myra said, smiling at me. "You just wanted to give the great American public an epic story?"

"That's all." I said. "Why should I worry about a little thing like 25,000 dollars? I'm a newspaper man."

"A minute." Pablo said, "I have not finished. I take the señorita now. Señor Millan writes of the kidnapping. Then we discuss the reward."

We all four stared at him. "You take the señorita?" I said, suddenly realizing the spot we were in.

"Certainly." Pablo returned, smiling at Myra. "The newspaper says she has been kidnapped, therefore I kidnap her. I shall hold her for ransom. I shall demand 50,000 dollars and you will pay. If there is much delay, I will send you her right ear and after three days I send you her left ear and then if I do not get the money, I send you a finger every day."

Myra went a little pale. "That'll make a swell headline in your rag." she said to me. "High rates for piecework or Blonde mailed in installments."

I said: "I don't think you'd better do that. It would mean U.S. reprisals. Maybe we'll send troops as we did a few years ago when we chased Pancho into the mountains."

Pablo laughed. "I go now." he said, and reached out, taking Myra's arm in his great hand.

She spun round. "Take your greasy paw off me!" she flared. "Who do you think you are? You can't scare me, you over-filled sausage!"

Pablo quaked with laughter. "Such spirit." he said and hit her across her face with the side of his hand.

She and the chair she was sitting on went over backwards. She sprawled on the ground.

The two Mexicans who had remained in the shadows, now pulled their guns and stepped forward. "Sit still." one of them said to me. The other threatened Bogle and Ansell who had stiffened when Myra went over.

I felt myself go white and ignoring the gunmen I bent over Myra.

Pablo hit me on the back of my neck with the jar of wine. The jar splintered and the wine splashed Myra's shirt. I found myself on my hands and knees and white hot lights seemed to be exploding in my head.

I heard Pablo laughing a long way away and then I shook my head clear and got to my feet.

Myra clutched at me. "Are you hurt?" she asked anxiously.

Before I could assure her, Pablo reached out and jerked her round to face him. "Never, mind him, my little rabbit." he said, drawing her towards him. "Now I am here, I like to have all your attention."

Myra caught her breath sharply. She moved in quickly and drove her clenched fist into the middle of his face.

One of the Mexican gunmen kicked her legs from under her. She hit the wooden floor of the verandah with a thud that shook the breath out of her body.

Pablo started to his feet, hissing like a snake. A patch of split skin just by his thick nose showed where Myra had hit him.

"Go for 'em, Sam." I bawled. And we both went into action together.

With a roar, Bogle tossed the table at the nearest gunman who was covering him. The gun went off; the slug shearing a furrow in the table. I jumped the gunman who had tripped Myra before he could regain his balance. We crashed over, almost on top of Myra.

Ansell who dodged into a neutral corner said afterwards that it was a pretty good scrap. While I was trying to pin my greaser, Pablo got hurriedly to his feet, tittering with excitement. "Come." he shouted to the other Mexicans in the Square. "They want to fight."

Sam had closed with the other gunman. Grabbing him round his waist he tossed him into the middle of the surging Mexicans below.

I got a grip on my man's hair and hammered his head on the boards. He seemed to have a soft head because he went out like a light. As I got up, I heard Myra scream. The Mexicans were pouring up on to the verandah.

Pablo grabbed Myra. She fought him, kicking and scratching like a wild cat, but he handled her effortlessly. He didn't even get up from his chair. He captured her hands in one of his, grinding and squeezing her fingers. White and furious, she dragged away from him, kicking at him wildly.

Giggling with excitement, he suddenly gave her a jerk. She came forward as if she had been shot from a cannon and thudded against him. With his free hand, he twined his great fingers, in her hair and pulled her head back steadily until Doc thought he was going to break her neck.

"If you had longer ears, I would pull them for you, too, little rabbit." he said, grinning at her. "Go down on your knees." and he forced her on to the boards.

Sam suddenly emerged from the heap of men. He looked like a massive bear attacked by wolves. He hadn't had a fight like this in years. With three men clinging to his legs, and a little greaser on his back, he stared round, looking for Myra. When he saw what Pablo was doing, he gave a great roar of fury. Bending down, he clubbed at the men holding his legs. His great fists, like two rocks, smashed down on their upturned faces. The greaser on his back redoubled his efforts, biting, scratching and thumping. Bogle didn't even notice him. He freed his legs, kicked the men clear and charged down on Pablo.

The little greaser shifted his hands and drove his fist into Bogle. Bogle bellowed like a wounded bull. One of his hands groped behind him and closed over the greaser's face. His thick fingers began to squeeze. The greaser clawed at the steel fingers. Then Bogle suddenly threw him away. He crashed against the verandah rail and went limp.

In the meantime, I was under a pile of Mexicans and one of them caught me a smack under the chin and I went out like a light.

These Mexicans scrambled to their feet and made for Bogle, but they were a little late.

Pablo found this immensely exciting and amusing. He dodged Bogle's first charge, then as he came in again, Pablo snatched Myra up by her shirt-front, gripping her ankles in his other hand, he slammed her at Bogle like a battering rain. Bogle went over with a thud, clinging to Myra. By holding her close to him, he saved her the shock of landing on the wooden floor.

"Go for him, you dogs." Pablo exclaimed, waving his men to Bogle.

The Mexicans piled on top of them.

Pablo skipped round the struggling mass of men, laughing until tears ran down his fat cheeks. He saw a leg and snatched at it. Pulling steadily he drew Myra out of the mass of kicking, flaying limbs. Before he could get her out, he had to drag away two Mexicans. This he did by seizing them one after the other by their hair and tossing them away as if they were kittens.

Myra came out of this struggling pile of men, more dead than alive. Leaving her on the floor, Pablo skipped back to the struggling men, ploughed his way down to Bogle.

The Mexicans got to their feet and drew off.

Pablo stirred Myra with his foot. She opened her eyes and stared at him. "You were nearly skinned that time, little rabbit." he said, quaking with laughter. "Ho! Ho! What excitement! What an evening! What beautiful fighting!"

He bent suddenly and knotted his fist in her shirt, then he heaved her to her feet. Holding her lightly, he walked across the verandah, straightened a chair and sat down. All the fight had gone out of Myra. He pulled her down on his knees. She just sat there limply, her head down and her face hidden by her hair.

The Mexicans gathered in a little bunch at the top of the steps. They talked excitedly together in whispers.

Bogle and I were still counting stars. Ansell edged further into his corner and hoped no one could notice him.

Myra suddenly began to struggle again. "Let me go, you fat toad." she gasped.

Pablo giggled. "Of course, little rabbit." he said and set her on her feet.

Without his supporting hand, her legs buckled and she nearly fell. He caught her as she was going over. "Come, come." he jeered at her. "Where is your strength?"

Making an effort, she pushed him away and tottered over to me. As she came, I began to sit up. I saw her through a dazed mist.

"How are we doing?" I asked feebly as she sank down on her knees beside me. "Did we win or do we start fighting again?"

"We lost, you dope." Myra said savagely. "Now, what do you think we're going to do?"

I looked round, spotted the bunch of greasers standing on the verandah steps, blocking our exit, looked sadly at Bogle who was beginning to move and then over at Pablo.

"As soon as I get my second wind." I said hurriedly, "we'll start another little session. But you've got to beat it. Make for the woods. Once you're there, you ought to be able to hide from them. Do you understand?"

"You don't think I'm going to run out on you three, do you?" Myra demanded fiercely. "We're all in this together."

"Famous last words." I said, thinking it was pretty fine of her. "You get out and don't be a little fool. They'll give you hell when they start on you and besides who's going to pay 50,000 dollars for you?"

"Why, you big drip!" Myra said angrily. "Wouldn't you pay that for me?"

"Look out behind." I said and tried to struggle to my feet. Pablo, losing patience, was coming over like an express train. He caught Myra before she could even begin to move.

"Now." he said, shaking her, "we talk no more and we go!"

"Take your hands off me!" she said furiously. "Do you hear? Get back into your skin, you fat sausage!"

Then it happened.

There was a sudden puff of white smoke that enveloped Pablo and when it had cleared away, he had vanished.

I had been watching the whole time. Pablo hadn't run into the lounge. He hadn't darted into the shadows. He had simply dissolved into smoke. It was the most terrifying thing I've ever seen.

Myra backed away with a little cry, then she spun on her heel and ran to me. I held her while I watched the wisp of smoke trail slowly into the darkness.

You ought to have seen those Mexicans. They gave one look at us and then they stampeded for their horses. And what a stampede! The bigger greasers trampled on the smaller greasers in their mad panic to get off the verandah. In under four seconds, they and their horses were pounding out of Orizaba. The Square was deserted.

"What happened?" I asked, holding Myra tightly. In spite of my scare, I liked holding her tightly. She was the kind of girl to be held tightly and I was doing a swell job. "What in Pete's name happened?"

Of course, Bogle had seen it all. "I can't stand it." he wailed, beating the floor with his fists. "First, she floats in the air and now he disappears into smoke. I tell you, I can't stand any more of it. I'm going nuts! Lemme get out of here. I wanta go home!"

"Quiet!" Ansell said, coming out of his corner. "Hold your noise!" He came over to Myra and me. "I saw what happened." he went on in a low voice. "Now do you believe in witchcraft? He just vanished into smoke, didn't he? You both saw it." He looked at Myra searchingly. "What did you do?"

Myra shivered. "Do?" she said. "You're not trying to pin this on me?"

"Of course, it's you." Ansell returned sharply. "I suspected it when Sam saw you floating. You've become a Naguale. Don't you understand? Quintl did pass on his secrets to you without you knowing it. You have the Nagualism power of witchcraft."

Myra backed away from him. Her eyes wide in horror. "I don't believe it!" she said, then turning on me "Tell him he's crazy! I won't believe it!"

"Then what happened to him?" Ansell persisted. "Men don't just vanish into smoke."

"Maybe he's hiding somewhere." I said, looking round, but knowing that it was a waste of time. Then I suddenly saw something on the floor and I moved forward. "What's this?" I said.

Under the table was the longest and most appetizing sausage I had ever seen. I picked it up. "Where the devil did that come from?"

Myra took one look at it, gave a little moan and fell at my feet in a faint.

Ansell clutched my arm. "Didn't you hear what she said?" he gasped, pointing a trembling finger at the sausage. "That's Pablo. That's all that's left of Pablo."

I dropped the sausage as if it had bitten me. "Am I going nutty or are you?" I demanded.

"She told him to get back into a sausage skin." Ansell screamed, his eyes bolting out of his head. "She's got the power to do it!"

"You're mad!" I said backing away. "Such things can't happen."

Bogle came limping over and gaped at Doc. "What the hell are you squealing about?" he said, then looking down at Myra. "What she think she's doing?"

I jerked my attention from the sausage to Myra. "I'll take her inside." I said, and picking her up I carried her into the lounge. When I had laid her on a couch, I yelled for Doc. "Come on." I shouted. "Help me, will you?"

Ansell came in white and trembling. "I can't believe it! It's the most fantastic …"

"Aw, shut up!" I said roughly. "There's plenty of time to talk when we've taken care of this kid. After all, we were in a damn tight spot before this happened. We should be grateful."

It took some little time to bring Myra round. She opened her eyes at last and blinked unhappily up at me. "I've had such an awful dream." he said sleepily. "Such an awful dream."

"That's all right." I said soothingly. "You go to sleep. I'm right by your side, so there's nothing to be soared about."

She smiled at me and then closed her eyes again. In a moment she was breathing regularly.

"I'd be a hit as a father." I said, pleased. "Did you see that piece of technique?"

Bogle came in. "How's she doing?" he asked.

"She's okay." I said abruptly. "What have you done with the sausage? I want it in here."

"I've given it to the innkeeper's dawg." Bogle said indifferently. "He's a good dawg and I've been promising him something …"

"Given it to a dog?" I shouted, grabbing him by the arm.

"Why not?" Bogle said, on the offensive. "Want to make anything of it? Do you think it's too good for a dawg?"

"Listen, you fat jerk." I exclaimed. "That wasn't a sausage. It was Pablo."

Bogle's eyes opened. "What was that?" he asked, starting.

"That sausage wasn't a sausage at all. It was Pablo turned into a sausage." I explained, trying to keep my voice down.

"The sausage wasn't a sausage, it was Pablo?" Bogle repeated in a dazed voice. "Was that what you said?"

"Yes, you fat fool!"

"Iszatso? Well, it certainly looked like a sausage to me."

"I don't care what it looked like to you! It's Pablo done up like a sausage."

"Done up like a sausage?" Bogle's eyes looked scared. "I see."

"No, you don't." I said savagely. "You don't see at all. Where is the dog? Tell me that and we won't argue."

"You'd better take a look at this guy, Doc." Bogle said to Ansell. "Something's got loose in his dome."

"Try to understand." Ansell said. "Myra has turned Pablo into a sausage."

A look of horror came into Bogle's eyes. "You, too?" he whispered, backing away. "Don't you think you guys ought to sit down or something?"

"I tell you Pablo's in that sausage!" Ansell snapped. "You've got to get it back at once."

Bogle shivered. "Maybe I'm going bats, too." he said hoarsely. "Maybe it ain't you two but me. Maybe I'm just hearing voices in my brain."

"What are you drivelling about?" I stormed at him.

"Someone keeps telling me that Pablo's a sausage." Bogle wailed. "I've gone nuts! I knew I'd go nuts and by God I've gone nuts!"

"I tell you, Pablo has been turned into a sausage." Ansell hissed, pushing his face into Bogle's. "Now will you do something about it, you large lump of useless blubber!"

Bogle closed his eyes and sat abruptly on the floor. "This is going to be a pretty sad day for my old lady." he said, as if to himself. "I wouldn't like to be the guy to tell her her only son's gone bugs." and he lay flat on his back and began making humming noises.

"Come on, Doc." I said. "We've got to find the dog by ourselves."

We didn't have to go far. Just outside on the verandah there was an enormous wolfhound lying on the floor who glanced up with bored overfed eyes as we came out. There was no sign of the sausage. As we stood staring, the wolfhound closed his eyes luxuriously and licked his chops.

"He's eaten Pablo." I said in a hushed, horrified voice. "That's something I wouldn't wish on my worst enemy."

Doc took off his hat and lowered his head.

Then a sudden thought struck me and I gripped his arm in alarm. "Doc!" I gasped. "Do you realize what this means? She's got the whip hand over us all. We won't be able to open our mouths."

Doc put on his hat again and blinked at me. "What do you mean?" he asked, bewildered.

"Can't you see what she can do if she decides she doesn't like any of us?" I looked furtively over my shoulder, then lowering my face close to his, I whispered: "She might even turn you into a pork pie and give you to me for my lunch. How would you like that?"

Doc just fainted away in my arms.

EIGHT

I woke the next morning to see the sun streaming through the grass blinds. I could hear the sing-song chatter of the Mexican waiters preparing breakfast in the patio below. I glanced at my wrist-watch. It was 6.40.

Not much use going to sleep again, so I reached for my cigarette case. Then I propped myself up in the hard little bed and brooded.

Once I got to thinking, I realized just how much there was to think about. It was terrific.

In twenty-four hours the whole set-up had so completely changed that I was up the creek without a paddle. When planning a newspaper campaign, a modern newspaperman can't take miracles into consideration. But, on the face of it, that was what I had to do. The kidnapped blonde story was as dead as a mummy. The blonde who could work miracles was front-page news. But how would Maddox react? I thought gloomily that he'd can me before I could give him a demonstration. On the other hand, of course, I might be able to persuade Myra to give him a little scare and get my job back.

What about Myra anyway? I couldn't imagine either Ansell or myself persuading her against her will. It'd take all my time, anyway, to keep on the right side of her. It wasn't as if she were a soft cookie. She'd always been difficult and now with powers such as she possessed, she was going to be a definite menace.

I came out in a cold sweat when I thought of Pablo. His was a story that could never be written. There was no proof and no one would believe it. If I even hinted to Maddox what had happened he would have sent me to the booby-hatch. I wouldn't blame him at that. So the Pablo episode had to be forgotten.

The next point was to find another approach to the kidnapping angle. How to make Maddox and Myra happy at the same time. Not easy. The 25,000-dollars reward complicated matters. I regretfully decided that I wasn't going to see much of that. Knowing Myra, I was pretty certain that she'd grab all of it. I couldn't see myself arguing about it either. What was 25,000 dollars if I were turned into a hamburger or a breast of chicken?

I ran my fingers through my hair. This was driving me screwy. I played with the idea of getting up, packing quietly and sneaking off to Mexico City. I'd lose my job, but at least, I'd be clear of the whole thing. The thought tempted me.

Then there was a light tap on my door and Myra came in. She was in flame-coloured pyjamas and a scarlet dressing gown. And as she stood in the diffused light, with the little bolts of sunlight in her hair, I thought she was the loveliest thing I'd seen for a long time.

She closed the door gently and leaned against it.

We looked at each other as if we had met for the first time and I was conscious of a new feeling for her. Up to now, she had been a subject to write about. But, seeing her there, her big eyes serious, the sun in her hair, the way she held her head, well, I guess she sent a tingle through my veins. At that moment, she came alive and looking back, now that it is all over, I guess that this was the time I really fell for her in a big way.

"I'm scared." she said. "Something's happened to me."

I sat up on my elbow. "Come here." I said. "What's happened to you?" I didn't like the bewildered look in her eyes and she seemed to have lost a lot of her confidence.

"I don't know what it is." she said, sitting on the end of the bed. "I feel— oh, I guess you'll think I'm crazy."

"I won't." I said, reaching for the cigarettes and offering her one.

We didn't say anything for a while. Smoke haze drifted in the sunbeams and the Mexican waiters chattered outside. Then she said: "It wasn't a dream last night, was it?"

I shook my head. "No."

"I hoped it was." she went on, tapping ashes on the floor. "I wish it all was a dream. It's frightening."

"I can't tell you there's nothing to be scared about." I said, "All I can say is I'm sorry we got you into this mess."

"I've been trying to remember what happened." she said. "I'm putting it together, but it still doesn't make sense. I can remember the old Indian more clearly. I can remember sitting in that little hut with him. We didn't speak. We read each other's minds. That was frightening. I couldn't lie to him, you see. Not talking like that. I just had to keep my mind blank when I felt he was finding out too much about me. I still don't know how far I succeeded. We talked with our minds for a long time. He told me a lot of things. I know that, but I can't remember what they were. He gave me some horrible stuff to drink and after I'd got it down I remember seeing some black smoke coming from the corner of the hut. It was quite terrifying. There was no fire or anything, just the black smoke building up into a shadow. I thought at the time it looked like the shadow of a woman, but it was dark in the hut and I couldn't be sure. But all the time we talked, the shadow was there, hovering close to me."

I lit another cigarette. I felt there wasn't much I could say, so I just lay there and listened.

"The shadow was behind Pablo, just before it happened." she shuddered. "I'm scared even to think of anything now, in case something happens."

"Snap out of it, kid." I said reaching out and pulling her to me. I put my arm round her and she stretched out with her head on my shoulder. I liked the smell of her hair and the feel of it against my face.

"But there's something else." she said in a small voice.

I wondered what was coming. "Tell me." I said.

"I don't think you'll understand." she returned speaking reluctantly. "I don't understand it myself. But, last night, when I got into bed, something happened to me. I thought I saw a shadowy figure get up from my bed and go out of the room. It—seemed to come from me. It—it looked like me, and when it had gone I felt different."

"You were dreaming." I said, patting her arm. "You've been through enough to have series of nightmares."

"But, I *feel* different." she repeated. "Oh, Ross, what *is* happening to me?"

"But, how different?" I turned so that I could look into her troubled eyes. "Don't get in a panic, kid. What do you mean … different?"

"Oh, lighter, happier—as if I'd been through a mental bath and become clean. Oh, I don't know how to tell you."

"Well, if you feel happier, why worry?" I said, and kissed her.

She drew away quickly. "If you're not going to concentrate, I'll have to leave you." she said severely.

"But, I am concentrating." I said, with my mouth against her hair.

She pulled away, "No, you mustn't." she said. "I wish all this hadn't happened."

"You wait until you get that reward." I said. "You'll think differently then."

"But, I don't want it." she returned emphatically. "That's another thing I can't understand. Yesterday, I was furious with you, but now—well, I just don't want it. I can get along without it and besides, it's not really honest."

This shocked me. Something *had* happened to her.

"Not honest?" I repeated stupidly. "What's the idea?"

"You know as well as I do." she said impatiently, "I wasn't rescued and you have no right to try to claim the reward."

"This is too much for me." I said, lying back. "Coming from you, that's rich!"

Just then Bogle opened the verandah door and stuck his head round. "Don't mind me, if you're busy." he said, leering at Myra. "I'm scared of my own company, this morning."

"Come in, Sam." I said wearily. "If you've any friends, bring 'em in too. I always work best when I've a room full of people."

"There ain't no one but me and Whisky." Bogle said, coming in. He was followed by the wolfhound. "Whisky's taken a liking to me."

Myra and I looked at the wolfhound uneasily. The dog clicked its teeth in an absent-minded kind of way and lay down near the bed. It eyed us with sleepy insolence and then stretched out with its head on Bogle's boot.

"Whisky?" I repeated. "Is that its name?"

"That's what I call him." Bogle said. "He seems to like it and it's the sort of name I wouldn't easily forget. Nice dawg, ain't he?"

"I don't know." I said, with some feeling. "Perhaps he is. I can't forget that he ate Pablo. That rather preys on my mind."

Bogle sneered, "Ate Pablo?" he said. "You're nuts! He ate a sausage. You and Doc ought to have your ears blown out!"

I considered this. I thought if that was the only thing necessary how absurdly simple everything would be.

"Never mind, Sam." I said. "You aren't the only one who won't believe it."

While I was speaking, Whisky turned over on his back and folded his legs across his chest like a crab. His tail straightened and he closed his eyes.

Myra said quietly, "I don't like that dog's attitude. It's unhealthy."

"I wouldn't say that." I returned, pulling the bedclothes a little higher. "But, it's disturbing, if that's what you mean."

Bogle unfolded Whisky's legs gently and turned him on his side. "Relax, fella." he said. "You can't rest that way."

Whisky opened one eye and looked at Bogle. Then he turned on his back and folded his legs over his chest again.

"Gawdamn it." Bogle said. "Did you ever see such a dawg?" and he bustled forward to unfold Whisky's legs again.

I suppose Whisky decided not to tolerate this interference. Opening one eye sharply, he regarded Bogle's hands with a sour look and then thrusting his nose forward he clicked his teeth with a snap like a mouse-trap.

I guess Bogle thought he'd lost his hand. He didn't dare look, but sat on the floor, breathing heavily until I had assured him that Whisky had missed him by an eighth of an inch. Then he removed himself to the far end of the room, where he sat in a chair and scowled at the dog.

"Listen." I said. "Don't think I'm unsociable. I'm not. I've always been sociable. I'm the guy they laughed at when I sat down at the piano. But, right now, my nerves are on edge and I'd like you and Whisky to take a little walk. I don't want you to go far. I'd even stand for seeing you at a distance, but I can't stand much more of your heavy breathing and the dog's affected attitude. So, would you drift… the pair of you?"

"Every time you open your trap, you write a book." Bogle said. "I'm waiting for Ansell. He's coming to have a talk. Besides, I've ordered breakfast to be sent up. You've got the best room, ain't you?"

"Well, Precious, you see how it is." I said to Myra. "We'll have to postpone our little talk. I just can't keep my mind on anything so long as Whisky's with us."

Myra got off the bed and stretched. "I don't think we would have got anywhere." she said, a little wearily. "I'm afraid talking won't help me."

"Did you say you'd ordered breakfast?" I asked Bogle.

"Yeah." Bogle's face lit up. "Eggs and fruit and cawfee. I didn't get much to eat last night. There was so much talking and shouting and people going off into faints."

"You wouldn't like to cover up Whisky, would you?" I said. "He really is getting on my nerves."

"Maybe he ain't well." Bogle said, looking at the dog with puzzled eyes.

"With Pablo inside him, I don't wonder at it."

Whisky rolled over on his side and looked at me. There was something strangely human about the expression in his eyes. "How right you are, old dog." he said in a deep, guttural voice. "He lies like a rock on my stomach."

"There you are." I said to Sam. "I knew he couldn't be well." Then I clutched my pillow and looked at the dog in horror.

Myra stifled a scream and stood petrified, but Bogle didn't seem to be moved.

"You know it sounded almost as if that dog spoke." I said a little feverishly.

"Sure." Sam returned. "What of it? He's been talking to me half the night."

"What of it?" I repeated, stupefied. "Have you ever heard a dog talk before?"

"Well, no, but then anything can happen in this country, can't it? What I mean is if a parrot talks, why not a Mexican dog? That's the way I've been reasoning." He suddenly noticed my strained expression and fear came into his eyes. "It ain't possible? Dawgs don't talk? Is that what you're trying to tell me? This is another of these freak things … floating women … disappearing men … now talking dawgs?"

"Yeah, along those lines."

"My Gawd! And I talked to it half the night!" Bogle shivered edging back in his chair and half raising his hand to protect himself.

"And a lot of rot you talked too." the dog snapped. "Of all the illiterate, prissy-mouthed, dyed-in-the-wool nincompoops I've had to listen to, you take the biscuit."

Myra said in a low voice, "I think I'll go now. Somehow, I don't feel like breakfast."

"For goodness sake stay where you are." Whisky said peevishly "There's so much yapping in this hotel, I'm leading a dog's life."

"It wouldn't be someone practising ventriloquism, I suppose?" I asked hopefully, feeling that any second I'd have to run out into the desert and keep running for some time. "Someone wouldn't be trying to make fools of us?"

Whisky yawned. He had the most astonishing collection of fangs I'd ever seen. "To improve on your mothers' efforts would be a difficult task." he observed. "Just because I happen to talk your horrible language, there's no need for you to behave like dolts."

"Look, old fellow." I said nervously. "Would you mind going away? It's not that I don't like you, but I've had all I can stand for one morning. Come back later on, will you? Maybe I'll be adjusted to the idea by then."

Whisky shook himself. "As a matter of fact I have something rather important to do." he said, getting to his feet. "And besides, it's time for my own breakfast." He walked to the verandah door, his nails clicking on the polished floor. "I've got to see a dog about a man, if you'll pardon the cliché." and he strolled out on to the verandah and then disappeared out of sight.

There was a long silence while we endeavoured to recover.

"Like a nightmare, isn't it?" I said, at last. "Maybe we'll wake up and have a good laugh over this in a little while."

"Naw." Bogle said, mopping his face with his handkerchief, "I wouldn't laugh at it even if it was a dream."

"I'd rather have a disappearing man and a floating woman to a talking dog." I said reflectively. "Do you think if we packed our bags and skipped, we'd be able to shake him off?"

"That dawg wants to stay with us." Bogle said gloomily. "Anyway, that's what he said last night."

"Then I think you had better take him away and leave us to mourn for you." Myra put in. "I don't see why we should all be driven mad."

Doc Ansell came in. He was looking a little tired, but there was a light of battle in his eye. "There you are." he said. "Breakfast is on its way up. I want to talk to you all this morning. We've got to make plans."

"Have you heard about the dog?" I asked.

Ansell sat down. "What dog?"

"The dog that ate Pablo." I said. "He's befriended Samuel."

"Well, that's all right." Ansell looked at me sharply. "There's nothing like a good dog to keep one company. You don't object I hope?"

"No, no, nothing like that. But the dog talks. He's just been in. He even makes little jokes like going to see a dog about a man. Whimsy stuff and he clicks his teeth."

Ansell looked at me closely. "Talks." he said. "What do you mean ... talks??"

"Just that." I returned, stretching out and making myself comfortable. "I thought you might have an explanation. I wish you could have heard him. At the moment, I'm suffering from general collapse."

"I see." Ansell said thoughtfully. "Well, maybe I will hear him. Actually, of course, I'm not at all surprised. I've been thinking things over and I've come to the conclusion that we mustn't be surprised at whatever happens. You see Myra has now the full powers of Nagualism concentrated around her. It is likely to set off the most unlikely things."

I smiled, "Oh, so Myra's at the bottom of it, is she?"

"Why, certainly." Doc returned. "None of you would believe me when I told you about the powers of the Naguales, you're seeing for yourselves. The great thing, of course, is to try to control it. That's really what I want to talk to Myra about."

The little Mexican girl came in with a tray and put it on the table by my bed. It was quite a relief to see someone who looked completely normal and who hadn't fear lurking in her eye.

When she had gone, and Myra had poured out the coffee, Ansell picked up his threads. "Now look, young woman, I am perfectly convinced that you have unlimited powers. It's no use your trying not to believe this. You've got to face it. Rather than let those powers control you, you've got to try to control them. I know a little about this business. I've studied it and I know that you can't do things unless you're in the right frame of mind. For instance, as you are now, relaxed and worried, you'll never be able to evoke the powers. But, last night, when those bandits arrived you were frightened and without knowing it, you were in the right atmosphere to perform. There are no limits to what you can do. I don't think you ought to waste your talents."

Myra put down her coffee cup with sudden determination. "All I want is to get back to my normal life. And more than anything, I want to have some peace and quiet."

Ansell sighed, "Disappointing." he said, half to himself. "You don't seem to realize that with your powers you could become mistress of the world. Haven't you any ambition?"

"Not that kind of ambition, thank you." Myra said shortly. "It's no use talking. I'm just not going to do anything about it."

"I think she's right." I said. "The whole thing doesn't bear thinking about. How long are these powers likely to last?"

Ansell scratched his ear thoughtfully, "I'm not quite sure." he said. "The Naguales used to begin their rituals at the beginning of the full moon. It may be that the power is influenced by the moon. If that's so, she's got to the end of the month before she returns to normal. Why not make hay until then? It's not long. She'll never be able to regain the power now that

Quintl's dead."

"And a good thing too." Myra said firmly. "I'm going to be very careful of how I act for the next few weeks. If I can get through that time without anything more happening, I'm going to be quite contented."

I threw up his hands in disgust. "What about my snake-bite remedy?" he demanded. "Am I to get nothing out of this?"

"I'm sorry, Doc." Myra returned, "but I don't want anything more to do with this business. It's all very well for you, but ..."

"Can't you do something?" Ansell appealed to me.

I was already racking my brains, "I don't think so." I said at last. "You see, she ain't interested in the reward any more."

"What?" Bogle said, sitting up. "What about us? Ain't we considered?"

"That's up to you, Myra." I said, looking over at her.

"Don't you see we can't claim the reward?" she said. "We're not entitled to it."

"It wouldn't be honest." I said, grinning at Bogle.

"Wouldn't be what?" he snarled, growing red in the face. "What's this ... a gag?"

"I'm afraid our Myra's become honest overnight." I said. "A girl's got to have her conscience, you know."

"Yeah?" Bogle bellowed, "I'll tell you something. She's trying to gyp us!"

"You can believe what you like." Myra said quietly, "but I'm not having anything to do with it. I want to go somewhere quiet and wait until the end of the month."

I thought of all the publicity I'd lose and I thought of Maddox. What he'd do to me if I didn't get this kid back to New York would be nobody's business.

"Now, for the love of mike, don't be in such a hurry." I said. "Here, you two, get out. I want to talk to her."

"It's no good." Myra said firmly, "I've made up my mind." and she turned to the door.

"Can't one of you think of something?" I demanded.

"Really, Ross, I mean it." she said over her shoulder.

As she opened the door, the little Mexican girl came bustling in. She had a telegram which she handed to me. I took it and then waved her away. She seemed glad to go.

"Hold on until I've read this." I said to Myra. "It might be important."

"Hurry." Myra said, standing by the door. "I want to change."

I was staring at the telegram in astonishment. It was from Paul Juden:

Maddox cables girl has been found stop. What are you diddling with stop Civic reception to be held today stop Girl's father claims reward stop Maddox loves you stop Juden.

"Well, fan me with a plate of soup!" I said and offered the telegram to Myra.

Bogle and Ansell crowded round her and read over her shoulder. There was a moment's silence which was immediately after exploded by a general uproar.

"What does this mean?" Myra demanded. "Is this something you've hatched up?"

"Now don't set yourself on fire." I said hastily, "I don't know any more about this than you do."

"Yeah?" Bogle said, jerking Myra round. "So you don't want the money, huh? You double-crossing little hooker! How the hell did you manage it?"

"Don't be a damn fool!" I said. "She's got nothing to do with it. It's her father trying to pull a fast one over Maddox. It sticks out a yard." I turned to Myra, "What kind of a man is your father?"

She hesitated "He—he's a bit of a crook." she said reluctantly. "But there's no vice in him. He was just born that way."

"Well, it looks to me like your father's trying to gyp Maddox. What's to stop him palming off some other girl as his daughter? You know, precious, that's about what he's doing."

She stared at me, "But the photograph in the paper. They'll know she's a fake."

"Maybe he's found someone who looks like you."

"Yeah, that wouldn't be hard." Sam put in. "Any one with a Veronica Lake hair-cut would do."

This seemed to annoy Myra. "So I look like any one, do I?" she said angrily.

"Now don't get up in the air." Ansell said hastily.

I suppose it was the association of ideas. I don't really know, but thinking about it afterwards, I guess that was what it was. Myra left the ground.

It was an unnerving sight. One minute she was sitting on the bed and the next she was sitting on nothing, about three feet above the bed.

The most astonished person in the room was Myra herself. "Now, see what you've done." she said in alarm, "Don't stare at me, do something."

But we all just sat and stared.

"I don't think I'll be able to stand a great deal more of this." I finally jerked out. "Will you calm down, Myra, and stop messing around?"

The first initial shock over, Myra reached for the bed rail and anchored herself. Then she pulled herself back to the bed. She settled on the bed with the lightness and instability of a thistle down.

"Levitation." Ansell said. "It'll pass off if you don't excite yourself."

"It's rather fun." Myra said, still looking a little scared. "Would any of you mind if I cast off?"

"Don't do it." Bogle pleaded. "Please don't do it."

"Oh, nuts!" Myra snapped. "Why shouldn't I enjoy myself." and she very cautiously pushed herself away from the bed.

She immediately rose in the air in a sitting position and then she over-balanced and turned upside down. Her feet shot up towards the ceiling and she hung suspended a few feet from the floor.

"Help!" she cried. "What am I going to do now?"

Ansell went to her rescue and got her straightened out. After a little balancing, she managed to float, lying full length.

"This is rather fun." she said. "But it's an effort to keep straight. Pull my feet down, Doc, I want to see if I can walk."

"I can't and won't stand it." Bogle said, closing his eyes and screwing up his fists.

"You shut up!" Ansell said, pushing Myra's feet down and helping her upright. "She's doing very well."

Myra took a few hesitating steps and managed to cross the room some three feet above the floor. It was a shocking sight and I could hardly bring myself to watch her.

"I think I'd prefer to lie out." she said, drawing up her feet and stretching out.

"I'll give you a push." Doc said and he did so, sending her floating across the room where she bumped gently against the wall. She was like a toy balloon and she bounced off the wall and came floating back to me. I reached out and dragged her back on the bed.

"Please stop." I pleaded. "You'll drive me crazy."

"But, it's marvellous." Myra said, her face alight with pleasure. "You're only jealous. Let me go once more across the room and then I promise I won't do it again."

"Well, if it means so much to you." I said and shoved her off into space again. I must have given her too hard a posh because she shot across the room narrowly missing Doc who threw himself on the floor with a squeal of fear. She banged against the wall, ricocheted like a billiard ball and whizzed over Bogle, who cowered down in his chair. Then the power that held her up seemed to be snatched away, for she came down on the end of her spine with a thud that made the coffee cups rattle.

Ansell hurried over to her and helped her up.

"Ooch!" she said, limping across to the bed. "There's nothing for you to laugh at."

"If you could have seen yourself." I said, wiping the tears from my eyes. "You'd have laughed too."

"Next time I take to flying, I'll pad my undercarriage." she said feelingly, as she sat down on the bed.

Bogle peered at her between his fingers. When he assured himself that she was sitting quietly, he took his hand away and sucked his teeth noisily. "Don't ever do that again." he said. "A sight like that doesn't belong anywhere."

"Think of the shoe leather I'll save." Myra said, smiling happily. "That was really something to experience."

"Can't we get our minds down to business?" I asked. "Not that I can think clearly. This's about the craziest moment of my life, but we've still to settle about your father. Can you discuss him without becoming inflated?"

Myra's face clouded, "I was forgetting him." she said. "There's nothing to discuss. I'm going to see him."

"Now, don't be in too great a rush." I said. "The first thing to do is to get hold of Juden. He'll have details. Then we can decide what to do. We'll get packed up and go to Mexico City as quickly as we can. We ought to get there by to-night. Then we can talk things over with him, make plans and see what it's all about."

"Sam and I are coming." Ansell said firmly. "Don't you get any ideas about stopping us."

I looked questioningly at Myra. She shrugged. "Oh, well." she said, "I suppose they'd better."

Just then the verandah door pushed open, and Whisky came in. "Mexico City?" he growled. "I haven't been there since I was a pup. I'll come along too."

I shook my head. "Listen." I said firmly. "I'm not interested in your puppy life. We haven't room for you and none of us like dogs. If you want to go to Mexico City you make your own arrangements."

Ansell was staring at the dog in delight. "My goodness! He's worth a fortune. Of course, he must come with us." he said.

Whisky eyed him suspiciously. "If you've got any ideas of exploiting me." he snapped, "forget them I'm against any form of sweatshop labour. I'm coming with you because I'm tired of the other dogs in this town. A change will do me good."

"He talks like a real gentleman, doesn't he?" Bogle said in awe.

Myra went to the door. "I think I'm going mad." she said in a firm voice.

Whisky eyed her thoughtfully, "Upon my word that's a pretty trull." he said. "Whoever gets her *will* be a lucky dog."

Myra looked at him, her eyes wide with horror, then she disappeared, slamming the door behind her.

NINE

We reached Mexico City at dusk and had an argument outside the *Plaza* Hotel. I wanted to go straight to Juden while Myra wanted to stop off at the hotel, change and get Juden to come down to us.

Myra got her way in the end. So we trooped into the *Plaza,* registered for rooms and had another argument about Whisky. At first, the reception clerk wouldn't hear of him coming into the hotel, but Bogle managed to persuade him.

Whisky got restive while Bogle and the clerk were wrangling, and I was scared that he was going to open his mouth. I knew that if he talked out of turn we'd all be tossed into the Street. I guess he was smart enough to realize that too. In the end, it was agreed that Bogle should have a double room and it would be okay for Whisky to share it with him.

Going up in the elevator, there was a further argument about who was going to pay the hotel bill. The only person—if you can call him a person— who didn't get excited was Whisky. We were still arguing when we reached the third floor and examined our rooms.

It was finally decided that Juden should be invited to meet the bill and since the others didn't know Juden this made them happy. I knew that to get money out of Juden was as easy as getting a running commentary on the Santiago handicap from a Tibetan deaf-mute. Anyway, I was tired of arguing.

"I'll get Juden on the 'phone." I said. "Suppose we all meet downstairs for dinner, say in half an hour?"

"Make it an hour." Myra said. "I'm not going to be rushed. I haven't been in a decent hotel for months and I'm going to make the most of it." She turned on Bogle. "And for goodness sake, dress yourself up, Samuel, right now you look like something put out for salvage."

"You don't look so hot yourself." Bogle snapped. "There's nothing about you that'd give a scarecrow an inferiority complex."

"Break it up." I said hastily. "We'll meet downstairs in an hour."

As soon as I had shut myself in my room, I had a bath, changed and then grabbed the telephone.

Juden didn't sound glad to hear me. "What the hell have you been do-ing?" he demanded. "Maddox's as mad as a hornet."

"Never mind about Maddox." I said. "Get your car and come over to the Plaza fast. I've got a sweet surprise package for you. No, don't ask ques-tions, just come down."

"Okay." Juden replied crossly. "But it's got to be good."

I laughed. "If only you knew just how good it is." I said and hung up.

I met Juden in the bar a half an hour later. He came in with the light of battle in his eye and a scowl on his face. "There's a load of grief piling up for you." he said, shaking hands in a half-hearted sort of way. "What's the matter with you? Do you realize that you've set Maddox back 25 grand? Right now, he's spitting rust and steel filings."

"Take it easy." I said. "Sit down and reduce steam. Let's have a drink and be reasonable."

He sat down, but I could see that he'd got a lot on his mind. "Make it a double Scotch." he said. "I've done a full day's work and I'm not feeling so good."

When the drinks came, I hitched my chair close to his. "So the girl's been found, eh?" I said. "And Maddox has had to fork up?"

"That's it." Juden said. "The poor old geezer didn't stand a chance. I tell you parting with all that dough's broken his heart."

"He never had a heart." I said grimly. "The thing that gets his blood circulating is a rock wrapped up in gristle. How did it happen?"

"Well, as far as I know." Juden returned. "It seems this Shumway bird bounced into Maddox's office with his daughter early this morning. His story is that she was rescued by a guy called Law Kelly. They brought Kelly with them.

"Maddox wouldn't play at first, but Kelly seems to be a tough egg. He'd seen the story about the reward and he remembers seeing this Shumway girl with a greaser. He set off right away and didn't have any difficulty in getting her away from the greaser. Then he grabbed a 'plane and reached New York this morning. He took her to her father and the trio turned up to collect.

"As I say, Maddox was wild, but Kelly persuaded him to part. So Maddox's blaming you for the whole thing."

"Who's Kelly?" I asked.

"Why, I guess he's one of those guys who's always around when someone's giving away 25 grand. You know how it is."

"Meaning you don't know?"

"Well, I can't know everyone, can I?"

"Swell." I lowered half my drink. "Now, we're getting places. Let me tell you, Kelly's yarn is a damn lie from soup to nuts."

"You ask Maddox." Juden returned grimly. "He'll tell you whether it's a lie or not in twenty different languages … all of 'em bad."

"You may be interested to hear that Myra Shumway's upstairs right at this very minute." I said, emphasising each word by stabbing the air with my finger.

Juden finished his drink and snapped his fingers for the barman. "The girl gets around." was all he said.

"She hasn't been to New York." I said patiently. "She's been right by my side from the time I told you I'd found her."

"Has it ever occurred to you that some young woman is kidding the pants off you?"

I thought about this, then I shook my head. "The girl's Myra Shumway." I said. "You gave me her picture. Remember?"

Juden opened a brief case, lying by his feet and produced a full plate glossy print. "Take a gander at that." he said, handing it to me.

There was Maddox looking like a well-fed turtle, another oldish man I hadn't seen before and Myra. They were standing in Maddox's office and Maddox was handing Myra a slip of paper. By the glassy smile that Maddox had hitched to his face, there could be no doubt that the slip of paper was the cheque for the 25,000-dollars reward.

I stared at the girl in the photograph. If I hadn't known that Myra hadn't been out of Mexico for the past week, I'd have been prepared to take an oath that the girl in the picture was indeed Myra Shumway. There were the same obvious points of similarity. The blonde hair down to her shoulders, half hiding her left eye. The same way of standing and the same way of tilting her head. The features were the same although the expression was a little puzzling. There was a look on her face I had never seen before, but then I'd never seen her receiving a cheque for twenty-five grand and that amount of money is enough to change anyone's expression.

I handed it back to Juden in bewilderment. "Something's wrong here." I said. "I don't know what it is." I shrugged helplessly. "When was this photo taken?"

"Eleven o'clock this morning." Juden said promptly. "It was flown out and I got it this afternoon."

"At eleven o'clock this morning, Myra Shumway was with me." I said firmly.

It was Juden's time to look startled. "Are you drunk?"

"Not with you handling my expense sheet." I returned bitterly. The barman came over at this moment and Juden ordered a second round. When he had gone away, Juden said, "So she was with you, was she?"

I nodded.

"Yeah." he said. "But who's going to believe it? Look, why don't you admit that you slipped up? Maybe, I can put things right with Maddox. I'm not promising, but …"

"Hold everything." I said waving my hand to the door. "Snatch a peep at that."

Myra was standing by the bar waiting for me to spot her. I've told you from time to time that this kid was a looker. I don't want to keep on at it or you'll think I've got something to sell. But I'll put this on record. She made anything that Earl Carrol had ever put up to dazzle the tired U.S. business men look like a wallflower in red flannel.

Maybe it was the dress. It was gold lame and the full skirt was lined with scarlet so that as she moved the scarlet showed in sudden unexpected flashes, making the dress look as if it were on fire. From the knees up, it clung to her curves like a nervous mountaineer.

She practically caused a riot. The men sitting around paused in their conversation like someone had jabbed them with a skewer, while the women radioed hate on a short wave length.

Myra didn't care. She came over, took the seat I offered her and settled herself with all the self-assurance in the world.

I said, "I'd like you to meet Paul Juden of the Central News Agency. Miss Myra Shumway." I went on to Juden.

He was like a man cut off at the knees. He managed to get to his feet and when Myra sat down, he collapsed into his chair. But he didn't seem able to say anything.

"He's not always like this." I said to Myra. "As a matter of fact he has a pretty good head on him."

"So have some umbrellas." Myra said. "But, it doesn't mean anything."

"Now, look, sunshine, don't let us have any unpleasantness, Juden is suffering from delayed shock He thought you were in New York."

"I hope we're not going to have all that all over again." Myra said.

The barman came over and stood admiring her.

"Something that would resurrect a corpse, please." Myra said, smiling at him. "Nothing small. Serve it in a brandy glass."

The barman blinked. "Yes, madam." he said, and went away.

"I'm going to get tight." she went on to me in a confidential undertone. "I haven't been in a decent hotel for months and I haven't been tight for years. I am pandering to my whims tonight."

By this time, Juden began making croaking noises. "Twins." he said feebly. "Twins."

Myra looked at him with interest. "No wonder you look like such a sad man." she said. "Should I congratulate you or buy you a wreath?"

Before I could stop him, he gave her the photograph. There was a long electric silence while she looked at it. Then she turned to me. "Who's this delightful little blonde trollop?" she asked, pointing with a trembling finger at the girl in the photograph.

"To all intents and purposes." I said as gently as possible, "it's you."

Myra drew a deep breath. "Have you ever seen me wear such an expression on my face as this over-dressed, sex-ridden, over-ripe, two-face hag is wearing?" she demanded, furiously rattling the photograph under my nose.

Even Juden shrank away from her fury.

But like all women, she had hit the nail on the thumb. That was the difference between this girl in the photograph and Myra. Whereas Myra had character, this girl had none. She had that loose, cruel expression on her face that you so often see in the face of a wanton woman. Make no mistake about it, this girl was bad right through, but it wasn't until it was pointed out to me, that I realized it.

"Take it easy." I said. "The red light's showing on your pressure gauge."

"So this is the hooker who's impersonating me." Myra said, controlling herself with an effort. She studied the photograph intently. "And look at that smug, I've-got-the-bone expression on my dear parent's face. This is some of his work. I'll make him suffer for this!"

Juden was clawing at his collar nervously. He quite expected that she would turn on him at any moment.

"Well, P. J.," I said. "Do you see how Maddox's been fooled now?"

"What can we say to him?" Juden groaned. "You know Maddox. The other papers would rib him for weeks. Besides, he wouldn't believe it."

"He wouldn't?" Myra twisted round in her chair so that she faced Juden, who shrank as far away as he could from her. "Don't you think I could persuade him?"

"You might." Juden returned feebly. "Yes, I guess with your character you could do pretty near anything."

"And that's what I think." Myra said ominously.

"It's going to be difficult." I said, finishing my drink. "If your father says she's you, you'll have a hard job convincing anyone."

The barman brought Myra's cocktail. There was a lot of it in a large brandy glass. He put it on the table beside her. "It is my own invention, madam." he said.

Myra picked up the balloon glass and took a long pull from the blue-green liquor. Then she shut her eyes, held her breath and her feet traced quick little patterns on the carpet. When she could speak, she said faintly, "Any smoke escaping from me?"

"You like it, madam?" the barman asked anxiously.

"That is the wrong word." Myra said, putting the glass on the table and staring at it. "You don't like a thing like that. A corpse doesn't like embalming fluid, but it does it good. What do you call it?"

"The breath of a Tiger." the barman said, not knowing whether to be complimented or not.

Myra shuddered. "I'm glad it's only his breath." she said. "Somehow, I don't think I could have managed the tiger itself."

"If madam does not like it, I will bring her something else." the barman said, looking hurt. "I have another specialty which I call the Panther's spit."

Myra waved him away. "Some other time perhaps." she said, and he returned behind his bar with a puzzled expression on his face.

Doc Ansell and Bogle came into the bar. They were wearing tuxedos. Bogle looked like an Eastside waiter.

"There you are." Ansell said, drawing up a chair. "We've been having a little trouble with Whisky, otherwise we'd've been down before."

I introduced Juden who nodded vaguely.

Myra examined Bogle thoughtfully. "What you need is an ermine dicky, Sam." she said. "It would set off that dress suit."

Sam was looking at her with undisguised admiration. "Gee!" he exploded. "That dress you've nearly got on is the horse's hoofs!"

"Never mind that." I broke in. "We've got a little brain work ahead of us." and I gave Ansell the photograph.

He studied it and then passed it to Bogle. "That's Mr. Maddox handing over the reward, I suppose." he said.

I nodded. It surprised me he didn't say anything about the girl in the picture. He just glanced thoughtfully at Myra, pursed his lips and then studied his small brown hands.

Bogle, however, had plenty to say. "What's she doing in this picture?" he demanded. "How did she get to New York anyway and if she's got the cheque, where is it?"

"That isn't me, you dope." Myra snapped. "Haven't you got eyes in your head?"

Bogle blinked. "Sure." he said. "Well, if it ain't you, that dame's certainly borrowed your geography. Who is she?"

"That's what I want to know." Myra returned grimly. "And when I find out, even a plastic surgeon won't be able to put her right." She reached for her drink and lowered a good two inches of the liquor down her throat.

I looked over at Juden. "We've got to do something, P. J.," I said. "For one thing, if I don't put myself right with Maddox, he might have a grudge against me. I wouldn't like that to happen."

"He's got one already." Juden returned. "You may as well know, Ross. I'm sorry, but you're out."

I stared at him. "What do you mean … out? How about my contract?"

"That falls due at the end of the month." Juden returned, looking unhappy. "He's not renewing it. He says you've cost him plenty as it is."

"The ungrateful rat." I said bitterly. "After all I've done for him too!"

"Anything might happen to change his mind by the end of the month." Ansell broke in. "I shouldn't let it prey on your mind."

"I know that kind of a guy." Bogle added. "You ought to call on him and kick his teeth in. That'll give him different ideas."

"I think you'd better keep away from him." Juden said, shaking his head. "He could get you on the blacklist if he wanted to." He got to his feet, scratched his head and then said, "Before I go, wasn't there something about a story? Wasn't that why I came down?"

"Yeah." I said. "But, now I'm out, I'm sticking to that story. Catch me making a present of anything to Maddox."

"That's not the way to go on." Juden said. "If you've got a story, you'd better let me have it."

"Not now. Maybe, later."

He studied my face and decided that it was no use pressing me. "Okay." he said, "I'll be getting along." He looked over at Myra, frowned, and ran his fingers through his hair. "I don't know what to make of her." he said, almost as if he were talking to himself. "You wouldn't have a twin, would you?" he asked her hopefully.

"No." Myra said.

"Then, I just give up. You can waste a lot of time with a problem like this. Time's money to me."

"Well, so long, P.J.." I said, shaking hands. "If I'm broke I'll look you up."

"Sure, anything like that."

"Okay. Keep out of hospital."

"Sure, last time I was in there, I took a turn for the nurse." he returned and went off laughing like a hyena.

"That guy's got nurses on the brain." I said, relaxing. "Oh well, let's forget him. I guess we'll all get drunk. It's a fine welcome to find your job's been thrown in your face."

Myra finished her drink, gasped, and then waved violently to the barman. "Don't you dare blame me." she said. "I didn't lose you your mouldy job."

"I never said you did." I said wearily. "Well, I've got to think of something …"

"You're going to help me find this blonde harridan. How would you like that?" she asked.

"It's an idea." I said. "But, not a very profitable one."

The barman came over.

"Four Tiger breaths." Myra said. "And make them large ones."

"You like it, madam?" The barman showed his pleasure.

"No." Myra said, with a shudder. "But it likes me."

I looked at the other two. "What have we got out of this so far? A couple of miracles and a talking dog. Surely, we can turn that little lot into hard cash?"

Ansell said, "We've got a great deal more than that. The first thing to do is to find Hamish Shumway and the girl who's impersonating Myra. We must waste no time in doing it."

There was an odd note of urgency in his voice which made me glance at him sharply. I had not seen him look so worried before.

"What have you got on your mind?" I asked.

"Plenty." He paused while the barman came with the drinks and then when he had gone he went on "There's evil in Nagualism. I feel some of that evil has broken loose."

"I wish you would be quiet." Myra said crossly. "You're always the skeleton at the feast. To-night, we enjoy ourselves. To-morrow we go to New York." And she raised her glass, "The toast is frustration and confusion to killjoys!"

We drank.

PART TWO—NEW YORK

TEN

It wasn't until we had been in New York for three days and we had more or less settled down in a Brooklyn apartment that I began to realize that Doc Ansell's presentiments might have some foundation.

During those three days, we were all busy trying to find Myra's father. Consequently, we didn't see much of each other.

In spite of this, I was aware of a subtle change that had come over Myra. She was kinder and she did not pick quarrels with Bogle. She looked different somehow, although I did not stop to analyse just why she did look different. She also clung more strongly than ever to her policy of honesty, which unsettled us all.

The first real indication that things weren't right happened on the third night of our stay in New York. I had been around the various Press Clubs hoping to pick up some clue to Shumway and I guess I must have been doing myself rather well. I wasn't exactly tight, but I'd had enough to make me hesitate about ascending the stairs in the dark. Also, I couldn't find the light switch.

I was standing in the lobby trying to make up my mind whether I'd go up on my hands and knees or sleep in the living-room, when I heard the sound of someone coming up the steps to the apartment. A moment later the front door opened and someone came in.

"Who's that?" I said, peering into the darkness.

There was a faint gasp and I recognized Myra's voice.

"Put the light on, will you?" I said, "I've been searching for the switch for the last five minutes."

She didn't say anything, but ran upstairs. I could just make out her shadowy form as she slipped past me.

"Well, that's a nice way to treat a guy." I said, "can't you even say hello?"

By this time, she'd reached the top of the stairs and had disappeared.

Feeling a little mad and wondering what made her behave like this, I took the stairs with a rush and eventually got to the top. I went straight to Myra's room and knocked on the door.

There wasn't any sound, so I opened the door and put my head round. The room was in darkness.

"Myra?" I called, "What are you up to?"

A sleepy voice came from across the room, "What is it?"

I groped for the switch and turned it on.

Myra sat up in bed. She was in a pair of gay pyjamas and she looked at me crossly. "What's the big idea?" she snapped, "take that drink sodden face out of here and put it under a pillow."

I stared at her. "But, you passed me a moment ago." I said, feeling startled, "do you usually get into bed in two seconds?"

She sat further up in the bed. "You're tight." she said. "I've been asleep since eleven o'clock. Go away!"

I came into the room. "Seriously, sweetheart." I said, "someone came upstairs. I thought it was you. Damn it, I'll swear it was you."

"This sounds mightily like the silk-worm gag." she said, "get out of my room before I toss you out, you drunken heel!"

This brought me up short. I looked at her. This was the Myra I'd known in Mexico. A sudden change had come over her from the Myra I'd known during the past three days.

"Take it easy." I said, "I'm not as tight as all that." and I walked over to where her clothes were lying. I touched her dress. It was warm. "You've just got out of this." I said, picking it up.

"Where did you get that from?" she asked, startled, "I put all my clothes away before I went to bed."

"Yeah? Well, there's a complete outfit on this chair. Look, one of us is nuts and it ain't me."

She climbed out of bed and came over. "But, I haven't had these things out of my trunk since we came here." she said, uneasily.

"Okay." I said dropping the dress. "Forget it. I don't want to know where you've been tonight. You don't have to lie so hard."

"I'm not lying!" she said angrily, "you're trying to make a fool out of me!"

"I couldn't do that." I said, suddenly feeling too tired to argue. "Go to sleep." and I walked out and left her.

I don't mind telling you it preyed on my mind. I couldn't get to sleep and I began imagining all kinds of things. I could have swore that whoever it was who'd gone upstairs had been Myra. Yet it didn't seem possible for her to get into bed and feign sleep in so short a time. Yet, that was what she must have done.

Why had she pretended to be asleep? What had she been up to? Or was she speaking the truth? That's how it went on in my mind for nearly the rest of the night. But, I did eventually get some sleep.

The next morning, while I was shaving, Doc Ansell came into my room.

"Hello there." I said as I mowed my beard with an electric razor. "Have I got a hangover or have I?"

"I've been thinking." Ansell said, sitting on the foot of the bed. "I'm not happy about certain things."

"What things?"

"That girl in the photograph." Ansell said slowly, "how do you explain she's the image of Myra?"

I selected a necktie and wandered over to the mirror. "I don't." I said.

"That's just the point. She hasn't a twin and you'll never make me believe that some other girl, no relation of hers, could look like her."

"Well, that's what's happened." I said. "Maybe, Shumway got hold of an actress who's made herself up to look like Myra. A guy like him would do a lot for all that dough."

Ansell shook his head, "I think there's more in it than that." he said, "I'm not saying you haven't hit on the explanation, but I don't think so."

"Quit beating about the bush." I said, facing him, "what are you getting at?"

"Haven't you noticed a change in the girl recently?" he asked.

Then I remembered what happened last night. "There was a change." I said slowly, "but now she's back where she started."

"I don't understand." he said. "What happened last night?"

I told him.

He sat listening, his face grave and his eyes worried. When I'd finished, he smacked one hand into the other. "Then I'm right!" he said. "There are two of them. Strange and powerful influences are around."

"Now, don't start that." I said irritably. "It's bad enough …"

"Did you ever read a book called 'Dr. Jekyll and Mr. Hyde'?"

I stared at him, "I guess so, but what has that …?"

"Plenty." Ansell broke in, "you remember it's a story of the separating of the good and evil in man. Did you know that the Naguales have this power? I think that's what's happened to Myra."

I put my coat on slowly and looked at myself in the mirror. I wasn't looking too good in the hard sunlight. I looked pale and there were smudges under my eyes.

"If you can't talk sense, you'd better shut up." I said at last.

"It's only because you refuse to believe." Ansell said quietly. "Ignorance breeds fear. You're becoming frightened."

I sat on the edge of the bed. I could see he wouldn't let it go, so I thought we might as well have it out.

"Give me a retake." I said.

"This is what I think's happened." Ansell said. "Quintl has separated the good and bad in Myra and has put each of these components into materialized form. The form naturally follows the original pattern. So we have two Myras, both of them exactly alike, but one has all the good qualities that a human being possesses while the other has all the bad ones. Now, do you understand?"

"It's crazy." I said, hating every bit of this.

Ansell shook his head, "It isn't, if you know about these things. If I told you that the dog would talk, you wouldn't have believed it. Now, you admit you accept it as a fact."

"Yeah." I said, thinking again of what happened last night. "So you really think she can become two people or rather possess two different bodies when she wants to?"

"I think so. Perhaps not when she wants to, but when she's not aware of what's happening and is off her guard. Let's put it that way."

"That would account for what happened last night. They've become one again."

"But what has the other one been doing?"

"That's something we've got to find out. That's where Myra's danger lies."

"What do you mean?"

"Let's go back to first principles." Ansell said. "We have all latent evil in our make-up. Some of us haven't the same control over this instinct as others. It depends on our training, our environment and our strength of character whether this instinct gets the upper hand. If the evil in us is segregated without the restraining influence of our instinct for doing good, then something entirely primitive has been created and may cause a lot of destruction. I'd hate to see Myra suffer for something she hasn't done."

This was beyond me. "Something she hasn't done?" I repeated.

"Yes. Suppose now, the other Myra, the Myra in the photograph, takes it into her head to commit a crime. Might not the Myra we know get the blame for it?"

"Why should she?"

"It depends if the other Myra is seen while committing the crime." Ansell returned.

"They're exactly alike. The finger prints would be the same. Both girls are easily recognized. Can't you see what danger there might be in all this?"

I drew a deep breath, "You're looking for trouble." I said. "This business is too much for me. What we've got to do is to get after Shumway. Now, come on, I smell breakfast."

"Wait." Ansell said. "What about this fellow Kelly? Maybe, we can get on to him."

"Maybe, we can." I said. "We'll talk it over at breakfast."

In the living room, Bogle was setting the table "All ready, Bud." he said to me. "Fried ham and eggs, whaddayssay?"

"Sounds fine." I said. "Isn't Myra coming down?"

"Naw." Sam said, going into the kitchen. "A dame like that likes to lay around in bed. Besides, it takes her half the morning to get up. I like to get breakfast over with."

When he had gone, I said to Ansell, "Old Sam's getting like a gawdamn housewife. Do you think he's going soft or something?"

Ansell shook his head absently. "He always wanted to have a place of his own." he said. "Many a time, in the desert, he'd talk about setting up home. Funny thing, isn't it? Yet he's mixed with the toughest thugs of Chicago. And now look at him, running around, keeping the house clean, cooking and waiting on Myra."

Just then Sam came in with a tray and put the food on the table. He then shot back into the kitchen, came out again with a smaller tray and carried it off to Myra's room.

"Kelly." I said, with my mouth full. "That's an idea, Doc. I wonder if we can get a line on him."

"Maybe your paper would know." Ansell returned, pouring out the coffee. "Anyone there you can ask?"

I thought for a moment, "Yeah, Dowdy's the guy. He's sort of secretary to Maddox. He ought to know something."

Sam came back, whistling cheerfully and pulled a chair up to the table. He sat down, "That dog murders me." he said "Jeeze! You never seen anything like it. He's in with the kid and they're talking away like a couple of professors. What they find to talk about, beats me."

"Never mind about them." I said, pushing the plate of fried ham over to him. "So long as they don't fight, what does it matter? I admit I don't find Whisky too easy to talk to. Maybe, it's because he kind of embarrasses me."

"He's a smart guy, that dog." Bogle said, spearing the ham with his fork. "He's got a political mind."

"You wouldn't know this fellow Kelly?" Ansell asked. "The one who's helping Shumway."

"Kelly?" Bogle repeated. "There's millions of Kelly's. I know two or three of 'em, but unless I saw the guy, I couldn't say."

"Don't worry about it, Doc." I said, helping myself to more coffee. "I'll go down to the *Recorder* as soon as I've finished. Maybe, I'll get something."

"Yeah." Bogle broke in, "ain't it time we found this Shumway guy? When we do get him, he'll have spent all that jack."

"We're doing our best." Ansell said. "You don't seem exactly full of ideas, Sam." He pushed his plate away and wandered over to an armchair. He sat down and began to read the newspaper.

Whisky wandered in, "Hey-ho." he said, with a flick of his tail "What's buzzin', cousin?"

"Don't." I said, pushing back my chair and lighting a cigarette. "Try to speak pure English if you're going to speak at all. I think Sam's accent is affecting you."

"Don't be a prig." Whisky returned, wandering over to Sam, "Well, my old." he went on to Sam, resting his long muzzle on Sam's knee, "What have you got for my breakfast? That ham looked a little fat to me."

"I'll cut the fat off." Sam said. "Don't worry about a little thing like that, or I've got a steak. Howjer like that?"

"Mmm." Whisky said. "Let's go find it. That sounds like something." They went off into the kitchen.

"The airs and graces that dog gives himself kills me." I said. "Steak for breakfast! He'll get too fat."

"Too fat for what?" Sam asked, putting his head round the door. "You be careful what you're saying. You ain't no hour-glass yourself."

"From where I'm standing." Whisky added, pushing his snout round the door, "that bulge in your waist line looks like a six-course lunch the waiter forgot to take out of the casserole."

"Aw, beat it, you two." I said grinning. "My waist line's all right. Well, I'll get over to the *Recorder*. So long, Doc."

Ansell waved, "So long." he said.

I thought I'd say hello and good-bye to Myra so I tapped on her door.

"Come in." she called.

I pushed the door open and walked in. I didn't see her in bed and I looked round the room blankly.

"Hello there." I said, "where've you gone?"

"Good morning, Ross." Myra said, and patted me lightly on my head.

She was floating near the ceiling, a book in her hand and a cigarette between her lips.

"Holy Moses!" I said, starting back. "Must you do that?"

"Why not?" she said, "Haven't you heard the saying 'I'm walking on air'? Well, I'm lying on it. It's very comfortable and restful."

She floated slowly down until her face was level with mine then she put her arm round my neck and lowered her feet to the ground. She stood with difficulty.

"I'm feeling very light, this morning." she said, "As light as a thistledown."

I looked at her thoughtfully, "Apart from that." I said, "How do you feel?"

"Oh, all right." her eyes clouded, "you were awfully drunk last night. I'm still a little angry with you."

I wasn't sure but this seemed the new Myra again. "I wasn't so bad." I said, "tell me, what happened? You know what I mean."

She went over and sat on the bed, "I'm scared." she said, "I dreamed things again. I dreamed that someone came into this room and got into my body. Then you woke me up. Weren't some clothes on that chair when you came in, or did I dream it?"

"There were." I said, looking at her uneasily. "Why do you ask?"

"Because they're not here now." she returned, "Oh, Ross, what's happening?"

"I don't know." I said, sure now that Doc Ansell was right. There were two of them. It seemed incredible, but everything pointed to it. "You're not to worry. Look, I've got to go out. Maybe we might lunch together."

Her face brightened. "Lovely." she said, "what time and where?"

I looked at the clock. It was already late. "Meet me at Manetta's in a couple of hours and we'll talk."

"All right." she said. "But, do you think it'll do any good?"

"I don't know, but there are things I want to discuss with you." I turned to the door, "Don't worry, and leave Whisky home, will you? I want you to myself."

"I'll tell him." she said, "but, he won't be pleased."

"And I couldn't care less." I said and left her.

ELEVEN

The doorman at the entrance of the *Recorder* Offices seemed embarrassed when he saw me.

"Hullo there, Murphy." I said wondering what was biting him. "It's good to see your ugly mug again. How's tricks? I haven't seen you in months."

"I guess that's right." he said, shuffling his feet like he was standing on a boiler plate of an overworked tug-boat, "you wouldn't be coming in here, would you, Mr. Millan?"

"Yep." I said cheerfully. "That's the idea. I'm one of those big-minded guys. I'm not afraid of catching anything in this joint although it ought to have been fumigated years ago."

He laughed like a very sad man, "Well, Mr. Millan." he said, "you know how it is." and he shuffled his feet some more.

It occurred to me suddenly that he wasn't going to let me in. "What's cookin', Murphy?" I said sharply, "has someone died in there or something?"

"Well, no, Mr. Millan, but Mr. Maddox has given instructions that he don't want you in the office. We all feel pretty sore about it, but that's the way it is."

"Maddox!" I said. "Well, how do you like that?" I pushed my hat to the back of my head and looked at Murphy more in anger than in sorrow.

"Well, don't let it get you down. You're only doing your job. Look, I want a word with Dowdy. Will you get hold of him and tell him to come over to Joe's?"

"You bet, Mr. Millan." Murphy said, brightening up. "I'll tell him. I'll tell him right away."

I went over to Joe's poolroom, behind the *Recorder's* Office end I felt sore. I'd worked for this sheet for almost ten years and it was like my second home. It was like being one of the orphans in the storm.

McCue of the *Telegram* was the only guy in Joe's. He was sitting at the bar on a high stool thumbing through a telephone book when I blew in.

Both he and the barman stared at me as if I was something out of a zoo.

"Hey, Mac." I said with a grin, "isn't it your bed-time?"

He screwed up his big rubbery face and then offered a limp hand, "Ross Millan." he said as if he couldn't believe it, "I thought you'd committed hara-kiri in the desert."

"Mornin' Willy." I said to the barman, "how about a coffee?"

"Nice to see you again, Mr. Millan." he said, going over to the urn, "we miss guys like you."

"Only because we pay our way." I said, pulling up a stool and sitting down. "These desk newshounds want everything on the cuff."

McCue took out a dollar and laid it on the counter, "Willy." he said, "I'm paying for that coffee. I consider it an honour to pay for anything that'll sustain the guy who cost Maddox twenty-five grand."

I grinned, but I wasn't feeling so good. "Quit ribbing me." I said, "and hang on to that dollar. You know it's the first piece of money you ever earned."

McCue put the dollar back into his pocket, "I was forgetting." he said. "Anyway, it's as good as a tenement fire to see you again. I hear you're out."

"The *Recorder's* washed me out, if that's what you mean." I said, lighting a cigarette. "But, I've got a great future ahead of me."

"That's what the guy said when they stuck him on the hot seat. But, then he was only foolin'." McCue said dryly. "What kind of a corny stunt was that you and Maddox thought up?"

"Never mind." I said, stirring my coffee. "Let the dead rest in peace. What's cookin' now?"

McCue returned to the telephone book, "We've got a new lead on the Wilson killing." he said. "I've gotta phone a dame." He found the number and pulled the battered telephone that stood on the bar towards him. It had no mouthpiece and the cord was frayed and knotted.

"When did you get back from Mexico?"

"A few days ago." I said, watching him dial. "You want to try Mexico sometime. It's a swell place."

"You can have it." he said, "I wouldn't know what to do with sand and horses." The telephone went plop and I heard a faint tinny voice snap something in McCue's ear. He shifted forward on his stool, "Is this the residence of Miss Gloria Hope-Dawn?" he asked.

"For cryin' out loud." I said astonished. "Is that a long distance to Hollywood?"

"Naw." he returned, grinning, "just a little tarnished glamour from the East Side." He turned his attention to the telephone, "Hello, there. Miss Gloria Hope-Dawn? This is Mr. McCue of the *Telegram*. Yeah. Is it true Harry Wilson gave you a mink coat last year?"

She seemed to have a lot to say about that, because McCue closed his eyes and glued his ear to the receiver and listened.

"All tight, all right." he said at last, "I've got to ask questions. It's part of my job."

He listened some more, then suddenly broke in, "Listerine's about the best kind of mouth wash. You ought to try it sometime." and hung up. He mopped his face with a dirty handkerchief, "Where these dames learn all their language beats me." he said mournfully. "I guess I'll have to go round and see her. Wilson couldn't have bought her that fur coat to keep her warm. She's like a blast furnace."

I told myself that I was going to miss working on the *Recorder*. You only had to smell a little press atmosphere to realize just how much it all meant. In Mexico, it was different, but right here in New York, it was a swell game.

"Well, I'd better be moving." McCue said, sliding off his stool. "You'll be around, won't you? Got any plans?"

"Don't worry about me." I said, "I've got more than my arm up my sleeve. It'll take a battalion of punks like Maddox to rattle me."

He looked at me thoughtfully, "Yeah." he said, "I suppose it will." and waving his hand, he went to the door. He nearly banged into Dowdy who came hurrying in, an anxious expression on his thin hatchet face.

McCue said, "You'd better watch your till, Willy, here's another guy from the *Recorder*." and he went off down the street.

Dowdy refused coffee and sat on the stool with a miserable expression on his face and his eye on the door. I could see that I wasn't going to get a lot of help from him and the sooner I let him get back to the office the better he'd like it.

"Where's Shumway?" I asked, abruptly.

Dowdy blinked, "Shumway?" he repeated, "I don't know. Why should I?"

"Listen." I said patiently, "if you were to tell me all the things you don't know, we'd be old men by the time we got out of here. I don't know why you should know where Shumway is, but, there's no harm in asking, is there?"

"Don't get sore, Ross." he said uneasily. "Maddox has told us to leave you alone. If he hears you and I have been talking, there'll be hell to pay."

"Don't worry about a crum like that." I said, "you inside men worry too much about punks like Maddox. I've got to find Shumway. It's important."

"Well, I'm sorry." he said, shaking his head, "I don't know where he is. He and his daughter collected the reward from Maddox and beat it. We haven't their address on file." He looked longingly at the door.

"This guy Kelly." I went on hurriedly, seeing that I wasn't going to hold him much longer, "What do you know about him?"

109

"Not much. He was the fellow who found the girl. By rights, I suppose, he ought to have had the reward, but they agreed between themselves to split it. I only saw him once and that was after Shumway and the girl had drawn the money."

"What did he want?" I asked, feeling that we might be getting places.

"He wanted to get in touch with Kruger." Dowdy replied.

I stared at him, "Peppi Kruger?" I asked, startled.

"Yes, Peppi's a big shot now, Millan." Dowdy returned. "He's president of the Brooklyn Motor Company and an important political figure in lower East Side politics. About six months ago he got control of the Taxi Chauffeurs' union. You know the racket. He scared the pants off the taxicab companies and made a pile of jack. Any company that doesn't pay up, gets into trouble. He's got them eating out of his hand at the moment, but something tells me that the D.A.'ll get on to him before long. Anyway, he's made enough money now to retire."

I whistled, "A guy like that." I said in disgust, "when I knew him he was running rum for Brescia. What did Kelly want with him?"

Dowdy slid off his stool. "I don't know." he said, "I wasn't having anything to do with it, but I guess he could get in touch with Kruger easily enough." He looked longingly at the door, "Well, I've got to get back." he went on, "Maddox might want me."

"Okay, Dowdy." I said. "You've given me a lead."

He looked at me suspiciously, "What's the idea? Why are you interested in Shumway?"

"Wouldn't you be interested in some guy who lost you your job?" I said, meeting his eye.

He looked a little scared, "You aren't going to start trouble, are you, Millan?" he said nervously. "Maddox wouldn't like that."

"Do you think I care what Maddox likes or dislikes?" I said. "Why a midget wouldn't be scared of a rat like him."

He gave me another troubled look, shook hands and went off across the street to the *Recorder* Offices.

I finished my coffee, lit another cigarette and then reached for the telephone book. Kruger had a house on East Seventy-eight Street. That made me think. To have a house in that narrow territory bounded by Lexington on the east and Fifth Avenue on the west meant something. It meant more than something. It meant money. Stacks of money.

"Remember Peppi?" I said to Willy, who had just got through preparing the free lunch sandwiches.

"Yeah." he said, "that punk used to worry me. He didn't come in here much, but when he did, he sure started a draught. Well, I guess he's had a successful career, but he didn't come by it honestly. I don't envy him."

I shook my head. "It wouldn't make a lot of difference if you did." I said with a grin, "Peppi wouldn't care."

Willy grinned back, "I guess that's right." he said. "You wouldn't be interested in Peppi now, would you, Mr. Millan?"

"I don't know." I said, "I've got time to be interested in anyone."

"Out of a job?" The big barman's face showed sympathy.

"Resting." I said, yawning. "When I want work, I'll get work. Well, so long, Willy, I'll be in again."

"So long, Mr. Millan." Willy still looked worried, "I hope you get a break."

Walking down the street, I hoped so too.

Anyway the morning wasn't wasted. I had something to think about. Why did Kelly want to get into touch with Peppi? That was interesting. Had Shumway and the girl double-crossed Kelly? Maybe Kelly had once worked for Peppi and wanted him to put some pressure on Shumway to divide up the dough.

I remembered Peppi well. You couldn't easily forget him. Last time I saw him was about two years ago. He was on trial for murder. I remember him sitting with his Counsel, listening to the opening address by the District Attorney. He never batted an eyelid throughout the two-day trial and he got away with it without the jury leaving the box. As far as I knew, he'd stood trial four times for murder and four times he'd been acquitted. Now, of course, he could pay some other guy to do his killing for him.

Peppi was a little guy with big bulging eyes. When he was a kid he contracted a skin disease that had stripped off his hair. He'd been as bald as an egg ever since. Apart from looking like a second cousin of Lugosi, he had a mean disposition.

So it came back to the problem. What did Kelly want with him? The only thing I could do was to call on Peppi and find out. If I went with a good enough story I might get somewhere. I didn't exactly relish the visit, but I argued that if a guy had a house on East Seventy-eight, then he wasn't likely to cut my throat. Or was he?

Anyway, thinking along those lines didn't get me anywhere so I hailed a cab and gave Peppi's address.

The driver knew him all right.

"Friend of yours, Bud?" he said, pushing the taxi through the traffic like he was anxious to get rid of me.

"You ask him. He'll tell you if he wants you to know." I returned.

"Wise guy, huh?" the driver snorted. "A dime a dozen. A dime a dozen."

"I heard you the first time." I said.

He didn't say anything for a couple of blocks, then he ventured again, "That Kruger guy ain't doing us any good in the taxi business. Somebody ought to stop him."

"Come in with me and stop him." I said, putting my feet on the spring seat in front of me.

"Yeah?" he said, "I like that kind of advice. It's like saying why not bop Joe Louis on the snout."

"Just drive me." I pleaded. "I would the rest were silence."

That held him and I didn't get a yap out of him until he'd stopped outside Peppi's house. I gave him a dollar. "Hang on to the change." I said. "You look like you could use some relief."

He put the dollar away slowly. "Some of you smart guys love yourselves." he said, spitting on the sidewalk. "I bet you've got chapped lips kissing mirrors." and he drove away before I could think up a comeback.

I concentrated on Peppi's house. Well, it was a nice joint. It looked like it belonged to Vincent Astor or J. P. Morgan or some high-powered magnate like that. It was solid, big and cool-looking with burgundy brick walls, a terra-cotta tile roof and bay-cottage windows of white stone.

I went up the three broad steps to the massive oak and iron-studded door and rang the bell.

An elderly man, got up to look like a butler, opened the door "come in, sir." he said, without even asking me what I wanted.

I followed him into a large lounge which was furnished in the most modern style I'd seen this side of Lexington. I can't say I liked it a lot, but it stank of money and I guess that was all Peppi ever worried about.

The butler looked at me questioningly. He was big with white hair and faded blue eyes. One side of his face was lifted as if he'd had a stroke at one time. It gave him a disagreeable look. "Did you wish to see anyone in particular, sir?" he asked.

"Yeah." I said, "I'd like a word with Mr. Kruger."

"Mr. Kruger, sir?" The butler's eyebrows shot up as if I'd asked to see the President.

"That's right." I said, smiling at him.

"I'm afraid, sir." the butler returned with dignity, "Mr. Kruger never sees anyone except by appointment. Would his secretary do?"

"Look." I said, "I'm sorry about the appointment. I couldn't care less about the secretary. I want to see Kruger. Go tell him that Ross Millan of the New York *Recorder* wants to see him and tell him it's important."

The butler studied me for a second. "Very good, sir." he said and floated away upstairs, leaving me standing in the lounge.

After a while, I began to think that he had completed his stroke and was lying upstairs making noises. The hands of the big old-fashioned grandfather clock kept moving forward with little jerky jumps and I got more and more tired of standing there.

Then I heard someone coming. It wasn't the butler. Whoever it was came along the passage quickly and lightly and then a girl came down the broad staircase. She was thin, fragile and dark. Her eyebrows were unusually straight and her eyes were very large, cobalt blue with big irises and a vague expression. She wore a pair of biscuit-coloured slacks, a burgundy sweater and a biscuit-coloured handkerchief round her head. She was all right until you came to her mouth. That gave her away. It was a tight, lipless slit of red. I could imagine her sitting up in a half dark room pulling the legs off spiders and getting a lot of fun out of it. Back and front her figure looked like she had been fed through a mangle.

"I'm Mr. Kruger's secretary." she said. Her voice was deep and musical.

"Well, well." I said, "well, well, well."

One of her eyebrows went up and she tried again, "you wanted to see Mr. Kruger?"

"That was the idea, but I've changed my mind. My doctor only lets me have one meal a day." I said, adjusting my necktie. "What do you do with your evenings?"

"You're Millan, of the New York *Recorder*, aren't you?" she asked. The cobalt blue eyes had darkened.

"Yep." I said, "Ross Millan. Just plain Ross to you. How about dating me up? The demand's brisk, but I can manage to-night."

"What did you want to see Mr. Kruger about?"

Somehow I didn't feel I was making much headway, but I wasn't discouraged, "I'll tell him that." I said gently. "No offence meant, but this is a little matter between men. Women have their secrets too, you know."

"Then you'd better come upstairs." she said and turned and walked back the way she had come.

When we reached the top of the stairs I drew level and walked by her side. "I was just kidding." I said suddenly. "Don't let it get your vitamins in an uproar."

She didn't say anything.

"Could I have your name?" I went on, "I'd like to know how to introduce you to my friends."

"Lydia Brandt." she said, without turning her head, "and I don't expect to meet your friends."

"You never know." I said. "Strange things happen."

She opened a door that led off the passage and stood aside, "Mr. Kruger will be in a minute."

"But, you're not leaving me?" I said, wandering into the room.

The cobalt blue eyes looked sultry, but she didn't say anything. She closed the door behind her and left me in the room which was large and lined with books.

I glanced round with interest. The library was made up of the most complete collection of crime books I'd ever seen. Even police headquarters couldn't compete with it. The books ranged from sixteenth century crime to modern crime. There were books on poison, forensic medicine, murder, blackmail, kidnapping, assault and, in fact, something of everything.

I was just getting interested in the second volume of Havelock Ellis when the door opened and Peppi came in.

All right, I admit I startled me. I hadn't seen him for a couple of years and then, as I've already told you, that was when he was rum running.

Now, of course, he had come up in the world. I expected a change, but not such a change as this.

He was dressed in a grey silk dressing gown with a scarlet cord. Under this, he seemed to be wearing white silk pyjamas. His face was smooth and unwrinkled as if he'd had all the electric massage in the world working on him. His small white hands were soft and well cared for and his finger nails manicured. But his eyes were the same. They were the same small pebbles of blue stone and his large bald head was the same except it shone as if he had polished it with beeswax.

We looked at each other, then he shut the door and came further into the room.

"You've got a swell library, Peppi." I said, saying the first thing that came into my head. "Who put it together for you?"

He stroked the side of his nose with his thumb. That was something new. In the old days, Peppi hadn't time to affect mannerisms. "What do you want?" His voice was high pitched and soft. Rather like the tones of a Jap and the sound of it brought back a host of memories. I'd forgotten that high pitched, hissing voice.

"What a success story." I said, admiring him. "I remember you a couple of years ago. And look at you now!"

"What do you want?" he repeated.

I paused and regarded him. The dead pebbly eyes told me that this wasn't going to be a love feast, so I decided to get to the point.

"Where's Kelly?" I asked.

"Kelly?" he repeated and frowned. "What Kelly? What are you talking about?" There was a thin edge of anger in his voice.

"There's a fellow called Kelly I want to get in touch with." I said, half sitting on the big oak reading table. "I hear he wanted to find you, so I thought if you two had made contact you wouldn't mind putting him in touch with me."

He studied me carefully. "I don't know any Kelly." he said, at last.

I shrugged, "Well, that's too bad. Okay, then I'll drift. I was under the impression that you did."

"What do you want him for?" The question suddenly shot out like the forked tongue of a snake.

"I wouldn't take up your time." I said, pushing myself away from the table. "It's nothing that'd interest you."

He said, "Don't go. Sit down." There wasn't any invitation in his voice. It was an order. Well, I had nothing to lose, so I sat down in a big armchair and relaxed.

He fidgetted with the cord of his dressing gown and I could see he was thinking about something.

"You've left the *Recorder?*" he said abruptly.

I inclined my head, "Yep." I said. "Maddox tossed me out. That's gratitude, after all ..."

"What are you doing now?" he broke in.

"Living on my wits and capital." I said carelessly. "I'll get by. Why the interest?"

"I could give you something."

I looked at him. The frog-like face, the blue stoney eyes, the bald glistening head told me nothing. All the same, I didn't like it. I knew the kind of racket Peppi went in for. It wasn't my line, but I had to be careful how I told him.

"I'm not looking for anything right now." I said slowly.

"It's a good job." he said simply and sat down in an armchair opposite me. "There's nothing you wouldn't like."

I made grunting noises. "What would it be?" I asked.

"Lu Andasca is running for election." he said. "He wants someone to handle his publicity. It's worth two hundred and fifty dollars a week for the right man. You could do it."

I was startled. "Lu Andasca?" I said, "I don't know him."

"He's all right." Peppi said, examining his neat finger nails. "He's fine."

"What makes you think I could do it?" I asked, playing for time.

"You could do it." he repeated. "Two fifty dollars isn't bad, is it?"

"It's swell." I said, "but, right now I've got one or two things …"

"I wouldn't bother about those things." Peppi said carefully.

We looked at each other.

"After all, what do they amount to?" he went on "Shumway wouldn't interest you. He's an old man and finished. Kelly wouldn't interest you. He's a crum. Leave the girl alone. You don't want girls. They mess up the works."

Well, that was telling me. I didn't know what to say.

He sat back in his chair and stared up at the ceiling, "If Andasca gets in, there'll be a lot of work to do." he said. "I'm interested personally."

I took a quick gander at my watch. It was nearly lunch time. "Look." I said, "I've got a lunch date. Will you let me think it over?"

"There's plenty of time. I'll get my chauffeur to drop you. Where are you going to eat?"

I said "Manetta's," without thinking.

"I see." he said. "Do you think she's good looking?"

I stared at him "Her?" I said. "What …?"

"Myra Shumway. She's your date, isn't she?"

"What do you know about Myra Shumway? What's the idea, Peppi?" I sat up. He was talking too many riddles.

"Excuse me a minute." he said and got up and went out.

I sat there wondering what the hell it was all about. Then he came back after a minute and smiled for the first time. "So you want to think it over?" he said.

"Now look, Peppi." I said, "what do you know about Myra Shumway? Let's get this straight."

"I read the newspapers." he said indifferently, "I hear things. I always hear things. Andasca is more important to me. Can you say yes or no?"

I stood up. "Give me until to-morrow. Where can I meet the guy?"

"To-morrow then." he said. "Call me. I'll fix a meeting. You want my car?"

I shook my head. "No." I said, "I'll take a taxi."

He suddenly seemed bored with me and anxious for me to go. "Then you'll call. Two fifty is worth thinking about." and he went out of the room.

He hadn't been gone three seconds before the butler came in. "This way, sir." he said and took me downstairs to the front door.

I was on the street and the door was closed behind me before I could collect my bewildered wits. I stood staring up at the big house and I felt someone was watching me.

So I waved to a cab and told the driver to take me to Manetta's.

TWELVE

There was no sign of Myra when I got to Manetta's, so I went into the bar.

"I'll have a mint-julep." I said to the barman. "And listen, I belong to the crushing school. Don't just soak the mint leaves, crush 'em. Do you get it?"

"We always crush them here, sir." the barman said, smiling, "and we wipe the rim of the glass with mint as well."

"That's fine." I said, "I don't have to tell you anything, but there are guys who soak their mint."

"They're just ignorant, sir." he returned and went to the end of the bar to fix my drink.

I lit a cigarette and thought about Peppi. I just couldn't make out why he had offered me a job. Knowing Peppi I guessed there was something behind it all and I wouldn't mind laying a bet that he knew Kelly and that Kelly had been to see him.

While l was thinking, a girl came in. A girl in a flame coloured silk dress that reached an inch below her knees. Across her shoulders she wore a white silk scarf-handkerchief with large red spots and her cute little hat of red and white felt was perched on the side of her head in a saucy tilt.

It was Myra.

And yet, somehow, I didn't recognize her for a moment. There was something in the way she moved and an unfamiliar expression in her eyes that made her almost a stranger to me.

As soon as she saw me she waved, smiled and came over.

"There you are." she said. "Have I kept you waiting?"

"I—I didn't recognize you." I said, "maybe it's the new dress."

She gave me a sharp glance, "Do you like it?" she asked, smiling again. "Especially for you."

"I think it's swell." I said, wondering what was different about her. "Let's sit down. I've had a strenuous hour."

She went over to one of the tables and sat down. I followed her.

"Well." I said when we were settled with our drinks, "it's nice to rest my eyes on a beautiful woman." I looked at her knees with interest, "You've got pretty elbows." I went on, "I don't seem to have noticed them before."

She laughed. "You've developed an awful squint since we last met."

"Yeah." I said, watching her closely. "You got rid of Whisky then?"

"I got rid of him." there was a little note of grimness in her voice that made me stare still more intently. She smiled, but her eyes weren't amused.

"Did you have an interesting morning?"

"I certainly did." I said and I told her about Peppi.

She sat quietly listening and when I was through she said, "What are you going to do?"

"You mean about the job? Why, I guess nothing. I wouldn't want to work for Peppi."

"But, isn't it a good job?" she asked, surprised.

"I don't know. The money's all right. But Peppi's a bad guy to work with. He won't last."

"But you're not working with Peppi." she pointed out. "You'd be working with this Andasca, wouldn't you?"

"It's the same thing. Andasca would be Peppi's stooge."

"You ought to think about it." she went on, "what will you do otherwise?"

I finished my drink, "I'll think about it but let's eat now." I said, getting up.

We went into the restaurant.

After the waiters had fussed around, and we had chosen our meal, I said, "Seriously, don't you think we ought to find your father first?"

She lifted her shoulders, "Oh, I've been thinking about that. You know, I don't care very much one way or the other."

I looked at her, "You don't, huh?"

"No."

"What about this girl who's impersonating you?"

Again she shrugged. "She can't hurt me, can she? If my father wants a cheap victory, I'm big enough to let him have it. But, don't let's talk about that. Let's talk about you. Don't you think you ought to look around for a job?"

"So you're considering me now, are you?" I said. "That's new, coming from you."

She looked up and I caught a look in her eyes that set my blood jumping in my veins. "Why shouldn't I think about you and your future?" she asked, putting her hand on mine.

"You wouldn't suddenly have taken into your head that you could like me a little?" I said, squeezing her hand.

"I might." she said, "I might like you quite a lot. But, you'd have to have a steady job."

"So what?" I said, "I can get a steady job. A guy with my experience …"

"Why not see Andasca and find out if you could work with him?" she suggested, a little too anxiously.

"Aren't you giving this guy an awful build up?" I asked suspiciously, "I believe you want me to work for him."

"I want you to get fixed up in a good job."

"Well, it seems to me you're pushing Andasca on me." I returned. "I've already told you what I think of Peppi and his set-up. I can get a job, but it won't be with Andasca."

"You're being pig-headed." There was a note of anger in her voice. "Where else do you think you can earn two fifty a week?"

"That's not such a lot of dough." I returned. "Just shooting in articles would get me double that."

She bit her lip and looked away. "Well, if that's how you feel about it." she said and jerked her hand from under mine.

It struck me that the lunch wasn't going to be a success and I wanted to get her somewhere where we could have this out. There was something at the back of her mind she hadn't told me and I wanted to know what it was.

We finished lunch almost in silence. When we did speak it was about the people in the room and stuff like that and all through the meal she didn't once look me in the eye. By the time I got the check and followed her out of the restaurant I was feeling a little low.

We stood waiting for a taxi in silence, then when one drew up, I said, "Well, what do we do? Shall we go back and take Whisky for a walk? Or shall we sit in the park or what?"

"The park." she said.

I hadn't been in Central Park for two years. It was nice to get back there. It was just like it always was. I guess in another fifty years it'll be the same as it is to-day. Mothers and nursemaids, minding children on roller skates, wagons, scooters and bikes, will be reading and gossiping in the sun long after I've been put under ground. Row-boats were lying on the lake as thick as water bugs and they'll be there too. Your born and bred New Yorker with a modest income doesn't miss the country much. He's got Central Park with thirty tennis courts, nineteen ball fields, six hockey fields and four-and-a-half miles of bridle paths to take his girl along in the evening. That's enough for him and it's enough for me.

We sat on a seat in the shade and watched the people mill around. It was nice just to sit there, but at the back of my mind I had plenty to think about. When I tried to take her hand, she shifted away from me.

"Don't make an exhibition." she said sharply.

"Who cares?" I asked, surprised. "Let's talk about ourselves, Myra."

"Of course." she said, "what about ourselves?"

"Do we get married?" I said, not knowing whether that was what I wanted or not, but anxious to see how she would react.

"I don't think so." she said, staring across the lake at the distant couples walking close together on the other side. "Why get married? Anyway, I wouldn't marry a man who hasn't got a position. Why should I? I've been getting on all right on my own."

"People don't get married for position or money." I said gently. "They get married because they love each other."

"Who told you that?" she glanced at me quickly and laughed. "That sounds like 'What Every Girl Should Know.' That love stuff went out with the Civil War."

"There are times." I said crossly, "when I'd like to throw you into a lake. Can't we be serious once in a while?"

"Not until you get a job. Then I might."

"Okay, if I get a job, you'll think about it?"

"If the job's good enough."

"You know, Angel skin, I'm getting a little tired of your mercenary outlook."

She pouted. "Will you go see Andasca?" she said, "just to please me?"

"What about you?" I said, hoping to side-track. "What am I to tell Doc and Sam? Don't you want to find your father or Kelly or the girl who looks like you?"

"Ross." she said, gripping my hand tightly "so long as we have each other nothing matters. I just want you and I to be together always. Can't we forget about the other two?"

"Well, we could drop them." I said slowly, "but we'd have to tell them."

"Then let's tell them." she said eagerly. "Let's tell them now."

"Okay." I said, "I don't mind," and I glanced at my watch. It was just after three o'clock. "They should be in, unless Sam's gone down to the poolroom."

As we walked towards the long flight of stone steps that led out of the park, she said, "Will you see Andasca?"

"Yeah." I said, "I'll see him sometime this evening."

"Promise?" she said, pressing my arm against her side.

"Promise." I said. "If it means all that to you."

As we entered the apartment, Sam came out of the kitchen with a worried look on his face.

"There you are." he said, relieved. "Is Whisky with you?"

"Why, no." I said, "Myra didn't take him."

Sam looked distressed, "Hell!" he said. "Then he's lost. He went out soon after you'd gone." he went on to Myra. "He ain't been back. I've looked up and down the street, but there's no sign of him. I thought maybe he followed you and you'd taken him for a walk."

Myra shook her head, "I haven't seen him." she said.

"Oh, he'll turn up." I said, tossing my hat on the chair, "you know Whisky. He's found a lady friend and is getting acquainted."

Doc Ansell came in just then. "Found Whisky?" he asked anxiously.

"Don't get excited." I said. "He'll turn up. He's just finding his feet. A big dog like that wants some exercise and he's having a look around."

Ansell looked at Myra, "Well." he said, smiling, "how pretty you look this morning. Did you have a nice lunch?"

"Yes, thank you." she said, pulling off her hat. "It was very nice."

Sam said, "Ain't you worried about Whisky?"

She blinked, "Why, no. If Ross thinks …"

"Ross?" Sam's eyes opened, "Gee! Have you two gone soft on each other?"

Myra turned on me. "You'd better tell them." she said and ran out of the room.

Ansell and Sam looked at me suspiciously. "What's buzzin'?" Sam demanded.

I wandered over to an armchair and sat down. "I don't know." I returned. "A lot's happened since I last saw you." and I told them about Peppi and Andasca and Lydia Brandt.

They sat listening in silence, then Doc said, "I've heard of Andasca. He's no good to anyone."

"So have I." Sam said, "he used to carry a gun for Jo-jo in Chi when I was there. You don't want to get mixed up with him."

I jerked my thumb at the ceiling. "That's what she wants." I said, slowly. "She wants me to drop you two and live with her. She says nothing else matters so long as we have each other and I work for Andasca. What do you make of that?"

They didn't make anything of it.

"She doesn't want to be bothered with her father. She doesn't mind being impersonated. Almost as if she was someone else." I went on, looking hard at Ansell.

"Yes." he said, "I see what you mean. Now, I wonder …"

"It wants looking into." I said, closing my eyes. "Maybe I'd better see Andasca."

"I think so." Doc said. "Take Sam with you."

"Where'll I find him?" I said. "Either of you know?"

"Last time I heard of him." Sam said, "he lived in a joint off Mulberry Park. Maybe someone knows what he's doing now."

"We'll go to Mulberry Park." I said. "In the meantime keep an eye on the girl friend. Don't let her leave the apartment. I may be wrong, Doc, but I'm suspicious of her change of heart."

"Leave it to me." Doc said, and we went out into the street, leaving him on his own.

Now, Mulberry Park lies north of the Brooklyn Bridge and a hundred yards or so from Chinatown. Right now it is a tree-shaded square which the city has equipped with swings, wading pools and showers for the kiddies. It looks quiet and faded but a century ago it was the toughest spot in Manhattan; Five Points was situated there and nearby a huge rambling building called the Old Brewery where swarms of Negroes and whites used to live. Seventy-five men, women and children once lived in one room of the Old Brewery. That ought to tell you how tough the place was. Murder was a daily occurrence and the kids in Old Brewery lived for years without leaving the rooms because in the halls they might get themselves knocked off by some guy with the blood-itch. The young punks who were strong enough to stand up for themselves met their pals in alleys and there formed the first gangs of New York.

For the next hundred years the stretch from Mulberry Bend through Chatham Square and up the Bowery remained the centre of the sin industries of the metropolis. The gangs flourished.

So in those days the Mulberry Park district was plenty tough. Now the old gangs were dead, Chinatown and Mulberry Bend had faded into seeming innocence, but the district was still the breeding ground for thugs.

Anyway, it was like a breath of home to Sam as we into the Square and picked our way through the kids that cluttered up the sidewalk.

"Where do we go from here?" I asked, feeling the eyes of the slatternly women hostile on my back as they stood in open doorways of their drab, dirty apartments.

"There's a guy I used to know." Sam said, head, "who had a gin mill around here some place. Now, what was his name?" He screwed up his face while he thought.

I waited patiently, trying to pretend I wasn't there. Even the kids had stopped playing and were watching us.

"Good-time Waxey." Sam said suddenly. "That's the runt. He'll know about Andasca. He knew every punk around here."

We found Good-time Waxey behind the bar of an evil looking dive at the corner of Mulberry and Kenmare. He was lolling over the bar, the midday sporting sheet spread out before him, looking down the list of horses for the three o'clock handicap.

He looked up suspiciously as we fumbled our way into the dark little tavern.

"Hey, Waxey." Sam said, grinning, "still carrying your corns in a snood?"

Waxey stiffened. His fat, brutish face, glistening with sweat, lit up and he shoved out a fist the size of a mellon. "Bogle!" he said, shaking hands, "where ta hell yuh spring from?"

Sam grinned as he pumped the big man's arm up and down. "Thought I'd look the old dump over." he said. "How's tricks, Waxey?"

Waxey lost his smile, "Looka." he said, "six years I work in dis burg, an' where does it get me? A lousy handout a thoity bucks a month! Starvin' an' freezin' ... fuh what? Peanuts!" and he spat disgustedly on the floor.

"Gees!" Sam said, his eyes opening. "I thought this burg was all right."

"It *was*." Waxey returned darkly, "when da boys were around. Lucky ... remember Lucky? ... When he was around, dat was somethin'. But, now ... Hell, might as well wait for Santa Claus tuh take care of me."

"Meet my pal Millan." Sam said, pushing me forward. "He's an all right guy, Waxey. We work together."

Waxey looked at me sharply, then stuck out his hand. "Any pal a Sam's pal a mine." he said, crushing my hand in a grip that made me shuffle my feet.

"We looked in 'cause we thought you might wise us up." Sam said, lowering his voice.

Waxey stroked his shapeless nose and his little green eyes showed interest. "Yuh in a racket, Sam?" he asked, hopefully.

"Not right now." Sam returned cautiously. "But, it looks like it was headin' that way. What do you know about Andasca?"

Waxey blinked. "What yew mean?"

"Just that. This guy's going to work for him." Sam said, jerking his thumb in my direction. "But he wants to know what line he's in first."

Waxey studied me. "Lu's gettin' somewhere." he said at last. "Twenty buck shoits. A hundred an' fifty buck custom tailored suits. Da fat a da land he live off of. An' he's got a flock a dames at'd make youse guys water at da mout'."

"But what's the set-up?" Sam persisted.

Waxey lowered his voice, "Peppi Kruger's behind him." he said "Between da two a dem, dey have da Bowery sewed up tight, see?"

"How tight?" Sam asked, looking hopefully at the row of dusty bottles behind Waxey's head, "and how about a drink, Waxey?"

"Sure." Waxey produced a black bottle without a label from under the counter. "Dis is da McCoy." he went on, slapping the bottle down in front of us. "Help yuhselves."

While Sam poured the drinks, I said, "I heard Kruger's almost washed up, that's why I'm nervous about going in with them."

"Hoid what?" Waxey gasped, "yuh crazy? Looks yew, both dese guys are tops, see? Nuttin's goin' tuh stop 'em. Dere ain't any punk tuh touch 'em now."

But I wasn't listening any more. I was staring out of the tavern into the street. "Hang on, Sam." I said suddenly, "I'll be right back." and I left them gaping after me.

From across the street I had caught a glimpse of a dog, moving along the shadows of the wall. That in itself wasn't anything, but the dog was a wolfhound and you don't see many wolfhounds in Mulberry Park.

I was certain it was Whisky.

By the time I got into the open he had disappeared, but I knew which way he had gone and I chased across the street, ducked down an evil smelling alley and ran on. Something on the ground made me pause and looking down I found that I was following a trail of bright bloodstains in a disjointed string of small circles.

I increased my pace and began calling. At the end of the alley I could see Whisky dragging himself forward painfully and slowly.

"Whisky!" I shouted and ran forward, just as the dog dropped wearily to the ground. "What's the matter, old dog?" I asked, bending over him anxiously.

There was no need to ask. There was a great patch of hardening blood on his shoulder. Across his head was a livid gash as if he had been hit very hard with a stick. Blood ran from his foot where he must have got himself a pretty severe cut. Whisky was in a bad way and from the exhausted look in his eyes I could see he was in need of some quick attention.

"Take it easy." I said, kneeling beside him, "I'll get you out of here."

"Don't waste time with me." Whisky growled. "They've got her. They kidnapped her when she was going to meet you. That wasn't Myra who was waiting for you at Manetta's … that was the other one."

"The other one?" I repeated stupidly. "Who kidnapped who? What are you talking about, Whisky boy?"

Whisky struggled to speak, then a look of terrified dismay came into his eyes. His teeth clicked and he half struggled to his feet, only to flop back exhausted.

"Take it easy." I said, "I'll get Sam and we'll fix you up, you poor old devil. But, I've got to know what you're talking about. Why should anyone want to kidnap Myra?"

Whisky still clicked his teeth as if he were struggling to speak and then to my shocked and horrified surprise he began to bark.

THIRTEEN

By the time I got back to Waxey's dive and had collected Bogle the full meaning of what Whisky was trying to tell me had sunk in. It was completely fantastic. But, then again, the whole thing was fantastic.

So the girl hadn't been Myra and Myra had been kidnapped. The sooner I got back to Ansell and put the screws to the girl the better. Now that Whisky had lost the power of talking, I wasn't going to get much help from him. I would have to wait until he was well enough to take us to the place where he had been attacked. That might give me a clue.

It was no use telling Bogle that there were two Myras. He would only think I'd gone crazy. Besides, it would be a waste of time trying to convince him.

So I left Whisky in his charge and grabbed a taxi. I had told Sam to get Whisky to a dog hospital as quickly as he could and then get back to our apartment pronto. Sam, when he saw how badly hurt Whisky was, became wildly angry and upset. I managed to convince him how important it was for him to return immediately to the apartment without actually telling him details.

It was about the longest ride I ever had in a taxi and I kept urging the driver to greater speed. I don't know why but I had the jitters all right.

When I reached our apartment block I tossed the driver his money and ran up the steps.

A moment later I was standing inside our apartment and for some un-accountable reason I felt scared. There was the same eerie atmosphere that I felt when I found Quintl's body.

No sound came to me and I called Ansell in a voice that I hardly recognized as my own.

I walked cautiously into the kitchen and looked round. There was no one there. More assured, I returned to the living room. Maybe Doc and the girl had gone out. I was just going to have a look in the bedrooms when something caught my eye which brought me up with a jolt.

From under the sofa I could see something red. I knelt down and looked. It was Myra's flame coloured dress. It had been screwed up into a bail and shoved under the sofa. This startled me for a moment. I hooked it out and stood up.

As I unfolded it I touched a wet, sticky patch and looking at my hand I found blood on it. Right down the front of the dress was a large blood-stain, still damp.

Just for a moment I thought that she'd been killed and it gave me a tremendous shock. But when I examined the dress there was no sign of a bullet hole or a slit from a knife. It looked as if the blood had come not from her but from someone else.

Throwing the dress aside I went upstairs and blundered into Ansell's bed-room.

He lay across the bed. There was blood on the floor and on the walls. I hadn't realized what a little guy he was until I saw him lying like that. The front of his coat was bloodstained and his face was blue-grey. Until I touched him I thought he was dead.

And when I touched him and felt his cold hand I realized just how fond

I had become of him and a wild, destructive rage swept through me. If I could have laid hands on the person who had done this I'd have killed without hesitation.

"Doc." I said gently, scared to lift him, "what is it, Doc?"

He opened his eyes and blinked up at me, but no look of recognition came from him.

"It's me … Millan." I said, kneeling close to him. "What can I do? Are you badly hurt?" I knew the answer to that one before I said it. I didn't think he'd last another two minutes.

He tried to speak, but couldn't quite make it. I watched his lips move and I put my ear close to them, but I couldn't hear what he was trying to say.

But he had to talk. He couldn't go like that without telling me what had happened and who had done this. So I bolted to the sitting room and poured two inches of Scotch into a glass and rushed back to him.

"Come on, Doc." I said, lifting his head. "Get hold of yourself."

The whisky did the trick, but I could see he was going fast. My only hope now was to keep him alive long enough to hear what had happened.

I could see he wanted to talk and I could see he was making a tremendous effort.

"You were right. She wasn't Myra." he whispered at last. "She attacked me soon after you left. I asked for it, I should have waited. Look out for her, Ross, she's dangerous. It's the way I thought. She's the bad one." He closed his eyes and I thought he had gone, but he was only resting for a second or so.

I couldn't really believe that it was possible and yet I knew the Myra we had worked with and fooled with could never have done this to him.

He began speaking again, "They'll try and pin this on Myra." he said falteringly. "You've got to cover it up somehow, Ross. I told you this might happen. Where's Myra? What's happened to her?"

"Now don't worry, Doc." I said. "I'll fix it. You just relax. I'll get a doctor for you. You'll be all right."

"You've got to find her and get her an alibi." Doc went on. "Don't call the cops until you've been through the place and cleaned up anything that might connect her with this. The other one's bad. You've got to catch her and get rid of her before the end of the month. Don't let her merge into Myra again. She'll try and do it after the full moon."

I couldn't understand what he was talking about, but there was nothing else to do but to listen. His voice was getting weaker and he died as Sam walked in.

When Sam saw Doc he ran over to him, his eyes scared.

"He's gone, Sam." I said, getting off the bed. And then I realized the hopelessness of trying to explain to him how it had happened. But, I had to do it. Sam already knew too much and the thought of trying to get this fantastic business into his thick head appalled me.

Bogle took one look at Doc, then he turned and grabbed me. His grip nearly ripped the coat and shirt off my back. I thought he was going to have some kind of a fit. His face was dark with congested blood and his eyes were wild.

"Who did it?" he said, ramming me against the wall. "Open up, you punk, who did it?"

I knew it wouldn't do to tell him. He wasn't in a state to cope with a story like that. So I said I didn't know and tried to break his grip. It was like heaving against the teeth of a bear-trap.

"Take it easy, Sam." I said, "this won't get you anywhere."

He gave a snort and then shoved me away. I banged against the wall and nearly went over. He returned to Doc and kneeling by him he took his hand. Then he began to cry, so I went out quietly and left them together.

When I got downstairs, I didn't know what to do. I felt sick about Doc. I felt scared for Myra and I wanted to get my hands on the other girl. I didn't really think of her as the other girl, but as someone who had killed Doc. I went into the sitting room and poured myself out a stiff glass of whisky. Then I sat down and tried to think.

A murder had been committed. That meant the cops. It meant trying to explain something to them that I couldn't explain to myself. If I didn't get my explanation over, then Myra would be on the spot. The bloodstained dress was enough to set the law working on her right away. I finished my whisky and picked up the dress. Doc had said to destroy any clue that might point to her. Well, this was the first one to go.

Then the dress was snatched out of my hand by Bogle who had entered silently. He took one look at the bloodstain and he knew she had done it. "Where is she?" he said quietly.

I always looked on Bogle as a harmless sort of a jerk. But not now. He looked like a killer and he looked half crazy.

"We've got to talk about this." I said. "Have a drink, Sam. It'll pull you together."

"So she killed him, did she?" he said, through his teeth. "She ain't going to get away with it. That little punk was good to me. Him and me got along fine until you came along. You and her. You think a lot of that broad, don't you? Well there won't be much of her to think about when I'm through."

"Don't be a fool, Sam." I said. "I know how you feel about Doc. He was a swell guy. But she didn't kill him."

"What's this?" he held up the dress.

"Oh, I know it looks like she killed him, but she didn't."

"The cops can work it out." he said, "I'm going to get a load of law here and let 'em find her. Then if she slips off the hot seat, I'll fix her." and he went over to the telephone.

If the cops came and found that dress, then I knew nothing could save Myra. She'd be hounded all over the country.

I jerked him round, "Leave the cops out of this." I said, "we'll handle it, Sam. Kruger's behind it. Can't you see that?"

Bogle wrenched himself away. "Do you think I'm crazy?" he said, "I know you're nuts about her, but that ain't stopping me. If we don't bring the cops in, how do you think we'll explain about Doc."

I shrugged. "Well, if that's how you feel about it." I said, and moved so that I was behind him.

I didn't like doing it, but it was the only way. I had to have a little time to clear things and make sure that Myra hadn't left anything for the police besides the dress.

But Bogle was expecting trouble. He turned and faced me. "Don't start anything." he said viciously. "It won't get you nowhere."

"There's no harm trying." I said and swung over a punch that caught him on his cheekbone.

He swayed back as my fist landed, so he rode most of the steam out of it. Then he moved in and his fist caught me in the ribs, sending me against the wall. Bogle could punch all right.

He lowered his hands. "Cut it out." he said, "I don't want to hurt you and if you make me mad you're going to get hurt plenty."

I thought that was likely. But I could see the mess that was ahead if I didn't stop Bogle.

I edged forward, "Can't you use your head, Sam?" I pleaded, looking for an opening to land my right. "I tell you Myra didn't kill him. She loved that old guy as much as you did. She wouldn't touch him. You ought to know that."

"Yeah?" Bogle said. "Then how come that dress? We left her with Doc, didn't we? Where is she now?"

"Kruger's got her, you fat fool." I said, suddenly realizing that we were both wasting time. "Don't you see?" I went on, "Kruger or some of his mob came here. For some reason they wanted Myra. Doc tried to stop them and they killed him. While we're bellyaching, they're taking her further away."

For a brief moment, Sam looked as if he was going to fall for it, then his eyes darkened again. "The dress." he said impatiently. "Why should Kruger want her? A guy as big as him wouldn't want her."

Then we both saw it at once. How I missed it in the first place I don't know. I guess it was the shock of seeing the dress and then finding Doc that had blinded me to it. On the mantelpiece was a white envelope, propped up against the clock.

We both made a rush for it. I nearly reached it, but Bogle suddenly lashed out and his fist caught me below the ear, sending me over. It was like the Empire State Building had fallen on me and I don't know how long I was out. It couldn't have been more than a few seconds, but it was long enough for Bogle to open the letter and read it.

I sat up slowly and one look at Bogle's face told me that nothing further I could say would convince him that Myra hadn't killed Doc.

"It's for you." he said in a cold flat voice. "She says she knocked him off and that she's going away. She'll write you again when things have eased down." and he slipped the letter into his pocket. "Talk yourself out of that!"

I shook my head clear and stood up. I had to get that letter. That was enough to send Myra to the chair. That and the dress. I realized the full significance of what Doc had said. The girl who had killed Doc was determined to pin it on Myra. With Bogle as a witness the cops had an open and shut case.

Somehow, I had to explain about the two Myras to Sam. It was the only way to save her.

"For the love of mike." I said, "will you listen to me? Doc told me what happened. When I reached him, he managed to say enough for me to know how it went. The girl who met me at Manetta's was not Myra. It was the girl who's been impersonating her. She's exactly like her." and I went on to tell him about Whisky.

Bogle said, "You're soft on that girl, ain't you? You'd do anything to save her neck. Well, you're not kidding me with a yarn like that. Tell it to the cops."

I never hoped he'd believe it, but I had to try. There was only one way to settle this. I had to destroy both the dress and the letter. So I went into action with both hands. But, I went in much more cautiously this time. I feinted with my left and then hooked with my right. Bogle knew all about that kind of fighting. He took the right on his forearm and came back with a heavy punch to my face. But, I was getting mad now and I rushed him, smothering his punches and driving him across the room. I forced him against the wall and slammed in two solid punches before he drove me away with a stunning uppercut.

I went in again and ran into a haymaker that nearly took my head off my shoulders. I felt myself floating and then I whammed against the wall with a jolt that knocked the wind out of me.

Bogle shuffled across the room after me. As I crawled to my feet, I caught a glimpse of his face and that sent me cold. He was fighting mad now and

I'd be lucky to get out of this alive. He banged me one on the side of the head before I was half up and then pumped a couple into my stomach.

Being hit by Bogle was like being beaten by a sledge hammer. My ribs bent every time he hit me in the body. Those slams hurt more than when he caught me in the face.

I managed to shake myself loose and got in a lucky one that sent him back. Somehow I went in and landed one on his mouth. He grunted and I knew he was hurt. But, I couldn't stop him. He was too tough and he was twenty pounds heavier.

He got in close and hit me four times in the ribs with punches that didn't travel more than a couple of inches. It felt like being under a pile drive. I felt my knees going and I grabbed hold of him to stop myself falling. He shoved me off and dimly I saw something coming at me. It looked like a football whizzing through the air. I couldn't do anything about it. I couldn't even try to get out of the way. Then it exploded on the side of my jaw, and that was that.

I was alone when I came to the surface. I sat up slowly and felt my jaw. It was swollen, but I was relieved it wasn't broken.

I got to my feet and wandered over to the whisky bottle. The liquor did me a lot of good and a second shot did even better. I wasn't mad at Bogle. From his point of view he had done the right thing. I'd have done the same if I'd been in his place.

I went into the bathroom and bathed my face. It looked a little better by the time I was through, and as I was leaving the bathroom I heard the wail of police sirens.

Sam was standing in the hall. His face was bruised and puffy, but he looked almost handsome beside me.

We looked at each other. Then he said a little shamefaced, "I'm sorry, Bud, but you had to stick your neck out. My beef ain't with you, but I'm not letting that dame get away with this. I can't help it if you're soft on her, can I?"

I said, "No, but you're making an awful mistake, Sam." and went into the sitting room.

Then the law walked in. There was Clancy of the Homicide Bureau, who I knew quite well, and a couple of patrolmen and a cameraman.

I heard a lot of talking going on outside in the hall, but I was past caring what happened. I had to wait to see how things shaped, then try to get Myra out of the jam.

I heard Clancy go upstairs to look at Doc. They were up there some time, then Clancy came down with Bogle, leaving the others to work on fingerprints and stuff like that in Doc's room.

Clancy was a little fat guy, with eyebrows like overgrown shrubs and a blue-black jowl which made him look tough. He usually dwelt behind a dead cigar and modelled his manners along motion picture lines. He wasn't the brightest star of the Homicide Bureau, and I was sorry he was handling the case.

He came in and stood over me. "Well, well." he said, surprised, "Ross Millan! What are you doing here?"

"Hello, Clancy." I said, leaning back in my chair, "I haven't seen you for a Long time."

He stared in astonishment at my face, then he looked at Bogle, "Hey!" he said, "what's this? You two been fighting?"

"Fighting?" I said. "What makes you think that?"

"Don't stall." he snapped, "look at your face."

"Oh, that." I shrugged. "That's the way I wear my face these days. You pick up odd habits in Mexico. Some guys wear beards, some wear ear-rings, I wear bruises. It's considered the thing in Mexico, isn't it, Sam?"

Bogle didn't say anything. He wasn't quite at ease with the cops.

"Still smart, eh?" Clancy said. "What have you two been fighting about?"

"Oh, we like to keep tough." I said, "it's got nothing to do with this business. All kidding aside, Clancy, it's just our form of self-expression."

Clancy chewed his cigar and eyed me suspiciously. "Okay." he said, "we'll skip that for the moment. How are you tied up in this business?"

I told him in a few words how I had met Doc and Bogle in Mexico, but I didn't say anything about Myra.

"What do you know about this girl?" He shot the question out as if he'd got a half a dozen cameras focussed on him and a bunch of admirers waiting for his autograph.

"Which girl?" I asked, carefully.

"You know." he said darkly, "Myra Shumway."

"I know that." I said, "but which Myra Shumway? There are two of 'em."

That slowed him down.

"What are you talking about?" he asked, "what do you mean ... two of 'em?"

"Look, Clancy." I said, "there is a lot behind this business that you don't know. It's going to be difficult for you to understand, but if you'll take the weight off your feet and lay off pulling the tough copper on me, I'll try and explain."

"Don't listen to him." Sam said savagely. "He's nuts about the girl."

Clancy hadn't much use for Bogle, "Clam up!" he snapped. "When I want a commentary from you I'll let you know." He turned to me, "Now, what is it?" he said.

I waved to a chair, "Sit down." I said. "It's going to take time and you'll need all your energy to keep your brain working."

"Leave my brain out of it. You be careful of yourself Millan. I know you think you're smart, but if you're trying to make a monkey out of me I'll slam you in the cooler as a material witness. How would you like that?"

"Now don't let's have threats." I said, but I was a little dismayed. If I were in jail there would be no one to help Myra.

"Come on, Millan, don't stall." he said.

I wasn't going to be rushed. The idea of telling a guy like Clancy the whole story of the Mexican business appalled me, but I had to do it.

So I sat and talked. Clancy sat listening with a drowsy expression in his eyes. He even put a match to his cigar, which let off a rank smell. He didn't seem to like it himself, because he let it out after a couple of drags. At that rate a cigar could last him a couple of weeks. This one smelt like he'd had it for years.

I nearly gave up half way, because I could see it was hopeless. He didn't know whether I was crazy or whether I was stringing him. So he just got hotter and hotter until I thought he was going to catch on fire.

"Well." I said, "that's the way it is. Someone's kidnapped Myra and her other half killed Ansell."

I didn't mention Kruger. I knew Kruger had a lot of influence and I wanted to go for him on my own without police interference.

"What a story to take to a judge!" Clancy said, drawing a deep breath. "If I didn't know you, Millan, and if we hadn't knocked around in the past, I'd toss you into jail right now for wasting my time. Do you think anybody but a lunatic would believe a yarn like that?"

I waved my hand to Bogle, "Your witness, Clancy. He'll bear me out. Sausage, talking dog, floating woman and the whole set-up."

"Well." Clancy snarled at Bogle, "what have you got to say? Did you see this guy turn into a sausage?"

Bogle looked at me and then at Clancy, "I told you he was trying to gum up the works." he said. "I didn't see any of that stuff, because it just didn't happen."

I half rose from my seat, "Why, you dirty heel!" I said furiously, "you know as well as I do it's all true!"

"Like hell it is!" Clancy suddenly roared. "I've had enough of this, Millan. You either talk turkey or you'll come down to headquarters."

"But, I tell you ..." I began.

"Okay." Clancy said, getting to his feet, "come on, the pair of you. I've had all I can stand of this. We'll see what the chief s got to say."

I looked at Bogle, "So that's the way you're going to play it."

Bogle's face twitched, "She's going to pay for this." he said viciously, "and you're not talking her way out of it. If these flatfeet don't pin it on her, then I'll fix her, but she don't knock Doc off without footin' the bill."

"Who are you calling a flatfoot?" Clancy demanded angrily.

Bogle sneered, "What makes you think you're anything but a fallen arch?" he demanded.

Before Clancy could come back on this the wagon rolled up to take Doc away.

We all stood silently watching, and when the stretcher came down Sam began to cry again.

FOURTEEN

The police captain was a guy named Summers. I knew him pretty well and he wasn't a bad guy if he felt like it. Otherwise, he had a temper like a flea on a hot stove and was liable to fly off the handle without warning.

They kept me waiting nearly four hours before they took me to his office and the wait nearly drove me crazy.

"Hullo, Millan." he said when Clancy pushed me into the room. "I'm sorry we had to keep you. Sit down."

Clancy stood behind Summers and gnawed dismally at his dead cigar.

I sat down after shaking hands. "That's all right." I said, trying to look as if I hadn't a care in the world. "It's just one of those things."

"Yep, I guess so." he studied me for a long minute, then took out a box of cigars and pushed them over, "Help yourself." he said.

When we had lit up he said, "Not like you to be mixed up in murder. I thought you were too smart for that."

"I'm not mixed up in anything." I said firmly. "Don't go making any mistake about that. I just found the poor little guy."

"Yeah, you just found him. Why did this girl leave a note telling you she had knocked him off?"

"This is a tough story to tell." I said slowly. "But, she didn't kill him and she didn't write that note. The other girl did both those things."

"The other girl?" He hid behind a cloud of oily smoke. "Oh that! Man into sausage, talking dog and floating woman. Yeah, Clancy was telling me."

Clancy shifted from one foot to the other and then a silence fell so that I could hear the watch on my wrist like it was an alarm clock.

"You've got to do better than that." Summers said at last. "I wouldn't want you telling me a whopper like that. Maybe, it amused you to kid Clancy, but it wouldn't amuse you for long to kid me."

We eyed each other and I decided that I had to think up something else.

"Okay." I said. "Why not ask the girl? Why ask me?"

"We will when we've found her." Summers returned. "We'll ask her a lot of things, then we'll sit her on a nice hot seat and fry her."

Well, anyway, they hadn't found her yet. That was something.

"She was your girl, wasn't she, Millan?" he went on casually.

I shook my head. "No, I liked her. She was good fun, but that's all."

"This guy Bogle says different."

"You don't want to believe what he says." I returned. "You see, he was the little guy's pal. He thinks Myra killed him and he'll say anything to get her convicted. He's prejudiced."

"Don't you think she killed him?"

"I've told you already." I said sharply. "Of course she didn't."

"I guess you're the only guy who thinks so. Why, she even says she killed him herself." and he tapped a sheet of notepaper which I recognized as the note Bogle had taken.

"Well." I said, uncrossing my legs. "You've got what looks like a confession and you've got the stained dress. There isn't much I can do about it."

"The knife had her finger-prints on it." Summers said, caressing the back of his head gently. "We found a strand of her hair in the old guy's coat. Nope, it's a cinch, Millan, so you'd better be careful."

I shrugged. "Well, I can't help you. I would if I could, but if my story's too much for you to swallow, I give up."

He eyed me thoughtfully. "Okay." he said. "Give. I've known you a long time, Millan, and I don't think you're a liar. So tell me. I'll listen anyway."

Clancy groaned, but neither of us took any notice of him.

So I told him what I'd told Clancy, only I gave him a lot more details.

Summers listened, caressing the back of his head the whole time. His cold, blank eyes never left my face, and when I was through he nodded.

"Well, I have to hand it to you, Millan. It's some yarn."

"Yeah, it's some yarn, like you say."

"So the dog talks, huh? A real honest to gawd dog—talking. Where's the dog now?"

"He's in a dog hospital some place. Bogle took him. Ask Bogle. He'll tell you."

"We've already asked Bogle about the dog. He says it never talked."

"Then telephone the dog hospitals. The nearest one to Mulberry Park ought to find him."

Summers brightened a little. "Do it." he said to Clancy. "I'd like to hear a dog talk."

Then, with a sudden feeling of sickness, I remembered. "Wait." I said. "He doesn't talk any more. Someone hit him on the head and he just barks now."

There was a long, painful silence and Summers' beefy face grew dark. "Oh, so he just barks now." he repeated, then seeing Clancy hesitate, he snapped. "Get after him all the same. I want to know if an injured dog's been picked up recently."

Clancy went out.

"I'm sorry Summers." I said. "This sounds phoney, but he did talk yesterday. I swear he did."

"So the dog doesn't talk any more and maybe the woman's given up floating." Summers said, his eyes glinted with anger. "If I didn't know you, Millan, you might be in for a bad time. I might even get some of the boys to give you a shellacking."

I shifted restlessly. "Give me a chance to prove it." I said suddenly. I remembered that Summers used to stake all his pay on a single cut of the cards. I've even seen him gamble with his next month's salary. He was far more likely to play along if I appealed to his sporting instinct. "Look, Summers, if I bring these two girls to this office and let you see them, will that convince you?"

"How would you do that?" he asked, but the glint went out of his eyes.

"Give me a couple of weeks. I've got to find them first and that'll take some digging around. But I'll find them all right if you call off your bloodhounds and give me a free hand."

"What do you think the newspapers'll say if I don't get action in the next day or so?" he asked, pulling at his short thick nose and looking at me old fashioned. "You're in the business. You know what a ride I'll get."

"I've been in the game long enough to know that if you want to stall the newspapers you can do it." I returned, feeling that I had the thin end in the crack and it only needed one good smack to drive it home. "There's something much bigger than murder behind all this. It's going to be a whale of a story and it'll do you a hell of a lot of good to be tied up in it on the right side. I tell you, if you grab Myra Shumway and try to pin the murder on her, you'll be passing up something that someone on top is trying to cover up. Let me handle it for a couple of weeks and I'll give it to you on a plate."

"What someone on top?" he asked, interested.

"That's my affair, Summers." I said. "I may be wrong, but I don't think so. I'll tell you when I'm ready."

"I suppose you realize that I could hold you as an accessory after the fact on that statement." Summers said, his voice suddenly cold.

"Where are your witnesses? I didn't say anything."

He tried to get mad, but then grinned. "I'll give you a week." he said. "You've got a week from now to bring the two girls to this office. If you don't, then I'll issue a warrant for your arrest as an accessory and we'll see if we can't persuade you to talk. How's that?"

I didn't hesitate. "Suits me." I said and put out my hand.

He shook it casually. "Okay, Millan." he said. "You can beat it. Remember, I want you here this time next week with the two girls. You're not to leave the City unless you tell me where you're going. Okay?"

"Okay." I said, and made for the door.

"I don't think you're going to be very lucky." he said as I was going out. "I don't think there are two girls."

"We'll talk about that when next we meet." I said, and closed the door behind me.

Clancy was coming along the passage and he stared at me. "Where the hell do you think you're going?" he demanded.

"Summers doesn't want me until next week." I said cheerfully. "Any news of my dog?"

"Yeah." he said. "There was a wolfhound at the Eastern Dog Hospital with a bang on his dome, but he took it on the lam before anyone could take care of him. Maybe that was your dog."

"Maybe it was." I said. "Now, will you have a talk with Bogle about that? It looks like I'm not the only guy who can tell stories."

Clancy's face became grim. "I'll talk to him." he said sourly.

"And Clancy, if you can keep him on ice for a week, you'll be doing me a favour."

"I will, will I?" he looked at me hard. "What are you up to?"

"Never mind that." I said. "You ask Summers, he'll tell you. But Bogle's got the wrong idea and he'll be better off out of the way. Do what you can for me, will you? I'll give you a good write-up if I handle the story."

"That reminds me." Clancy said, snapping his thick fingers. "Maddox 'phoned through a couple of hours back. He wanted you to go around to his office right away."

This startled me. "Maddox?" I repeated. "Wants to see me?"

"Yeah." Clancy said.

"Okay, thanks, Clancy. Be seeing you. So long." and I beat it out of Headquarters as fast as I could travel.

As I got into the street a cruising taxi slowed down and the driver looked at me hopefully. I nodded and he stopped.

"*Recorder* office." I said, and jerked open the door. Then I paused.

There was a girl sitting in the far corner.

"What's the idea?" I demanded, turning on the driver. "You've got a customer, you pudden-headed monkey."

"Get in, Mr. Millan." the girl said. "I want to talk to you." The voice was familiar and I looked back into the cab. Lydia Brandt was sitting there and in her hand she held a small, businesslike automatic. Its snub nose was pointed at my waistcoat.

"Why, hello." I said, because I couldn't think of anything else to say.

"Get in." she repeated. "Unless you want another belly button."

"Not outside police headquarters." I said hastily. "It'd be bad for their nerves." and I got in and sat down gingerly beside her.

The driver shot the cab away from the curb and took off down the street.

Lydia Brandt was dressed in a smart olive green dress, and cerise turban, gloves, handbag and shoes. She looked like Fifth Avenue.

"Didn't I tell you I was susceptible to your feminine lure, you beautiful butterfly? I don't need kidnapping at the point of a gun." I said, watching her closely because I didn't like the efficient, almost careless way she handled the automatic. From that range a slug from that pop-gun could make me awfully unhappy.

"Mr. Kruger wants to see you." she said indifferently. "I thought you might not be anxious to come."

"What, not see Peppi?" I said. "You don't know me. He's a guy I dream about. I want his autograph and I'll wear his old clothes."

"Very funny." she said, her eyes darkening. "You'll laugh the other side of your face before long."

"Don't threaten me." I returned, smiling at her. "Peppi wants to give me a job. I was going to call him anyway."

She put the automatic on top of her bag and folded her long, slim fingers over it. Its barrel still pointed at me, but she had taken her finger off the trigger and that gave me more confidence. "You want to be sure to pick someone smaller than yourself next time you start fighting." she said, eyeing my bruises.

"Never mind that." I said, relaxing. "You know it was a dumb trick to pick me up outside police headquarters. Both from Peppi's and my own point of view. It's not the smartest thing to let the cops know that we are interested in each other."

"What do you mean?" She looked searchingly at me.

"I've been turned loose, but I'm willing to bet my last pair of socks that I've got a load of law tailing me and I'll be tailed from now on."

I'd hit the right note. She looked alarmed.

"Tailing you?" she repeated and looked hastily through the little rear window.

There was a lot of traffic on the road and she didn't see any particular car that attracted attention.

But the movement was enough for me. I had her gun before she knew what I was doing. I put it in my pocket. "You'll excuse me." I said. "But that heater made me nervous."

She sat glowering at me.

"And now." I went on. "Let's be sensible. Tell the driver to take us to my apartment. I want to talk to you."

"You can talk here." she said, her voice off key.

"Don't be a dope." I said sharply. "You've had your fun. I'm going to have mine." I leaned forward and told the driver my address. "And make it snappy, Happy." I added.

He made no move to change direction, but kept on towards Fifth Avenue.

"One of your boys?" I said, looking at her.

She didn't say anything, but I could see I was right. I took her automatic out of my pocket and rammed it into the driver's neck. "Maybe you didn't hear me the first time." I said.

He swung off the main street and I sat back.

"You'll pay for this." she said angrily.

"Be smart." I returned. "Look back now." and I indicated a large black car sitting on our tail. "That's the law, and let me tell you something: I'm tied up in a murder case. If they think Peppi's in on this, they'll take him apart just for the fun of it."

I could see she didn't know what to think.

"You don't have to get your girdle twisted." I went on. "I just want to have a little talk with you, then I'll go over and see Peppi. But, before I do, I've got to shake these coppers."

Neither of us said anything until we reached my apartment, then as she got out of the taxi I cautioned her, "Don't make a fuss." I said, "just go straight in."

The driver, a thin, weedy youth looked at her enquiringly but she crossed the sidewalk without saying anything to him and entered my apartment. I gave him a half a buck. "Tell Peppi I'll be along in a little while." I said, and left him staring after me.

As Lydia and I entered the apartment house the big black car swept by. I caught a glimpse of Clancy, looking back through the window then I shut the front door quietly.

"Sit down and make yourself at home." I said, waving to the armchair.

She faced me. "What do you want?" she demanded angrily. Her cobalt blue eyes were dark and the lines of her mouth hard.

I took her arm and shoved her gently into the chair. "I want to talk to you." I said and stood over her. "Ansell was murdered this afternoon. He was killed by a girl who's impersonating Myra Shumway."

"He was killed by Myra Shumway." Lydia said softly.

Well, anyway that told me where we stood.

"Where is she?" I asked.

"With Mr. Kruger."

"The other one's with him too?"

"There's no other one."

"Oh yes there is." I said grimly. "This talk's off the record. Neither of us have witnesses and I want to get things clear."

"There's no other one." she repeated.

"Okay, there's no other one. What is Kruger going to do with her?"

"He'll tell you when he sees you."

"That's what he wants to see me about?"

"Yes."

"Why did she kill Doc Ansell?"

"You'd better ask her that yourself."

"You tell me."

She didn't say anything.

I pushed myself off the table and wandered to the window. There was a guy on the opposite side of the street, hiding behind a newspaper. He had copper written all over him from his hard hat to his flat feet. I turned back to Lydia.

"Where does Andasca come into all this?"

"You'd better let me go." she said suddenly, gathering up her bag and gloves. "This has gone on long enough."

"So it has." I said. "So it has."

I didn't like doing it, but the idea only occurred to me as she stood up. It was one of those ideas that come like a bolt from the blue and are so good that you've just got to play them without thinking.

I hit her on the point of her chin with a short tight. I'll swear she never felt it and she was on the floor before I had regained my balance.

I knelt beside her, lifted her eyelid. She was out for a long count. Well, if Peppi had Myra, I certainly had Lydia. In playing with a rat like Peppi it was just as good to have one of his toys if he had one of yours.

I took a quick gander out of the window. The copper was still there. That was going to make things difficult but not impossible.

I went into the bathroom and found a long roll of adhesive tape. Then I came back into the sitting room and taped Lydia's hands and ankles. I gagged her with my best silk handkerchief and put her on the sofa.

Then I lit a cigarette and did some thinking. The moment Peppi knew I had her he'd send a bunch of strongarms to my apartment. So she'd have to be moved from here. The question was where could I put her? And when I'd found the right place, how was I going to get her out with that copper nesting on my doorstep?

This certainly called for a little thought.

There was the back way out of the apartment block. But, I guessed there'd be a copper watching that too. I went into the kitchen and looked out into the alley. I was right. A big beefy man loitered at the entrance of the alley.

How I was to get out of this building with Lydia and not be seen baffled me. I couldn't imagine her going with me willingly, now that I had clipped her. And to carry her out with the law looking on just wouldn't do.

I had to work fast. I had to get her out of the place before the taxi driver could wise Peppi up that I'd taken her gun and forced her into my apartment. In a way, the cops guarding both entrances prevented Peppi sending a bunch of toughs to beat me up. That was about the only consolation I had.

I wandered upstairs, trying to think of a way out. I went into my room, saw nothing to give me an idea and wandered out into Myra's room.

It was lucky I did. Propped up in a corner was a life-size dummy of a girl, modelled along Myra's lines. It was a prop she used as a magician and it gave me an idea.

The dummy was in an evening dress and was made so that it could stand up or sit down. I went over to it and lifted it. It wasn't heavy.

I carried it down into the sitting room and laid it by Lydia's side.

Then I had another look at the copper standing out in front. I'd never seen him before and that meant he wouldn't be familiar with my looks.

Then I went into my room and selected a light suit in contrast to the one I had been wearing, dug out a slouch hat which I jammed over my eyes. Then I went over to the bed and stripped off the two sheets and went downstairs again.

In the room there was a small, round table, the top of which measured about a foot and a half in diameter. This would just suit my purpose. I got a screwdriver and took it apart.

Then I sat on the floor and swapped a table leg behind each of Lydia's knees with adhesive tape. I strapped the other two legs to her body.

I stood her up. The wooden table legs kept her rigid and that was just what I wanted. Putting her back on the floor, I took off her shoes and went into the kitchen where I found some long screws. I screwed her shoes to the table top. Then with some difficulty I put the shoes on her feet again and laced them securely.

Then I stood her up again and stepped away from her. She looked like a wax dummy on its stand that you see in any dressmaker's shop.

All this had taken about ten minutes and I had to hurry. I put some more adhesive tape round her mouth and fastened her arms to the table legs. I didn't think, if she did come to the surface, she could move or attract attention.

Then I covered her with one of the sheets and tied the sheet round her waist with a length of string. I did exactly the same with the dummy.

Side by side, under the sheets, you couldn't tell which was the dummy and which was Lydia.

Now the tricky part of the business began. The apartment house was divided into wings. We lived in the West wing and each wing was connected by a long corridor. There were four entrances all leading out to the same street, so the copper who was watching outside could see all entrances at once.

But I reasoned this way. He saw me go in with Lydia by the West entrance. He knew I was wearing a dark suit. I had to hope that if I came out of the North entrance with a light suit on he might not connect me with the guy he saw going in the West entrance. Anyway, that was how I had to play it.

I picked Lydia up under one arm and the dummy under the other. Together they were plenty heavy, but I managed. I walked out of my apartment down the corridor, until I came to the North hall. I left Lydia and the dummy there and giving my bat another jerk over my face, I walked out into the street.

I felt as if every eye in the police force were watching me. I glanced right and left. The cop, who'd parked himself outside the West entrance was moving slowly towards me. He wasn't suspicious, but I guess he just wanted to make sure.

I turned and walked very slowly towards him. I saw him hesitate and then turn back to the West entrance. Who said that attack wasn't the best form of defence?

I looked back over my shoulder and then paused on the curb. When a taxi passed, I yelled and the driver crammed on his brakes.

As he nailed the taxi beside me, a patrolman wandered past. He looked at me casually and I took a chance.

"Hey, officer!" I called, moving towards him, "I want some help and your protection."

He looked puzzled, but his face brightened when he saw the five bucks I was folding carefully. That's one language all cops understand.

"Sure." he said. "Any little thing."

I slipped him the dough. Out of the corner of my eye, I could see the copper who had been watching the West wing suddenly show interest in what was going on. He began to move towards me.

I grabbed the patrolman's arm, "Come in, officer." I said, leading him into the lobby. "This is a gag. I've got a couple of dummies to put in my pal's bed. I've been waiting to get even with him for some time and his wife's a jealous woman."

While I was speaking I'd got him up to Lydia and the dummy. I took the dummy and opened up the sheet so that he could see the papier mâché face. "Doesn't she look like the real thing?" I asked.

He gaped at it. "You're going to put that in some guy's bed?" he said, astonished.

"I'm going to do a lot better than that." I told him, "I'm going to put both of them in a guy's bed."

I thought he'd break a blood vessel. I haven't seen a guy laugh so much in years. All the time he was smacking his leg and bellowing I had to stand by and pretend I enjoyed the joke.

But I was losing weight every second wondering if Lydia was coming to the surface and whether if she moved he'd spot her.

"Give me a hand." I urged, when he stopped laughing to mop his eyes, and I shoved the dummy into his arms. "Will you put her in the taxi? If the driver sees this without the law around he'll think I'm kidnapping someone. And listen, don't let your lack of chivalry take advantage of a lady who can't protect herself."

That set him off again. He gathered the dummy up in his arms. "Do you waltz, madam?" he asked, and then locking at me he said, "Her breath smelts of Scotch."

"What of it?" I demanded, "you'd smell of something too it you were as stiff as she is."

"Yeah." he said, "I hadn't thought of that." and he staggered out into the Street, snorting with mirth.

I grabbed Lydia, who stirred as I picked her up. I felt the sweat running down my back, but I had to go through with it. Moving fast, I joined the patrolman by the taxi.

At that second, the copper drifted up and stood looking at us with a disapproving eye.

"What goes on?" he demanded, staring at the two shrouded figures and then at the patrolman.

"Well, if it ain't O'Hara." the patrolman said, losing his good humoured expression. "Holy Moses! Don't I ever get any privacy on my beat?"

"I'm on a special job." O'Hara said. "What have you got there?"

"You look after your special job." the patrolman said shortly. "I'm just helping this guy kidnap a couple of dames." and he began laughing again.

Both O'Hara and the taxi-driver were staring now with eyes like door-knobs.

I tried to edge round O'Hara and get into the taxi, but he was too near the door and I couldn't quite make it. I was scared of attracting his attention. Up to now he hadn't even looked at me.

"Kidnapping?" he repeated stupidly, "I don't get it. That's a Federal offence."

The patrolman turned to me, "This guy started the rumour that dicks were dumb." he said, and went off into another spluttering guffaw.

O'Hara began to get mad. He turned on me. "What the hell is this?" he demanded. "What have you got here?"

"Show him, officer." I said, trying to smile. "We shouldn't keep it to ourselves. He might run us in."

"These are dummies, you big sap." the patrolman said to O'Hara. "This guy's going to put them into his pal's bed. Ain't that funny?"

"Dummies?" O'Hara repeated blankly. "How do you know they're dummies?"

"What the hell else do you think they are … corpses?" The patrolman began to get heated, "Are you nuts? Think I'd help get corpses in a cab?"

"You might do anything." O'Hara said, darkly. "I've heard things about you."

The patrolman thrust the dummy into my arms and clenched his fists. "Yeah?" he said, pushing his face into O'Hara's. "What kind of things?"

"Never mind what kind of things." O'Hara returned airily. "But I've heard enough to know you ain't so hot."

Lydia stirred in my arms and then she made a small grunting noise.

Both O'Hara and the patrolman stopped glaring at each other and turned to me.

"That was the cucumber I had for dinner." I said hurriedly.

"Well, you cut out eating cucumber." O'Hara said, "I don't like that kind of noise."

"Why shouldn't the guy eat cucumber?" the patrolman demanded fiercely. "Who the hell do you think you are?"

O'Hara scowled, "I know who I am." he said with a sneer, "that's more than I can say for some people."

By this time, the taxi-driver was losing patience. "Listen, you guys." he said plaintively, "are you using this cab or ain't you?"

Both O'Hara and the patrolman rounded on him.

"You stick around and like it." the patrolman snarled. "We'll tell you when we're ready, see?"

The driver began to tremble with temper, "I ain't scared of a couple of coppers." he said.

O'Hara turned his attention to me. "How do I know they're dummies?" he demanded, fixing me with a cold eye.

I suddenly lost my own temper and shoved the dummy at him. "Look and see." I said angrily, "I'm getting fed up with this. I ask this officer to give me a hand and the whole damned police force has to come along and shoot its mouth off."

"Yeah." the patrolman said, ranging himself on my side, "what he says is right."

O'Hara felt the dummy gingerly, took a peep at its face and seemed satisfied. "Well, it's a crazy trick, anyway." he said, handing the dummy back to the patrolman.

"Who wants your opinion?" I said, opening the cab door.

As I began putting Lydia into the cab, she grunted again.

O'Hara said, "Cucumber, huh?"

I looked back over my shoulder, "You must be psychic." I said and got into the cab.

"Just a minute." O'Hara said, pushing forward, "I want to look at the other dummy."

That nearly brought me out in a rash.

"If you think I'm going to unpack this just to satisfy your curiosity, you're crazy." I said, slamming the door.

"Leave him alone." the patrolman said, "you pain in the neck."

I could see O'Hara was determined. He yanked open the door again. "I'm seeing that other dummy." he said between his teeth, "and if you start anything, I'll take you to the station."

I got out of the cab again. At least, it would give me a chance to run.

Then just as he was laying hands on Lydia, a guy came out of the West entrance of the apartment block and set off fast, walking away from us.

"Isn't that the guy you're watching?" I said, jerking O'Hara out of the cab and pointing excitedly.

He took one look, cursed under his breath and broke into a frantic run.

I turned to the patrolman, "Can I scram before he comes back?" I rustled another five-buck note because I didn't think he could see it in the darkness.

"Sure." he said, reaching out his hand, "you get off."

"West Forty-fourth." I said, saying the first thing that came into my mind. "And step on it."

As the cab shot away I sank back between Lydia and the dummy and drew a deep breath of relief. Even when Lydia began to wriggle violently and let off a few grunts I couldn't care less.

"That's some cucumber you've been eating." the driver said chattily. "Yes, sir, your grocer sure must have an uneasy conscience."

I put my hand over Lydia's mouth.

"If you don't shut up." I said to her fiercely, "I'll strangle you."

The car lurched and the driver said, "Was you talking to me?"

"Don't be a dope, I can talk to my stomach if I like, can't I?" I returned, squeezing Lydia's face between my fingers.

"I wish you wouldn't, mister." the driver pleaded. "It makes me kind of nervous. Besides, you don't strangle stomachs, you kick 'em or you poison 'em, but you don't strangle 'em."

"I hadn't thought of that." I returned, wiping the sweat of my face with my free hand, "Thanks, pal, I'll know next time."

"You're welcome." the driver returned airily, "It's guys who use their brains that get places."

I agreed with him.

FIFTEEN

Pappi's butler showed no surprise when he opened the front door and found me on the doorstep.

"Come in, sir." he said, stepping to one side.

"Peppi in?" I asked, tossing my hat on the large mahogany table that stood in the hall.

"Mr. Kruger's in, sir." he corrected me. "He's expecting you."

"Swell." I said, fingering my tie.

He closed the front door, "I trust Miss Brandt is in the best of health, sir?" he said quietly.

I eyed him, but his face was Inscrutable. "So far as I know." I returned. "But, the modern woman varies from hour to hour. Shall we say, she was all right when last I saw her?"

Just for a second, he looked as if he wanted to slug me and then the poker face came back again. "Miss Brandt has been very kind to me in the past." he said, as if to explain his curiosity.

"I'm glad." I said. "One of these days you must tell me all about your love life. It should be very, very interesting."

"Yes, sir." he said, and I could see that he was hating my guts. "Will you come this way, please?"

I followed him up the stairs and into the library.

"Mr. Kruger won't keep you long." he said.

"Tell him not to stop to brush his teeth. I ain't particular." I said.

"Very good, sir." the butler returned, and went out, closing the door behind him.

Peppi came in a moment later.

He stood looking at me and I could see he liked me a lot less than when we had met previously.

"There you are." I said, admiring his suit "What a well-turned-out guy you've turned out to be."

"Where is she?" he said.

That's one thing I liked about Peppi. He didn't waste time getting to the point.

"That's the question I was going to ask you." I said, looking up at him from my chair.

It was certainly a smart idea when I grabbed Lydia. I had no idea that both the butler and Peppi would start running round in circles.

Peppi drew a hissing breath through his teeth and controlled himself with an effort. "I'm talking about Miss Brandt." he said, his small hands clenched at his sides. "Where is she?"

"And I am talking about Miss Shumway. Be your age, Peppi, this won't get us anywhere. Turn Myra over to me and you can have Lydia. I'm just trying to even the odds."

"I see." he said, and suddenly smiled. "Very clever of you, Millan, very clever." He drew up a chair and sat down. "You are taking a chance on getting me mad, but I think we can come to an agreement."

"I hope so." I returned, watching him carefully. The change round was a little too sudden.

"You haven't hurt her?" There was an anxious note in his voice.

"I tell you what I haven't done." I said, looking at him coldly, "I haven't framed her for murder. So you're still one up on me."

He examined his finger nails, "No one's been framed for murder." he said. "You still haven't answered my question."

"We're wasting time." I said. "I want Myra and you want Lydia. That's all there's to it. Do we make a deal?"

"If I had Miss Shumway, then, of course, we'd make a deal." he said smoothly. "But she got away."

"Then maybe Lydia will get away, but I doubt it." I said, not believing him.

"I could call the police." he said, moving restlessly.

That was a joke. Peppi going to the police was like a snake dropping in to see a mongoose.

"You could do that." I said, lighting a cigarette. "They might be glad to see you."

"If you found Miss Shumway." he said, "what would you do with her? She's wanted by the police."

"I'll look after that when you turn her over." I said, "and look, Peppi, I'm getting impatient."

Then the door opened and Lydia Brandt walked in.

It was a shock, but I managed to smile at her. It looked like the breaks were not in my favour in this game.

"There you are, Peacherine." I said, "we were just talking about you."

I was almost sorry to see she had a small black bruise each side of her jaw where I had tried to stop her talking in the cab. There was also a graze on her chin where I had hit her. And, what was worse, she looked as mad as a hornet in a paper bag.

Peppi was as startled as I was. He took her arm and stared at her as if he couldn't believe his eyes.

"What happened?" he demanded.

She pushed him aside and came over to me. If there's one thing that makes me nervous it's a dame in a temper. You never know what they're going to do. They might stab you with a hat pin or scratch your eyes out. They might try and make you bald. They might kick you. You just don't know which way it's coming.

I held up my hand, "Now, don't bust your brassiere." I said, hastily. "Remember your upbringing and act like a lady."

She caught me a sizzler on the shin with her pointed shoe. "You heel!" she said, "I'll kill you for what you did to me!" and back went her leg to post me another bone-crusher.

I caught her foot as it shot towards me and lifted it sharply. She sat down with a thud and I guess the jar cooled her fever. Anyway, she just sat there, her eyes snapping and her mouth twisted with pain.

As I got to my feet, someone grabbed me by my shoulder spun me round and I ran into a punch that sent me crashing into the table. I tried to get my balance, but couldn't quite make it. The table and I went over on the floor.

I touched my chin with a grimace and looked at the guy who had hit me. He was one hundred per cent muscle and brawn, with a face moulded on Epstein's lines and a pair of shoulders as wide as a barn door.

"It's a funny thing." I said, "but no one seems to like me."

Lydia, seeing me close, lashed out again and caught me on the knee. I hurriedly got to my feet. "Will you quit kicking me around?" I said, stepping away from her.

The guy who had hit me was bearing down on me again, but Peppi stopped him. "Wait." he said, "don't hit him again. I want to talk to him."

He then turned and helped Lydia to her feet. She looked as if she were going to make another rush at me, but he jerked her round, "Cut it out!" he said. "What happened?"

It came out like a bursting dam. She told how I had got the gun, taken her into my apartment and knocked her cold; how I had taped her up and taken her to the top floor of an empty warehouse by the river and left her there, and how some bum had found her and released her.

All the time she was talking she was glaring at me, and when she was through she made a sudden dive in my direction, but Peppi grabbed her arm and shoved her back. "Get out." he said, in his little hissing voice, "you're not hurt and you've had a lucky break. I want to talk to this guy. Maybe I'll let you at him later."

She gave a look that'd stop a runaway horse and then she went out, leaving me alone with Peppi and the muscle man.

"Okay, Lew." Peppi said, "just watch him. If he acts dumb, you can have him."

I sat down again. "Go on." I said bitterly, "don't mind me. Put me up for auction."

Peppi came over and helped himself to a cigar from a box on the table. "You don't seem to be so clever after all." he said.

"Can I help making mistakes?" I said, shrugging. "I'm just good at 'em, that's all."

"Well, this makes a big difference." he went on, blowing a cloud of smoke into my face, "we can talk now." He began wandering about the room. "I've got this Shumway girl. You were right."

I looked at him in disgust "You always were a liar." I said, "you got the other too?"

Peppi smiled, "Arym, do you mean?"

"Is that her name?"

"Why not? She's just the opposite to Myra. I think it's a good name, don't you?"

"Myra backwards?"

"Yeah, Myra backwards in every way. Your girl's a good girl."

"Where do you get that my girl stuff?" I asked, trying to look bewildered.

"I know." Peppi smiled, "otherwise I wouldn't have bothered. Now there's no chance of you getting away until I say so, you may be interested in some details. Then we can talk business."

"Go ahead." I said airily, "I've got nothing to lose."

For all that, I was interested. There was a lot to clear up and if Peppi wanted to talk I wouldn't stop him.

"Ansell was right. There were two girls." Peppi said, flicking ash into the empty fireplace. "It wanted believing, but it didn't take me long to see how it all added up."

"I bet it didn't." I said bitterly, "you were always a smart guy. Didn't some columnist say you had more brains in your little finger than you had in your head?"

"Shall I hit him?" Lew asked casually, puffing a short rubber club from his hip pocket.

Peppi shook his head, "Not yet." he said, "there's time for that." He turned back to me, "You remember this guy Kelly?"

"Sure." I said, "you'd never heard of him when I was here the other day."

Peppi smiled, "I wasn't ready to talk then." he explained. "Kelly told me about the Shumway girl. She interested me. She gypped Kelly and he wanted me to get the 25 grand out of her. I didn't help him. It wasn't my line, but I wanted to see the girl. I quite liked her." Peppi flicked more ash,

"She's quite a dish. So, I got rid of Kelly and kept her here for a while. Her father got in the way, too. But, I gave him a little money and got rid of him. Then she told me about you, and what happened in Mexico." He moved over to the window, glanced out and then wandered back to the middle of the room. "I didn't believe it at first, but she convinced me. She's a restless dame." He shook his head. "I don't know where she gets to. Now, there's this trouble about your pal Ansell. She shouldn't have rubbed him out, but, in a way, it suits me."

"Let's have it." I said, interested, "I feel this is where I get dragged in."

Peppi nodded, "I'd fixed a substitute Arym for your girl because she said she could persuade you to work for Andasca. I wanted that. It was easy after you told me you were taking Myra to Manetta's. All I had to do was to send Lew along and snatch Myra while Arym took her place." He shrugged "Then she loses her head when this Ansell guy gets nosey and kills him. Well, it's still all right with me. If you don't play along, I'll turn Myra over to the cops."

"Don't talk in riddles." I said, "what do you mean?"

"I've got a job for you. Now, listen, Maddox wants you back."

"Maddox? Did he say so?"

"Sure, he wants you back. And I want you to go back because Maddox has a set of photos I want. You see, I'm being frank with you." He smiled, and when Peppi smiled it was the most unbeautiful thing in the world. "I want you to get those photos. It shouldn't be hard. Andasca got tight some months ago and got himself in a jam. Some guy photographed him. He was talking to me. I didn't want him to talk to me, but he was tight. If those pictures get in the press Andasca's finished. If anyone knows I'm behind him he might just as well throw in his hand. Maddox's going to print those photos the day before the election. You've got to get 'em before then, or I'll turn Myra over to the cops."

There wasn't much to say to that. It was a straightforward proposition.

"I want more than that." I said, "I want both the girls. If I'm to get Myra out of a jam, the other one's got to be given to the cops."

Peppi shrugged, "That's okay with me." he said. "She's no use now. All I want is the photos. You can have 'em both."

"That's on." I said, standing up, "I'll see Maddox right away."

Peppi stubbed out his cigar, "You've got three days before the election." he said, tapping the calendar. "It's no use talking to Maddox. I've offered him fifty grand for those photos. He ain't selling. You've got to find where he keeps them and lift 'em, do you get it?"

I could see myself stealing anything from Maddox. He'd have all the law in the country after my hide quicker than a flea's hop.

"That's okay by me." I said. "I owe him something and this'll about even things up."

Peppi jerked his head to Lew. "Okay." he said, "don't try and be smart. Crossing me won't get you any place."

I smiled at him, "You wouldn't let me have a word with Myra?"

He shook his head.

It was no good arguing with him. So I walked out into the hall where the butler opened the front door.

"So long." I said, "be careful of that brunette. She ain't always kind."

He said something under his breath, but I didn't catch it. Then he closed the door sharply behind me.

Within fifteen minutes I was in Maddox's office.

Now Maddox wasn't the kind of guy you invited to your home. He looked the kind of guy who was put in a home. Maybe his blood pressure bothered him. I don't know, but he looked like he had swallowed a volcano and was uncertain of future events.

With him was his personal secretary, who most of the boys knew as 'Whalebone Harriet.' That dame was so straight laced her figure suffered from arrested development. But in spite of this she was smart and she'd always been a good friend of mine.

Right now, she was trying to calm Maddox down while I stood by the door waiting to see how safe it was to advance further.

Maddox left off scrumpling up his blotting pad and breaking his pens and pencils, so I guessed that the first spasm was over. I advanced cautiously across the wide expanse of carpet until I was within six feet of his desk. "Hello there, Mr. Maddox." I said, smiling.

Maddox half rose from his chair, but Harriet pushed him back firmly, so he had to be satisfied with a lot of lip twisting stuff.

"So you've come back, you incompetent, useless, pin-headed baboon." he exploded, with a roar that rattled the windows. "Call yourself a newspaper man? Call yourself a special correspondent? Call yourself a …!"

"Mr. Maddox, please." Harriet broke in, "you promised you'd behave! You can't expect Mr. Millan to help you if you begin by calling him names."

"Help me?" Maddox repeated, wrenching at his collar, "do you honestly think this brainless ink-slinger can help me? He's cost the paper twenty-five thousand dollars! Twenty-five thousand dollars!! And look at him! It means nothing to him!"

"That wasn't my fault." I said, edging back a couple of feet. "You ask Juden. He'll tell you what happened. You were double-crossed, Mr. Maddox. You've got Shumway to blame for that."

Maddox began to swell, "I was double-crossed all right." he said, leaning over his desk, while Harriet hung on to his coat, "you fell down on the job, you hollow-headed monkey! I know all about it … if you think I believe that stuff you told Summers you're crazier than I thought. Floating women! Talking dogs!! Man into sausage!!! Bah!"

"Never mind about that." I said, "I want to talk to you about Andasca."

"Andasca?" He stopped tying his face in knots and stared at me. "What do you mean? What do you know about Andasca?"

"I know what you've got on him," I said, cautiously, "and I know Kruger wants you to lay off."

He sat down abruptly, "How do *you* know?"

"Kruger told me. Now listen, Mr. Maddox, forget the twenty-five grand. After all this paper can afford to lose twenty-five grand once in a while …"

I thought that would start him all over again, but Harriet anchored him to his chair.

"Kruger's framed Shumway's daughter with murder. Unless he gets those photos he's going to give her to the cops. He wants me to get those prints from you and in return he'll turn the girl loose." I went on. "He's got enough on the girl to send her to the chair."

Maddox drew in a long, deep breath. "So you want those photos, do you?" he repeated, struggling to get the words out. "You want to give them to Kruger, do you? Well, you're not having them! I don't care if he's got enough to send every man, woman and child in this country to the chair! Do you understand that?"

I didn't expect anything else. "Now, look, Mr. Maddox." I said, "can I give you the whole story? Will you listen?"

"Will I listen?" he snarled, "why do you think I sent for you? Do you think I wanted to look on your cretinish face?"

"Okay." I said, drawing up a chair, "it'll take a little time, but at least you'll know where you are."

"At least I'll know where I am." he repeated, "and by the time you've finished, you'll know where you are!"

I didn't let him rattle me, but went straight into the story and told him everything from the meeting with Myra to the meeting with Kruger.

He sat drumming on the desk, looking as if he could eat me, while Harriet took the story down. When I was through, he just sat looking at me. There was a long painful silence. Even Harriet looked doubtful.

"What a dream!" he exploded at last. "That settles it. Young man, you're a menace to the citizens of this country. Do you know what I'm going to do to you? I'm going to have you sent to a nut house. If I spend my last dime, I'll have you put away before the end of the week."

I got hastily to my feet. "Hey." I said, "you can't do a thing like that!"

"I can't, huh?" Maddox snarled. "Well, you wait and see. This time next week you'll be in a strait jacket!"

A knock sounded on the door.

"Come in." Harriet called.

Murphy, the doorman, walked in. I've never seen a guy look so altered. His face was pale and lined and he carried himself as if he'd got a ton weight on his back.

"What do you want?" Maddox snapped, "get out, I'm busy."

"I'm sorry, Mr. Maddox, sir." Murphy said in a low voice, "but, I'm leaving. I've just come to say good-bye."

"What do you mean … you're leaving? You've been with me twenty years." Maddox said, startled.

"I know that, sir." Murphy replied, shaking his head sadly, "it'll be a blow to the wife when she hears about it, but I've got to go. I'm conscientious, sir, and I don't think I'm fit any more for the job."

Maddox got to his feet. "What are you drivelling about?" he roared. "What *is* this? I warn you, Murphy, if this is a gag, I'll make you sorry. I won't have people wasting my time. Now, go downstairs and look after the doors. If you've been drinking, sleep it off. You're an old trusted servant and I'll overlook this, if you'll get out."

Murphy approached him. "It's not that, sir." he said mournfully, "my brain's given way."

Maddox took a hasty step back, "Your brain?" he repeated uneasily.

Murphy nodded. "Yes, sir." he said, "it was all right this morning, but it's gone now. I've got to go. I might do something I'd be sorry for."

"How do you know your brain's given way?" Maddox asked, behind his desk by now.

"I'm hearing things, sir." Murphy said. "Voices in my head."

Maddox appealed to Harriet. "Do people hear voices in their heads when their brains give way?"

Harriet lifted her square shoulders. "It's not an encouraging sign, Mr. Maddox." she said softly.

Maddox wiped his face with his handkerchief. "I suppose not." he said. "But what kind of voices?"

Murphy shivered. "There's a big dog downstairs." he said. "I thought he spoke to me. That's why I say I'm hearing voices."

"Spoke to you … a dog? What did he say?" Maddox demanded.

"He wanted to know if I changed socks every day."

I jumped to my feet, "What?" I shouted, "a dog?"

Murphy shrank back, "Yes, Mr. Millan, a big dog. I shouldn't ought to bother you with this…"

"Where is he?" I shouted. "It's Whisky." I turned on Maddox. "Now, I'll show you something. Get that dog up here! Where did you leave him?"

"I don't want him up here." Murphy wailed. "I couldn't bear to have him up here."

I rushed to the door and jerked it open. Half the office staff, who had been listening at the keyhole, fell into the room, but I didn't stop. I trod over them, shoving the others out of the way and rushed for the elevator.

Downstairs, I found a group of people standing round the door, but there was no sign of Whisky.

"Anyone seen a dog around here?" I demanded.

"Sure." a big guy said, pushing his way towards me, "a big wolfhound. He came in here a few minutes ago and then Murphy suddenly seemed to go crazy and ran for the elevator. The dog went off like he was offended."

"Which way did he go?"

"To the right. What's it all about?"

I didn't wait, but bolted out into the street.

There was no sign of Whisky anywhere. That didn't worry me a great deal. There was only one place where he'd go and that would be home.

I signalled a passing taxi and gave him my address. "Keep near the sidewalk." I said, "I'm looking for a pal of mine."

The driver, a wizen little punk with suspicious rat-like eyes, touched his cap. "I'm ready to stop when you are." he said, and drove along the street, hugging the curb.

I was nearly home, when I spotted Whisky trotting along. He looked in better shape. Someone must have cleaned him up, but he still had a nasty wound on his head.

"Stop!" I bawled to the taxi driver and bundled out of the cab. "Whisky, old boy!" I called, running towards him, "Gee! Whisky, it's nice to see you."

Whisky turned quickly, "Well." he said, "I've been looking all over for you."

"Come back in the cab, Whisky." I said, patting him gently. "We've got a lot to talk about."

We crowded back into the cab. "Just drive around, will you?" I said to the driver. "I've got a lot to say to my dog."

The driver eyed Whisky. "He's a nice dog, ain't he?" he said, "you ain't been beating that dog, have you, mister?"

"Now listen." I said, pushing Whisky in a corner so I had room to sit down, "I just want to talk to my dog. I don't want to get tied up in a conversation with you. I haven't got the time for it."

"I don't like guys who beat dogs." the taxi driver said, turning in his seat. "I got plenty tough with the last guy I saw beating his dog."

"Yeah?" Whisky said, pushing his face into the taxi driver's, "then he must have been a midget."

"Well, he was, but that don't change the idea of the thing." returned the driver and started up his engine.

Whisky and I settled back and we regarded each other affectionately. "Well, pal." I said, "you've certainly had a bad time. What did they do to you?"

Before he could reply, we were both thrown in a heap on the floor as the driver trod on his brakes.

"What's the idea?" I said, angrily. "What do you think you're doing?"

The driver turned in his seat. His face was the colour of a fish's underbelly. "Hey!" he said in a trembling voice, "didn't that dog speak?"

"What are you talking about?" I said. "Get on with your driving, can't you?"

"Now, wait a minute." the rat-like eyes glared at me. "I've got to get this straight. Did that dog speak to me?"

"Well, what if he did? That's nothing to be ashamed of."

"Yeah, yeah, I know. But dogs don't talk. They bark, see?"

"Oh, I get it. Well, there's nothing to worry about. He's just that kind of a dog."

"Well, if that's all it is." the driver said, relieved, and be began driving again.

"I thought you'd lost your voice." I said to Whisky.

"So I did." he growled, "and damned inconvenient it was too. I hope I never go back to barking again; you just don't get anywhere like that. But, we're wasting time, I know where Myra is."

"So do I." I said gloomily, "with Peppi."

Whisky shook his head. "She's in a top front room in Waxey's dive." he said.

I stared at him. "She's with Peppi." I said, "let me get you up to date." and I told him about Ansell and Peppi and the whole set-up.

He sat looking at me with alert eyes and when I'd finished, he said, "Don't bother about those photos. I tell you she's at Waxey's dive. We can get her out of there and then turn Peppi over to the cops. Tell the driver to turn around."

"You're sure?" I said, half convinced. "What has Waxey to do with Peppi?"

"Will you stop yapping." Whisky said fiercely, "and tell the driver."

"Okay." I said, and leaning forward I said, "take us to Mulberry Park, will you?"

"Sure." the driver said, "and listen, I've been thinking. I don't believe that dog talked, see? And nothing you say'll convince me." and he swung the cab off the main street.

SIXTEEN

While we were driving to Mulberry Park, Whisky explained what had been happening to him. He had seen Myra kidnapped when she left our apartment and he had followed the car. He had seen her taken to Good-time Waxey's dive and he went after her.

But Waxey and Lew had been too much for him. He only managed to get away by the skin of his teeth and not before Lew bad nearly brained him with his rubber club.

I listened grimly to all this. "I'll settle that heel." I said. "He's nor going to knock you around and get away with it."

"Better be careful." Whisky said mournfully, "he's a mighty big guy."

"I'll be careful." I said. "If I get a chance to slug him when he's not look-ing, I'll take the chance."

As the cab slowed down, Whisky said, "Well, here we are."

"Yeah." I said, getting out and paying the driver. He didn't look at me when he took the money, but he eyed Whisky suspiciously, then he drove away fast. "I don't think that guy liked us." I said. "Now, listen. We'll get nowhere if they see you, Whisky. You watch the building. If I don't come out in half an hour, you'd better get the cops."

"No good doing that, unless the two girls are there." Whisky said. "If the cops get Myra and not the other one what sort of jam will we be in?"

"You've got something there." I said, "but, what if something happens to me? What'll you do?"

"I'll send you a wreath." Whisky returned. "What else can I do?"

"Never mind about the wreath." I returned sharply. "You better come in after me if I'm longer than a half an hour."

"I'll think about it." Whisky returned. "I'm not worked up about the idea."

"I can understand that." I said. "You're sure she's in the place?"

"She's upstairs in the room facing the street. I saw her look out of the window."

"Swell. It just means getting up there."

"That's right. If anyone tries to stop you, just don't take no for an an-swer."

I didn't feel I was getting all the encouragement I needed, but apparently Whisky wasn't an encouraging kind of dog.

I left him at the corner of the square and wandered towards Waxey's dive. The place seemed deserted and when I got inside I found a thin weedy youth half asleep over the counter.

"Where's Waxey?" I asked.

"Out." the youth yawned and put his head on his arms again.

I glanced round the dim room. Over to the right was a door which I guessed led upstairs.

"I'll wait." I said, sitting on an upturned box near the door.

The youth didn't say anything. He was nearly asleep. I sat there watching him and after a minute or so he began to snore.

I shifted my box closer to the door, but he didn't look up. I gave him a few seconds just to be on the safe side and then reached the door. It opened silently and, leaving the youth spread over the counter, I peered into the gloom of a passage that led to a flight of stairs.

I'd have felt a lot more confident if I had a gun with me. All the same, if Myra was up there, I was going to get her out. I went up the stairs quickly.

The first room I entered was obviously Waxey's bedroom. It was empty except for a rough cot and a lot of dirt. Waxey certainly lived the hard way.

The next door was locked. I hadn't time for any fancy stuff, I drew back and caught the door a peach of a kick just below the lock. The door flew open and I sprawled in the room on my hands and knees.

Myra twisted over on the bed so that she could see who it was. I sat up and grinned at her.

"So you've come at last." she said, trying to sit up. I could see that her wrists and ankles were bound. "Don't sit there like a big drip. Hitch up your truss and get me out of here."

"Kid." I said, getting to my feet. "It's grand to hear your voice again."

"Never mind that stuff." Myra snapped, bouncing up and down on the bed. "Get me undone. We can have our little cry together later on."

"I'm right with you." I said, going over to her. "They haven't hurt you, have they?"

"Don't talk so much." Myra returned. "They haven't had time, but they've promised all kinds of things."

I examined the cords that bound her. Whoever tied her had made a swell job of it. But when I found my knife, it didn't take long to free her.

"There you are, sugar." I said, sitting beside her. "How does it feel?"

"Lousy." Myra said moving her legs and wincing. "I've got a cramp."

"I'll fix that." I said, pushing back my cuffs. "I'll get some life in them."

"Hands off!" Myra said sharply. "I like to do my own massaging."

"That's a pity." I returned. "I was looking forward to that."

While she began restoring her circulation, I glanced round the room. It was empty except for the bed and a table. On the table stood an odd looking contraption. There were two large springs, a handcuff on a long chain and one or two cogwheels. They were all joined up together and they intrigued me.

"Someone's going to pay for this." Myra said angrily. "Why should they want to kidnap me?"

"I'll tell you in a second." I said, picking up the handcuff, "what's this thing?"

Myra gave a little scream, "Don't touch it!" she cried.

"Why not … is it a man-trap?"

There was a sudden sharp click. The springs moved forward, the cog-wheels spun and I found the handcuff on my wrist.

"You big sap!" Myra said furiously.

"Why, it *is* a man-trap!" I said, admiring the thing. "That's smart. There might be a fortune in it."

Myra swung her legs off the bed and hobbled over to me. "Didn't I tell you not to touch it?"

I took hold of the handcuff and jerked at it. "I'll get it off." I said calmly. "I was glad to see it work."

"You won't get it off." Myra said, nearly crying. "Oh, I could brain you!"

And she was right. The handcuff had me tight round the wrist and nothing I could do would shift it. The chain to which it was fastened only allowed me a few feet from the wall.

"Hey!" I said in alarm, "get this off, will you?"

"But I can't." Myra wailed. "You stupid dope! What am I going to do now?"

I wrestled with the thing silently. After a while, I gave up. "Don't let's get into a panic." I said. "If this chain thinks it can hold me … why it's crazy!" I put my feet against the wall and holding the chain in both bands, I threw my weight backwards. It ought to have wrenched the staple that held the chain out of the wall. But it didn't. But it did nearly give me a hemorrhage. I sat on the floor and mopped my brow.

"You're right, sugar." I said in disgust. "I'm a sap and a dope!"

"They'll kill you if they find you here." Myra said anxiously.

"Don't talk that way." I said hastily. "Someone might hear you and get ideas. Now listen, you're in a jam and I'm in a jam, but it's a lot worse for you than for me."

"What do you mean?"

So I told her in a few words about Doc Ansell and the cops and how they were looking for her.

"So you see." I said, "you've got to hide some place. Don't wait for me. Get going. Take Whisky with you and tell him where you're going. He'll tell me later."

"I'm not leaving you here." she said, "I'll get a file or something and break that chain."

"You're wasting time. Find me a rat to talk to and I'll pretend I'm in jail. Go on. They won't do anything to me."

"I'm not leaving you." she said, and then she gave a sudden sharp cry.

"What's the matter? Why are you looking like that?" I asked as her expression changed.

She put out her hands towards me and I saw she was shivering.

"You're not going to faint, are you?" I asked in alarm. "Here, hold up, kid." and I tried to reach her.

"Something's happening to me." she said wildly.

The look in her eyes scared me and then I saw something that made me start back. You won't believe this. I didn't believe it myself. It was like something had gone wrong with my eyes.

Myra was becoming blurred. Her figure was smudgy, like a blurred photograph and even her features seemed to be dissolving.

"What's happening to you?" I exclaimed, feeling my heart pounding.

She didn't say anything, but just stood swaying before me. I could see something filmy in front of her. Something that moved. Then a shadowy figure stepped from her.

You've seen those trick films where people become transparent? Well, that's exactly how this figure looked. It sent my blood pressure up and gave me the scare of my life.

As I watched, the figure became more distinct and then there she was— Myra the second, the spitting image of Myra except she was dressed only in white satin panties and brassiere.

I knew it must be Arym. But, even seeing the two together, it didn't make it possible.

Myra backed away. She was as startled as I. Then she clutched at her frock and gasped.

"You—you've got on my underwear!" she said.

Arym admired her figure. "Well, I had to have something." she returned airily. "After all we aren't alone." She looked at me archly. "Aren't you staring a little too much?" she asked.

I hastily averted my eyes. "You're not a sight for anyone to pass up." I said feebly.

"But … you're me!" Myra exclaimed, looking stunned.

"Of course, I am." Arym said. "At least, we share the same body."

Myra put her hands to her face. "This is awful." she said, "what am I going to do?"

"It's all right once you get used to it." Arym returned with a giggle. "Every one has two sides to their natures."

"I know." I put in, "but they don't have two bodies. This is driving me batty."

"Oh, that's Quintl." Arym went on, "he had a swell sense of humour. In a way, it's been a good thing. I've got tired of sharing a body with someone else. It's nice to have one of my own."

Myra came over and clutched at me. I put my arm around her. "Take it easy." I said. "We'll wake up in a minute and find this is just another nightmare."

"Oh no, you won't." Arym said. "Why don't you get wise? I'm just part of you and I've decided to leave you."

Myra looked at her fixedly. "You're bad." she said quietly. "I can see you're bad."

"What of it?" Arym said, shrugging. "We can't all be good, besides no one would be interesting if they didn't have a little bad in them. Think how prissy you're going to be now that I've left you."

"So you're the one who's been making a mess of my life." Myra said, stepping away from me and confronting Arym.

"It's been mighty hard work. I tell you, it's quite a relief to get away from you for a while."

"You'll never get back again." Myra said. "So don't you think you will."

"If I want to, I shall." Arym returned, wandering over to the bed and sitting down. "You can't get along without me."

"Yes, I can… and I'm going to."

"How do you think you'll live?" Arym scoffed. "I made all your money by stealing it. Remember Joe Krum? What a time I had to get you to break the ice!"

Myra flushed scarlet. "Oh, I wish I'd never listened to you."

"You've got quite a strong character really." Arym admitted reluctantly.

"You won't need to worry about my character now." Myra said grimly. "I've got you out of my system, and this time I'm keeping you out."

Arym shrugged, "I don't want to come back." she said. "You don't have to get so worked up. I don't think it would be safe any more. In fact, I'm certain it wouldn't be." and she laughed.

Myra stared at her. "What do you mean by that?" she demanded.

"If it wasn't for that silly little man, I suppose I wouldn't have left you for good. I think I was getting the upper hand of you although it was a tough struggle. But be had to interfere and so I had to kill him. You see Peppi says they'll put me in the chair if they catch me. He's going to hide me until they find you. They think you killed him, so when they've dealt with you, I'll be able to start all over again."

Myra suddenly saw what a jam she was in and looked desperately at me.

"If I could only get this handcuff off." I said, jerking furiously at the chain, "I'd know what to do."

"There's nothing you can do." Arym said, curling up her long bare legs under her. "This is the proverbial struggle between good and bad. I've tried to get along with Myra, but it's been too uphill. Why should a girl with such a nice body and looks lead such a dreary life as she makes me lead? I'm sick of it. Since she met you, she hasn't stolen a thing. How does she expect us to live? Why, I had to leave her to get after that reward. She wouldn't have bothered about it. Now, I've salted it away where no one can find it." and her eyes lit up at the thought. She put her arms behind her and leaned back. I don't want to stress the point, but that dame would certainly have made Petty a swell model. "Are you still going to marry me like you said, when all this is over?" she went on looking at me with an arch smile.

"I'll have you understand he loves me, you horrid little hooker!" Myra broke in before I could say anything.

"That's what you think." Arym said, waving her away. "But he's actually proposed to me. Haven't you, darling?"

I didn't know what to say.

"That settles it." Myra said grimly. "I won't let you get your claws into him. You've talked too much already. I'm going to take you to the police. They can choose between us."

Arym looked alarmed, "Oh no, you're not." she said, sliding off the bed. "That wouldn't do at all." and she made for the door.

"Don't let her get away." I shouted, trying to reach her.

Myra made a dash towards her, but Arym was too quick. As she opened the door, Lew came bounding in.

Then things happened. I kicked over the table in front of Lew. Arym disappeared out of the room, slamming the door behind her and Myra suddenly swooped up to the ceiling.

As the table went over, the man-trap apparatus crashed on the floor. The fall set the mechanism working; there was a whirr of wheels and the handcuff clicked open. I just managed to get it off my wrist as Lew came at me.

I stopped a punch on the side of my head that made my teeth rattle, but I managed to slow him down with a counter to his belly.

He stepped back and Myra grabbed his hair. She twined her fingers almost lovingly in his locks and pulled.

I thought he was going out of his mind. He looked right and left and then behind him. He couldn't see anything because Myra was above him. While he was occupied, I stepped in and hit him pretty well where I liked. I remembered Whisky, so I let him have it. He tried to back away, but Myra, exerting all her strength clung to him like a leech. Then he looked up and saw her. He could only gape in horror and I had no difficulty in hanging a punch on his jaw that came up from my ankles.

He gave a tired little smile and folded up on the floor.

"Very nice work." I said, blowing on my knuckles. "And now let's get out of this fast."

I reached up to take Myra's hand and I pulled her gently to the floor. She was as light as a thistle down and I had difficulty in keeping her by my side.

"She's gotten away." she said desperately, holding on to me, her feet a few inches off the floor.

"Never mind that." I said, "at least, I've got you and that's something." As I moved to the door I heard the sound of heavy footsteps pounding up the stairs.

"The window." Myra said. "Quick!"

I let her go and dashed to the window. As soon as I released her, she shot up in the air and banged against the ceiling.

"Ooch!" she exclaimed from up there. "That hurt!"

I didn't pay any attention. I was leaning out and looking down into the street. It was a long drop and we'd only break our necks if we went that way.

"It's too high!" I said, coming away from the window. "What the hell are we going to do now?"

Myra floated down and drifted out of the window. She hung suspended just outside. It was an unnerving sight to see her standing calmly on nothing thirty feet or so above ground.

Already a number of people had stopped and were staring up at her. Several were clutching each other and one fat woman began running madly down the street, screaming like a train whistle.

"Don't stand there." she said impatiently. "Give me your hand. I won't let you fall."

"What? You want me …" Then I heard the door crash open behind me and Myra grabbed me.

I don't mind admitting that I shut my eyes as I stepped into space. But she had no difficulty in keeping me from falling. I felt a rushing sensation and I opened my eyes timidly.

We had flashed over some buildings, leaving Waxey's dive far behind.

"Do you like it?" Myra asked, holding my hand firmly and smiling at me.

"Only because I trust you." I said, taking a firmer grip on her. "Otherwise, I'd just go crazy at the thought."

We swooped over a crowded street. I noticed a loiterer below. He glanced up casually, stiffened and then hid his face in his hands. I guess that guy would go off liquor for the rest of his days.

"Pick a quiet spot and let's get down." I said. "We'll start a riot in a minute."

We circled some buildings, spotted a deserted alley and floated gently to the ground. As we recovered our balance, we noticed an old man standing in a doorway staring at us with fixed concentration.

"Do you do that often?" he quavered, plucking nervously at his beard.

"It only happens when we're a bit light-headed." I returned, dusting myself down. "Think nothing of it."

"I wish I could." the old man said, wistfully. "It'll haunt me for the rest of my days."

"That won't be long." I said, kindly, "so it won't be hard to bear."

"Don't tease him." Myra said. "He looks as if he's been through rather a strain."

"I have, lady." the old man said eagerly. "The trouble is no one will believe me." and he went into his house and shut the door.

"Phew!" I said. "We're lucky to get out of that."

Myra suddenly faced me. "Did you really propose to that blonde?" she said, looking at me accusingly.

"But, darling." I said hastily, "I thought it was you. There was a look in her eyes and …"

"You mean, I haven't encouraged you?" Myra said seriously. "I suppose I haven't." and she reached up and kissed me.

"The proposal still stands." I said, a few minutes later. "Will you consider it?"

"I will." she said. "And now I want some undies. Will you take me somewhere where I can buy them?"

"We've got to be quick." I said. "If the cops …"

"I can't go around like this." Myra said firmly. "We've just got to take a chance."

At the end of the alley, I spotted a taxi and I waved. Just as we go in, Whisky came bounding up. He scrambled in as we drove off.

SEVENTEEN

"Where to, boss?" the driver asked, as soon as we had settled down.

"Keep driving." I returned, shoving Whisky's foot out of my chest. "I'll tell you when I've had time to think."

Myra and Whisky were making a great fuss over each other, and I had to tell Whisky that when I wanted his tongue over my face I'd let him know.

"It's certainly nice to see you again." Whisky said, panting with excitement. "I'd given you both up for lost."

"We'd given ourselves up for lost." I said, taking Myra's hand. "It's a good thing you learned to float, sugar."

"You know, I just can't help it." Myra said apologetically. "But I must get some undies. I just haven't any confidence without them."

"What have you done with them?" Whisky asked, pricking up his ears.

"Don't tell him." I pleaded. "It'll take too long. Never mind about your undies. The cops are looking for you. They've only to hear I've been seen with a blonde and a dog and they'll come after us like bats out of hell."

"Very well." Myra said, settling back. "But you've no idea how it preys on my mind."

"The point to concentrate on is where do we go from here?" I said.

"That, I think, is for you to decide." Myra said, slipping her hand into mine. "I'll go where you say."

"I've got to put you in some place where the cops won't find you. Then I've got to get hold of Arym."

"Who's Arym?" Myra asked, puzzled.

"Your other self, my pet." I said lightly. "That's what she calls herself. If I get her, then you'll be in the clear."

"But how are you going to do that?"

"I don't know. I'm not even going to think about it. I must first find a hide-out for you." Then I remembered Harriet. "I know." I said, and leaning forward I told the driver to stop at the first public telephone.

"This do you?" he asked, cutting across the traffic and drawing up outside a drug store.

"Yeah." I said, then to Myra, "wait here, I've got to 'phone."

I found there was only one telephone booth when I got into the drug store and some dame was using it.

I went over to the soda-jerker behind the counter. "Is that lady going to be long?" I asked. "I've got a taxi outside and I'm in a hurry."

He shook his head. "She's about through." he said. "Anyway, I figure it that way. She's been in there since noon and she must have used up most of the air in that little booth by now."

I thanked him. He had a pretty good grip on his business because the woman suddenly hung up and stepped out of the booth. She nodded to the soda-jerker and went out into the Street.

"What they find to talk about." he began, leaning on the counter, but I didn't wait to hear any more. I shut myself in with the telephone and put a call through to the *Recorder.*

Harriet was tied up with Mr. Maddox, I was told.

"Well, can't you send someone in to cut her loose?" I demanded. "This is important."

"How important would you say?" the switchboard girl asked. She didn't sound impressed.

"Her apartment's on fire and her old man's trapped up on the roof." I lied. "If that's important to you, I guess you might do something about it."

"I can't interrupt Mr. Maddox for that." she replied. "How long has he been upon the roof?"

I would have liked to have been right behind that baby. I'd have surprised her.

"Look." I said. "It doesn't matter how long he's been up there. The point is the place is on fire and he gets dizzy when he's high up. He wants to see his daughter before anything happens to him."

"Well, I'll tell her when she's through with Mr. Maddox." the girl replied curtly and rang off.

Maybe she didn't believe me.

I had to leave the booth to get some change and when I got back some guy was entering the booth.

"Look, mister." I pleaded. "I've got a priority. Would you mind giving way to me?"

He shook his head. "I've got a priority too." he said. "My wife's apartment's on fire ..."

"I know and she's up on the roof." I skid, in disgust.

He looked at me sharply. "I wonder how you knew that." he returned, then he suddenly shrugged. "Well, hell I'll wait. There's plenty for her to look at up there."

I thanked him and got back to the *Recorder*. "If you don't put me through to Miss Halliday." I said when I got the operator, "I'll fix you good some dark night."

"Let's make a date." she replied promptly. "The trouble is the nights are never dark enough these days."

"How can they be?" I said, wanting to strangle her.

"Well, you know what I mean. How dark does it have to be?"

"I don't know and I don't care. I'll just choose the first dark night that comes along." I said, snarling.

"I can't do business on those lines." she replied, giggling. "I like something definite. How about to-night? To-morrow there's a new moon and it'll be too light for fixing."

Something jogged my memory. "New moon?" I repeated. "Did you say there'll be a new moon to-morrow?"

"Sure, I have to watch little things like that. They make an awful difference in a girl's life."

"Never mind about your life." I said quickly. "What's the date?"

"July 31." she replied. "Have you been shipwrecked or something?"

I nearly dropped the receiver. The end of the month. I remembered what Doc Ansell had said. Myra would lose her influence at the end of the month when the moon changed. I looked hurriedly at the clock on the wall. It was just five-fifteen. I had only seven hours to get everything fixed up.

"Hello … hello … hello?" the girl said. "Are you still there?"

"I think so." I said cautiously. "Will you see how Miss Halliday's getting on?"

"How about that date?"

"Sure, make it to-night. I'll pick you up."

"But how shall I know you?"

"Who, me? You'll know me all right. I'll be wearing a Zoot suit and I carry my left leg over my right shoulder. No one's mistaken me yet."

There was a moment's silence. "Can't you do anything about that left leg?" she asked at last.

"I can leave it at home."

"Couldn't you be a little rough with it for to-night?" she asked hopefully. "I'd stand the Zoot suit but the leg gets me down."

"That's the idea." I pointed out.

She thought about this for a moment. "It's a date." she said briskly. "Miss Halliday's free now. I'm putting you thr-r-r-ough."

Harriet was all brains. I didn't have to go into details. She got what I wanted almost before I had started. She told me where her apartment was and how to get in and she promised to be back early. I thanked her and rang off. I felt I'd lost ten pounds by the time I got out of the booth. I collided with the guy waiting to put through his call. He apologized.

"Excuse me, pal." he said. "Can you remember what I wanted to telephone about?"

I told him.

"That's right." he said. "I've got the darnedest memory. Do you know I just can't remember whether the fire was to-day or last week. Ain't that a hell of a thing?"

I shoved past him and went out into the street.

I found Whisky lying on the floor of the taxi, but Myra wasn't there.

"Where is she?" I demanded.

"Get inside." Whisky said. "Where have you been?" The urgency in his voice startled me, so I got into the cab and shut the door.

"What's the matter?" I asked.

"How much longer are you keeping me here?" the driver asked angrily. "I've got a home if you haven't."

Whisky showed his teeth. "Sit there and like it." he snarled.

The driver got out of his cab hastily. "Come on, legs." he said, clutching at his collar. "I'm going to start running."

"Come back when you're through." I said. "You've got a nice evening for it."

The driver didn't listen. He began running madly down the street.

I turned my attention to Whisky. "Now." I said, "where did she go?"

"Keep down." Whisky said in a mysterious mutter. "The cops have moved in."

"What?" I exclaimed, startled. "What do you mean? Have they got her?"

"A couple of minutes and it'll all be over." he returned with ghoulish gloom. "She's in that lingerie shop across the street. The moment you'd gone, she spotted it and made a dart for it. I hadn't time to reason with her. There was a copper on the corner and he saw her. It took him just five seconds to call the riot squad. They've just moved in."

I looked across the street. Two patrolmen stood outside the smart modiste shop, looking with interest at the various garments displayed in the windows.

"Why don't they bring her out?" I said, feeling a little sick.

"How do I know?" Whisky said peevishly. I could see he was as worried as I was.

"Well, I'm not staying here." I said, "I'm going to see what's cooking. You wait here." and I left the taxi and crossed the street.

The two patrolmen looked like they were going to stop me, but I kept walking and they let me through.

The first guy I set eyes on was Clancy.

"Well, well." I said, smiling at him. "Buying something for the little woman?"

"There you are!" he said, swelling with rage. "I've been looking all over for you. Where *is* she?"

I took a quick gander round the shop. It was certainly a nice place. The guy who'd put it together had taken a lot of pains to get it just right. It was all chromium furniture, mirrors and concealed lighting. The carpet was so thick that it tickled my ankles. There were a number of alcoves round the room containing life-size models on which were displayed bathing suits, lingerie and evening gowns. Some of these models were so snappy that I took a second look to make sure I wasn't passing anything up.

At the far end of the room, a patrolman stood guard over a group of girls. He seemed to be enjoying his job. I could understand that. The girls looked like they had been lifted straight out of the front line of the Follies. There was a nervous looking guy in morning clothes, fussing around. I guessed he was the manager of the shop.

But there was no sign of Myra.

I turned my attention to Clancy. "Where's who?" I asked. "Why don't you relax sometimes, old boy? Life ain't *all* work. Take a gander at those wenches huddling in the corner. Don't they stir your pulse?"

"Don't give me that stuff." Clancy said, looking fierce. "She was seen coming in here and now you turn up. Do you think I'm dumb?"

"She ... she ... she?" I repeated. "What are you talking about? What she?"

"This Shumway bird." Clancy said, clenching his fists and looking homicidal. "You'd better be careful, Millan. She's wanted for murder."

"I know, I know. But, what have I got to do with it? I just got here." I said. "Haven't you searched the joint? And listen, Clancy, while we're on the subject, *you'd* better be careful. My paper won't stand for me being kicked around."

That slowed him up. He vented his temper on the cops.

"Don't stand there like a bunch of stuffed eels." he snarled. "Look for her. Turn this joint upside down. Take it to pieces. She's here, so find her!"

The manager came rushing up. "I won't have it!" he spluttered. "You can't go into the dressing rooms. My customers wouldn't stand for it. This is an unpardonable, unwarranted outrage!"

"Wait a minute." Clancy said to the cops. Then he turned on the manager. "Do you think I care what you've got to say? A woman came in her five minutes ago and she's still here. Where did she go?"

The manager wrung his hands. "I put her in that dressing room." he said, pointing to an empty room near one of the alcoves. "She's vanished. I didn't see what happened to her."

"Well, she's somewhere around." Clancy said, between his teeth. "Send one of your dames into all those rooms and get every woman out of 'em."

"This should be good." I said. "A great outdoor playboy like you wouldn't know that dames go in those rooms to undress."

"Keep out of this!" Clancy bellowed. "I'm going to find that dame if it's the last thing I do."

"It certainly will be the last thing you do if you drive a lot of undressed society dames out of hiding." I returned. "Captain Summers' wife buys stuff here."

He pushed his face into mine. "If you don't pipe down, I'll make you sorry you were born." he said violently, but I could see that I'd shaken him. "You want this girl to get away, don't you? Well, she ain't getting away."

I shrugged. "Go ahead." I said. "It's your funeral."

He turned back to the manager. "Get 'em out!" he ordered. "Everyone of 'em. She's hiding somewhere in those rooms and she's wanted for murder!"

The manager hesitated, then he decided that there was nothing he could do about it. He told off a couple of the girls and they went from cubicle to cubicle.

In five minutes about six women, in wraps, were standing indignantly before Clancy, who looked as if he were going out of his mind. Myra wasn't among them.

While he was staring at them, I wandered round looking at the wax models. I began to suspect where Myra was hiding. Sure enough, one of them looked familiar. I looked again and Myra met my eyes imploringly. She had on a smart black frock and a large floppy hat which hid her face. Standing with the other models, it was impossible to spot who she was until you got right up to her.

"Go away." Myra hissed. "Don't look at me."

"But I *must* look at you." I said in an undertone. "I love you for one thing and you look terrific for another. Are you scared, sweetheart?"

"Terribly." she said. "But, do go away."

"I'm going." I said, "but I'll be back."

As I turned away, one of the saleswomen came to me.

"Hello." she said.

I looked at her and paused. She was a red-head. Now, I like red-heads. I like them particularly if they have a nice creamy skin, green eyes and a lot of curves. This one had everything, so I said, "Hullo." and raised my hat.

"Were you thinking of buying that dress?" she asked, smiling. "I'd just love to help you."

I glanced over at Clancy. He was still trying to explain himself to the indignant women.

"It did cross my mind." I said cautiously, "but I've got nothing to fill it with when I get it home."

"You don't have to worry about that." she said, sidling a little closer. "The trouble is having too many girls and not enough dresses to go round."

"I like it that way." I said simply. "I'm a man of nature."

She blinked just once, but it didn't stop her entirely.

"There's something in my book of rules about men of nature." she said, looking puzzled. "I just can't remember what it was right now."

"Lady." I said earnestly, "you don't need any rules. You ought to get along all right by your instincts."

"That'd be like driving a car with no brakes." she said. "I know my instincts better than you."

She began to interest me.

"Maybe we'll go for a drive together one of these days." I said hopefully.

"Let's not make too many plans." she returned. "Let's concentrate on this dress." She turned back to Myra. "Don't you think I'd look cute in it?"

"Not half so cute as without it." I said hurriedly.

"I don't think I like that remark." she said. "It doesn't indicate a sound business footing."

"Who cares about a business footing?" I returned. "Let's go somewhere and forget business."

"Keep concentrating on this dress." she said insistently. "I know I'd look good in it. Let me put it on and show you."

"Some other time," I began, and stopped because she had put her hand on Myra's arm.

"It's awfully attractive." she said wistfully. Then a look of puzzled fright entered her eyes and she pressed Myra's arm.

I hastily took her hand away. "I used to be a palmist." I said. "Let me read your lines."

"So long as we're thinking of the same lines." she returned, trying to smile, but all the time she kept staring at Myra with growing uneasiness. "Do you know that dummy felt almost human." she went on in a low voice.

"Yeah?" I said, patting Myra's hip. "Isn't it marvellous what they do with papier mâché these days?"

I still kept hold of her hand and she began to calm down. Then out of the corner of my eye, I saw Myra move. Still keeping her fixed pose, she rose a foot into the air and remained there. I came out in a cold sweat.

The red-head had her back to Myra, so she didn't see what was going on. I put my hand on Myra's shoulder and pushed her back on her stand again and held her there.

"Can you really read my lines?" the red-head asked.

"Well, I took a correspondent course a few months back." I said, feeling like hell. "I can only read the past up to now, but I hope to get around to the future sometime next week."

I released Myra for a second. She began to rise off the ground, so I hung on to her again.

The red-head hastily snatched her hand from mine. "I'll wait until next week." she said, "I know all about my past. That's something I like to keep to myself."

That came as no surprise, but I didn't tell her so.

"You seem to like that model." she said, "or can't you make up your mind?"

It was becoming increasingly more difficult to hold Myra and just for a moment, she succeeded in rising a few inches before I slammed her back again.

The red-head drew in a sharp breath. "Is—is it trying to get away?" she said fearfully.

"There's a draught in this joint." I explained. "These models are mighty light."

She backed away. "You know I don't like that old model." she said. "I just don't like it at all."

Clancy, who had got rid of the indignant women, joined us. He was sweating freely and he looked mad.

"What are you pawing that dummy for?" he demanded.

"I'm that kind of a guy." I said desperately. "I go for dummies in a big way."

The red-head said, "There's something about that old model. It's trying to fly away."

Clancy looked at her suspiciously. "What do you mean … fly away?"

"I don't know." she said. "But that's what it's trying to do."

"Pay no attention to her, Clancy." I said quickly. "She's not herself to-day."

Clancy looked at me and then he looked at Myra. "So that's it." he said between his teeth. "I might have known it. So that's where she's hiding." and before I could stop him he'd whipped off Myra's hat.

Myra didn't blink an eye-lash. She just stood there, her eyes blank and her body rigid.

Clancy stared at her. "Yeah." he said, "it's her all right. You can cut that dummy act out. You're under arrest." he went on to Myra.

I took my hand from Myra's shoulder and stepped back. As Clancy moved forward to grab her she floated out of his reach. Still keeping her stiff pose, she rose about ten feet in the air.

It certainly upset Clancy. He closed his eyes.

"Gawd!" he said. "What a horrible sight!"

"What's worrying you?" I asked. "Haven't you heard of the new lighter-than-air models? It helps solve the transportation problems." and I patted him on the back.

"Never mind about the transportation problems." he said, looking at Myra from between his fingers. "I've got my own problems to worry about just now."

Then Whisky wandered into the shop.

In the general confusion no one noticed his entrance. The saleswomen were screaming, while the shop manager had collapsed on the floor and was jerking feebly at his collar. The cops just stood rooted, staring at Myra in horror.

To make matters worse, the red-head had thrown her arms round my neck and was screaming wildly in my ear.

It was a pretty good time for Whisky's entrance. He came straight over to me. "You haven't been long getting yourself fixed up." he said approvingly. "That's quite a pretty trill you've got there."

The effect of this speech was electrifying. The red-head gave a stifled moan and slid to the floor in a faint. Clancy backed away, his face like a flour bag, while everyone else in the room stopped making noises and clutched one another.

"And now do you believe my story about talking dogs and floating women?" I said to Clancy. "It's all here for you to see."

"I'll believe anything." Clancy said, shivering. "This is too much for me. You've all got to see the captain."

Whisky peered into the red-head's face "Odd how these dames pass out, isn't it?" he said and began to lick her face energetically.

I caught him a quick kick where it'd do him the most good. He gave a startled curse and removed his tail hurriedly.

"Leave her alone." I said sternly. "Besides, all that make-up might poison you."

"As a matter of fact." Whisky said with a leer, "it was extraordinarily tasty. But apart from that, I was just trying to revive her."

"She doesn't need reviving." I returned. "She's happier the way she is."

"Can't you stop him?" Clancy pleaded, gaping at Whisky as if he was some monster. "I can't stand any more of this."

Myra swooped past me. "What do we do now?" she asked. "Shall I run away?"

"No." I said. "We can't go on like this. We'll all go along to Summers and let him sort everything out."

She settled lower and then stretched out within my grasp. I pulled her to me and kissed her. "It'll be all right." I promised. "They'll have to listen to reason."

Clancy tried to pull himself together. "Can't you persuade that dame to stand on her feet?" he pleaded. "It's doing me no good at all seeing her that way."

Myra frowned at him. "I'm not considering you." she said. "You've never done anything for me."

"You remain like that." I urged. "The more people who see you like that the more witnesses we'll have. Let's go, sweetheart."

I took her by her shoulders and began pushing her towards the door.

It must have been a pretty upsetting sight. Myra lay full length, suspended in the air, with her hands folded across her chest. It was like pushing a perambulator that hadn't any wheels.

Whisky fell in step beside me. "Going through the streets like that, old pal?" he asked.

"That's the idea." I said firmly, leaving Myra in mid-air while I opened the shop door.

"Hey!" Clancy said, running up to me. "You can't do a thing like that!"

"I'd like to see you try and stop me." I said grimly.

He looked round desperately. "You guys!" he shouted to the cringing patrolmen. "Get these two into the wagon."

The patrolmen hesitated and then approached us warily.

"I think we're going to have a little trouble." I said to Myra. She lowered her feet to the ground. "Leave this to me." she said, her eyes snapping fire, "I've been very good up to now. If they're going to be nasty then I'll be nasty, too."

Now she was on the ground, the patrolmen seemed to regain some of their courage. They came towards us in a body.

Myra flickered her fingers at them and they suddenly paused. "It's beginning to rain." one of them said uneasily.

"What are you talking about?" Clancy snarled. "It doesn't matter if it rains! Arrest that woman!"

A big Irish cop extended his hand and then went a little pale.

"Holy Moses!" he said in a strangled voice. "It's raining in here!"

I thought Clancy would go out of his mind. "It don't rain indoors, you punk!" he stormed. "I'll tear that badge off your coat if you don't do what I tell you!"

Myra flicked her fingers in his direction and almost immediately he stiffened. "Gawd!" he said looking up at the ceiling. "It *is* raining!"

"Didn't I tell you." the Irish cop said feverishly. "I think I'll get out of here."

This intrigued me. Over each patrolman and Clancy I could see a light sprinkle of water falling. It didn't come from the ceiling but seemed to start a few feet above them.

As they moved uneasily the shower of water followed them. It was the damnedest thing I'd ever seen.

"Are you doing this?" I whispered to Myra.

"Certainly." she said. "Didn't you know I could make rain? It's an old Naguale custom."

She suddenly spied the red-head who was sitting up in a dazed kind of way. "And a little rain might improve that young woman's complexion." she went on grimly.

She flicked her fingers in the red-head's direction.

There was no question of a sprinkle of water this time. It began to rain in torrents. The red-head screamed wildly and getting to her feet, she dashed round the room. The narrow ribbon of pouring water followed her ruthlessly. In a few seconds she was soaked to the skin.

"I think that will do." Myra said, looking pleased. "She's not nearly so attractive, is she?"

Right now the red-head looked like something that'd got lost in a river.

"You're right." I said, wondering if I was losing my mind. Myra flicked her fingers and the rain stopped.

The cops and Clancy began mopping themselves with their handkerchiefs. The red-head lay on the floor and drummed hysterically with her heels.

"If there's any more talk about wagons." Myra said coldly, "it'll begin raining again."

"Do what you like, lady." Clancy said brokenly. "I ain't making trouble."

Myra resumed her suspended position. "Push me through the streets." she said to me. "All the way to police headquarters. Then we'll have lots of witnesses, won't we?"

As I began to push her to the door again, Sam Bogle entered the shop.

One look was enough to see that Sam had been hitting the bottle. He didn't look at any of us except Myra.

"Don't think you're getting away with it." he said. "Doc was a pal of mine and no jury can kill a pal of mine and get away with it."

We were all so startled that no one moved. Myra lowered her feet to the floor and faced him.

"I didn't kill him." she said quietly. "You ought to know that, Sam."

"You killed him all right." Sam said, his eyes gleaming evilly. "Well, this is where you get yours."

"Look out!" Whisky shouted and sprang forward.

He was too late. Sam fired from his hip. I saw the flash from the gun. Myra took two tottering steps forward. Then she spread out on the floor.

No one could do anything but stare. Sam let the gun slide out of his hand.

Then I ran to Myra. As I bent over her, I heard Sam's voice wailing.

"I didn't mean to do it." he kept saying "Honest to Gawd, I didn't mean to do it."

EIGHTEEN

We waited at the hospital for more than an hour before the doctor had any news for us.

There was Clancy, Summers, Whisky, Bogle and I, as well as a handful of cops who were keeping an eye on Bogle.

Summers and Clancy kept throwing looks at Whisky like he was something they couldn't believe. Summers had now heard the whole story and after the first shock of hearing Whisky talk, he had been big enough to apologize to me.

"You've got a free hand." he said, "Hell's bells! What a case to bring before a jury! I hope that girl lives. It's the damnedest thing I've ever run into. You can't blame me for being suspicious, can you, Millan? But, if you want to get after the other girl, it's okay by me."

I hadn't the heart to go after Arym. The thought of Myra lying in the little room across the way struggling for her life, knocked the ground from under me. I just wanted to be near so if anyone could see her I'd be the first to go in.

Whisky felt the same way.

We just sat and waited, and when the doctor came out I was too scared to go over to him.

"Which of you is Mr. Millan?" he asked.

Summers went over and said something. The doctor shrugged. The gesture chilled my heart. Then Summers nodded at me and the doctor beckoned.

I got up and walked the few yards with legs that felt like they'd been mashed by a trolleycar.

Whisky followed at my heels.

"How is she doc?" I asked, looking anxiously at his tired face.

"Not so good." he replied. "She's asking for you. Don't excite her. I don't think she's going to make it."

I clutched at his arm, "She's got to make it." I said. "You must save her."

"We're doing all we can." he pulled his arm away with a grimace of pain, "but, she just won't try. There's not much we can do when a patient throws up the sponge. That's what she's doing. She doesn't seem to have the will to live."

"Can I see her?"

"For a minute, but be careful what you say."

I went into the little room with Whisky.

Myra was lying flat. She looked small and white and just to see her turned my heart over.

I sat down and took her hand.

She opened her eyes. "I was afraid you wouldn't come." she said.

Whisky pushed his long muzzle on the bed. She touched his ears for a moment before turning to me again.

"There was no one big enough to keep me out." I said, trying to smile. "Please get well, sweetheart, I can't get along without you."

"I'll get well." she said, "only, I'm tired. I'll be better when I've had some sleep. I don't want to stay awake any more."

"Listen, kid, the doctor says you're not trying." I went on, stroking her wrist, "you must fight. There's Whisky and me wanting you. You can't pass us up."

"It's awfully hard." she said drowsily. "I have only half my resistance. If my other half were here I know I'd be all right."

Then I realized why she couldn't get well. She had to have Arym to help her fight. Before I could say anything, a nurse came in and beckoned to me.

I petted Myra's hand. "I'll be back." I said. "Promise you'll wait for me."

She kept her eyes open with an effort. "Come back soon." she said urgently.

I went out into the hall again.

Summers said, "She's pretty bad, isn't she?"

"I guess so." I returned. "Can I take a walk around the block! This place gives me a pain."

"Sure." he said sympathetically, "I know how you feel."

I went over to Bogle. "Cheer up." I said, "I'm doing all I can for her."

Sam had tears in his eyes. "I don't know why I did it." he said miserably. "I guess I was crazy."

I couldn't help feeling sorry for him. "I know how you felt about Doc. He meant as much to you as Myra does to me. I'd have done the same thing in your place."

He shook his head, "I wouldn't have hurt her for anything, but I got good and mad."

There was nothing I could say to him that'd do any good, so I left him and went out into the street.

"Whisky." I said, "we're going after Arym. She's the only one who can save Myra."

"How can she help her?" Whisky asked hopelessly.

"Don't you understand? She's got half of Myra's willpower and strength. Get them together and they can both make a real fight for it. Peppi will know where she is. I'll see him first."

"You're taking a chance with Peppi, aren't you?"

"I have to take a chance. If he doesn't know where she is, I'm sunk."

"He won't talk without those photos." Whisky said. "Why not get 'em and trade with him?"

I glanced at my watch. It was seven fifty. Maddox would have gone home by now.

"It's an idea." I said, waving down a passing cab. "If we can get into Maddox's office, I think I can bust his safe."

As we drove off Whisky said, "I don't think I want to be mixed up in this. I was merely giving advice."

"You'll come with me and like it." I said shortly. "It all depends whether we can reach Maddox's office without being seen. If we can, then the rest's easy."

Whisky clicked his teeth uneasily. "They wouldn't put a dog in jail, would they?" he asked.

"No, they'd take you some place and shoot you."

"I was afraid of that." Whisky returned mournfully.

"Why worry? They can't do that more than once to you." I said, trying to cheer him up.

Maddox's office was on the top floor of the *Recorder* building. I stopped the cab at the corner of the street and we walked the short distance to the entrance. There was no doorman on duty at that time of night, but I had to get pest the man at the information desk just inside the hall to reach the elevator.

We paused at the entrance and I took a quick gander through the glass doors.

"We're in luck." I said to Whisky, "I don't know the guy. Come on in."

The man at the desk just glanced at us without interest.

"I want to talk to the night editor." I said. "I'm a friend of his. Can I go up?"

"Sure." he said. "Know your way?"

I nodded and we went over to the automatic elevator. "Well, that was easy." I said, as the elevator shot up.

Whisky heaved a sigh. "You can get five years for this." he returned. "Even Summers couldn't do anything for you."

"Quiet!" I said and stepped out onto the eighth floor. At the end of the passage was the door that led to Maddox's offices. As we approached, Whisky cocked his head on one side.

"Wait a minute." he said sharply.

"What's up?"

"Someone's in there." he said, "I can hear 'em."

I listened, but I couldn't hear a thing. "Sure?"

"You bet I'm sure." Whisky said, lowering his tail.

I crept to the door and listened. A man's voice sounded faintly through the thick door.

"Hell!" I said, stepping back. "What do we do now?"

"We go some place and wait." Whisky returned.

I put my hand on the doorknob and turned it softly. The door gave a few inches and I looked into the outer office. There was no one there, but voices came from Maddox's office across the room. His door stood open.

"Wait here." I whispered, and entered the outer office silently.

I crossed the room and edged up to the open door. One quick glance brought me up short.

Peppi was standing by Maddox's safe. With him was his muscleman, Lew, and two other men I hadn't seen before.

Peppi was smoking a cigar, his hands in his pockets and his hat pushed to the back of his head. He watched Lew, who was trying to open the safe.

I backed away, crossed the office once more and started to join Whisky. Then I paused.

Standing on one of the desks was a press camera complete with a flashgun. I picked it up as I passed and then joined Whisky in the passage.

"What's up?" Whisky asked, eyeing the camera nervously.

"Peppi and his gang are cracking the safe." I said. "Now look, I'm going back in there and I'm going to get a picture of them. If we can get away with this we've got Peppi just where we want him."

"You don't think he'll let you take a picture of him and then walk out, do you?" Whisky demanded. "He'll probably be a very mad man."

"That's where you come in." I said.

"They've tried to brain me before." Whisky returned uneasily. "I'd prefer to remain neutral, if it's all the same to you."

"Pipe down." I said. "As soon as I've taken the picture, I'll give the plate to you and you beat it. I'll hold them off until you get away. They won't do anything to me so long as we have the picture."

"That's what you hope." Whisky said. "They may have different ideas."

I thought that was likely, but I had to take the chance.

"When you get outside, go to Miss Halliday's apartment and wait for me." I said. "I've told her about you and she's expecting us. If I don't come out within an hour, turn the picture over to Summers."

Whisky looked worried. "Aren't you being unnecessarily heroic?" he asked. "Can't we work out something better than that?"

I shook my head. "I've got to put the screws to Peppi and this is the only way to do it. Get in the elevator and wait for me."

"Well, I'd rather it was you than me." Whisky said, enter in the elevator.

I adjusted the shutter of the camera and set the lens-stop. Then I went back into the room.

Peppi was cursing Lew when I arrived at the door.

"If you can't get that can open." he snarled, "why don't you say so? We've been here twenty minutes."

"Gimme a break, will you?" Lew grunted, his ear against the safe. "I gotta have quiet to hear these tumblers."

Peppi drew in a deep breath and stood over him. That was how I found them.

I shoved the camera round the door and braced it. Then I said sharply: "Hold it!"

I gave them time to look round and then I released the shutter. There was a blinding flash as the flashlight exploded and I didn't wait to see what happened.

I whipped across the outer office, slammed the door and jerked the plate out of the camera.

Whisky watched me with startled eyes.

"Here you are." I said and shoved the plate holder into his mouth. Then I pressed the elevator button and the door snapped shut as Lew and Peppi tumbled into the passage.

Lew had a gun in his hand and he looked mean.

"Grab some air." he said, pointing the gun at me.

I raised my hands, holding the camera above my head.

Peppi, snarling with rage, snatched the camera out of my hand. He took one look at it and flung it to the floor.

"Where's the plate?" he snapped.

"On its way down." I said. "Now, don't get excited." I went on hurriedly as Lew made as if to slug me. "That picture'll give you a lot of grief if you don't wise up."

"Who's got it?" Peppi snarled.

"Never mind who's got it." I returned. "All you have to worry about is who's going to have it in an hour's time."

"That's it, is it?" Peppi's voice was soft and menacing. "You're crazy to try that stuff on me."

"Okay, so I'm crazy." I said. "But I've got something on you, Peppi, that you won't get out of in a hurry."

"Let me slug this punk." Law said.

Peppi jerked his head to the office. "Come in here." he said, "I want to talk to you."

I went into the office with Lew crowding me.

"What's the idea?" Peppi said. "Come on—give."

"If I'm not at a certain address in an hour's time." I explained, watching Lew out of the corner of my eye, "that picture's going to the police chief. And then you can talk yourself out of it."

"What address?" Peppi asked, fiddling with his cigar.

"Be your age." I returned, wandering over to the desk and sitting on it. "Now listen, Peppi, here's the deal. Give me Arym and I'll give you the picture."

While I was talking I glanced over Maddox's desk. I remembered there was a button concealed somewhere which let off the burglar alarm. Maddox had had it fitted when some hood had threatened to scramble his brains in the old days of prohibition.

Peppi turned to Lew. "Get that safe open." he said. "We'll fix this guy when we're through."

That didn't suit me. I spotted the button and rammed my thumb on it.

One of the other men caught me a full swing behind my ear, but he was a shade late. As I went over on the floor a bell began to ring somewhere in the building.

I struggled to my feet as Law went for me.

"Cut it out!" Peppi said, his face white with rage. "Take him and let's get out of here."

Lew dug his gun into my spine and herded me into Maddox's private elevator. The others followed.

As we shot between floors, Peppi said: "You'll be damned sorry you stuck your neck out." And I didn't like the look in his eyes.

The elevator landed us at the side entrance, away from the main doors. There was a big closed car waiting and as soon as we had bundled in it shot away towards Fifth Avenue.

No one said anything all the way to Peppi's house. Law sat by my side with his gun sticking into me and a hungry look in his eyes. I felt that I'd only to flicker an eye-lash and he'd plug me. So I sat still and sweated plenty.

When we got inside Peppi's house Lew shoved me into the sitting room.

The butler was in there fussing with a decanter. He looked at me with a tight smile on his crooked face.

Peppi said: "Get Miss Brandt."

The butler went out.

Peppi and Law left me standing in the middle of the room and went over to the window. They whispered together and then Law gave a low laugh.

"Don't waste too much time." I said, feeling uneasy. "You've only got another thirty-five minutes to turn Arym over to me."

"That'll be long enough." Peppi said.

"I'm not bluffing." I said. "I've got you where I want you. Give me the girl or that picture goes to Summers. Where is she?"

Peppi shook his head. "I don't know." he said. "And I don't care. I warned you not to double-cross me. Now you're going to get your lesson."

The door opened and Lydia Brandt came in. She looked at me much the same way a tiger looks at its dinner.

"I want this guy to talk." Peppi said. "I thought maybe you'd like to soften him."

Lydia smiled. "Yes." she said. "That would amuse me."

"What are you going to do with him?" Peppi asked.

"I want to try that experiment again. I made a mess of it last time." she answered.

Peppi shrugged. "She thinks she can cut a guy. I tell her she can't do it."

Lew sneered. "Let her try." he said. "It don't matter if she makes a mess of this punk, does it?"

I began to sweat.

Lew went to the door and called in the other two birds who had been in Maddox's office.

"Tie this lug up." he said. "If he starts anything, beat his brains out."

Before I could make up my mind what to do they grabbed me. I waited until they began to twist my arms behind me, then I let them have it.

I wrenched one of my arms free and slugged the bigger of the two guys in the eye, then as the other swung at me I stepped close and hit him low.

That was as far as I got. Lew came up and slammed me over the head with his gun-butt. By the time I'd cleared my head I was sitting in a chair trussed up like a Houdini act.

Peppi was looking at the clock. "We ain't got a lot of time." he said.

"It's not going to take me long." Lydia said. She held a thin, sharp knife in her hand. She looked across at me. "You won't have many dates after this." she said viciously.

"Let's be reasonable." I said hurriedly. "You wouldn't really want to do that to me."

She held up the knife, then she came over. "You won't feet it for a while." she said, standing over me. "I've done it before. If you stay still you might save your eyes." Her face was white and stony and I could see she was getting a big kick out of seeing me sweat.

Peppi said to me. "Are you talking?"

"I'm talking." I said, shrinking away from the knife.

"Where's the plate?"

I gave him Harriet's address.

"Let's go." he said to Lew. "We've still got ten minutes."

They made for the door.

"Hey!" I shouted, "don't leave me with this dame. She might start something."

Peppi paused and smiled at me, "She will." he said, "maybe you won't be in such a hurry to double-cross me next time." He looked over at Lydia, "When you're through, tell Toni to park him in the river."

She nodded.

"We'll be back pretty soon." Peppi said, and they all went out leaving me with Lydia.

I admit, right at that moment I was losing a lot of weight. I strained on the cords that held me but I couldn't budge them.

There was a cold efficiency about Lydia that told me she was going through with this.

"I don't want to lose my eye-lids," I said desperately, "I wouldn't know how to sleep without them."

"Oh, that'd be easy after a while," she said, turning the knife in the flame, "it's just a matter of concentration."

She was batty, of course. As crazy as a bug, but that didn't help me.

"Well." she said, "we're ready to go. All you have to do is to sit still. I'm quick and it won't hurt for a few hours, anyway." she chuckled. "Then it'll hurt plenty."

I believed her.

She came over and twined her long fingers in my hair. I rammed my chin on my chest so she couldn't get at my eyes.

"Don't make it difficult." she said, pulling at my hair. It scared me to feel how strong she was.

I braced myself and kept my chin down. She kept pulling and it felt like the top of my head was coming off.

"Damn you!" she said suddenly and touched my ear with the knife.

I jerked away with a yell and the next second I was staring up at the ceiling with the knife hovering a few inches from my eyes.

Then the door burst open and Arym marched in.

Lydia released my hair and stood away. Arym stared first at me and then at Lydia, and I could have hugged her if I'd been free.

Lydia was the first to recover, "What do you want?" she said in a flat, sullen voice, "go away!"

"What do you think you're doing?" Arym demanded, her eyes flashing. "What's happening, Ross?"

"She's taking off my eye-lids." I said feverishly, "it's an old family custom."

"Is she?" Arym laid her gloves and bag down on the table. She took off her hat with deliberation. "Not so long as I'm standing on my two feet." she said.

"Get out!" Lydia said furiously, "you've no business being in here. Go upstairs and wait for Peppi. He wants me to do this."

"He's mine." Arym said, moving towards Lydia. "No one touches him but me."

Lydia went for her with the knife.

I yelled a warning, but it wasn't necessary. Arym was quite capable of taking care of herself. She simply vanished in a puff of white smoke.

Lydia stopped in her rush with a startled scream. She looked around the room, her knife held ready and her eyes wild.

Just behind her a large vase containing flowers suddenly floated off the table. It shot high into the air and descended on Lydia's head. She flattened out on the floor and the vase flew in a hundred pieces.

"And that's that." said Arym's voice.

Invisible hands gathered the flowers into a bunch and laid them on Lydia's chest.

"She only lacks a wooden overcoat." Arym said, suddenly reappearing. "But I haven't time for that now."

I felt unnerved. "I just can't get used to your tricks." I said, staring at Lydia with morbid fascination.

"Didn't you like that little exhibition?" Arym asked, not without pride.

"I thought it was swell." I said, "but I can't stand a lot of it. Look, sweetheart, will you untie me?"

"Oh, no." Arym said firmly, "I want to talk to you first."

"But we haven't time." I said desperately. "Peppi'll come back any minute."

She shrugged, "I couldn't care less about that." she returned, putting her arm round my neck. "I can do to Peppi what I did to her and think nothing of it."

"Arym, you must let me loose." I said feverishly, "I want you to do something for me."

"I know." she said, "but you're going to hear what I want first." She sat on my knee and began fondling my ear. That's a thing I can't stand, but I wasn't in the position to tell her so.

"You're going to marry me."

I stared at her, "Of all the crazy things!" I said angrily. "This is no time for fooling."

"But, I'm not fooling." she said, "you're marrying me or it'll be the last thing you refuse me."

"I'm marrying Myra." I said, trying to push her away, "Be reasonable for the love of mike. Myra's desperately ill. She needs you. You can't refuse to help her."

"I know all about that." she said carelessly, "I've just come from seeing her. She knew what was happening here and she sent me to get you out of the mess. I agreed on one condition—that she would give you up. Well, she's given you up. If you want me to save her, you must promise to marry me."

"I'm not going to." I said, hardly believing my ears. "Of all the dirty tricks! You ought to be ashamed of yourself."

"Don't get upstage." Arym said, putting her face against mine. "I'll let Peppi handle you, if you don't play along with me. And I'll let Myra fend for herself, too."

I drew a deep breath, "You can't do this." I said, "think what it means. You don't really think you could hold me to such a marriage. Why I'd leave you in a week. What do you think I am—a mouse?"

A look of doubt came into Arym's eyes, "But, don't you like me a little?" she pleaded, hugging me to her.

"I like you all right." I said, "you've got everything Myra has except her nice nature. That's something you'll never have."

"I could be nice to you." she wheedled, "and you would be good for me."

I had a sudden idea.

"I'll agree on one condition." I said.

She looked suspicious, "What condition?"

"You return to Myra, give up your body and I'll marry you both."

"No." she said, getting off my knee. "I want to have a body of my own."

"But, you'll never really be happy." I urged, feeling that I was persuading her. "It's the only way you'll ever get me. If you can't share me with Myra then I'm through with you."

She began to pace up and down. "You don't understand what this means to me. As I am now, I can do what I like, go where I like and love whom I like."

"And where's it getting you?" I asked. "Can't you see it's the only possible way out? Ask yourself, have you been happy? You're only half yourself. Myra has all the good qualities. If you go back to her you'll be complete and you'll have me."

She stopped pacing and stared at me. "You devil." she said, "I hadn't thought of it like that. You're right. I have missed Myra. I've missed tempting her to do the wrong things. I've missed fighting with her. I guess I'm being a sucker, but I'll do it, if she'll have me back."

"I warn you." I said, "you're going to behave. No more stealing. I'll be around to keep you in order."

"I'll do it—for no other man in the world but you." she said, and picking up the knife she cut me free.

I stood up with a grimace. "We must get over to Myra." I said, stamping life into my legs. "I've left her too long as it is."

"Don't fuss." she said. "She'll be all right."

I suddenly remembered Whisky. "My goodness!" I said hobbling to the telephone. "Maybe Peppi's cutting poor old Whisky's throat right now."

"You worry too much." Arym said calmly. "He'll have his throat cut sooner or later, he's that kind of a dog."

I got through to police headquarters.

When Summers came on the line I shot him the story. "Get a squad over there." I said feverishly, giving him Harriet's address. "And make it snappy. You'll have Kruger and his mob on ice if you get that picture."

"We'll get it." Summers said excitedly, and hung up.

"I hope they do." I said. "Well, let's get over to the hospital." I put my arm around her and kissed her. "You're a nice kid." I said. "And you won't have any regrets. Now, come on. Go into your vanishing act. The cops mustn't see you."

"Consider it done." she said, and a wisp of smoke indicated where she had been standing.

When we reached the hospital we found Clancy and a couple of cops still waiting outside Myra's door. Bogle had been taken away.

I went up to Clancy. "How is she?" I asked anxiously.

Clancy looked mournful. "She's bad." he said. "The doc's in there now."

"Can I go in?"

"Not yet." Clancy said, shaking his head. "Maybe when the doc's through."

I turned away. I was tempted to burst into her room, but I knew it wouldn't do, so I wandered over to a chair and sat down.

"Who's the guy with a face like a tomato?" Arym whispered in my ear. I told her.

"He looks like a heel." Arym said. "I think I'll throw a scare into him."

"Lay off." I said hurriedly. "We don't want any trouble here."

"It wouldn't be any trouble to me." she said wistfully. "It'd be fun."

"Now for the love of mike behave yourself. Haven't I enough on my mind without you adding to it?"

Clancy had drawn near and was staring at me with startled interest. "Do you have to do that?" he asked suspiciously.

"Why not?" I returned. "Can't I talk to myself without you horning in?"

"I guess so." he returned, looking at me old fashioned. "But, I don't like it much. It shows softening of the brain."

"That's better than having no brain at all, you cretin." Arym's voice snapped.

Clancy stiffened. "What's that?" he said, glaring at me.

"I didn't say anything." I returned hurriedly.

"Don't tell lies." Clancy said. "One more crack like that and I'll toss you in the can. And cut out that falsetto voice. I don't like it."

Just then a young and pretty nurse came down the corridor.

Clancy, who never passed up a nice-looking girl, swallowed his wrath. He adjusted his necktie and smirked at her. "Evening." he said, swelling out his chest.

She paused and smiled brightly. "Good evening." she said. "Is there anything I can do for you?"

Before Clancy could reply, Arym's voice said from behind him, "You can wipe that smile off your insipid face."

Clancy couldn't believe his ears. He looked around wildly, his mouth gaping.

The nurse tossed her head. "If it comes to that." she said, "your face isn't so much, and from the sound of your voice you should be shuffled and dealt again."

As she passed Clancy there came the sound of a sharp slap. The nurse gave a convulsive start and stifled a scream. For a moment she stood rigid and then turned, her face scarlet.

"That wasn't a nice thing to do." she said. "Do you call yourself a gentleman?"

Clancy blinked at her. "I ain't done nothing." he said uneasily.

"It may seem nothing to you." the nurse returned. "But, I'll have you know that back in my home-town gentlemen don't do such things."

Clancy began to get mad. "You're not the only one who has a home-town." he snapped.

"I shouldn't like to visit yours, if you're a specimen of what comes out of it." the nurse returned, putting her hands carelessly behind her and edging away.

This remark hurt Clancy's pride. "I'll have you know." he said, "my home-town's the oldest in the country."

"That doesn't surprise me." the nurse said feelingly. "You have some of its oldest habits." and tossing her head, she went off down the corridor.

"What kind of hospital is this?" Clancy demanded, glaring after her. "Even the nurses are nuts!"

While he was speaking, Myra's door opened and the doctor came out.

I jumped to my feet. "Can I see her?" I asked anxiously.

He looked at me gravely. "I'm sorry." he said. "But I did all I could for her."

My heart went cold. "She's not …?" I began, but the look in his eyes told me.

"She wouldn't fight." he said. "I can't make it out. She just didn't seem to have the will…"

I pushed past him and went into the room.

A nurse had pulled the sheet over Myra's face. She glanced at me sympathetically and left the room.

I stood looking at Myra's small form under the sheet and I felt pretty bad.

"So she quit." Arym said, suddenly appearing at my side. "Can you beat that?" she jerked the sheet off Myra's face.

Myra looked very peaceful. Her hair framed her small white face and there was a faint smile on her lips.

"Of all the smug, two-faced, prissy-mouthed fugitives from a convent." Arym said in disgust. "She's it."

"Don't." I said, sitting wearily on the bed. "She wanted to live, but we were too late to help her."

"Phooey!" Arym snapped. "She's putting on an act. Cut it Out, Myra." she went on. "Or I'll grab that body and leave you without one."

"Try it and I'll haunt you." Myra's voice said close to me.

I looked round with a startled gasp. Standing at the foot of the bed I could make out a filmy shadow.

"Don't materialize any further." Arym exclaimed. "You haven't got any clothes on."

"As if I didn't know." Myra sounded annoyed. "Where have you two been? I was just going to look for you."

"Wait a minute." I said. "Aren't you dead after all?"

"Of course, she isn't." Arym said. "I told you not to worry."

"Has the darling been worrying?" Myra asked eagerly.

"You know how men are." Arym replied airily. "But never mind him. Get back into your body. We have things to talk about."

"I'll be right with you." Myra said, and the shadowy figure climbed on to the bed and melted out of sight.

A second later what had been Myra's remains sat up abruptly in bed.

I shied away from her. This, I felt, was a little too much.

"He wants me to come back to you." Arym said sulkily. "That's the only way he'll marry me."

"Certainly not." Myra said firmly. "I've had enough of your influence to last me a lifetime. I'd rather be dead."

I pulled myself together. "Myra." I said, taking her hand, "you must be sensible. The new moon rises in an hour. If Doc was right, that's when you'll lose your supernatural powers and then it'll be too late to do anything. You have to take her back. Think of me. Think of having her around all the rest of our days. Think of the mischief she could do us if we thwarted her."

"That's all very well." Myra returned. "But what about Doc? She did kill him. I draw the line at sharing a body with a murderess."

She had something there.

Arym pouted "If I fix Doc, will you do it?" she asked.

"What do you mean?"

"I didn't kill the old fool. I wanted to have a hold on you so that Ross would work for Andasca."

"Now look here, Arym, it's no use lying. You did kill him. I saw him die." I said coldly.

"You thought you saw him die." Arym said, smiling. "Haven't you heard of mass hypnotism?"

I ran my fingers through my hair, "What are you getting at?" I said. "Mass hypnotism? I don't know what you're talking about."

"You're not being very bright, are you darling?" she said patiently. "All I did was to put Doc in a coma and hypnotize you and Sam into believing he was hurt. The letter and the dress were planted to give the right atmosphere."

"I don't believe it." I said, "the cops saw him too."

"So what?" she returned "I was there all the time, although you couldn't see me. It was as easy to hypnotize the cops as you."

"Do you really mean Doc's alive?" I still couldn't believe it.

"Of course, but he doesn't know it." she said airily. "Right now he's in the City morgue and he thinks he's as dead as George Washington but we can soon fix that."

"Then what are we waiting for?" I exclaimed "Look at the time, we've only a half an hour before midnight."

Arym looked over at Myra, "Are you going to take me back?" she asked.

"I suppose I'll have to," Myra said, a little doubtfully "Are you going to behave?"

"She'll behave." I said, "I know how to handle her."

"All right." Myra said, "I've missed her too. Come on back." her eyes lit up, "it'll be just like old times."

Arym hesitated, then she came over to me. "You won't ever see me again." she said sadly, "not as I really am." She put her arms round me. "This is the last time I'll hold you like this."

I pulled her to me and kissed her. "Be good." I said, "I'm trusting you."

"I'm ready when you two are." Myra said, a little waspishly.

Arym gave me a quick hug and pushed me away. "Look out of the window." she said, "I have to undress."

I hadn't turned my back for ten seconds when the door opened and Clancy walked in.

"So she's dead, eh?" he said, "well, Bud, I'm sorry."

I took a quick look at the bed and then stiffened. Myra and Arym were lying side by side, their blonde heads sharing the same pillow. Even though I knew what was happening, the sight unnerved me.

Clancy saw them at the same time. He blinked and passed his hand over his eyes. Then he had another look and went pale.

"She looks nice, doesn't she?" I said, deciding to bluff.

Clancy made gurgling noises. Beads of perspiration appeared on his forehead. He moved closer to the bed and stared. "Yeah." he said, in a cracked voice, "but it ain't the kind of thing I want to see every day."

"Nor do I." I said feelingly, "but she does look happy."

"That's more than I do." Clancy said, supporting himself against the bed rail, "my eyesight's giving me a little trouble. You wouldn't say there are two dames in that bed, would you?"

"No." I said firmly, "I wouldn't say that at all."

"I didn't think you would." he returned, with a groan, "Maybe I've been working too hard."

"You'd better go away some place quiet and lie down." I said.

"Yeah, yeah." Clancy said, "but I can't imagine any place quiet enough." and he went out of the room with dragging steps.

I turned back to the bed in time to see Arym merge into Myra.

"I'll sure be glad when this business is over." I said, mopping my face with my handkerchief.

Myra sat up in bed. "Wait for me." she said, "I'll be with you in a few minutes."

"Don't let them see you." I said, and went out into the corridor.

Clancy was sitting in a heap with his head in his hands. The two cops were watching him uneasily.

"Don't worry him." I said to them, "he has a lot on his mind right now."

"We ain't worrying him." one of the cops returned uneasily, "he's worrying us."

I moved down the corridor and stood waiting. Myra didn't keep me long. Her voice sounded in my ear after a few minutes, "Let's go." she said.

We reached the city morgue a quarter before midnight. A thin, querulous looking bird with a heavy moustache and a network of veins over his sharp, hooked nose sat behind the counter. "What do you want?" he snapped.

"You have a body here I want to look at." I said, taking out a *Recorder* press card and handing it to him, "a guy named Ansell. Doc Ansell."

He flipped the card back to me, "Come to-morrow." he said, and picked up his newspaper.

"Wait a minute." I said, "I have to see this guy right now."

The morgue attendant glared at me over his glasses, "No one's going in there to-night. Beat it." he said.

I turned to Myra, "One of those nice helpful guys." I said, "maybe you'd better do something about it. Look at the time."

It was ten to twelve.

Myra said, "I'm on my way." and she vanished.

On the floor where she had been standing were her clothes in a neat little pile. Her hat rested on top and her shoes were at the bottom of the pile.

I lit a cigarette and watched the effect on the morgue attendant with interest.

He got up deliberately and peered at the pile of clothes with glassy eyes.

"Astonishing how little these girls wear." I said chattily, "just a handful of silk here and a wisp of silk there and yet they look marvellous."

"Where is she?" he whispered, clawing at his throat.

"In the morgue by now." I said, "but, she'll be back."

He gave a long sigh and fell down behind the counter. I didn't blame him. It was a shock for a guy his age.

I left him there and ran round the counter. As I reached the head of the stairs that led to the morgue I saw Doc Ansell come stumbling up.

I ran down and grabbed him, "Doc!" I cried, "am I glad to see you!"

"Take care of him while I dress." Myra's voice said, "he's still a little dazed."

"Don't hold that against me." Doc said, gripping my hand, "I've had a very trying experience."

The morgue attendant still lay behind the counter, but as we passed he sat up and peered at us.

"You won't want this stiff any more." I said to him. "I'm going to take it away and buy it a meal."

Myra flashed into her clothes.

"Come on, Doc." she said, slipping her arm through his, "let's get out of here."

As we went out, the morgue attendant gave a low wail and collapsed once more on the floor.

NINETEEN

I really don't think that I need keep you any longer. If you have read this far you'll probably be like Maddox who never could bring himself to believe my story and if I hadn't left New York, I'm sure he would have shanghaied me into a nut house.

The only defence I offer is that strange things do happen. I'm not suggesting that you should believe everything you read or hear, but if you make a habit of doubting everything you will miss much of the fun in life.

It was nice to have Doc Ansell with us again. It was nice for me to have Myra without Arym and to know that she wouldn't suddenly shoot into the air or vanish without warning. She meant a lot to me and if I'd had to have her with her black magic, I wouldn't have hesitated. But after the new moon she settled down to normal life again.

There was no trouble in getting Bogle out of jail. Summers was so pleased to have Kruger and his mob on ice that he was willing to give way of a small matter like releasing Sam.

I cannot close this story without telling you what happen to Whisky. The police rescued him from Peppi and held him for us. At midnight as we were hurrying with Doc to the police headquarters, there was a sudden uproar in the room where they had put Whisky. On going in they found Whisky trying to gnaw an immensely fat Mexican who had mysteriously appeared out of thin air.

The Mexican had been so abusive and violent that the police kept him for us to see. You can imagine our feelings when Pablo was brought in, looking as if he could make mincemeat of us all.

Yes, Pablo had come back. He wasn't any nicer and I can't say I blamed him. To have been turned into a sausage and then eaten by a large wolfhound is a pretty harrowing experienced. He was inclined to blame Myra and me for it, and I felt, that if he were at large, he might resort to his hornet trick some dark night when we weren't expecting him.

I had a word with Summers and he sent Pablo back to Mexico under an armed escort. There, he was handed over to Mexican authorities who put a rope around his neck and strung him several feet into the air.

I never liked Pablo anyway.

Now that his influence had been removed from Whisky the dog was unable to talk. We regretted this because Whisky had been a sensible kind of dog and he invariably had a number of sensible things to say.

At first, Whisky was depressed because he couldn't express himself, but, fortunately, he ran into a lady dog who took to him and they settled down quite happily together.

Myra and I decided to set up home on the Pacific coast. This decision was largely influenced by finding among Myra's clothes twenty-four thousand-dollar bills. It was the reward that Arym had hidden on the night she met me for the first time on the stairs, three days after we had arrived in New York.

It seemed a waste of good money to return the money to Maddox. He had plenty of his own and we could use it to advantage ourselves. Besides, Maddox never really forgave me and as he spent much of his time making inquiries about lunatic asylums, it seemed safer to have a change of air.

Doc set himself up once again as an herbalist and Sam helped him. They insisted on sharing our house. It seemed only right to have them after all we had been through together and we invited Whisky and his lady friend to join us.

It is an odd thing, but I never did meet Myra's father. We heard he had married a midget from a travelling circus, but we never had confirmation of this. Anyway, he dropped out of Myra's life which was a good thing. I had enough on hand without having a midget for a mother-in-law.

I found a profitable market as a short-story writer and Myra was busy preparing for Ross Millan junior.

I always wanted a son. And, after the inevitable alarming span of months, a son arrived. He was a nice-looking kid, more like his mother than me. We were all crazy about him.

On the face of it, it looked like we had finished with black magic, policemen and hoodlums and were all set for a nice quiet trip to old age, but it didn't work out like that.

One Sunday morning I was sitting at my desk trying to invent a situation for a story, when a sudden wild scream brought me to my feet. Throwing down my pen, I rushed into the garden.

Myra, Doc and Sam were staring into the sky with horrified expressions. I followed their gaze and my reason almost crumbled.

Thirty feet or so in the air sat Ross Millan junior. He waved his toy Mickey Mouse excitedly when he saw me.

"Look, Pop." he shouted happily, "I'm flying!"

THE END

James Hadley Chase at the Movies

(listed by book title in chronological order of original film release)

Compiled by Dr. PC Sarkar and Gregory Shepard

MOVIES & TV PRODUCTIONS

No Orchids for Miss Blandish

Chase's first novel was the subject of two films, *No Orchids for Miss Blandish* (1948) and *The Grissom Gang* (1971). The former was directed by St. John Legh Clowes and starred Jack LaRue as Slim Grissom and Linden Travers as Miss Blandish. According to *Wikipedia*, "the film caused enormous controversy on its release, because of the high levels of violence that had got past the film censors." Condemned by the critics, it was nonetheless very successful.

It was remade by Robert Aldrich as *The Grissom Gang*, starring Scott Wilson as Slim, Irene Dailey as Ma Grissom, Robert Lansing as Dave Fenner, Tony Musante as Eddy Hagen and Kim Darby as Miss Blandish. An excellent rural gangster film.

I'll Get You For This

Produced in England in 1951 by Joseph M. Newman as *Lucky Nick Cain*, the movie portrays a successful American gambler who acts as an advance man for a posh Italian casino. Kay, played by Colleen Gray, is a tourist who loses all her money at the casino, but Cain, played by George Raft, falls in love with her and tries to make good on her debts. The critic quoted on the IMDb website calls the film "dreary."

The Last Page

This 1946 play by Chase was filmed by Hammer Film Productions (pre-horror days) in 1952 in black and white, the first Hammer film directed by Terence Fisher. Written by Chase and Francis Knott, it starred George Brent as John Harman, Marguerite Chapman as Stella, Raymond Huntley as Clive Brent, Peter Reynolds as Jeff and Diana Dors as Ruby. It was released in the U.S. as *Man Bait*. Still very effective.

Tiger by the Tail

An 1957 Italian movie, *L' Homme à l'imperméable*, or *The Man in the Raincoat*, directed by Julien Duvivier, starring Bertheau, Bernard Blier, Albert Dinan, Judith Magre and Fernandel, was a rare humorous adaptation of Chase's book, although the novel itself was grim and fast-paced, and there was nothing humorous about it.

The novel was also the subject of two Hindi films: *Kashmakash*, directed by Feroze Chinoy, starring Feroz Khan, Shatrughan Siinha, Rekha and Padma Khanna (1973); and *Akalmand,* directed by Raj Bharat, starring Jeetendra, Ashok Kumar, Sridevi and Sarika (1984).

More recently, the Hindi movie, *88 Antop Hill,* directed by Kushan Nandy, starring Jackie Shroff, Rahul Dev, Lisa Ray and Shweta Menon (2004) was inspired by this Chase classic as well.

Miss Callaghan Comes To Grief

This complex effort from French filmmaker Yves Allégret in 1957 was distributed in English-speaking countries as *Young Girls Beware* and *Look Out Girls,* and as *Mefiez-Vous Fillettes* in France. Miss Callaghan (Michèle Cordoue, starring as Fan in the movie), has the bad luck to witness a gangland murder, and is promptly kidnapped by the killers' cohorts. She is then abducted by a rival gang, only to be re-kidnapped by her original captors. Held hostage to allow the murderer to escape, Fan's ordeal is compounded when the police begin closing in. Only the fact that the killer, Raven, played by Robert Hossien, falls in love with her saves the girl from further outrages. Also starring Pierre Mondy and Gerard Oury.

There's Always a Price Tag

The 1957 black and white French production, *Retour de Manivelle,* was based on this novel. Also known as *Delitto sulla Costa Azzurra* in Italy, the film starred Michele Morgan as Helen, Daniel Gélin as Nash, and Peter Van Eyck as Dester.

A 1998 Hindi version of the novel was *Maharathi,* directed by Shivam Nair, with Naseeruddin Shah playing the role of Dester, Paresh Rawal as Glyn Nash and Neha Dhupia as Helen.

The Sucker Punch

A 1957 French production, *Une Manche et la Belle* (Beauty Up His Sleeve), directed by Henri Verneuil and released in the U.S. as *A Kiss For A Killer.* In this version of the book, the protagonist, Chad Winters, renamed as Phillippe (played by Henry Vidal), marries an heiress Vestal Shelly, re-named Stella (played by Isa Miranda). Phillippe has a roving eye and soon falls for Betty's secretary, Eve, played by Mylene Demongeot. But Eve has her own sinister agenda.... Given high marks for excellence by the critic at IMDb.

More recently, the novel was the subject of a 1994 film in Hindi, *Aar Ya Paar,* directed by Ketan Mehta, with a Bombay star cast of Jackie Shroff as Chad, Kamal Siddhu as Vestal and Deepa Sahi as Eve.

A Dead Ringer

Produced for the TV series *Studio One in Hollywood,* and directed by Robert Stevens, it aired March 10, 1958 on CBS. The cast included Valerie Allen, Robert Carson, Marguerite Chapman, Elizabeth Montgomery and Gig Young.

The Things Men Do

Made into a French movie, *Ça n'arrive qu'aux vivants* or *It Only Happens to the Living*, directed by Tony Saytor in 1959, starring Raymond Pellegrin, Giselle Pascal, Magali Noël, Emile Prud'homme, Marc Valbel and André Valmy.

Hit and Run

First made into a French movie, *Delite de Fuite* by director Bernard Borderie in 1959. Ches Scott of the novel became Fred in the movie, played by Felix Martin, with Aimé Clariond as Aitkin and Antonella Lualdi as Lucille.

More recently, the book was the subject of a 1986 West German production filmed in the U.S (specifically, Galveston, Texas) called *Rigged*, directed by Claudio M. Cutry, with an uncredited assist from Jefferson Richard. It was released in Germany as *Tödliche Sucht*. The cast included Ken Roberson, George Kennedy and Pamela Jean Bryant. The screenplay was adapted by Jill Gurr and John F. Goff. The IMDb critic called it "painfully eighties" and made this suggestion: "Do yourself a favour and, instead of searching for the movie, introduce yourself to the work of James Hadley Chase." Always good advice.

Dark as the Night (?)

Produced for the TV series *Playhouse 90*, directed by Terence Young, and starring Ronald Allen, Sheila Allen, Hermione Baddeley, Michael Hordern and Michael Wilding. It aired in the UK on June 18, 1959. A British politician finds himself open to blackmail because of the indiscretion of his American wife. Marc Brandel wrote the teleplay from one of Chase's novels (the original title of which, so far, eludes us).

You Find Him - I'll Fix Him

Produced as *Les Canailles* (1960), directed by Maurice Labro and writing credits by Rodolphe-Maurice Arlaud. Also known as *Le Canaglie* (Italy), *Riff Raff* (U.S.) and *Take Me as I Am* (UK). The movie starred Robert Hossein as Ed Dawson, Scilla Gabel as Gina, Claire Maurier as June Chalmers and Alexander Gauge as Chalmers.

Don't Stop—You're Killing Me

Produced for the TV series *Spectacular*, and written by Chase, with additional material by Denis Goodwin. It aired in the UK on August 20, 1960, and starred Michael Adrian, John Citroen, Jerry Desmonde and Bob Monkhouse. Does not appear to have been adapted from a particular novel, or if so, the title was certainly changed.

The World in My Pocket

This was made into the movie, *An einem Freitag um halb zwölf*, released in the UK as *On Friday at Eleven* and in the U.S. as *The World in My Pocket*, by director Alvin Rakoff in 1961, with Nadja Tiller playing the lead role of Ginny. The cast also includes Ian Bannen as Kitson, Jean Servais as Gypo, Peter Van Eyck as Bleck and Rod Steiger as Frank Morgan.

This was also turned into a Latvian/Soviet Union TV mini-series called *Mirazh* (Mirage), produced in 1983 and directed by Aloizs Brencs. It stars Paul Butkevich, Martins Verdins and Romualds Ancans. The plot involves the stealing of an armored vehicle with a huge sum of money, which each character is sure will bring them happiness. It doesn't turn out that way, of course.

In 1986, the French movie, *Pouvoir intime*, directed by Yves Simoneau, also known as *Blind Trust* and *Intimate Power*, starring Marie Tifo and Pierre Curzi, was loosely based on this novel as well.

Just Another Sucker

A 1961 black-and-white French production, *Dans la gueule du loup* (In the Lion's Den) was directed by Jean-Charles Dudrumet, and adapted by Jean-Charles Dudrumet. It stars Felix Martin as Harry Barber, Magali Noel as Barbera and Francoise Vatel as Odette.

This Chase book was also filmed as *Bonbast* by Iranian director Mehdi Mirsamadzadeh in 1965. This was Mirsamadzadeh's second Chase film, the first being an unauthorized adaptation of *But a Short Time to Live*, listed three entries below. *Bonbast*, also known as *Dead-End*, stars Iraj Ghaderi, Parvin Ghaffari and Mohsen Mahdavi, and is apparently a fairly faithful rendering of the book.

Another version is the more recent 1998 U.S./German production entitled *Palmetto*, directed by Volker Schlondorff, from a screenplay by E. Max Frye, starring Woody Harrelson as Harry Barber, Elisabeth Shue as Rhea Malroux, Chloe Sevigny as Odette Malroux and Gina Gershon as Nina. Reviews were somewhat tepid.

Eve

Filmed as *Eva* by Joseph Losey in 1962, starring Stanley Baker as Clive Thurston (rechristened "Tyvian Jones" in the movie), Jeanne Moreau as the fatal Eva and Virna Lisi as Carol (re-named "Francesa"). Adapted by Hugo Butler. A good film, but not a great film, flawed by serious miscasting, and occasional overacting from Baker.

Filmed again in France by director Benoît Jacquot as *Eva* and released in 2018, this version stars Isabelle Huppert (in the title role), Gaspard Ulliel, Julia Roy and Marc Barbé. Adapted for the screen by the director and Gilles Taurand, it was co-produced by Luc Besson. The critic at IMDb said "it felt a bit unfinished at times because there was so much going on but a lot of it remained untouched and unresolved" and gave it six out of ten stars. This was the first new Chase-based film in 20 years.

Miss Shumway Waves a Wand

A French film, *Une Blonde Comme ça!*, directed and adapted by Jean Jabely 1963, also known as *Miss Shumway Goes West*. It stars Taina Beryl as Myra and Jess Hahn as Alex.

The novel was also filmed in the U.S. as *Rough Magic* in 1995 by Clare Peploe, starring Bridget Fonda as Myra Shumway, Russel Crowe as Alex and Jim Broadbent as Doc Ansell. An uneasy mixture of film noir and magic realism, it was reviewed on *Rotten Tomatoes* as "an entertaining mess."

But A Short Time To Live

Produced in Iran in 1963 as *Tare ankabout* and directed by Mehdi Mirsamadzadeh, this film stars Iraj Ghaderi, Victoria and Houshang Kavoosi. It is also known as *The Spider's Web*. According to an article called "Dead-End of a Career: Mehdi Mirsamadzadeh's Crime Thrillers" on the British Council website, the film was both unauthorized and "marred by both technical ineptitude and a humdrum script."

This Chase novel was also made into a 1968 French film, *La petite vertu*, directed by Serge Korber, starring Dany Carel, Robert Hossein and Jacques Perin. Main adaptation credit goes to Michel Audiard.

Come Easy, Go Easy

The subject of a 1963 French movie, *Chair de Poule* (Goosebumps), or *Highway Pickup*, from director Julien Duvivier (famous for *Pepe le Moko*, 1937), this movie stars Robert Hossein as Chet Carson (Daniel in the movie), Jean Sorel as Roy (Paul in the movie) and Catherine Rouvel as the sensual Lola Jensen (Maria in the movie).

Mission to Venice

Originally titled *Agent spécial à Venise*, this 1964 French film directed by André Versini is also known as *Voir Venise Et...Crever*, *Mission to Venice* (U.S), *Mord am Canale Grande* (West Germany) and *La Spia che venne dall'ovest* (Italy). It stars Sean Flynn (Errol Flynn's son) as Don Micklem, (renamed Michel in the film.), Madeline Robinson as Mrs Tregarth and Pierre Mondy as Tregarth. The IMDb critic calls it "stylish and well paced."

Mission to Siena

Made into the 1964 b&w German film, *Wartezimmer Zum Jenseits* (Waiting Room to the Afterlife), directed by Alfred Vohrer, released in the U.S as *Mark of The Tortoise* (USA), and starring Gotz George as Don

Micklem and Carl Lange as Crantor. Also features Klaus Kinski in a supporting role. Sometimes thought to be based on an Edgar Wallace novel due to the similarity of tone and storyline.

A Coffin From Hong Kong

A 1964 German film directed by Manfred R. Köhler as *Ein sarg Aus Hong Kong,* released in the U.S. as *A Coffin From Hong Kong,* it stars Heinz Drache, Elga Anderson, Ralf Wolter, Sabine Sesselmann, Willy Birgil and Angela Bo.

One Bright Summer Morning

Made into the French film, *Par un Beau Matin d'été,* directed by Jacques Deray in 1965, starring Akim Tamiroff as Big Jim Kramer (Frank in the movie), Jean Paul Belmondo as Riff (Francis in the movie) and Geraldine Chaplin as Zelda (no name change here).

The basic theme of the novel was also adopted in the Hindi film, *36 Ghante,* directed by Raj Tilak in 1974, starring Raj Kumar as Vic Dermott (Ashok Roy in the movie) and Mala Sinha as Carrie (Deepa in the movie).

Lay Her Among the Lilies

Adapted as *Die Katze im Sack* for a German TV mini-series broadcast that premiered September 18, 1965, starring Hanns Lothar, Hanne Wieder, Helmut Förnbacher and Renate Ewert. It was directed by Jürgen Roland and written by both Chase and Wolfgang Menge.

The Wary Transgressor

A brief situation in the novel, where the protagonist Chisholm confronts General Costain, who murders a prostitute and frames the former, was developed into an entire movie, *The Night of the Generals,* directed by Anatole Litvak in 1967. Set against the backdrop of WWII, and told in flashback, the story begins in Warsaw in 1942, with the murder of the prostitute. The prime suspects are three German generals. When the investigating officer, played by Omar Sharif, becomes too determined in his pursuit of the culprit, he is transferred.

Two years later in Paris, another prostitute is killed. Again Sharif is on hand, but when he confronts the psychotic general, played brilliantly by Peter O'Toole (presumably the maniacal Costain of the novel), the general frames his driver, played by Tom Courtenay (presumably Chisholm of the novel) and then kills Sharif. An impressive movie, with brilliant performances by all, even though the main plot of the novel is cast aside. Also stars Christopher Plummer, Philippe Noiret, Joanna Pettet and Donald Pleasance.

A Lotus for Miss Quon

This novel was made into a German-Italian-French co-production in 1967, called *Lotosbluten fur Miss Quon* (Lotus Blossoms for Miss Quon), directed by Jurgen Roland with a cast that included Lang Jeffries, Francesa Tu and Christa Linder.

You Have Yourself a Deal

A 1967 French/Italian/West German film, *La Blonde de Pekin* (The Blonde from Peking), directed by Nicolas Gessner, was adapted by noir author Marc Behm (who also wrote the script for The Beatles' *Help!*) and Nicholas Gessner. Mark Girland became Gandler in the movie, an out of work actor played by Claudio Brook. Mireille Darc starred as Carlota Olsen (Christine in the movie), Georgia Moll as Ginny, Francoise Brion as Erika Olsen, Edward G. Robinson as John Dorey (Douglas in the movie) and Jean-Jacques Delbo as Erich Olsen. An IMDb review calls it "some of kind of spy thriller verging on a spoof on Bond and Co."

Not Safe To Be Free

A French production released as *Le démoniaque* by director Rene Gainville in 1968, this film stars Anne Vernon as Sophie, Jess Hahn as Floyd Delaney, Francois Gabriel as Jay Delaney and Anna Gael as Lucille. Also released as *Meurtre en liberté* (France) and *The Woman Is a Stranger* (English). Writing credits go mostly to Jean-Louis Curtis.

The Way the Cookie Crumbles

Chase was tremendously popular in France, and here is another French production, *Trop Petit mon Ami* (Too Small My Friend), released in 1970 and directed by Eddy Matalon. It stars Jane Birkin, Michael Dunn and Bernard Fresson. One of the writers, Sady Rebbot, plays an inspector in the film.

Lady - Here's Your Wreath

A 1971 Hindi film, *Memsaab*, directed by Atma Ram, starring Vinod Khanna and Yogita Bali and Johnny Walker.

There's a Hippy on the Highway

Another Hindi film, *Victoria No 203*, directed by Brij, released in 1972, starring Ashok Kumar, Navin Nischol and Saira Bano, with only a small element from the novel.

The 1991 Russian film, *Bukhta Smerti*, (also known as *The Bay of Death*), directed by Grigory Cohan and Timofei Levchuk, was based on this Chase classic as well, starring O. Shtefanko, I. Krikunov and O. Fomicheva.

Just a Matter of Time

This 1972 French/Italian/West German movie, *Pas folle la guêpe* (He's No Fool), was directed by Jean Dellanoy and adapted by Daniel Boulanger and Jean Delannoy. The principal character of Alice Morely-Johnson was played by Francoise Rosay. Others in the cast include Anne Duperay as Sheila Oldhill, Bruno Pradal as the disinherited nephew, Gerald, and Phillipe Clay as the sinister chauffeur, Bromhead.

I Would Rather Stay Poor

Made into the German film *Pittsville - Ein Safe voll Blut* by director Krzysztof Zanussi in 1973, the film starred Horst Buchholz as Calvin, Ann Wedgeworth as Kit Loring, Louise Caire Clark as Iris Loring, Patricia Joyce as Alice Craig, Chip Taylor as Ken Travers and Rod Browning as Easton. The film was reported to be interesting, if somewhat amateurish, without any major changes in the plot or principal characters. It was filmed almost entirely in Bennington, Vermont, and was released in the U.S. in 1975 as *The Catamount Killing*. Dennis Schwartz, reviewing it in *Ozus' World Movie Reviews*, called it "an awkward crime film that derails when it goes from film noir to an unconvincing moralistic tale about society losing its moral integrity."

Shock Treatment

An obscure 1973 Hindi film, *Joshila*, directed by Yash Chopra, starring Dev Anand, Hema Malini, Pran and Bindu, where only the core subject of murder through electric shock was adopted. Noted for its musical score.

The Flesh of the Orchid

Another French production, this one from 1975 and directed by Patrice Chereau as *La Chair de L'Orchidée*. It stars Charlotte Rampling as Carol Blandish (Claire), as well as Bruno Cremer, Simone Signoret, Edwige Feuillère, Gunter Meisner and Alida Valli. Adapted from the Chase novel by Jean-Claude Carrière, a number of characters were added and unnecessary changes were made in the plot. According to a critic at IMBd, this sequel to *No Orchids for Miss Blandish* is "typical of the neo-noir revival of the era."

An Ace Up My Sleeve

Directed by Ivan Passer in 1976, this West German film was re-titled *Crime and Passion* for moviegoers. It stars Karen Black as Helga Rolfe (Susan in the movie), Omar Sharif as Archer (Andre in the movie), Joseph Bottoms as Larry and Bernhard Wicki as Rolf. Actually in the novel, Rolf was not portrayed at all and Helga only had telephonic talks with her husband throughout the book. Jesse Lansky Jr. was one of those responsible for adapting the Chase novel. Vincent Canby, reviewing it in the *New York Times*, called it "a grossly disoriented and disorienting shaggy dog of a movie that seems to have no point, and no point of view, whatever."

The Vulture is a Patient Bird

This multi-starrer Indo-US film, *Shalimar*, directed by Krishna Shah—starring Rex Harrison, John Saxon, Sylvia Miles, Dharmendra and Zeenat Aman, released in 1978—was loosely based on this Chase thriller. Music by R. D. Burman. The film was released in two versions: Hindi and dubbed in English for the U.S. release. Both were unsuccessful when they were released. However the Hindi version later gained cult status in the DVD-Video circuit, and is now seen as ahead of its times.

Also made into an Italian film in 1991 as *L'avvoltoio può attendere*, directed by Gian Pietro Calasso, and starring Donald Pleasance, Valeria D'Obici, Massimo Serato and Sasha D'Arc. The storyline reads like pure Chase: "A brilliant but sadistic safe-breaker; a beautiful seductress; an expert young hunter and an ace pilot with a shady past—this is the team that undercover operator Armo Shalik assembles to steal the priceless Borgia ring from millionaire Max Kahlenberg's closely guarded fortress in the remote and deadly African bush. But when Kahlenberg finds out they are coming, the gang's expedition turns into a strictly one-way safari—to slaughter."

The Paw in the Bottle

A Czechoslovakian TV film version from 1978, *Pracka v láhvi* was directed by Jan Matejovský and stars Ilena Steinmasslová, Petr Cepek and Regina Rázlová. It was adapted by Milos Rehák.

Goldfish Have No Hiding Place

Another Czechoslovakian TV film, this one called *Zlaté rybicky* (Goldfish), was produced in 1979 and directed by Karel Pokorný. It stars Frantisek Nemec, Hana Maciuchová and Jana Sulcová, and was adapted by Jaroslav Merunka.

You Have Yourself a Deal

An Italian mini-series called *Patto con la morte* from 1982, starring Luc Merenda, William Berger and Francesco Carnelutti. Written and directed by Gian Pietro Calasso, with no listed character credits, we are taking a best guess at which Chase novel this is based on.

Grandeur et décadence d'un petit commerce de cinema (?)

This French film—*Grandeur et décadence d'un petit commerce de cinema* (Rise and Fall of a Little Film Company)—directed by Jean Luc-Godard, was made in 1986, poking fun at the follies and injustices of small-time filmmaking in this drama-comedy about two apparent has-beens who are trying their best to get together the funds and the cast for a last, desperate bid for cinematic fame and fortune. The duo (Jean-Claude Mocky and Jean-Pierre Leaud) and their assistants mull over the meaning and purpose of cinema, but at the same time, the cattle-call for their proposed new production does not rise above its bovine metaphor. While eyeing beauteous new actresses with a dash of lasciviousness, the pair are also keeping track of would-be backers with more than a dash of cunning manipulation. The film had Marie Valera as the lead female character. Although Chase is credited as the book author, the book cannot be identified, and was probably only a very loose adaptation at best.

The Soft Centre

Chantons en choeur (Let's Sing in Chorus) is a French TV movie directed by Maurice Dugowson and broadcast as part of the television series Série noire on July 30, 1987. It stars Pascale Rocard, Hippolyte Girardot and Jean-Pierre Bisson.

Tell It to the Birds

An Italian/French TV movie production from 1987, *Assicurazione sulla morte* (Insurance Death), was directed by Carlo Lizzani and stars Giovanni Vettorazzo, Patricia Millardet and Augusto Zucchi. Plot: A scrupulous insurance agent comes into contact with a woman. Together they plan her husband's murder to scam the insurance company. But something goes wrong. Of course.

Also released as part of the Série noire as *Cause à l'autre* (Cause to Another) and broadcast on October 13, 1988.

Have a Change of Scene

A 1988 Italian TV production, *Cambiamento d'aria* (Air Change) was directed by Gian Peitro Calasso, starring Luigi Amodeo, Bruno Bilotta and Linda Christian.

Try This One For Size

A movie of the same name, *Try This One For Size* was produced in the U.S. in 1989, directed by Guy Hamilton; also known as *Sauf votre respect* in France and *Con perdon de Usted* in Spain. The movie starred Michael Brandon as Lepski, David Carradine as Bradey, Arielle Dombasle as Maggie, Mario Adorf as Radnitz and Valerie Steffen as Carol. The screenplay was written by Chase, Sergio Gobbi and Alec Medieff.

Have a Nice Night

A 1990 French TV production, *Passez une bonne nuit*, directed by Jeannot Szwarc, was also known by its book title, *Have a Nice Night,* in the U.S. It starred Michael Brandon as Lepski, James Booth as Warrenton, Marc de Jong as Bradey and Anaide as Carol.

Want to Stay Alive?

Another French TV production, *Le Denier du colt*, directed by Claude Bernard-Aubert in 1990, stars Michael Brandon as Lepski. Others in the cast included Jacques Toja, Mickey Sebastian, Catherine Erhardy, Guy Marchand and Olivia Brunaux.

Believed Violent

Présumé Dangereux is a 1990 French film directed by Georges Lautner, starring Michael Brandon as Lepski, Robert Mitchum as Forrester, Marie Laforet as Thea, Mario Adorf as Radnitz, Daniel Ubaud as Silk, Jean-Marie Lemaire as Keegan, Steve Kalfa as Craige, and Andre Oumansky as Lindsay. Not one of Mitchum's finer moments, it is said that he plays his role like a sleepwalker, and that the rest of the cast surpasses him in mediocrity.

We'll Share a Double Funeral (?)

Mais qui arrêtera la pluie? (Who Will Stop the Rain?) is a French TV movie from 1990, adapted and directed by Daniel Duval. It stars Ricky Tognazzi, Gérard Darmon, Nathalie Nell and Albert Dray. We're guessing at the source book here.

Like a Hole in the Head

A 1992 Russian/Ukranian film, *Snajper,* directed by Andrei Benkendorf, stars N.Eremenko-Jr, A.Djigarhanyan and E.Strijenova.

Well Now My Pretty

Another 1992 Russian film, *Kazino,* directed by Samson Samsonov, stars A. Djigarhanyan, E. Martzevich, Olga Koposova, Leonid Kulagin, Olga Popovich and Edward Martsevich. The screenplay of the movie was written jointly by Chase and Samson Samsonov.

What's Better Than Money?

Requiem per voce e pianoforte (Requiem for Voice and Piano) is a 1993 Italian production directed by Tomaso Sherman and adapted by Gian Pietro Calasso. It stars Vittorio Amandola, Hartmut Becker and Toni Bertorelli.

My Laugh Comes Last

Produced as *The Set Up* and directed by Strathford Hamilton in 1995, the film starred Billy Zane as Larry Lucas (Charles Thorpe in the movie), James Coburn as Farrell Brannigan (Jeremiah Cole in the movie), Mia Sara as Glenda Marsh (Gina Sands in the movie) and James Russo as Edwin Klaus (Kliff in the movie). Apparently all this talent goes to waste, as the critic at IMDb claims it suffers from "horrific writing, truly absurd plot twists, a serious gem of stupidity and cliché movie-making."

Interesting side note:
Chase's only notable TV Guest Appearance was in *Cinépanorama*, playing himself (16th May 1957).

PLAYS

Get a Load of This
Written for the stage by Chase, *Get a Load of This* was performed in 1941 at the London Hippodrome in London, England, as a musical. It featured Vic Oliver, Jack Allan, Celia Lipton, Valerie White, Gaylord Brian and Harold Wilkinson in the cast.

No Orchids For Miss Blandish
On July 30, 1942, the play of the book, written by the author and Robert Nesbitt, with additional dialogue by Val Guest, was presented at London's Prince of Wales Theatre and ran for 203 performances. A tour of Britain ran from 1942 until 1949. The principal players were Robert Newton, Linden Travers, Hartley Power and Mary Clare.

A French adaptation by d'Éliane Charles and Marcel Duhamel was produced in Paris at the Grand Guignol Theatre on January 2, 1950, directed by Alexandre Dundas, featuring Nicole Riche as Miss Blandish, Jean-Marc Tennberg as Slim Grissom, Renée Gardes as Ma Grissom and Sasha Tarride as Inspector Fenner. Critic J. B. Jeener wrote in *Le Figaro*: "The audience feels trapped, embarrassed, and shameful; they hardly dared applaud."

Chase's classic first novel was again produced as a French play, *Pas d'orchidées pour Miss Blandisch* by Claude Barma in 1978. This play was written by Frédéric Dard and starred Sophie Deschamps as Miss Blandish, Robert Hossein as Slim, Candice Patou as Anna, Mario David as Eddie, Clément Harari as Doc, Gérard Lartigau as Bailey, Jean-Marc Fyot as MacGowan and Jacques Bouanich as Riley.

Also in 1978, Glasgow's celebrated Citizens Theatre mounted a production of *No Orchids* dramatized and helmed by its artistic director, Robert David MacDonald. This play starred Pauline Moran as Miss Blandish, John Breck as Riley, Pierce Brosnan as Eddie Schultz, Patrick Hannaway as Doc, Julia Blalock as Anna, Peter Jonfield as Slim and Sian Thomas as Ma Grissom.

And in 1990, this adaptation was presented on the American stage under the direction of Rosey Hay, starring Margaret Klenck as Miss Blandish, Roberto Fente as Riley, Tom Tammi as Eddie Shultz, John Hickey as Slim Grissom, Molly Regan as Ma Grissom and Steve Ryan as Fenner.

A new, well-received production of MacDonald's adaptation was also mounted as recently as 1999 for Evidence Room by Bart DeLorenzo, starring Ames Ingham as Miss Blandish, Jason Hall as Riley, Christian Leffler as Schultz, Mickey Cottrell as Doc, Ken Roht as Slim, Pamela Gordon as Ma Grissom and Randy Kovitz as Fenner. F. Kathleen Foley in the *Los Angeles Times* called it "a no-holds-barred melodrama that goes as far over the top as a vintage Cagney movie."

Last Page: A Play in Three Acts

Written in 1946 and published by Samuel French in 1947, but there is no information available about it having been staged.

PC Sarkar, is a Ph.D in organic chemistry, working as Principal Scientist, Indian Council of Agricultural Research. He has been a long time fan of James Hadley Chase, since his school days. He can be contacted at: dr_pc-sarkar@rediffmail.com.

Thanks also from Dr. Sarkar to Chase fans Amit Mehta (U.S.), Vladimir Matushenko (Russia), Ton Nieuiwenburg (Holland), Alberto Zylbersztajn (Italy), and Jorge Espinosa (Chile), for providing further updating material.

References:

"James Hadley Chase": http://www.angelfire.com/celeb2/hadleychase/index.htm

IMDb: https://www.imdb.com/name/nm0153777/

Wikipedia: https://en.wikipedia.org/wiki/No_Orchids_for_Miss_Blandish_(film)

British Council: https://iran.britishcouncil.org/en/underline/theatre/Iran-noir

Blood on the Stage, 1975-2000: Milestone Plays of Crime, Mystery, and Detection
by Amnon Kabatchnik

James Hadley Chase Bibliography
(1906-1985)

As James Hadley Chase

No Orchids for Miss Blandish
(1939; reprinted as The Villain
and the Virgin, 1948)

He Won't Need it Now (1939; as
by James L. Docherty)

The Dead Stay Dumb (1940;
reprinted as Kiss My Fist!, 1952)

Twelve Chinks and a Woman
(1940; reprinted as 12 China-
men and a Woman, 1950, and
as The Doll's Bad News, 1974)

Lady—Here's Your Wreath (1940;
as by Raymond Marshall)

Miss Callaghan Comes to Grief
(1941)

Get a Load of This (1941; stories)

Miss Shumway Waves a Wand
(1944)

Just the Way It Is (1944; as by
Raymond Marshall)

Eve (1945)

Blonde's Requiem (1945; as by
Raymond Marshall)*

More Deadly Than the Male
(1946; as by Ambrose Grant)

Make the Corpse Walk (1946; as
by Raymond Marshall)

No Business of Mine (1947; as by
Raymond Marshall)*

I'll Get You for This (1947)

Last Page (1947; play, filmed as
Man Bait)

The Flesh of the Orchid (1948)

You Never Know With Women
(1948)

Trusted Like a Fox (1948; as by
Raymond Marshall; reprinted as
Ruthless, 1955)

You're Lonely When You're Dead
(1949)

The Paw in the Bottle (1949; as by
Raymond Marshall)

Lay Her Among the Lilies (1950;
reprinted as Too Dangerous to
be Free, 1951)

Figure It Out for Yourself (1950;
reprinted as The Marijuana
Mob, 1952)

Mallory (1950; as by Raymond
Marshall)

Strictly for Cash (1951)

In a Vain Shadow (1951;
reprinted as by Raymond Marshall as Never Trust a Woman,
1957)

But a Short Time to Live (1951; as
by Raymond Marshall;
reprinted as The Pick-Up, 1955)

Why Pick on Me? (1951; as by
Raymond Marshall)

The Double Shuffle (1952)

The Fast Buck (1952)

The Wary Transgressor (1952; as
by Raymond Marshall)

I'll Bury My Dead (1953)

This Way for a Shroud (1953)

The Things Men Do (1953; as by
Raymond Marshall)

Tiger by the Tail (1954)

Safer Dead (1954; reprinted as
Dead Ringer, 1955)

The Sucker Punch (1954; as by
  Raymond Marshall)
Mission to Venice (1954; as by
  Raymond Marshall)
Mission to Siena (1955; as by
  Raymond Marshall)
You've Got it Coming (1955)
There's Always a Price Tag (1956)
You Find Him—I'll Fix Him
  (1956; as by Raymond Mar-
  shall)
The Guilty are Afraid (1957)
Not Safe to be Free (1958;
  reprinted as The Case of the
  Strangled Starlet, 1958)
Hit and Run (1958; as by Ray-
  mond Marshal)
Shock Treatment (1959)
The World in My Pocket (1959)
What's Better Than Money (1960)
Come Easy—Go Easy (1960)
A Lotus for Miss Quon (1961)
Just Another Sucker (1961)
I Would Rather Stay Poor (1962)
A Coffin from Hong Kong (1952)
Tell it to the Birds (1963)
One Bright Summer Morning
  (1963)
The Soft Centre (1964)
This is for Real (1965)
The Way the Cookie Crumbles
  (1965)
You Have Yourself a Deal (1966)
Cade (1966)
Have This One on Me (1967)
Well Now, My Pretty (1967)
An Ear to the Ground (1968)

Believed Violent (1968)
The Whiff of Money (1969)
The Vulture is a Patient Bird
  (1969)
There's a Hippie on the Highway
  (1970)
Like a Hole in the Head (1970)
An Ace Up My Sleeve (1971)
Want to Say Alive? (1971)
You're Dead Without Money
  (1972)
Just a Matter of Time (1972)
Knock, Knock! Who's There?
  (1973)
Have a Change of Scene (1973)
So What Happens to Me? (1974)
Goldfish Have No Hiding Place
  (1974)
Believe This, You'll Believe Any-
  thing (1975)
The Joker in the Pack (1975)
Do Me a Favour Drop Dead
  (1976)
My Laugh Comes Last (1977)
I Hold the Four Aces (1977)
Consider Yourself Dead (1978)
Can of Worms (1979)
You Must be Kidding (1979)
Try This One for Size (1980)
You Can Say That Again (1980)
Hand Me a Fig Leaf (1981)
Have a Nice Night (1982)
We'll Share a Double Funeral
  (1982)
Not My Thing (1983)
Hit Them Where it Hurts (1984)

Omnibus Editions

Three of Spades (1974; includes
The Double Shuffle, Shock
Treatment and Tell It to the
Birds)

Meet Mark Girland (1977; in-
cludes This is for Real, You
Have Yourself a Deal and Have
This One on Me)

Meet Helga Rolfe (1984; includes
An Ace Up My Sleeve, A Joker
in the Pack and I Hold Four
Aces)

(All titles originally published as
by Raymond Marshall were
reprinted as by Chase except *)

As René Raymond

(reprinted as by Chase)

The Mirror in Room 22 (1946;
story, appeared in Slipstream: A
Royal Airforce Anthology edited
by René Raymond and David
Langdon)

For further info on the works of
James Hadley Chase, visit
www.hadleychase.co.nr, compiled
by Dr. P. C. Sarkar. This is the de-
finitive Chase website.

Classic hardboiled fiction from the King of the Paperbacks...

HARRY WHITTINGTON

A Night for Screaming / Any Woman He Wanted
$19.95 978-1-933586-08-3
"[*A Night for Screaming*] is pure Harry. The damned thing is almost on fire, it reads so fast." — Ed Gorman, *Gormania*

To Find Cora / Like Mink Like Murder / Body and Passion
$23.95 978-1-933586-25-0
"Harry Whittington was the king of plot and pace, and he could write anything well. He's 100 percent perfect entertainment." — Joe R. Lansdale

Rapture Alley / Winter Girl / Strictly for the Boys
$23.95 978-1-933586-36-6
"Whittington was an innovator, often turning archetypical characters and plots on their head, and finding wild new ways to tell stories from unusual angles." — Cullen Gallagher, *Pulp Serenade*

A Haven for the Damned
$9.99 978-1-933586-75-5
"A wild, savage romp and pure Whittington: raw noir that has the feel of a Jim Thompson novel crossed with a Russ Meyer film."— Brian Greene, *The Life Sentence*. Black Gat #1.

Trouble Rides Tall / Cross the Red Creek / Desert Stake-Out
$21.95 978-1-944520-11-3
"If these three Whittington novels are the only westerns crime fiction fans ever read, they will have experienced some of the best the genre has to offer."
—Alan Cranis, *Bookgasm*

"Harry Whittington delivers every time." — Bill Crider

STARK HOUSE

Stark House Press, 1315 H Street, Eureka, CA 95501
griffinskye3@sbcglobal.net / www.StarkHousePress.com
Available from your local bookstore, or order direct or via our website.